Just Friends with a Prince

Becky Tzag

JUST FRIENDS WITH A PRINCE

First edition. June 2023

Copyright © 2023 Becky Tzag

Cover design by Kari March Designs

ISBN 979-8-3953-8669-4 (paperback)

This book is dedicated to anyone who has ever felt a little lost in life. Take some time to just be. Don't settle, and remember that you are fucking sunshine!

Chapter 1 - Harper

"I'm sorry Harper, but we're going to have to let you go."

Whoa, hold on here for just a minute. What the *hell* is Mr. Peters talking about? I've been working as an administrative assistant at Peters Designs for 5 years. I don't love my job, but I'm competent at it.

"Can you please explain why? Did I do something wrong?" Mr. Peters looks away from me. He's uncomfortable and doesn't like confrontation. I can tell he just wants me to accept this and leave. I'm so confused that I'll probably do just that.

"It's nothing personal, dear, but fewer people are hiring home designers right now. People are still recovering from the pandemic and are simply not redecorating as much right now. This truly is just business. If you can please tidy your desk and stop by HR, Anne will have your last paycheque ready for you."

And that was it. I was dismissed. Five years of loyalty. Five years of my life gone. Sure, I never actually wanted to be an administrative assistant. I never wanted to move up in the world of design and decorating, but this still sucks.

I place all my personal belongings in a box that just happened to appear on my desk while I was in Mr. Peters' office. I really don't even have too much. A few pictures, including one of me and my boyfriend Levi, one of me and my mom on a camping trip, and one of me and my sister at her wedding in Sova where she now lives with her amazing husband. Some pens (including my absolute favourite one that I once snarled at a co-worker over who asked to borrow it). A small succulent. And that's it. Five years of my life summed up in a box and it looks incredibly pathetic.

After a stop in HR, where sweet grandmotherly Anne gives me a hug, a chocolate chip cookie and my last paycheque, I'm now sitting in my car wondering what I should do now. I blow out a giant raspberry and rest my forehead on the steering wheel, hands clenching it so tight my knuckles have turned white. I feel a few tears escape my eyes and roll down my cheeks. I wipe them away angrily. I don't want to be sad. I'm angry, frustrated and shocked, but not sad.

What's done is done. Sitting here crying, fogging up my windows with my sobs, isn't going to change anything. I need to take these feelings and use them as fuel.

I jam the keys into the ignition and turn the car on. I make a plan with myself as I pull out of my parking space and leave the underground parking lot.

"Ok Harper, things will work out. Sometimes shitty things happen, but that's ok, because it lets us see how crappy the path that we were walking on really was. Time to choose a new, non-pothole ridden path."

I take a breath. Plan time. Having a set plan always helps me to feel calmer. I don't like not knowing what to expect. A step-by-step guide is exactly what I need right now.

"First, I will go home and do a deep clean of the kitchen. Clean all the grout on the counter and island and scrub the sink. Second, I need carbs and cheese, so obviously I'll make a lasagna and then shove a handful of chocolate covered almonds in my face. It's only ten in the morning. I'll have hours to scrub and think. Then when Levi gets home a little after five o'clock, I'll have some sort of plan to talk over with him."

I breathe out a giant sigh of relief as I make a left turn onto yet another busy Toronto street. It doesn't seem to matter what time or day it is, there are always people going somewhere. Watching everyone rush is kind of exhausting.

My mind wanders to what Levi is going to say. Levi hates surprises, but he hates deviating from *his plans* even more. Me losing my job definitely goes against *the plan*.

Levi has had his entire life mapped out for him, probably since his father was a child. His great-grandfather started one of the largest law firms in Toronto, Metz, Sherr, and Tillman. His grandfather, father and Levi all work there. Levi's *plan* consists of being a partner at the firm and marrying a beautiful, successful business woman. I used to feel honoured that he thought I fit the bill, but lately things have been strained between us. Less talking, less sex, less everything. No, me losing my job is not going to help. But, Levi loves me. He'll help me figure out my next steps.

I pull up to our house about twenty minutes later, finally leaving the never-ending lines of cars and people rushing to-and-fro. It's a modern looking two-storey detached house in a sought after neighbourhood. Our street is right off a busy road, but the neighbourhood itself is quiet. As I take the time to look at the house, I realize that I don't like it. Nothing about this house or the neighbourhood says *Harper.* We moved here because Levi said it's where we should buy a house. It'll impress colleagues and clients, he said. It'll make us look good, he said. This is where the important people live, he said. But, it's ugly. It's fake. It's all wrong.

I suddenly feel like I can't breathe. My chest feels tight. My heart is beating a million times too fast. My head is swimming. Sweat is beading on my neck and temples. I focus on the irises in the flowerbeds. The beautiful mixes of purples and yellows help calm me. I breathe in slowly, counting to four. I hold it in for eight, and then breathe it out for seven seconds. I repeat this a few times until I can feel my heart slowing down. It's ok. It will all be ok. I'm just freaking out because of my job. Panicking right now makes sense.

"Screw cleaning, I need a new plan. I'll make a giant cup of tea, put on sweatpants, eat a whole bag of chips and watch *Gilmore Girls*. Stars Hollow will help."

I take a breath and get out of my car. There's a grey SUV that I don't recognize parked in front of my house, but it's probably just someone visiting a neighbour. Not like I'm here often during the day, so maybe that car is always parked in front of my house and I just never knew.

Levi installed a keyless entry door lock, saying "keyless is the way of the future, babe. Just think of how nice it'll be to not fumble with your keys trying to get in!"
I hate when he calls me babe. But he has never listened to me when I tell him I didn't want to be called *baby* or *babe*, he would just huff a laugh and continue with his preferred pet name.
I also prefer keys to punching in a code to unlock my door, if we're taking stock of things I don't like but never got any say in. He made the code his birthday, which seems very unsafe. I roll my eyes as I put in 0217 and open the door.

My ears are assaulted with cries of pleasure as soon as I walk in the door. "Oh god, yes! Just like that, baby!"
Ummm…ok…so perhaps that car parked in front of my house *is* visiting my house.
I feel like a robot. I quietly close the front door, take off my pumps and walk down the hall towards the living area. Levi is naked. Completely naked except for a pair of black socks pulled up mid-calf. He has a fully naked woman bent over the side of the couch (a couch which I agonized over and finally chose after a month of

searching for the perfect one to pull the room together. I'm glad she seems to appreciate its sturdiness). I should probably announce my arrival. Say something. Throw something. *Feel* something. But nope. Nothing.

I turn around and go upstairs. I pull out clothes at random from our closet and toss them into a suitcase I find on the floor. The suitcase was a gift from Levi's father. Some expensive brand that I could never afford, in plain, boring black. Next is my drawers with socks, underwear and bras. I can hear their moans, grunts and that beautiful, sturdy couch being banged against the wall the entire time I'm packing. Ok, bathroom time. I grab my beautiful teal carry-on suitcase (one I actually chose and bought myself, which Mr. Snottypants Metz sneered at), I toss in my makeup, brush and lotions. I even add some towels and shampoo, because why the fuck not? Jewelry, sunglasses, headbands, basically anything I see that's mine or that I've recently used gets put into one of the two suitcases. Phone charger, Kindle, a couple of books. My file folder with all my important documents.

More moaning, more grunts, the tempo of the couch hitting the wall has sped up, telling me that they're almost done and it's time for me to go.

I go back downstairs and toss my bags by the front door as they finish.

"God, baby, that was incredible!" she gushes. He sucks at sex. She must be lying. That or he just sucks with me. Great, now I have something else to agonize over.

I walk into the living room just as he's climbing off her. They haven't noticed me yet, so I take the opportunity to really look at him. He's fairly tall at 5'11", blond hair kept cut close to his head. No beard, no stubble. He's not muscular but he's not out of shape per se. He's average. He's ok. And looking at him now, I realize that I'm not attracted to him. I used to be, but it's been a while since I felt that rush. At least I'm pretty sure I used to feel it. He's objectively attractive, but I'm not attracted to him. I wonder when that changed.

I clear my throat and they both whip their heads over to where I'm standing. "Well, I'm going to leave. Levi, don't forget to pick up your dry cleaning tomorrow, cause I sure as shit won't be doing it for you. I packed some of my stuff, but I'll be back at some point to get the rest. I'll let you know when and would appreciate it if you weren't here."

I spin on my heel to leave when I hear Levi call out, "Harper, wait! This isn't what it looks like!"

How stupid does he think I am??

"Excuse me?? I walk in and find you fucking some other woman against *my couch* and you have the audacity to tell me it's not what it looks like?!? Fuck you, Levi! And random woman, if you knew that he was in a relationship, for the last three years I might add, then fuck you too! But if you didn't know, I'm sorry you found out like this."

And with that, I grab my bags, throw them in the trunk of my blue Toyota Corolla and leave.

Chapter 2 - Harper

I'm driving aimlessly down the least busy streets I can find. What the fuck just happened? What the fuck do I do? Why the fuck am I swearing so much?! I'm usually a levelheaded person. I keep calm and cool. I'm a motherfucking cucumber. But not today. No, today I'm a goddamn sailor who lost her job, saw her boyfriend having sex with another woman, moved out of her house and now has absolutely no plans at all. I have no job, no house and no boyfriend, but mostly right now I'm sad that I'm still wearing the dress and stupid underwire bra I put on this morning and not my beloved sweatpants.

This is one of those times that living so far away from my sister hurts. I have a sprinkling of family around, but a cousin isn't going to cut it. I need my sister. My sister and I are very close. We're the stereotypical sisters that look alike, speak alike and borrow each other's clothing. Cara is almost exactly a year younger than me. She was born three weeks before my first birthday. Growing up, it was like I was living with my best friend, and I feel so incredibly blessed to have a sister like her. We both have medium length dark brown hair, but mine has a red shine to it, whereas hers is more multiple shades of brown. We both have blue eyes and are within an inch in height of each other (I'm an inch taller at 5'6", thank you very much). Cara's cheekbones are more prominent and she has a nicer butt, however, I have slightly bigger boobs, which I think evens us out. We get mistaken for twins quite a bit, and considering that she looks like an absolute goddess, I will happily take that comparison.

I call my sister on speakerphone as I continue to drive around. "Hey Harper, what's up?" my sister asks breezily. She sounds so happy. Sova is five hours ahead of us here in Toronto, making it just about 4 p.m. there. She must have just left her job at the daycare center.

"Hey Cara, I just needed to hear your beautiful voice. It's been a crappy day." I tell her everything that has happened this morning. I can tell she wants to jump in, maybe with her own sailor-inspired swearing tirade, but she manages to keep it in.

"So, now I'm just driving around, trying to manifest a new life. So far, all I've found is a coffee shop, so I manifested a tea and donut."

My life might be falling apart, but this apple fritter is absolutely amazing!

"What if you came here for a bit? A little vacation with your favourite sister?" she suggests.

"Yeah, hmm, no," I grumble. "I have no job, therefore taking a vacation and spending money probably isn't the best choice right now." As lovely as flying over to Sova sounds, I should be an adult about this. Right?

"I hear you, and I understand your point," Cara replies. "But, what if this is exactly the right time to get away? You don't really have any reasons to stay in Toronto at the moment, Harp."

"Gee, thanks for pointing out how pathetic my life is, sis. There's that moral support I was looking for."

"No, look, I'm not trying to make you feel bad. Let's find the positives here, just like Mom would have done".

"Ok, yeah, you're right." I think about my mom. She was an eternal optimist and absolutely would have found a silver lining.

"I don't have a job. I don't have a boyfriend. I packed my belongings and effectively moved out of the house. I have a couple of friends here, but they're mostly couple friends with Levi. I really don't have a reason to stay here right now. Maybe a European getaway will clear my head and help me come up with a new plan. A better plan. A Harper plan. Sunshine, mountains and time with you just might be the right things to soothe my soul. I'll book a hotel for the night and look into flights for later in the week".

"That's better," Cara says before yelling out, "Babe! Can you book Harper a plane ticket here ASAP?"

I can hear some shuffling around and her husband Theo answers, "Sure thing! There's a plane leaving today, can she be at the airport in a couple of hours?"

I am so lucky to call these people family.

Chapter 3 - Harper

I arrive at the airport with four hours to spare before I take off. It gives me some time to repack my suitcase after my hasty departure from the house. Thank goodness I had the foresight to grab my folder of documents, which includes my passport. It would have totally sucked if I had to sneak back into the house to find it.

I don't want to take too much, so I Marie Kondo-style fold and roll the necessities into my carry-on suitcase. Just the basics. I can do laundry at Cara's house and buy a few extra shirts while in Sova.

I sigh in relief as I find my beautiful sweatpants. These are the unicorn of sweatpants. Not too thick, not too tight around the ankles. Silky soft. However, the best part about them are the giant pockets! I can easily fit my Kindle in there. I own four pairs, and I am not ashamed about how often I wear them. I grab one of the black pairs, and then fold the other black and a dark grey pair and put them in the suitcase. They are totally necessary for my trip. The blouses and office appropriate dress pants can stay in a crumpled ball in my trunk. Screw business casual, I'll be living in sweatpants casual!

After filling my carry-on with sweatpants and other casual, comfortable clothes, I add in my makeup, pj's, a bathing suit, underwear, socks and some bras. Tossing in my chargers, a couple of books and a couple shoe options, I zip it up.

With a quick scan of the parking garage to make sure I'm alone without any creepers watching me, I dash into the car's back seat to change out of my dress and put on a comfortable pair of underwear, cotton bralette, a navy blue long sleeve cotton t-shirt and my beloved sweatpants. I actually sigh out loud. This feels so much better. Getting out of those clothes feels like peeling off a layer that I didn't even realize was too tight.

Was I even happy? My life wasn't exactly turning out the way I thought it would, but I was happy, wasn't I?

Ok sure, I'm thirty-three years old. Single (again, fuck you Levi!), jobless, homeless. I have a university degree, but it's in English, which wasn't exactly my dream. The job that I was working at was supposed to be temporary, just something to get me through until I found something better. But one year turned into five because staying somewhere ok was easier than taking a leap for something really exciting.

The same could be said about my relationship with Levi. He was ok. We were ok. He was someone to go to the movies with. Someone to eat dinner with. Someone to be with rather than be alone. He didn't make me feel alive. He didn't push me to grow and be more. I think he liked that I was boring and at his beck and call. I picked up his dry cleaning, cooked meals, and cleaned the house. With his work schedule being a lot more hectic and all over the place than mine, I was reliable for him. God, that makes me seem more like his personal assistant than his girlfriend. He paid all the bills, groceries were bought with his money and even the house was purchased in just his name since my credit score isn't exactly amazing. I still have some student loans to pay off and the price of gas is insane. I relied on him financially, and it made me feel safe knowing I didn't have to worry about the price of grapes. I guess we were using each other.

As I wheel my suitcase through the airport, I can't help but feel pathetic. I thought I was happy, but now I see that I was just pretending. Alive without living, I suppose. I used to have such big, fantastical dreams for myself. I was going to be rich, well respected in my field of study, always wearing the most beautiful clothes. I was going to be effortlessly classy. I would fall in love with a gorgeous, athletic man who made me feel like I was on fire. Fuck, when did I become such a disappointment?

Taking the easy way became a way of life for me. After mom got sick, I put all of my time and effort into helping her. I didn't leave enough space for me. At the time, I couldn't. If I stopped and thought about me, my life, my needs, I would break down. I shoved myself to the back of my mind and focused on mom's health and end of life care. Apparently, I left myself there.

Chapter 4 - Harper

Airplanes are absolute marvels and amazing and wonderful, but my god, they are horrible. I'm lucky that Theo was able to get me a seat, and I will thank him until he tells me to shut up since the plane is nearly full. I somehow have a window seat (hey universe, is this you apologizing for all the crap you've put me through today?). Unfortunately, the person beside me apparently thinks he has the rights to the window, judging by how many times he leans over to look out, shoving his sweaty neck into my face as he gazes out at the beauty of the tarmac. We haven't even left yet and he's already invaded my space six times. This is going to be a long flight.

"Why are you going to Germany?" sweaty neck guy demands of me. He doesn't ask. He doesn't politely inquire of my travel plans. No, sweaty neck guy demands my window and my life plans.

"Actually, I'm going to Sova, but I have to stop over in Frankfurt and Paris to get there."

I hoped my non-answer answer would be enough for Sweaty Neck, but oh no, Sweaty Neck barks back at me

"Why the hell would you go to Sova? Germany is way better than fucking Sova!"

Alright, Sweaty Neck likes Germany, got it.

"I'm visiting my sister. Germany is lovely though, and one day I would love to explore it more."

"Oh, yeah, well, you should do that." Sweaty Neck rubs the back of his neck. He seems bashful now. Maybe he's not so bad, just needs some polite conversation and a towel. New airplane friends offer airplane friends sweat towels, right?

"Does your sister live there?"

"Yep, she moved there with her husband. He's from Sova, but they met in Toronto when he was there for a conference. Love at first sight! I miss her so much, but she is so happy that I can't even hold this ridiculously long plane ride just to see her against her. I can't wait to see her and get some sunshine."

After that, Sweaty Neck becomes the perfect plane friend. He's nervous about flying, hence all the neck sweat and window stealing. He's going to visit his aunt and uncle whom he hasn't seen for ten years.

Sweaty Neck and I trade stories about having family so far away, places we've visited and places we want to visit. Sweaty Neck (whose name is actually Robert, but I will forever call him Sweaty Neck) listens to me as I relay the crapshoot that has been my life in the last twelve hours.

"He was not wearing fucking black socks while banging some chick *on your couch!!*" Sweaty Neck exclaims as we soar 35,000 feet over the Atlantic. "The absolute nerve of that dickwad!"

"He definitely was!! I know that I should be more angry about the actual cheating, but I'm more hurt that he felt the need to go behind my back and find someone else. If he wasn't happy with me and wanted to be with someone else, why couldn't he just break up with me first?"

"Well honey," an older lady sitting in front of me with stark white hair says, turning around in her seat. "Some men are, as your lovely seat partner has said, just dickwads. Cheating is cowardice. It would have taken bravery to talk to you about how he was feeling. Since he was at your house, *on your couch*, I would say that part of him wanted you to find him so that you would be the one to end things. He was a coward, and you, brave, sweet girl, are so much better off without him."

Tears well up in my eyes. This woman, whom I have never met before, made me feel so much better in a matter of seconds. She spoke to me just like my mother would have, and I feel like a part of my soul has been soothed.

"Thank you, that means a lot to me. And can I just say how great it is that everyone is just as appalled as me that they were having sex against my precious couch?! I really loved that couch. Levi ruined my couch. He owes me a new couch."

The rest of the flight is actually kind of nice. Sweaty Neck and I chat on and off. I read on my Kindle. I nap. I wake up with a sore neck because I didn't buy the overpriced neck pillow at the airport. Note to self: buy an overpriced neck pillow for the trip home.
I think about Sova. The last time I was there was for my sister's wedding. Summer in Sova is absolutely gorgeous. Sova is a small country nestled between France and Spain, right on the Atlantic coast. The air is warm, the sun is bright and it's full of old-world charm. The capital city, Croix, is the largest Sovan city with about a million people living in it. The entire country only has about ten million people. It's small but mighty. The official languages are French and English (thank goodness) and most people can speak both quite well. Spanish is also very commonly spoken, and there's a mix of German (Sweaty Neck will approve of that fact!), Dutch, and

Portuguese. Croix is home to the Sovan Royal Family, and they live in a real life castle on the beach. Theo works at Croix General hospital as an endocrinologist, so they bought a house in the capital city. If you look out their back window, you can see the castle.

It's May, so it'll be a little colder than last time I was here, but like ten degrees warmer than Toronto right now. I sigh. This will be good. Some sunshine and sister time to reset my life. I'll figure out what to do with my life and get a tan. Canadians can totally relax on a beach when it's 20° Celsius. It's a superpower. Then, I'll return home as a new woman with a purpose. I'll be that woman little me dreamed of.

By the time the plane starts its descent in Frankfurt, I feel as though an entire day has passed. I ate some mediocre food, had a nap, read, watched a movie and still had time to become BFF's with Sweaty Neck. In reality, the flight was just shy of eight hours. I'll have a couple of hours before I have to board the next plane going to Paris, so really enough time to get off, pee and get on the next plane. At least that flight is only an hour and a half before touching down in Paris. And then another plane. Air travel: a wonderful, helpful, amazing marvel, but still frustrating and cramped.

There's a collective sigh of relief when we land and are finally told we can get off the plane. Sweaty Neck, being the absolute gem that he is, gets my carry-on out of the overhead compartment for me. We make our way off the plane and into the airport, where Sweaty Neck wraps me in a giant bear hug. He's sweaty and huge, but I don't care. It feels so nice and protective. I can't remember the last time someone gave me such a warm, friendly hug. When's the last time Levi hugged me, like really hugged me? I think the last time that I felt enveloped by love like this was the last time I saw my sister. A year without a real hug would make anyone bitter and sad, especially when there was someone in my life who should have been giving me those hugs. Stupid fucking Levi.

"Now listen to me, Harper." Sweaty Neck pulls away just enough so that he can see my face. "Do not settle for any more blockheads. You are fucking sunshine, and deserve nothing but fucking sunshine in return. Got it?" Sweaty Neck stares into my eyes, with a slight grin on his face.

"Yes, I *am* fucking sunshine!! No more couch ruiners for me. Thank you, Robert. I can't even begin to tell you how glad I am that you were sitting with me. You are a true gentleman and I appreciate you so much!"

"Well, geez." Sweaty Neck lets go of me to rub the back of his neck, and I pretend that I don't notice his eyes glistening. "Be safe on the rest of your trip and have fun with your sister."

With that, Sweaty Neck walks one way to find his uncle who is picking him up, and I go the other in an attempt to find Terminal 2 and my next plane.

It's a good thing there are so many signs telling me where to go, otherwise I would be stuck in this airport forever. I'm directionally challenged and have gotten lost in the grocery store before. Yeah, I'm embarrassed for me too. The airport is huge, and while architecturally intriguing, I don't want to live here. Sure, there's tea and food, but I would like to see my sister soon. Making my way to my next plane, I text my sister.

Me: Hey, just landed in Frankfurt and on my way to Paris. I lead such a fabulous life *tosses hair behind me*

Cara: You're on European soil! Squeeeeeeeee I'll see you soon!

Me: Just a hop skip and a jump and then I'll be at your house!

Cara: You should pick up some German sausage to enjoy during your layover

Me: I don't eat sausage

Cara: Not that kind of sausage ;) German men are hot

Me: Ugh, no. I am done with any nationality of sausage for a while

Cara: Never say never

Me: I'll let you know when I'm in Paris. Love you!!

The rest of my journey flies by (ha! See what I did there?!? I'm hilarious!). On a plane, sit down, make polite small talk, read, get off plane. And repeat.

∎∎∎

Finally, I land in Sova. If I wasn't afraid of contracting some terrifying diseases, I would kiss the ground. But no one wants hepatitis, so it's only ground looking for me. I find my sister standing just outside of arrivals. And I'm going to murder her. Does Sova have an extradition agreement with Canada?! I could probably make my way to some other country and hide for a while.

Cara is holding a poster board sign with my name written in thick purple letters on it, covered in pink and yellow glitter. It looks like her preschool class threw up on it. She's waving it around and yells "HAAAAARRRRPPPERRRR! I'M WAITING FOR HARPER JONES!!"

Ugh, guess I'm choosing murder tonight.

Cara drops her poster and hugs me as soon as I'm within reach of her.

"Harper!!! I am so glad that you're here! How were all the planes? Did your ears pop? Did you get any German sausage? Did you sleep?" Cara asks me rapid fire. I'm guessing she's had about four cups of coffee today. I think coffee is gross, but Cara drinks it non-stop. It's probably how she has enough energy to keep up with her group of three-year-olds at work.

"Planes were planey, ears popped a bit, no sausage for me, I slept a little, and you're cut off from coffee," I reply.

"Theo is at home making us a delicious dinner, but you're welcome to go straight to the guest room we have set up for you and crash if you're more sleepy than hungry. Whatever you need, lovey."

Cara, although younger than me, has always been the more motherly of the two of us. She's always looked after me emotionally and still regularly checks in with me to see how I'm doing. A few months ago, she mailed me a care package filled with my favourite tea, comfy socks and the newest Lucy Score book, just because. No reason for it, just wanted me to get a box full of happy.

Cara leads me to her shiny red Audi S4 wagon.

"Holy moly, Cara!" I yell out. "This is a sexy car! Damn, marrying a doctor has its advantages!"

Cara just laughs at me. "Nice cars and a big dick, I'm a lucky woman!"

We giggle as we load my suitcase into the trunk, alongside the giant sign Cara was holding, aka exhibit A in my murder trial. The trunk is huge, and for a moment I consider crawling in and falling asleep. Probably illegal to ride around in trunks here too, though. My tiredness crashes into me. Even though I've really only been sitting down, I'm exhausted. Travelling is hard work, man.

As Cara drives us to her house, the purr of the engine puts me right to sleep.

■■■

"Hey, Harpy-love, we're here." Cara's voice pulls me out of my sleep induced fog.

"Ugh, sorry, I didn't mean to fall asleep on you. I didn't realize I was quite so tired." I rub my eyes and wipe drool away from my mouth. Gross. I am definitely no rom-com princess who wakes up with perfect hair and makeup. I drool, have knots in my hair and should not be conversed with for a good twenty minutes after waking up in the morning.

We get out of the car and walk into her beautiful home. They bought it about four months before their wedding, and have been remodeling it ever since. Cara is constantly sending me pictures of updates and getting my opinions on tiles, paint and countertops. It looks incredible in her pictures, but I'm sure it's going to look even more amazing in real life.

The house is about 250 years old, and they've tried to keep as much of the original features as possible, with a vintage French country vibe. Her foyer has this gorgeous cream and red toile wallpaper, printed with giant roses. A brass chandelier hangs above our heads, and its beauty is so breathtaking that I find myself standing in the foyer, staring up at it. Cara brought me along virtually to antique shop after antique shop looking for the perfect pieces for her house. I remember her finding this chandelier.

We were both speechless when she spotted it in a back corner of a little shop just outside of Croix that had way more things than space.

"Cara", I whispered to her. "You have to go touch that one! It needs to be petted and loved. Look at the detail!" She walked over to it, reverently, stroking the arms of the candle sconces. "This is absolutely perfect! If I have to choose between this and my hypothetical future children's wellbeing, I think I might just pick this chandelier."

Looking at it now, I can't blame her for her thoughts. My poor hypothetical nieces and nephews. At least they'll have a gorgeous chandelier to gaze upon while they're stuck in the house forever because they couldn't afford to move out or get an education.

The chandelier is from the 1920's, and the ornate sconces look like rose buds, just like in the wallpaper. The leaf bobeche drip pans make it look feminine and soften the harsh brass. It is perfection.

I make myself leave the chandelier and walk into the kitchen where Theo is indeed cooking our meal. That man is an absolute boss in the kitchen, and I'm pretty sure I'm going to put on at least fifteen pounds while I'm visiting. It'll be worth it.

The kitchen has white marble countertops and blue-grey cupboards. A giant island with black barstools takes up the middle of the kitchen, with a vase of beautiful white tulips in the middle. Another gorgeous vintage chandelier hangs over the flowers, this one in a softer, more delicate gold. Theo is standing at the marble apron sink finishing washing his hands and I rush over to him before he can even dry his hands completely.

"Theodore!! It's so good to see you! I've missed my pretend brother!"

Theo wraps his big arms around me. He smells like wood and vanilla, and it's the exact perfect scent for him. Masculine, yet soft and sweet.

"Harper! I'm so glad you made it! Were your flights ok? Do you need a drink?" Theo's deep, rich voice surrounds me like an embrace.

Theo immediately goes into host mode and gets me a drink of water. We chat about my flights, and I tell him all about Sweaty Neck. We avoid discussion of Levi, but I know they're both dying to talk about it. I appreciate them pretending that they aren't though. I need some time to be happy here first.

We eat perfectly cooked, locally caught fish, roasted potatoes and green beans. After crappy airplane food, this is absolutely heaven in my mouth. I even groan in a very unlady-like way.

The three of us spend the rest of the night sitting around the fire in their giant brick fireplace, chatting and catching up. It feels so nice to laugh with people who love me. At this moment, I feel truly happy.

Chapter 5 - Harper

Today is Friday, and though Theo is at work, Cara got a supply to cover for her so we could have an extended weekend together.

We start by going to brunch, our absolute favourite meal. Whoever invented brunch deserves a gold medal. Waffles and booze at 10am, yes please!

"Ok, Harp, time to spill. You gave me the quick version of what asshat Levi did, but I know you left out a lot. So, go, all the details!"

"Ugh, do we really have to talk about him? I'm happy eating," I whine. But I know she won't let me off the hook. She's always had a knack for getting me to spill all of my secrets.

"I really did give you all of the details. I got home early after being fired, feeling all kinds of embarrassed and pathetic, and I walked into our house to see him fucking some woman. I didn't recognize her and he tried to tell me it wasn't what I thought, while his dick was still half hard from the pounding he gave her." I shake my head, trying to get the image out of my head. It doesn't work. It's probably permanently burned onto my brain.

"Did you suspect he was cheating on you?" Cara asks.

"No, not at all. I never had a thought that he might be sniffing up someone else's tree. Looking back, I can see that we weren't happy or in love anymore, but there was never anything that made me think something was *wrong*. But honestly it didn't feel *right* for a long time either. Maybe I should have seen that as a red flag, but I didn't. It was easier to ignore the unhappiness and pretend like ok was good enough. It doesn't matter now though, we're over, and I'm actually ok with it. Hurt as shit about the way it happened, but not really hurt about the relationship ending."

Cara tilts her head and studies me for a moment. I appreciate that she's accepting my feelings and words. It feels good to know that I can tell her what I really feel. Levi used to try to tell me what I think or feel, instead of really *listening* to what I was saying.

"OK, so then, next hard question. Maybe take another drink of your mimosa before you answer this one." Cara motions with her hand to drink up, and you don't have to tell me twice. I gulp down a giant mouthful of deliciousness.

"So, what's the plan now? You are obviously very, very welcome to stay here as long as you want to as you sort out your next steps, but just wondering if you have any

36

next steps thought out?"

"Ummm…nope, " I reply, really popping the p. "I have zero steps thought out, which in itself is messing with my head. You know how much I like planning things out. I'm thirty-three years old and I have no idea who I am or what I want to do when I grow up. I'm such a fucking mess!" I can feel tears in my eyes and I blink a few times, hoping that'll stop them from falling.

"Oh, lovey, no you're not! I wasn't trying to pressure you, or make you feel bad! Not at all. I think sometimes not knowing what your next steps are is actually an important step. Sometimes you need that time to just *be* and allow yourself the space to grow. When we're just rushing and doing, we're not enjoying what we are and who we are. There's a proverb that says 'silence is full of answers', so now you just need to allow yourself to listen."

This time, I let the tears fall down my cheeks.

"Do you really think that it's ok that I don't know what to do? I feel like a coward running away and hiding in your guest room," I admit.

"It's not hiding if you're finding yourself. Now, let's finish our booze and go shopping!"

"This is the last store, I promise!" Cara tells me, and I grumble in response.

I love shopping. I really do. Malls are amazing, magical places full of joy and possibilities.

But, we've been out for hours, my feet hurt and I'm dealing with some major jet lag on top of all that. There's also a good chance that I'm a hobbit, because I've missed my second lunch and I am not happy about it.

"Okay, fine, this last one and that's it. You owe me a bath and chocolate after this."

"Deal! Come on!" Cara answers quickly as she grabs my hand and literally pulls me inside.

I can already tell that I am going to fall in love with a lot of things in this boutique, and then I'll have to deal with Cara gloating for the rest of the day.

"Oh, Harp! You totally need to try this one on! You deserve something to make you feel sexy!" Cara pulls a slinky, red dress off the rack. It's beautiful in its own right, and has a sort of femme fatale vibe to it, but it's not me at all.

I laugh at my sister, "Have you ever seen me wear something like that?!"

"No, but this is the perfect time to try something new! Just try it on, pleeeeeeeease!!!"

It's literally impossible to say no to Cara when she begs like that and looks at me with her big eyes, like a little blue-eyed seal cub. You cannot say no to a seal cub, it's absolutely impossible.

"Fine, I'll try it on, but only for you." I grab the dress from her and head to the dressing rooms.

This dress is insane. I'm pretty sure that the only person who could really pull this thing off is Jessica Rabbit.

"I'm coming out, and I'm sorry in advance if you see parts of my body that are usually covered by clothes." I walk out of the small dressing room, very, very carefully. I wasn't joking about exposing myself to everyone in the store. There is a slit that goes all the way up my left thigh. Like, *all* the way up.

"Cara, I can't even walk three feet in this dress. It's so low that a nip slip is inevitable, and my vajayjay is cold. My vajayjay needs more protection than this!"

Cara isn't listening to me though, she's staring at something on the other side of the store.

"I'm going to take this off, and then can we please go home?"

Cara continues to ignore me as she walks through the boutique. I make my way back into the dressing room and start taking off Jessica Rabbit's sex dress, when a blur of off-white thuds its way over top of the door.

"Put this on!" Cara squeals from the other side.

"Cara, I don't want to look like a sexy cartoon character again," I start, but Cara shushes me.

"Trust me with this one!"

I reluctantly agree, but once I have the dress on, I can see why Cara was so spellbound by it. It's beautiful. It's simple and elegant, but also relaxed. It's an off-white lace, with a white underlay. It has three quarter length sleeves and hits me just below the knees, while the gentle scalloping of the lace brushes against my shins like a lover's caress. The skirt flares out slightly, just enough to give it some shape, but not enough to be big. The sweetheart neckline accentuates my breasts without being pornographic like the red dress.

I step out of the dressing room, this time with a look of love and awe on my face.

"Oh my god! Harper! You look stunning!"

I have to agree with my sister. This dress is what dreams are made of.

"But, I don't really have a reason to buy this dress. I already bought clothes that I will actually wear and need while here. I don't need this dress," I say, feeling glum, but it's reality.

"OH! Oh! I know!" Cara is practically bouncing now. "You can wear it to the Sova Day party at the castle in a few weeks!"

"A party at the castle?! I don't know about that. I'm not exactly buddies with any royals, so I doubt they'll want me hanging out with them in their house. Even in this amazing dress."

"Everyone goes to this party! It's fabulous! The Royal Family invites everyone to the castle to celebrate. There is music and dancing, and so much food! There are family oriented games during the day, lunch and afternoon tea for everyone in the garden, and then an adults only event in the ballroom in the evening. And that dress is absolutely perfect for it!"

"It does sound like fun, but I might not even be here in a few weeks."

I still haven't made any plans to return home, but I probably shouldn't assume that I'll still be here. I should get back to reality at some point. Probably.

Maybe.

"Hush, you. I'm buying you that dress because I love you and you deserve it. I hope you're still here for Sova Day, but if not, I'm sure you'll have some other wonderful event to wear this to at some point."

"Well, in that case, thank you very much, Cara."

As the employee wraps the dress up and Cara pays for it, my mind wanders to what it would be like to stay in Sova for the summer.

Chapter 6 - Harper

Cara, Theo, and I spend the weekend lazing around the house, eating a lot of bread and watching episodes of *Are You Smarter Than a Fifth Grader?* Spoiler alert: we are not.

By the time Monday morning rolls around, I'm ready to get out of the house and breathe in some fresh air.

"Where would be a good place for me to go for a walk?" I ask Cara as she gets ready for work, making two travel mugs of coffee to bring with her.

"You could try Croix forest. There are some really easy hikes, and they go in a loop, so you can't get lost. It's beautiful in there this time of year. Peaceful."

My sister knows me well. Directionally challenged, with a need to be in silence and sunshine.

"That sounds perfect, I think I will head out there after breakfast."

Once Cara leaves for work, I help myself to some toast with a cup of tea, and enjoy the quiet morning.

I try to not make a plan for the week. I want to just *be* and enjoy living for right now, and a hike in the woods sounds like the perfect way to do just that.

I change out of my pajamas and into a pair of yoga pants (which have never actually experienced any yoga) and a long sleeve lilac t-shirt. I borrow a pair of shoes from Cara since they look sturdier and more hiking-friendly than my well loved Adidas I brought with me and head out the door.

Croix forest is only a fifteen minute walk away, located close to Croix castle. If I keep the castle's tower in my line of sight, I know I won't get lost. I also make sure the gps on my phone's map app is picking up my location. Lord knows that I've had to use it to find where I was going more than once.

When I make it to the forest entrance, I can see why Cara suggested I come here. It's like I'm stepping off a busy, modern day street into a forest from 300 years ago. There's a plaque at the entrance that reads: *This forest is considered Crown land. Any logging, disturbance of the ecosystem or harm to the animals that live in the forest is strictly prohibited. Citizens are welcome to enjoy the forest, and find calm within its walls".*

That explains why it feels like I'm stepping back in time. I feel like an explorer, charting new territory. There are a few paths leading off the main entrance. I choose to turn

right on random, and hope that Cara was correct when she told me the paths all connect and go in a giant loop. The ground beneath my feet is springy. The air is pure and cooler than outside the forest. I can hear birds and insects. Some squirrels scamper by as I take my time walking along the path.

I reach the summit of the hill I have been climbing. It overlooks a pond, and I can see swans gliding on the top of the water, like they're performing a ballet just for me. There is a small bench off to the side of the path, and I sit down to marvel at the resplendency of the moment.

Chapter 7 - Tate

I walk down the corridor, plush carpet underneath my shoes, and head straight for my rooms.

"How was your meeting, sir?" Gabriel, my assistant, asks as I reach my door.

"It was yet another meeting that could have been an email. I know I need to be present, and I really am honoured to be a part of most of the boards that I sit on, but a man can only be expected to sit through so many meetings where people just talk around each other."

I rub the back of my neck and sigh. My position is important, and it helps keep Sova running smoothly, but sometimes it feels more like I'm a pretty centrepiece than a valued member of the team.

"I'm going to head out for a walk. I need to get away for a bit before meeting with my father." I pull off my tie and toss it on the chair that has become a holding spot for clothes I don't want to wear, but will be expected to wear again soon around people, and therefore can't let them wrinkle. I roll my eyes. Sometimes the pageantry is too much.

Gabriel leaves me alone, and I change out of my suit and into my favourite pair of charcoal Patagonia hiking pants,

a navy henley and shove my feet into my Salomon hiking shoes. If I could live in clothes like this, I absolutely would. Unfortunately for me, I'm expected to sleep in my Tom Ford suit.

I quickly make my way to my favourite trail in Croix forest. I don't have much time between meetings today, but I need to get out. This trail has the best view in the entire forest, and luckily for me, people rarely seem to choose this particular one.

I breathe in as much fresh air as I possibly can in one breath. The meeting today rattled me. I love what I do, and know that these organizations help and will continue to help so many people. But lately, I've had this need to *do* more. I don't want to just be another person sitting in a room deciding on programs to help theoretical people, I want to *help the people*, children in particular.

I reach the top of the trail, and unfortunately for me, there is a woman sitting on my usual bench. Fuck, I really needed to be alone today. It's days like today that I wish I could just go wherever I want, be a normal person.

The woman hasn't heard me approach. Instead, she's sitting silently on the bench, leaning slightly forward with a small, private smile on her face. She tucks her hair behind her ear, giving me an unobstructed view of her profile.

And holy mother of god, she's fucking beautiful. The sight of her, with the sun shining on her, causing her auburn hair to look like it's glowing, sucks the air right out of my lungs. My hands are sweaty. My ears feel hot. I have never had a physical reaction like this to someone just from looking at them. She hasn't even seen me, hasn't even looked at me, and I'm an absolute mess. God, what would happen to me if she spoke to me? I'd be a goddamn puddle on the forest floor.

RIP Tate. But what a way to go.

I know I'm being creepy. I need to stop staring at her, but I can't seem to move or speak. I need to decide now whether to announce myself so I don't freak her out if she sees me, or call upon my inner ninja skills and leave as silently as I can.

Leaving would be the smart thing to do, unfortunately, my mouth decides against that plan and I find myself clearing my throat, saying "Bonjour, hello," the standard greeting here in Sova when you don't know the person and what language they speak.

"Oh! Goodness, I didn't see you there!" Her hand flies up to her chest, and it takes everything in me to not stare at her breasts as she takes a few big, deep breaths.

"No, no, I'm sorry. I didn't want to scare you with my approach, but it seems that I have done just that. Please, stay and enjoy the morning, I only wanted to say hello."

"Oh, ok, well hi!" She waves at me in the most adorable way. "Gah, that's dorky. I promise I am actually an adult and I don't usually scream or wave like a child to strangers. It's just so beautiful here, and I guess I got lost in thought."

Her words, her voice, are like magic. She has an accent that tells me she's from North America. A tourist then. She doesn't seem to recognize me. She doesn't recognize me! Maybe I can steal a few minutes of normalcy with her, and just *talk* like a person.

"I come here quite a bit. It's a favourite spot of mine."

"Do you want to join me? There's plenty of space on the bench." She pats the seat beside her and smiles up at me. This is probably a bad idea. I should thank her, tell her to enjoy her day and walk away. But, once again, my mouth is calling the shots. "That would be lovely, thank you."

I make sure to keep a respectable distance away from her, but what I really want is to grab her and see if her skin is as soft as it looks.

See if her skin is soft? Who am I today? I generally don't think like this, especially about a stranger, about a tourist.

I'm expected to remain in control of myself at all times, and I usually do. But not today, not with her.

"I can see why you come here a lot. It's gorgeous, eh?" She asks me. At least now I know that she's Canadian.

"It is. See that pair of swans down there? They're mates. I watch them whenever I come up here. They look out for each other, always staying in each other's orbits, like a beautiful dance only they know the steps to. They help to calm me when I need a moment to escape." Oh my god, why did I tell her that?! My goddamn mouth needs to learn to shut up around her. Can't just say *yes, it's beautiful. I agree.*

My hands are clammy again, and for the first time since I was a teenager, I'm blushing from the tips of my ears down to my chest.

"If I lived here, I'd be doing the same thing." She sighs.

I take the opening she gave me, "I take it you're a tourist, then?" She nods.

"Where are you from?"

"Canada. I'm visiting my sister. She and her husband are working today, so I'm enjoying the peace and sunshine."

I should leave. I should get up, tell her it was lovely chatting with her and go home.

Instead, I ask her, "Have you been here long and had a chance to sightsee much?"

"Not really. I got here on Thursday and have basically just hung out with my sister and her husband. Beyond shoving delicious brunch foods in my face at a cute little cafe and being dragged to store after store with my sister on Friday, this has been my first expedition. I was here last summer for Cara's wedding, and we visited some really cool spots though. I'm pretty sure I bored my sister when she made the mistake of asking my opinions on flowers for her wedding, and me and the florist geeked out over flowers for like three hours." She laughs, and fuck me, that sound goes right to my dick. I shift on the bench so she won't notice.

"Are you a florist yourself?"

"Oh, gosh no. I wish. I've always loved flowers, and for a while I thought that I would grow up to be a florist or botanist or something, but it didn't work out. I barely even gardened at my house." She frowns as she looks down at her hands clasped on her lap. Her shoulders sag and her eyebrows pull together. Well shit, here I was trying to talk to her casually and make her happy, and I've made her sad.

"There are really great gardens at the castle, some with very rare plants. I imagine you could spend entire days in there without getting bored."

The gardens are some of my favourite places to be, that is when I can't get away to the forest or my country home.

"I bet I could! I'd probably refuse to leave, and then the King would have to get the royal guards to throw me out. It would be quite the spectacle!" She laughs again. I only want to make her laugh. It's suddenly become my life's mission to make her smile and laugh.

"Pfft, they wouldn't throw you out. The Queen would probably bring you a cup of tea and join you in the rose garden." She would too. If the sun is out, she's with the flowers.

She looks at me, her eyebrows pulling together again, this time it looks like she's putting pieces of a puzzle together. Shoot, I need to cover that blunder.

"The royal family here are pretty relaxed and open with the citizens of Sova. The Crown Princess plays football on a local team, and the youngest Prince volunteers at animal shelters."

"There's a middle sibling too, right? What does he do to slum it like us regular people?"

"He likes pie. He can be found far too often at a little cafe downtown with a cup of tea and a pie. Not a slice of pie. A. Pie. And don't ask if you can have a slice, Prince Jerome does not share pie."

"Now, that is something I can get on board with! I'd probably challenge the prince to a pie eating contest over asking for a slice." She laughs that big, full of life laugh that she has. "Ok, no I wouldn't. I'd probably be too nervous to talk to a *prince*, but I'd think it!"

"I think you'd find it would be easier than you imagine. They're just people."

"Ha! Yeah, just regular people who are like gods among men, and are stupidly, incomprehensibly wealthy." She laughs, and I force myself to laugh along with her.

I change the subject quickly. "What's your favourite dinosaur?"

She blinks at me a few times, obviously confused by my sudden subject change.

"You want to know what my favourite dinosaur is? Are we five?"

"Hold on, dinosaurs are cool! I don't think the problem here is that we aren't children and shouldn't ask questions like that, it's that adults penalize simple curiosity. Oh sure, asking things about favourite vacation spots, what you would do if you won the lottery or what your dream car is are ok, because they're adulty curiosity questions. Which makes me wonder why we have collectively decided that asking another adult what their favourite dinosaur is or how fast their new shoes can make them run are no longer acceptable? Those things are going to tell me more about who the person is, and that's what I want to know."

She continues to look at me, with a crooked smile, like she's biting down on the inside of her cheek to stop a full smile from blooming on her face.

"Parasaurolophus. I've always been partial to hadrosaurs, and there's just something about their super long crest that makes me dream about riding one and holding tight to that crest that juts out towards their backs. Plus, they were found in Canada, something little patriotic me could not resist. When I was about nine, I went through a dinosaur phase. I even wrote a letter to Bill Nye the Science Guy to ask for more information about Parasaurolophus. It took months, but I actually got a whole package with information about them. Sketches, information about where they lived and what they ate. I think I still have that envelope in a box in the basement. Now it's your turn, what's your favourite dinosaur?"

"Well, the manly answer would be T-rex, obviously because I'm just as tough as one," I wink and she giggles. "But the real answer is the Ankylosaurus. I could sit here and tell you that I like them so much because they were basically walking tanks, with their armoured skin and giant wrecking ball tails, but that would only be half the reason, and not my main reason. The real reason is because I like to picture these massive, spikey, armoured dinosaurs just bumbling around saying 'dum de dum dum dum', not really having a care in the world."

We laugh together as I hunch my shoulders and arms and pretend to be an Ankylosaurus. I'm about to ask where she would ride her Parasaurolophus to when my phone rings.

"I'm sorry, I have to take this."

"It's ok. I don't mind. I'll just imagine Lionel, my Parasaurolophus swimming with the swans down there." She smiles up at me. Fuck she's sweet. I stand up, taking a few steps away for some privacy, but not wanting to take my eyes off her.

"Hi dad," I say when I answer my phone.

"Son! I hope you're still planning on making our meeting today. We're meeting in the small library, and Eliza is about to bring tea in. Simon wants to know if he can have your pie if you don't show up."

I had no idea it was already so late. I should have been back at least 20 minutes ago. I can't say I'm disappointed in the way I spent my time though.

"Tell Simon to stay away from my pie! I'll be there in ten minutes. No one touches my pie." I hang up and walk back to the bench.

"I'm sorry, but I have to go. Family meeting." I rub my upper lip against my teeth. I don't want to leave. I'd much prefer to sit here the rest of the day, just talking and laughing with her.

"I should get going too. I'm getting hungry for lunch. Thank you for this morning. This was honestly the most fun I've had in a long time."

Does she realize she's killing me with those words? She's making it impossible to leave, even though I know I have to. Perhaps, for her, this was just a pleasant morning spent in a pleasant place with some pleasant company. For me though, I feel as if my whole being has changed. The cells within my body have shifted. I'm walking away from this moment a changed man, a better man simply for making this beautiful woman laugh.

"Ok, so, I'm going to go. Enjoy your lunch. Lunch is good. I too should lunch."

Another giggle from her. At least my sudden inability to speak coherently is making her laugh. I give her a wave, holding my hand up, and she gives me a cute feminine fluttering of her hand.

"Bye! Enjoy lunching!"

I turn around to make my way back down the hill, when my mouth strikes up a partnership with my dick, deciding to work together to mess with my brain.

"I'll probably come for another walk tomorrow afternoon. A longer escape with my dogs. I have meetings all day, but I'll probably escape around three o'clock and the dogs like to run around here," I tell her, and since my dick is now taking this little speech over, I add, "If you're not doing anything, I'd love for you to join us on our walk. We could meet you here. I'd like to see you again."

She's going to say no. I've just embarrassed myself. I should have just walked away.

"You have dogs?! I will definitely join you! It's mostly for the dogs. And maybe a little because it would be nice to see you again too," she says.

"Ok, yeah. Yes. Ok. So, I'll meet you back here tomorrow at three. In the afternoon. I won't be here in the middle of the night. Unless that's when you want to meet, if that's better for your jet lag," I ramble on. Just say bye, you idiot!

"Three in the afternoon is perfect. It'll let me sleep in and get some stuff done before we meet up. Jet lag has indeed made my sense of time a little wonky, but not wonky enough that I'll meet a stranger in a forest in the dark."

She winks at me, and I shoot her some finger guns like the absolute fucking idiot that I am.

"I will see you tomorrow then. Goodbye."

I walk away before I give myself more opportunities to embarrass myself and make her change her mind about tomorrow.

I can hear her laughing as I walk away.

Chapter 8 -Tate

"And what exactly has you so smiley?"

I snap out of my daydream upon hearing my sister's voice. She's suspicious, like she knows I was thinking about pushing that woman up against a tree and fucking her senseless. I could almost feel the rough bark under my skin as I imagined shielding her body from getting scratched up as I pounded into her.

I clear my throat and force the thoughts out of my head. "Nothing much. Tell me about your meeting at the hospital today."

That shifts everyone's focus onto her as she tells us about the board meeting today and the planning for the new women's health wing at Croix General. It's her pride and joy and has her off and running as she described the spacious rooms, and how they plan on making it a welcoming space for everyone who identifies as female as well as their families. Women's healthcare and LGBTQ+ support are her two biggest causes, making this hospital project that much more important to her.

And with her taking everyone's focus, I can go back to my daydreams.

Once my sister is finished, my brother regales us with a story of how a volunteer at one of the animal shelters he volunteers at tried to clean out the kitten room, but ended up with seven kittens climbing literally all over him. I know he probably had little cuts all over his body from their sharp little kitten claws, but damn that would have been cute to see. Kittens are adorable as fuck, no one can deny that.

Mom and Dad are leaving on a weeklong trip to Switzerland tomorrow, having finalized all the details this morning.

"While we are gone, Marielle, you will need to meet with the ministers and run the meeting on Thursday."

"Got it, Dad. Don't worry about a thing. We'll be fine. I can handle the ministers. I have run the weekly meeting on my own plenty of times. Your job is to dine and laugh and make Sova look amazing. Focus on relations with Switzerland and spending some time with your friends," my sister tells Dad.

"Yes, yes, I know. You are all adults and amazing leaders. I know Sova will be in good hands while we are gone."

Once I eat all my pie, and mom gives me hers, and we're done talking about the important things, I get up to leave.

I'd like to go to my apartments and relax by the fire. Marielle however, doesn't like that plan.

"Tate! Wait up!"

I groan, I know what she wants to ask about, but I'm not sure what I can even tell her. I stop and wait for her to catch up, since she'll just follow me anyway.

"Where are you running off to so quickly?"

"I'm not running."

"Ok, fine, where are you walking speedily to?"

"I just want to go to my rooms and relax before dinner. Is it so difficult to believe that I'd like some peace and quiet?"

"No, not really, but I also know that the look that was on your face earlier wasn't just you lost in thought about the updates of infrastructure dad was telling us about."

"Ugh, fine, I was thinking about something else, but there's no story."

"You were thinking about something, or *someone*?" She does a little shimmy with her shoulders, wiggling her eyebrows up and down. She knows.

I usher her into my living space. It has a grey couch facing a large slate fireplace, with pictures from my travels on the mantle. Some are of scenery, moments in time when I was caught up in the beauty of a landscape.

Others are of me and my family on tours and trips around the world.

"I met a woman today while I was in Croix forest. She was beautiful and easy to talk to, and she had no idea who I was. We were able to talk, like, just talk like regular people. It felt nice to make someone laugh because they thought what I said was actually funny, and not because their Prince made a joke and they were worried about being thrown in the dungeons if they didn't laugh."

I sit down on the couch, resting the back of my head on the cushion and stretching my long legs in front of me. Marielle sits beside me, curling up into the opposite corner.

"She didn't know who you are? Are you sure?"

"Yeah, she had no idea. She's Canadian, over here visiting her sister. She was lovely. Probably the most beautiful woman I have ever seen. And funny. I didn't want to leave her." An image of her smiling pops up, and I find myself smiling along with her.

"God, Tate, look at you! Smiling and blushing like a teenage girl with a crush! Too bad she's just visiting."

"Yeah, too bad. I did very, very awkwardly ask if she'd like to meet me again tomorrow. I'll bring the dogs for a walk in the forest. They love the woods, and that seemed like a safe, easy way to ask to see her again."

"You're going to see her again? Are you sure that's a good idea?"

"It probably isn't," I admit. "But I couldn't seem to just walk away from her. I really had no control of my mouth. Words were coming out without my permission, and the next thing I knew, I was asking her to meet me tomorrow. I'll see her tomorrow, and then that'll be it. She'll likely be leaving soon anyway. If I see her anymore after that, she'll likely find out who I am, I'll end up heartbroken when she leaves, or she'll use me because I'm a prince."

"Not everyone is Celeste. It sounds like you made a real connection with this woman." Marielle smiles kindly at me.

"I thought Celeste and I had a real connection too. I don't want to talk about Celeste though. Ever. It doesn't matter anyway, this woman doesn't live here. We'll enjoy our afternoon together tomorrow, and when I'm old and grey, I can remember the time I made a beautiful woman laugh in a forest."

Chapter 9 - Harper

I can't cook much, but there are a few things that I can make well. Lasagna is one of those things, but now lasagna makes me think of Levi cheating on me. Stupid fucking Levi, ruining lasagna for me. Lasagna!

I can also make bread. It's a simple, no-knead recipe, but it's so delicious! Carbs are wonderful, and always necessary.

I pull out a large mixing bowl, flour, yeast, salt and a large wooden spoon. As I mix the ingredients with warm water, my mind wanders to the handsome stranger I met today.

He was beautiful. I don't know if I've ever thought of a man as beautiful before, but he was. His olive skin looked bronze in the sunlight filtering through the trees. His hair was so black it looked like a raven's feathers. His facial scruff was intentional. More than stubble, but not a beard, it was cleanly defined and looked effortless, but you knew he painstakingly made the effort to shave *just* the right amount. I'm not usually a facial hair gal, but oh lawdy, he pulled it off! His jaw was strong, nose prominent without being overbearing. He looked tall, probably over six feet. But his most striking feature were his eyes. They were blue, like mine, but that's where the similarity in colour ended. My eyes are what I refer to as watery blue. Light blue, kind of washed out looking, just blah. But his eyes were like a bright sky blue with a ring of navy surrounding them. They were mesmerizing and it took all of my willpower to stop myself from staring the entire time we were talking.

I cover the bowl and slide it to the back of the counter to let the dough rise for a few hours.

As I'm wiping off the counter, making sure to get all the flour I managed to get everywhere, Cara comes home from work.

"Hi honey, I'm home!" Cara calls out, laughing at herself. "How was your day?"

"It was nice. I went to Croix forest like you suggested. You were right, I loved it there. Then I came home, had a bath, had a nap, and started some bread!"

Cara eyes me carefully, looking me up and down.

"How come you said all of that really quickly? What happened that you don't want to talk about?"

"If you know there's something I don't want to talk about, then why are you making me talk about it?"

"Because I'm your sister and it's my job. Spill, what happened?"

"You're the worst. Fine, when I was in the forest, I met someone. A guy. A hot guy. He was so hot! Like, supermodel, what the hell are you doing in a forest where the dirt lives kind of hot."

I'm flushed now, sweaty all over. Maybe meeting him tomorrow isn't a good idea. If I'm this flustered just thinking about him, I can't imagine that I'll be charming company tomorrow.

"I'm the best and you love me. What happened with him? Did you kiss him? Ooooh, forget German sausage, you could try Sovan sausage!"

"There was no kissing, just talking. And you really need to stop calling it sausage." I roll my eyes, but laugh out loud at her. "He was nice. We talked about the forest and dinosaurs. He was unexpected, but welcomed. He made me forget about Levi and my life. We just *were*. He made me laugh. And then when he was leaving, he was so cute and awkward. He invited me for a walk in the forest again tomorrow with him and his dogs."

"Are you going to meet him?"

"I don't know. I told him yes, but now I'm thinking that maybe I shouldn't."

"Why not? You just said he was a nice, hot supermodel with dogs! Why would you pass on that?"

"Cara, you know me, I can't do casual. I fall in love. I'm only here for a short time, so getting together with him is a terrible idea."

"Who said anything about *getting together* with him?"

"You did. You told me to get his sausage!" I exclaim, my eyes going wide as I think about her suggestion.

But Cara just laughs at me, waving away any worries that I may have. "You don't have to go after him like that if you don't want to. You already spent time with him today, right? And you had a good time too. I don't see the harm in going tomorrow, even if it's nothing more than spending time with a person you get along with and forming a short-term friendship with them."

I think about what Cara's saying. It would be nice to have someone to spend some time with while I'm here and Cara and Theo are at work.

"Do you think he'll expect something to happen between us?" I ask.

"Maybe, but just because he wants something doesn't mean you have to let it happen. Make sure you have your phone on you, and we'll turn on location sharing so I can find you if need be."

"You have a point. And turning on location sharing is probably a good idea given how easily I can get lost. And he has dogs."

After gorging on bread, cheese and fruit for dinner, I collapse into the bed Cara set up for me. The room is gorgeous. Light, dove grey walls with white trim. The hardwood floors continue throughout the bedrooms. There is a white and cerulean blue carpet, with a looping floral-like pattern in the middle of the room, disappearing under the queen size bed. The sheets and pillows match the blue in the carpet and the duvet is a crisp white. This room has an attached ensuite with matching dove grey walls and accents in the same blue. The freestanding tub sits under the large window, with plants hanging down in macrame pot holders. The white and grey honeycomb tiles on the walls in the separate shower and above the sink add some interest, without being too dramatic. The drama is left to the giant, sparkling silver chandelier hanging above the tub. My sister sure does love chandeliers.

I fall asleep quickly, with thoughts of a certain blue eyed beautiful man taking over my dreams.

Chapter 10 - Harper

I allow myself to sleep in a bit. I am on vacation, you know. I heard both Theo and Cara wake up, but refused to get up with them. The bed is warm and soft, and mornings suck monkey butts.

By the time I roll out of bed, it's almost ten. After visiting the little girl's room, I make my way downstairs to the kitchen. Theo left out some muffins he must have picked up from the little bakery down the road. I choose a lemon poppyseed muffin and pick at it while I wait for the kettle to boil.

As I sip my life-giving black tea, I ponder what to do about my date in the forest. I don't even know his name. Shouldn't I know the name of the person I'm going to disappear into a forest with? What if he's a murderer with a murder shack in those woods? Or, what if he's some kind of sex maniac and has a sex shack in the woods? I like sex, sex is fantastic, but I'm not one to jump into bed with any random stranger who has a sex shack. No judgment for those that do that, you do you and get yours, all the power and love to you! But, that's not me. I get attached easily. I get my heart broken easily. I came here to heal and spend time with my family, not to meet someone new and start a relationship that will inevitably end.

But maybe Cara is right. Just because I find him extremely attractive, and I could feel tingles all over my body while he was talking, doesn't mean we can't be friends. Having a local buddy would be nice. He said he works a lot and has to attend a lot of meetings, but he was there yesterday in the middle of the morning, and he said he'll be free by three o'clock. Sounds like he has a decent amount of flexibility in his schedule for a friend, but he probably doesn't have time for a relationship. Sounds like a win-win to me!

I'll meet him today, suggest we be friends for the duration of my visit and just have fun. Just be.

I putter around the house for a bit. Putting away the dishes from last night's dinner and sweep the floors. They're feeding me and letting me stay in their house, so I figure I can help out by doing some chores.

With the house tidied up, I jump in the shower. I pretend that I'm taking extra care to scrub and shave and wash in all the crevices for me. Being clean and smooth is nice for me.

Not for anyone else's hands.

Yep. And the coconut lotion that I'm putting on now is all for me too.

Mmhmm. I like when my legs are soft and smooth.

I grab the hair dryer out from the cabinet under the sink and dry my hair, making it lay smooth and straight down to my shoulders. My hair has a slight wave to it if I let it air dry, but then it also gets frizzy, so I make sure to blow dry my hair when I'm going to see people.

I look at myself in the mirror. I don't usually wear too much makeup, just a quick application of foundation, some bronzer and mascara. If I want to get really fancy, I'll add some eyeliner. I also pretend that I'm not taking extra time blending in because of the mystery man.

Yes, fine, I'm lying.

Yes, I want to look good for him.

Yes, I want to be smooth and soft and smell delectable to entice him.

I can't help it. I know nothing can happen. My brain knows that nothing can happen, but my vagina is driving this bus, and she is a horny little bitch.

My brain manages to convince Ms. Vaj to dress casually, though.

I put on a pair of dark wash jeans and a cobalt t-shirt. I've now claimed Cara's hiking shoes as my own. After lacing them up, I head out the door.

Theo helped me set up location sharing on our map apps last night, so we can all see where each other is at any given moment. Knowing they could easily find me if I get lost helps to alleviate any worries I have about walking around alone in a strange city.

I have over half an hour to make the fifteen minute walk, but maybe that's a good thing. Some time to enjoy the fresh air and talk Ms. Vaj down.

By the time I get to the forest, I can pretend that I have successfully convinced myself that becoming friends with this man is a good idea.

I make it to our meeting spot about ten minutes early, but he's already there. He's dressed similarly to yesterday, but today he's wearing dark khaki pants paired with a white shirt. He's laughing at something that I can't see, and I feel like all the air has whooshed out of my body. His laughter surrounds me, squeezes me tight. It's a deep, melodic embrace.

Two giants come loping towards him from the trees. I have to assume that these are his dogs. Although they're huge, they're graceful. They bound more than run. One is mostly white with a light brown patch on its head and one near its hips. The other is also white, but with large black patches covering almost half of its body.

I walk towards them, stepping on a twig and snapping it, ruining my own graceful entrance.

"Hello!" I call out, with a little wave.

He turns around and as soon as he sees me, a huge, full smile takes over his face. The dogs start bounding over to me, but he gives a loud, sharp whistle and they stop. "Sit", he commands, and the dogs automatically sit down.

I understand the dogs immediately obeying him. His voice had dropped to a deeper, authoritative tone making even me instantly want to do as he said. To please him.

"Hi there! Would you like to meet the dogs? I promise they're gentle. Sometimes they forget how big they are though." He chuckles and scratches the head of the white and light brown one.

I walk right up to the dogs, trusting him when he said they're gentle. With the speed that their tails are wagging, the darker one vibrating with happy energy, I think I can believe him.

"This one here is Axelle and she will love you forever if you scratch her right here," he says as he scratches right behind the ear of the lighter one. "And this one is Mars. He wants to believe that he's his sister's protector, but in reality, he hides behind couches if he hears a noise. Any noise." Laughing, he gives the darker one some love.

I reach out and start petting Axelle, which makes Mars jealous, who shoves his long snout between my hand and his sister's head.

"What kind of dogs are they? They're gorgeous!" I ask "They're borzois, and they know exactly how beautiful they are. They believe they are royalty and that your job is to treat them as such. They're two years old, so still just babies and have a ton of energy. Hence why I bring them here to get all their sillies out. They are insanely fast, so I need to keep my eyes on them, and when we get deeper into the woods, they'll need to be leashed or they'll see a squirrel and be gone within seconds. They listen to my commands very well, but they are sighthounds and hunters by instinct. They'd be gone before you even realized there was something to chase." I pet the dogs more before I make myself shift my attention.

"What's your name? I realized last night that we never actually introduced ourselves, and continuing to call you 'that man I met in the forest' will probably get weird if we spend more time together."

His eyes search mine for a second, like he's having an internal argument with himself before he clears his throat a little and finally replies, "I'm Tate, and it is an absolute pleasure to meet you." He reaches out his hand to shake mine, and ohmygod, the gentleman act is making Ms. Vaj sit up straight and reach for the controls.

I take his hand in mine and squeeze. His hand is much larger than mine, and so warm. I can feel a zap of electricity between our palms. I need to let go.

I don't ever want to let go.

"My name is Harper. How about we get going? I didn't really see much of the forest, just the one trail up to this spot." I need to get moving and put a bit of space between us, or I might do something stupid like climb him like a tree.

Tate clips the leashes onto the dogs' harnesses and leads us further into the woods.

As we walk, we make small talk. We discuss the weather, I tell him about my flights, making sure to mention the gloriousness that was Sweaty Neck.

I explain why maple syrup is the best thing ever invented and that nothing tastes quite as good as maple syrup from Québec. He tells me of a Sovan pastry filled with cream and blackberries he likes to eat.

"How about a lightning round?" he asks with a grin.

"Sure, but I get to pass on anything that's too personal or too much for a new friendship."

"Ok, I accept your terms," he agrees with a quiet chuckle.

"Alright, first question, what is your favourite colour?

"That's your first question? Yesterday you asked about my favourite dinosaur, and today you're asking about my favourite *colour*?" I ask, confused and surprised. I was expecting something more in depth.

"I'm just warming up! Favourite colour?"

"Purple."

"What's your favourite shape?"

This was more what I was expecting from him and I smile. "Triangle."

"Favourite season?"

"Summer."

"Favourite holiday?"

"My birthday!"

He looks at me from the corner of his eyes, but doesn't comment.

"Ok, what is your house like back home?"

"Pass." I do not want to talk about anything connected to Levi and why I'm here. We're having fun, and that conversation would drag the mood way down.

"Interesting. Ok, then what do you do for a living?"

Shit, I don't want to answer that one either, but I need to give him something, and this seems slightly safer to answer than anything about Levi. I look down and bite the inside of my cheek, thinking about how to answer without sounding like a loser.

"I was an administrative assistant at a design company in Toronto."

"Was? As in you are no longer?" He clarifies.

"Hmm, yeah. You weren't really supposed to pick up on that," I huff out a breath. "I worked there for five years. I didn't really enjoy it, but it was a paycheque and I was good at my job. I was fired last week. My boss said not to take it personally, and it was just a numbers thing since they are getting less clients right now, but it's hard to feel ok about losing your job when you didn't expect it. It stings."

"Harper, I am so sincerely sorry. But, you said that you didn't like your job. Perhaps this is an opportunity for you to find something that you actually enjoy doing."

"Yeah, my sister said the same thing. I'm just not sure what that something is."

"What's your favourite flower?"

I am beyond grateful to him for changing the subject. I didn't want to continue down Poor Harper Road.

"Now that, sir, is a difficult question to answer. I don't think I have just one favourite flower. Choosing one would be like asking me to choose a favourite book or favourite song. I have a favourite for different moods, different seasons, different memories. They're all so spectacular in their own ways!"

"Ok, give me a list of five favourites, in no particular order," he amends and laughs at me. His smile reaches his eyes, telling me that he's happy and enjoying this conversation, rather than finding my inability to choose just one favourite exhausting or frustrating like Levi did. "Hmmm, if I had to choose five flowers, it would probably be lily of the valley, daffodils, tulips, roses and columbines. However, I reserve the right to change that list at any given moment."

"Tell me why you listed lily of the valley first."

"Well, when I was little," I start with a smile to my voice, already getting lost in some of my favourite memories of my mom. "We had lily of the valley growing along our house on the north side. They only bloom in spring, and only really for a short time, but every year, I would spend hours just sitting in the grass, smelling the flowers. They were my mom's favourite, and she would come out and sit with me at the side of the house, freezing in the shade in May in Ontario. But we were so happy there, talking about anything and everything. Now, whenever I smell them, I think of my mom and her beautiful smile."

"Those sound like perfect memories of an obviously beautiful person," Tate says quietly, looking at me with a tender smile. I know he picked up on the use of past tense when I mentioned my mom, but he doesn't ask, and I appreciate it.

Grief is hard, and sometimes it hits you right in the chest even in the middle of a happy memory, and I don't want to spoil this moment with him.

We continue to walk and he has to pull the dogs away from a rabbit, his arms jerking as the dogs attempt to give in to the chase. We make our way back to the bench we met up at. He takes both leashes in one hand and tells the dogs to sit, which they do immediately.

"Thank you for asking me to join you and the dogs today. I had a lot of fun with you. And the dogs." I stumble over my words.

"So did I. Thank you for joining us. Axelle and Mars must have been trying to impress you, they didn't pull my arms off nearly as much as they typically do." He laughs, but it's obvious he loves his dogs and doesn't really mind having his arms pulled off by them. "Do you remember when I mentioned the royal gardens? I was thinking that you should visit them."

"Are they open to the public? Can we just walk in and stroll around?" I ask, not really sure what the protocol is for visiting *royal gardens*.

"Some parts of the gardens are open, yes. You need to purchase a ticket, but then you can spend the day in the public areas of the castle grounds, exploring gardens and greenhouses. However, I was thinking more of a behind the scenes thing. If you'd like, I know the head gardener and I bet he would love to show off his babies."

"Are you sure that would be ok? I wouldn't want to go anywhere that I'm not allowed or anger the Royal Family." It would be incredible to visit and speak with an expert like the head gardener of the Sovan Royal Gardens.

"Yes, I am sure that it would be fine. Let me text Yves and see what would work for him." He pulls out his phone and taps a quick message to who I assume is the head gardener.

"So, then, is setting up visits to private gardens something you do for all your friends?" I ask, knowing I need to friend zone us quickly. I don't want to go into this as a date. I cannot date him. Friends can look at flowers and go on tours of gardens together.

Absolutely they can.

It wouldn't be romantic at all.

Mmhmm.

He looks up from reading the reply that has come in already. "Honestly, no, I have never asked Yves if he'd show the gardens to anyone before. But, I can tell that my new friend Harper would absolutely love to see them, so it's my job as a friend to make that happen." He grins at me, making any remaining just friends feelings I was holding on to disappear.

"Yves would be more than happy to show you around. I'm going to be busy over the next few days, but he said you can go to the garden entrance and ask for him by name. The staff will know to expect you and will let you in, free of charge."

"Oh my gosh! Are you serious right now? That is amazing! Thank you so much for setting that up for me. But I can pay the entrance fee, I really don't mind," I insist. It would feel weird to just stroll in.

But he just waves away my concerns. "Truly, do not worry about it, Harper. Yves might be more excited about it than you. He keeps sending me smiley face, flower, and heart emojis," he tells me, holding up his screen for me to see. There is indeed a screen full of emojis. I think I'm going to love Yves.

We say our goodbyes, much less awkward than yesterday, and I make my way out of the forest, and back onto the busy street. It's a lot busier than it was when I left, and I quickly find myself turned around and confused. I tuck myself into a little alleyway between a bakery and candle shop, pull out my phone and find the marker I added for Cara's house on my app. After studying the route for a bit, I turn the other direction than

I was heading and find their street within five minutes.
Thank goodness for technology, or I'd probably walk
myself into the ocean.

■■■

Theo is already in the kitchen preparing dinner when I get
back to the house. Cara is sitting at the island with a glass
of white wine and a book. They are the epitome of
domesticated bliss.

They aren't even really doing anything, and you can feel
the contentment rolling off them, permeating the air.

I'm not necessarily jealous of them, but I do want what
they have. They are true love. Every fairy tale I have ever
heard pales in comparison to the way that Theo looks at
Cara, like she is the sun and it is his life's purpose to
catch and hold onto her rays.

I never had that with Levi, not even in the early days. We
had lust. We had affection. We had agreement. But I
never felt adoration like I see with my sister and her
husband. Now that I can look back and examine our
relationship, I'm glad it's over. Not happy, but glad.

Chapter 11 - Harper

I'm positively vibrating with excitement as I walk over to Croix castle. I've been awake since 8 a.m., but made myself wait until ten before leaving. I don't want to appear crazy when I show up, even though I feel like I am right now.

Between the forest and the castle, there is a brick lined driveway leading up to a small parking lot and a smaller brick lined path leading up to ornate wrought iron gates. A live edge sign with "Sovan Royal Gardens" written on it in a beautiful cursive script hangs above them.

I walk right up to the little booth in front of the gate.

"Hello, my name is Harper Jones. I'm looking for Yves." I tell the young woman sitting in the booth.

"Oh, yes! Ms. Jones! Yves has been looking forward to your visit. If you could hold on for a minute, I will radio for him and he will come meet you just through the gates. You're welcome to go on in, but stay near the front so that Yves can find you. He'll pull up in a golf cart so you won't be able to miss him. I hope you have a fantastic day!"

She points toward the front gate, and I thank her and make my way to the gardens.

I walk through the gates, marvelling at the fact that they don't squeal like how I imagine old iron gates should, they must have a full-time gate oiler. Ye Olde Oiler.

I see a white golf cart coming right for me.

He's exactly what I imagine a head gardener would look like.

In his late 50's, he has salt and pepper hair, a bit more salt than pepper, and a bushy moustache, which has more pepper than salt in it.

He's wearing khaki cargo pants and a white golf shirt, although with the amount of green and brown stains on it from working in the gardens, I'm not sure if you can legitimately call it white anymore. He has a straw hat on, which is the only hat a gardener should be allowed to wear.

"You must be Harper!" Yves booms as he stops his golf cart a few feet from me, stepping out slowly, with his hand extended already for a hearty handshake.

His hands are rough, and his laugh is loud. He is full of life.

I absolutely do love him.

"Yes I am! And you must be Yves! I can't tell you how happy I am that you agreed to let me come visit you! This is a dream come true!" I'm way too excited, but I can't help it. Disneyland-schmisneyland, I dream of garden tours!

"Oh, it's not a problem at all. I am more than happy to have you here. Let's go for a ride in my golf cart and we can stop at the main greenhouse first, maybe get a sense of how many plants we have here, and then if there's anything specific you want to see, you just let me know. How does that sound?"

"Yves, that sounds positively superb!"

We get in the golf cart and Yves points out a few plants and trees as we drive. There's an orchard at the back that is starting to bloom, which includes some fruit that I've never even heard of. There's a hedge maze, rose garden, pond, wildflower fields and even beehives where they produce Sovan honey.

"Here we are! This is the main greenhouse, but we have a few smaller, more specific ones on the grounds as well. This is where I do most of my work. There is a front section that is open to the public, but we'll go to the back so you can see my messy house and how the magic comes alive." He smiles at me like a kid on Christmas. We pull around to the back and Yves leads me inside. It smells like soil and green. I'm not sure what exactly the green smell is, but it's heavenly. I take a big breath in and Yves does the same.

There are giant work tables with the biggest bags of soil underneath them. Pots, trowels and gloves are scattered all over the tables. To my right is a smaller table with a long, hanging light above it. Some geraniums in smaller pots sit on the table, along with some pansies, marigolds and daisies. There's a bougainvillea sitting in a large pot on the floor beside the table. On the other side of me are some begonias, impatiens and violas. The room seems to be separated into a full sun side and a shade side.

"We're prepping flowers to fill in beds and containers along the walkways. We spent all winter creating charts and plans on where to put flowers and create seasonal gardens. Every year is a little different. Queen Janelle helps decide which flowers to use every year, but trusts us with the design."

Tate did mention that the Queen loves the gardens and flowers. It sounds so otherworldly to imagine a *Queen* getting down and dirty with the plants and gardeners.

"Is there anything that I can do to help?" I ask Yves, crossing my fingers and toes that he'll let me get my fingers into some soil. It's the best, when you feel the silky soil between your fingers and give that little plant a home. I didn't realize just how much I missed this, how much I needed gardening.

"Absolutely, Harper. I would love it if you would help me fill these containers over here. We'll put these at the entrance, so they'll need to be dramatic and colourful. We'll start with the geraniums first."

Yves and I work together for over an hour. He shows me the plans the gardening team and the Queen created. It's going to look gorgeous when it's done.

"Well, I think we're done with these for now. How about we dust ourselves off and I'll take you on a tour of the rest of the gardens before we part ways?"

Yves drives us slower through the gardens and shows me where he plans on planting the marigolds, what gardens he wants to add some more native wildflowers to, and the spot he chose by the pond for the bougainvillea. His team is putting in a tall, wide arbour and some new benches, creating a private sitting area and will train the bougainvillea to grow up and around the trellis. He teaches me about their thorns and how his team will have to keep them meticulously manicured so people don't hurt themselves getting too close to the plant.

We arrive back at the main gates all too soon.

"Now, Harper, please tell me that you will be coming back to visit me again?" Yves asks earnestly.

"I don't want to overstep, but, Yves, I would live here if I could," I laugh. "Maybe I can come back in a couple of days?"

"Tell you what Harper, I'm here during the week, nine to five. You show up whenever you want, however often you want, and I will always be happy to see you."

"Sounds like a plan, Yves!"

Chapter 12 - Tate

It's been three days since I last saw Harper.

Not that I've noticed.

Or thought about her.

Or missed her.

Nevermind, I've been thinking about her nonstop.

It took all of my willpower to not run down to the gardens when I saw her walking into the greenhouse with Yves two days ago. I had to grab onto my chair to make myself stay sitting during a budget meeting, when all I really wanted to do was go see her.

I wanted to be there to see if her eyes lit up when she was in the greenhouse like they did when she was talking about the lily of the valley she sat by with her mom.

I imagined her smelling the flowers, feeling their petals with her dainty fingers.

I pictured her laughing and smiling in the sunshine.

I'm not sure if seeing her again would be a good idea or not. I want to see her, badly, but that doesn't mean it would be the smart thing to do.

"Yves was telling me about a visitor he had in the greenhouse. He is absolutely taken with her!" My mother announces as she glides into the sitting room I'm attempting to read a report in.

I clear my throat and sit up straight. "Oh yeah? What has he said about her?" I try to act casual, but this is my perceptive mother, and there's no way she's falling for it. "Just that she loves the flowers almost as much as he does, and that she was a friend of yours. Interesting how I have never heard of this friend before now."

"We met randomly while I went for a walk. She's here visiting her sister, and she mentioned that she likes flowers. I set up a meeting with Yves, it's not really a big deal," I shrug, hoping to get her off the scent.

Obviously, it doesn't work.

To make matters worse, my sister chooses that particular moment to join us.

I love my family, dearly, but they are a bunch of busybodies. If I give them any small details, or the inclination of details, they will latch on and won't let go. "Are we talking about the woman Tate met? Yves says she's lovely. And beautiful. Tell us Tate, is she as beautiful as Yves says?"

Well shit, what do I say now? My sister already knows how I feel about her, and will absolutely call me out on it, but I don't particularly want to have this conversation with my mother, especially since nothing can come from these feelings.

"Yes, she is good looking. But stop," I hold up my hand, knowing exactly where my mother's mind is racing to. "She is only here visiting. She does not live here. She doesn't even live on this continent. Whether or not I think she's pretty doesn't matter because she will be leaving soon. I was being nice and offered her an opportunity I know she would appreciate. That is all. Now, if you will excuse me, I have some work to do."

"Work, or daydreaming about a beautiful Canadian you want to *offer an opportunity to*?" My sister sings after me, giggling.

I choose to ignore her, and the fact that my mother joins her.

· ·

High school still smells the same. Bleach, paper, sweat and hormones. I have found that no matter where the school is, private or public, they all smell the same. Angst and cleaner.

"It is my absolute honour to introduce our guest today. He once walked these halls and listened to lectures in the same rooms as you. Please put your hands together and give a big Crembois welcome to His Royal Highness Prince Jerome!"

I stand up from my chair on the stage, button up my jacket as I take the few steps to the podium and wave to the students.

I enjoy doing things like this. I would much rather come to a school and speak with a group of teenagers about what they're working on than sit through another meeting about strategic planning and infrastructure. That's my sister's jam, not mine.

"Thank you everyone for such a warm welcome. It is my honour to join you here today. I cannot wait to see what you have created. And I promise that I will try to keep up as you explain what you've come up with, but if you see my eyes glaze over and I start nodding more than normal, you've probably lost me." Everyone laughs. "I, along with your teachers, will circulate the room and you will have the opportunity to explain your work. Remember that this is not a competition, but more of a gathering of creative and inquisitive minds. We will not be grading you or choosing a winner. I am here to learn from you, and we welcome you to walk around and see what your peers have created."

This became a pet project of mine a few years ago. During a meeting with the education minister, we were discussing ways to introduce more STEAM (science, technology, engineering, art, and math) experiences to students, especially those that may not have access to the materials, tools and resources to tinker, build and create. I approached tech companies and artists about running some workshops and providing materials to let the students learn to program, play around with electronics, motors, lights, paint, charcoal, and whatever else they may not otherwise have easy access to.

Some students have created elaborate structures, obviously taken more with the building and designing aspect. Others have created simple video games. One girl has created a rocket. A boy set up a light show to his favourite song, creating an impromptu dance party. One girl created a giant mural of abstract art to represent the feeling of community.

We make our way around the room, and listening to how passionate and enthusiastic these kids are about their projects fills me with excitement. Some of these kids have never done anything like this, and now they're thriving. I hope at least a few of these kids feel like pursuing a career in STEAM is something that they can attain after this. I know a few needed a boost to get their grades up and start thinking about the future.

■■■

I'm driving down rue Étoile, a main street in downtown Croix, when I see Harper. I almost swerve into the next lane when she throws her head back and laughs. She's sitting at a cafe, a cup of what I assume is tea in her hands, with a woman that looks a lot like her. It must be her sister.

The light changes to red, and I come to a stop at the intersection with her maybe thirty feet away. My car, a sleek black Mercedes AMG GT, is tinted so dark that I know she can't see in, and I struggle whether or not to pull over and go see her.

If I get out, people will address me as Prince Jerome, and that will cause some confusion. I know I'll likely have to explain to her who I am if we see each other again, but I like that she talks to me like I'm just Tate and not a prince. That might never even be a discussion we have to have. She's only here for a little while, not like she ever really needs to know. Maybe I'll never see her again.

My heart rate increases at that thought. I do not like the idea of never seeing her again. Never getting to look into her eyes. Never kissing her.

I shake my head and force myself to tear my eyes away from her and drive away when the light turns green.

Chapter 13 - Harper

I have been here in Croix for almost two full weeks now.
I set up a schedule with Yves for me to come help in the
gardens and learn from his infinite wisdom. I will go in
on Tuesdays and Thursdays. Today is Thursday, and as I
make my way into the gardens, giving Delphine at the
front gate a wave before I head in, I notice there is a lot
more hustle and bustle going on.

Yves meets me in his golf cart so I don't have to walk all
the way to the greenhouse, something my feet appreciate.
"What's up with all the extra people here today?" I ask as
we approach the main greenhouse.

"We're getting ready for Sova day!" Yves yells out
enthusiastically.

My excitement for Sova day comes nowhere near Yves'.
I doubt anyone could match his enthusiasm.

"We'll have all hands on deck until Sova day next
Saturday. Planting, sprucing up the main grounds and
gardens, getting flowers ready to cut for fresh
centrepieces. Mulching, weeding, trimming. It'll be a
busy week, but it's also my favourite week!"

"Alright, so where do you want me today to help?" I ask, mentally preparing myself for an intense, back breaking day.

"I have a special assignment for you. In the main private gardens there is a huge rose garden, and within the rose garden is the rose greenhouse. In there, we are able to grow a variety of roses year round. Every Sova day, the Queen selects a rose of the year to cut and use in floral arrangements during the evening ball. I need you to check on the roses for me."

"You're trusting me to do such an important job alone? I am not qualified to do that!" I start to panic. I don't want to ruin something so special for the Queen.

"Ah, no, do not worry at all. You will be assisting my top rose checker!"

Yves drives us around the gardens and up a path that I have never seen before. He has to get out and unlock a gate, making sure to lock it again when we are through. We make our way through some more beautiful gardens. I assume that we are now in the private, main grounds of the castle.

I can see our destination now. Up ahead I see a giant glass dome, surrounded by thousands of roses. Bushes, vines, reds, pinks, yellows. Rows and rows of roses.

We stop and Yves leads me into the greenhouse. I'm not sure if *greenhouse* is even accurate for this building. Glass castle is more like it.

Yves opens the door, and a wall of humidity, spiked with the unmistakable sweet scent of roses hits me.

"Looks like we beat her here. That's ok, it will give you some time to get acquainted with the space. This greenhouse was built in 1798 for Queen Selène by King Phillipe III. She loved roses and missed the greenhouse that she had back in Belgium. King Phillipe couldn't stand to see his bride so sad, so he commissioned this for her. It was said to be her favourite place, and rumour has it that she begged her husband to bring her here as she was dying, so she could be amongst her roses as she left this world for the next."

"I do wish we knew the accuracy of that story," says a woman's voice from behind me. "But in all my searching, I have not been able to find out if it is truth or myth. I would like to believe it to be truth. Much more of a romantic story that way."

"Your Majesty, I did not hear you come in." Yves turns around, smiling at the newcomer.

Your Majesty? That means this is the Queen! Shit! Oh my god. What do I do? How do you curtsy?

I do an awkward bow thing and bend my knees, kind of a curtsy, maybe?

"Your Majesty! Hello, hi!" And there goes any good impression I was hoping to make.

But she just smiles kindly at me, her eyes big and bright.

"Hello, you must be Harper. I have heard so much about you. I have to admit that I asked for you to join me here today. I hope that you do not mind."

"Oh, no, your Majesty, not at all. It would be an honour to help you. Your Majesty."

"Please, call me Janelle now that we have become acquainted. Yves, I hope we can chat later on about the progress of the gardens."

"Of course. Enjoy your time together and let me know how you feel the roses are coming along," Yves replies as he walks out of the greenhouse. And leaves me alone. With. The. Queen.

"Ok, I feel like I need to be upfront here for a moment," I begin to nervously ramble. "I don't know what I'm supposed to do right now, I have never been around a queen before. I don't know how to be casual and pretend like you aren't my sovereign. Wait! Oh my gosh, you aren't *my* sovereign! Is it ok that I talk to you? Like, is there some sort of sovereign rule that I just broke because I curtsied to you and I just enacted some sort of war between you and my King and Queen?" I'm panic rambling now. I know that I'm not making any sense, but I can't stop freaking the fuck out.

Queen Janelle glides over to me, like somehow queens just know how to glide, and takes my hands. God her hands are soft. Of course they are, dummy, she's a queen!

"Harper, I am a regular person who loves roses. I am here with you to look at roses and talk about roses and pet all the pretty roses. In here, we can just be Janelle and Harper, alright? You and me, just regular women. Got it?" She asks me, searching my eyes.

In that moment, I see it. This is probably her escape from reality, just as much as coming here has been mine. She needs this just as much as I do. I take a big breath. "Show me what to do."

"Come over here and tell me what you think of these ones. I love the colour, but I'm not sure how they'll look in a vase."

Queen Janelle leads me over to some big, bright fuchsia coloured roses. I study them for a moment, tilting my head to look at them from another angle.

"I see what you mean. The colour is striking, and they'll totally be noticed, but the flowers are big. Like, really big. I would be worried about them flopping over from lack of support and looking sad and droopy," I say as I hold one in my hand.

"Yes, I agree. Why don't we walk around and we can see what else is growing well in here," Queen Janelle suggests, as she hooks our arms together and begins walking towards some light, blush pink roses.

"These are a nice size, but the colour won't stand out as much as the first ones you liked," I comment.

"Agreed. So, we are looking for a rose with a smaller head, but bright colour."

I look around at all the roses. There are every shade imaginable in here. Toward the back, I see them. A fuchsia so dark they almost look red with a purply-pink sheen to them lending them a magical aura. They have tight blooms, holding the precious petals closely together.

"What about those ones?" I point toward them.

"Oh, you do have a good eye! Those are a hybrid tea rose, and I think they are perfect!"

We take some time to count the blooms to ensure that there will be enough to fill the vases on the main tables at the ball, and check the plants for any signs of ill health. The Queen proclaims them to be healthy, happy and perfect.

I know she must be busy, she is a very important person after all, but Queen Janelle insists she can stay and answer all of my questions about the roses here. She really is an expert and clearly loves these flowers. She tells me about their watering schedule, fertilizing, how to cut blooms, when to cut blooms, when not to cut blooms. I feel like I have learned more about roses in the last hour with her than I would have otherwise learned in my entire life.

"I'm sorry to say that I must leave now. I have had a lovely time with you, Harper," Queen Janelle tells me, as she once again takes hold of my hands. The Queen is a warm person, and I have gotten over all my worries and awkwardness from earlier.

Ok, maybe not all my awkwardness. I'm still awkward AF.

"I feel like I just lived a fairy tale here with you. Thank you for giving me so much of your time today," I tell her, and mean every word of it.

"It has been my pleasure. I do hope to see you again."

Then she winks at me.

■■

I fly into Cara's house. "Holy shit, Cara!!" I call out.

"Cara! I just met *THE QUEEN*!" I squeal as I run through the house looking for her.

Now that I've had the time to process the day, it's hitting me.

Cara comes out of her room, pulling a shirt over her head.

"What are you on about, lovey?"

"I met the Queen of Sova! Like, the actual *Queen* of Sova! She was nice and taught me about her roses and held my dry, cracked hands in her super soft ones, and probably thought I need to moisturize more, because, yeah I absolutely do, but even if I do, my hands could never be as soft as a motherfucking queen's hands!" I try to catch my breath after the word vomit that just poured out of my mouth.

"Ok, so, you met the Queen and need hand lotion?" Cara's eyes are big as she's staring at me, probably waiting for me to freak out again.

"Yes, and well, yes, but mostly I met the Queen! She was so nice, Cara!"

I fill her in on my day, and only ramble a couple more times about her soft hands.

"Speaking of Sova Day, are we still going to Theo's parents?" I ask.

"Yep! Every year, they host a big family party. The entire family comes, and so do most of the neighbours. It's the biggest party of the year in their neighbourhood. We'll leave late morning and can stay as long as you want. If you want to come back to experience the party at the castle and see all your hard work in the gardens come to life, we can totally come back before dark."

"I'm ok with staying at Theo's parents' house. I'll be at the castle helping with finishing touches on Friday, instead of just going on Tuesday and Thursday, so I'll see it all then." It would be nice to see everyone appreciate my hard work, but I won't pull Cara away from her new family, and I'm looking forward to hanging out with some of Theo's cousins I met at their wedding.

Chapter 14 - Tate

"Tate, honey, are you in there?"

"Yes, Maman, I'm in the office."

My mother sits down in one of the navy upholstered club chairs facing my dark cherry wood desk.

"And to what do I owe the pleasure of your visit today?" I ask, immediately suspicious of her.

"I just wanted to see my favourite son named Tate." She smiles up at me.

My mother is sweet and caring. She has always been very hands on with us, not something always typical or possible with a busy royal family. We had nannies and a full staff growing up, but Maman was set on being as present as possible, both her and my father. They attended every school event, helped us with homework and taught us how to ride a bike. Papa taught us how to drive, only asking the chauffeur to step in for lessons when he was abroad. They took us on diplomatic trips as much as possible, breaking all sorts of protocol. We always knew we could talk about anything with our parents, knowing they would never judge us for our feelings.

My mother loves me, but I know she is bullshitting me right now and there is a specific something she's here to talk about.

"Mmhmm, sure you did. And while you're here, what should we chat about?"

"Oh, nothing in particular," my mother tries to feign innocence. "Is there anything on your mind that you'd like to share?" She flutters her eyelashes, no doubt trying to appear more innocent, but it just makes her look more guilty. It's a good thing my mother became a queen and not an actress.

"Maman, if you're here to talk about Harper, just come out with it," I sigh.

"Well, now that you've brought her up, I did happen to meet her."

"What do you mean you *happened to meet her?* The Queen does not just happen to meet anyone she does not plan on meeting."

Oh god, what did she do?

"Yves has been so busy with preparations for Sova Day, and I knew he could use a hand, so I offered to look at the roses with Harper so he could be elsewhere. She helped me choose the perfect colour blooms for this year and we chatted a bit. She is absolutely lovely, Tate! But, of course, you already knew that, hmm?"

106

"Maman," I grumble. "I have already told you. Nothing will happen between Harper and I. She is only here visiting. So, unless you're suggesting we have a torrid, short-term fling, I recommend focusing your efforts elsewhere, like perhaps Marielle's wedding next year."

"I just want you to be happy. I see the way your eyes light up when you talk about her. I'm not sure I have ever seen you so happy at just the mention of a woman's name before." Maman looks down at her right index finger, drawing swirling patterns on her left leg.

"I am happy," I tell her. "Harper and I have become friends. She *is* lovely, and yes, ok, fine, I can't even remember how to walk when I'm around her, but, again, it doesn't matter. It's a crush, and I will move on. I'm thirty-one years old, I need you to trust me when I tell you that I'm happy and can manage my own love life. I'm happy."

I'm a filthy liar.

My mother smiles at me, the private smile she only gives to her children, the one that tells us she loves us no matter what, through and through.

"Ok, Tate. And I'm sorry, but I'm your mother, it's my job to worry and meddle. Marielle is getting married next summer, and Simon and Corvin married already last fall. I want you to find what they have, what me and your father have. And if you want to give me some grandbabies too, I wouldn't be upset about that."

"Geez, Ma, you're barking up the wrong tree about babies. I haven't met the right woman yet, and I still have lots of time to meet her. But for now, I need to work on this speech for this year's graduation from Crembois."

"Dinner will be ready in an hour. Simon and Corvin should be arriving in about twenty minutes. Marielle and Dax are already here having drinks with your father. We'll see you soon."

She walks out of my office, and I hear the doors of my rooms click shut behind her. I sag my shoulders and let a heavy breath out.

"I'm fine. I'm happy. This is fine."

I don't believe myself, but maybe in time I will stop picturing Harper wrapped in my arms whenever I imagine the future.

■ ■

I hear voices floating up to me, and a quick glance at the clock tells me that I only have fifteen minutes before dinner.

I was supposed to be working on my graduation speech for Crembois, something I have given every year for the last five years.

Instead, I spent the last forty-five minutes thinking about Harper.

How she'd moan as I kissed her neck.

How her breasts would feel in my hands.

How her nipples would get hard under my tongue.

How soft and warm she would feel as I slid my cock deep inside of her.

I needed to get control over my body and my thoughts, unless I wanted to eat dinner with my family with a raging boner.

I get up and walk around the room, forcing myself to breathe in and out.

Once I feel in control, I head downstairs and find my family already making their way to the smaller dining room we use for family dinners.

"Tate! How the hell are you, man?" Corvin, my brother's husband calls out when he sees me, grabbing me and hugging me tight.

"Hey Corvin, I'm good bro, how's it going with you?" Corvin releases me, and pushes his blond, curly hair out of his eyes. His hair is forever flopping in his eyes, yet he refuses to grow it longer or cut it shorter.

Simon makes his way over to us, throwing an arm around his husband's shoulders.

They are a beautiful dichotomy of opposites. Corvin is shorter than Simon by about five inches, blond, and athletic. He has broad shoulders, thick, muscular thighs and arms and a hearty laugh. Simon on the other hand, is tall at 6'3" and lanky. He has black hair, cut very close to his head. Has thick, black rimmed glasses and is the most academic one in the family. He has a Master's degree in biochemistry and is working on his PhD. They're different, but perfect together. They compliment each other and keep each other grounded.

We chat for a bit, them filling me in on their week. Simon visited three animal shelters this week. I think it relaxes him when his brain feels ready to explode, trying to process theories and experiments, filled with words that I can't even pronounce. Corvin tells me about his adventures in cooking last night. As in, how he burnt dinner beyond a crisp and they had to order pizza.

We make our way to the table. Michel, our head chef, prepared dinner for us, but we like to serve ourselves. When we aren't in the public eye, or hosting a state dinner, we're just a normal family eating chicken, egging each other on and trying to one up stories. Sunday dinner is family dinner. Whoever can make it is expected to.

"How's your speech coming along, Tate?" My father asks. He knows how important attending Crembois graduation is to me.

"Not so great, Papa. To be honest, this year I'm struggling with what I want to say. I don't want to repeat the same speech from previous years. I want it to be meaningful, fresh. Specific for this graduating class. But the words aren't forming, and I'm starting to get frustrated with it," I admit.

"You still have a few weeks yet, correct? What if you took some time away from the city and went to your house in Montfret to clear your head? Perhaps some country air and a different space will help," My father suggests.

"That's a good idea. I'll leave after Sova Day, maybe stay for a few days. The dogs would certainly like to get out there." I look at Axelle and Mars sleeping on their beds, cuddled in with my mother's springer spaniel, Violette. They would indeed love the freedom of the walled-in grounds to run. Six acres of privacy and peace is exactly what we need.

"So," Papa starts, and I see him glance at Maman. "Umm, how are Sova Day preparations coming along, Janelle?"

Shit.

"Wonderfully!" Maman claps her hands. "The flowers are beautiful, and Harper and I picked out the most beautiful roses. Harper also helped me choose flowers for the smaller vases around the room that will coordinate with the roses. She truly has a gift. She's so smart and beautiful and kind."

I glare at my mother. "I think that's enough talk about the flowers, how's the menu for the day coming along?"

But no one pays attention to me. They just keep talking about how brilliant Harper is, like I'm not even there. The fuckers.

"Tell me more about this Harper. Yves has been singing her praises since she came to help him. He said she's a blessing, sent down from the heavens." My brother is laying it on thick.

"Oh, she's certainly angelic. I like her quite a bit. I bet we would all like her quite a bit."

And that's my cue to get up and pour myself a lot more scotch.

"Guys, come on," I grumble and then down the scotch, focusing on the burn rather than the doe eyed stare of my mother.

"I know what you're doing, and it needs to stop. Obviously, you all know of my feelings for her, but, like I have already said, it doesn't matter. She. Doesn't. Live. Here." I pour myself another finger of scotch, tossing it back quickly. "Now, if you'll excuse me, I'm leaving because you're all jerks."

"We love you!" Simon calls out as I'm leaving the room.

"Yeah, yeah, I love you guys too. Goodnight, all."

Chapter 15 - Harper

Between helping Yves in the gardens, spending time with my sister and getting in some sightseeing, I haven't had the chance to get back to Croix forest. And maybe a part of me didn't want to go in there in case Tate was there. I want to spend more time with him, and that scares me. I just got out of a relationship. I don't know if I can trust my heart, and I really don't want to get my heart broken again. Plus, I'll be leaving to go back home. At some point.

But today is Wednesday. I don't have to help Yves, and the forest is calling my name. The sun is shining, the birds are singing and it's a beautiful day to spend outdoors.

I make it to the bench on the hill and sit to enjoy the little picnic lunch I packed myself. Ok fine, that Theo made and packed for me. I love Theo and his cooking.

I did however make the tea and put it in the travel mug myself, so I'm adulting enough.

After my sandwich, I watch the swans. What did Tate say about them? That they're performing a dance that only they know. He has a way with words, beautifully painting a picture with his prose. His voice melts around you like honey as he describes a scene. He could probably recite his grocery list and I would find it erotic. I pack up my containers from lunch, slipping them into my backpack.

"Well, isn't this a welcomed déjà vu."

I turn around to see Tate, standing ten feet away, like I conjured him here with my thoughts, his dogs sitting beside him.

"Tate! I haven't seen you in weeks! I need to thank you for hooking me up with Yves! I have had the most magical time working with him. I've learned so much from him. Thank you, thank you so much!"

He starts to blush, and looks away from me, clearing his throat.

"You are very welcome, Harper. I'm glad to hear that you're enjoying your time with him. Were you on your way out?" He asks me, with a hint of vulnerability in his voice.

"I was enjoying some lunch and was about to do a loop before heading home. Would you like to join me?"

"Yes, I would. As long as you're ok with it."

I walk over to them and crouch down to scratch the dogs' heads. Axelle flops down and I rub her belly. Mars shoves his long snout under my arm again, pulling my hand away from his sister. Jealous little guy.

"Shall we take a path that you haven't explored yet?"
Tate asks, as he switches Mars' leash to his other hand so
that he has a dog per hand.

Tate leads us in the opposite direction than I have
previously taken. I'm completely relying on him here,
because I have no clue where we are.

"Last time, I had to answer your lightning round
questions, so this time it seems fair that I get to ask you
questions."

"Yes, that does seem fair. But same rules apply. I get the
right to pass on any questions that are too personal," he
replies.

"Of course, kind sir! Question number one. What is your
favourite juice?"

"Good one. Let's see, probably apple. I know it's simple,
but I love the tartness of it."

"Growing up, what was your dream car?"

"Lamborghini Countach. It's over the top and exactly
what little boy dreams are made of."

"Favourite holiday?"

"Christmas. I like giving. And sparkly things."

I laugh. This man is ridiculous.

"Ok, hard one coming at you. If you could have a
superpower, what would it be?"

"Hmmm, ok, I need to really think about this. I'm assuming I can't make it something like the ability to have any superpower I want?"

"You would be correct with that assumption. That's like finding a genie and wishing for more wishes. Goes against the rules. One specific superpower."

"In that case, I would probably have to say teleportation. Think of how handy it would be to just *go* somewhere, anywhere. Not have to worry about sitting in traffic or taking three planes to come see your sister. Teleportation would be fucking amazing. That or flying, but teleportation *just* wins out."

"Wow, I was going to say telekinesis, but teleportation would be fantastic. It would save me so much time visiting, and I could do it more often. I was all set on wishing I could move things with my mind, but then you come in with your realistic argument and make me reconsider."

"Do you know when you're going back home?" he asks me, as he studies the trees in the distance.

"No. In a very un-Harper-like way, I haven't made any plans. I know I need to figure out what I'm going to do, find an apartment I guess, find a job, blah blah blah, but it's honestly been nice to just not. I haven't not had a plan since I was a teenager. When my mom got sick, I was only sixteen. After she went into remission the first time, we were so hopeful. But cancer is a deadly bitch. It came back, and by the time I was eighteen, and should have been starting university, I was a full-time caregiver to my mother. I put school and my life on the backburner so I could focus on my mom and sister. She put up a good fight, but the cancer was stronger." I stop to wipe tears from my eyes, finding tears welled up in Tate's eyes as well. "When I was twenty, I started university, but played it safe. I studied English, got good grades, and kept moving forward, even though I took two extra years to graduate. After a few odd jobs, I was hired at Peters Designs, where I stayed simply because it was a job. I met Levi a couple years after that."

"Is Levi your boyfriend? He'd probably want you to go home sooner rather than later," he says. He's clenching his jaw, moving it from side to side. I'm not sure if he's even aware he's doing it.

I can't help it. I laugh. Uncontrollable laughter. It's either laugh or cry, and my survival instincts are kicking in and choosing laughter over curling up into a ball and sobbing.

"S-sorry," I stutter between laughs. "It's just that that is a shitstorm kind of story." I huff out a breath.

"You don't have to tell me anything, Harper," Tate tells me.

"No, I want to. It actually helps to talk about it. After I got fired, I drove home and found Levi at home with another woman, having sex against my couch. I packed my bags and left right then and there. Theo got me a plane ticket and I left a few hours later. After losing my mother, it was the worst day of my life. Now I have nothing to go back to, and the more time I spend here, I wonder why I want to go back at all, even though Toronto has been home to me my entire thirty-three years of life."

"Holy shit, Harper. Did you punch him in the throat? Fuck, let's go right now, We can be back here for tomorrow. How dare he do that to you? You are goddamn perfection, how could he not see that?"

He's breathing heavily, hands clenched around the leashes he's now holding in a deathgrip. I put my hands on his chest.

"Tate, it's ok. Take a big breath for me."

His eyes fly up to mine, staring into them as I can feel his heart rate begin to slow down to a more normal pace. We stand there for a few minutes, lost in each other. He slowly looks down to where my hands are still resting on his hard chest. I can feel his defined pecs through the cotton of his t-shirt. He switches both dog leashes to one hand, and covers my left hand with his.

"Harper," he says my name like a prayer.

A small animal, probably a squirrel, scurries up a tree and Mars tries to take off after him, pulling Tate and Axelle with him. Mars is practically dragging them as Tate tries to regain control. No wonder his body is so muscular, he'd have to be to deal with those dogs.

He gets the dogs back on the path, our moment behind us.

"What's your favourite shape?" I go for an easy, light question after I brought the mood down.

"Oh, that's simple, an icosahedron."

"That's *simple*? How is that simple? What even is an icosdahedron?"

He laughs at me. "An icosahedron is a 3d shape with twenty sides."

"Dude, that's not simple." I flick my eyes to him, but smile broadly. "What's your hot drink of choice?"

"Tea, although I do occasionally crave a coffee in the mornings. My whole family loves tea. My sister actually has a secret breakfast blend she created. It's too dark for me, but she loves it."

"Oooh, I bet I would love it! Dark, black tea is my favourite! It sounds like I would get along with your family, or at least want to join them for tea time." I giggle. Sometimes I am really easy to please.

"What was your last relationship like?" Now I'm just being nosy. I don't need to know this, probably shouldn't ask, but I'm dying to know what kind of women he's attracted to.

"Pass." His voice is hard. Unmoving.

"Ok. No talking about the ex. What about your favourite colour?" I choose an easier topic.

He looks me up and down, then quickly away from me. "Ice blue."

It looks like asking about his ex has completely soured the mood. I need to lighten the mood. By a lot.

"Tell me the weirdest fact you know."

His lips tip up, clearly enjoying what he's about to tell me.

"There was once a form of divination that used cheese to predict the future. It was called tyromancy."

"What? Are you serious?" I ask, blinking a few times. "Why cheese? I mean, cheese is fantastic, let's be honest here, but how on earth would it be used to predict the future? Would someone eat moldy cheese and have hallucinations, claiming visions from God?"

"Ha! No, although I'm sure some people may have tried that. Tyromancy was more about reading the way cheese matured, changed over time. Mold spots, scent and shape would all tell the person something about the future. Similar to reading tea leaves."

"Huh, well, there's my something new for today. Oh! I have one! Sunsets on Mars are blue! Because of the dust in the Martian air, the light from the sun scatters in a different way than here on earth, and us humans perceive that as looking more blue, even though daytime hours on Mars look more red."

"Whoa, for real? That's cool. We'll go to Mars one day and see it for ourselves."

Mars the dog stops and looks at us, his head tilting side-to-side, trying to figure out why we keep saying his name.

We chat easily as we loop our way back around to the bench.

"Hey, Harper. I know you're busy with Yves lately, and leaving soon, but do you think maybe I could get your phone number? Maybe text you and we can meet up intentionally for a walk?" he asks me, foot scuffing up the forest floor. He looks bashful. Adorable. I want to hug him.

"Yeah, sure, friends text each other, right?"

Friends. We are friends. I can be just friends with him.

"Here, put your number in my phone, and then I'll text you so you have my number too," he says as he hands me his phone.

I take it and put my number in and he immediately texts me.

"I should get going. Cara is probably home by now and wondering where I am."

"Bye Harper. I'm glad I ran into you again. Have a good night," Tate waves at me and he and the dogs make their way down the path they take home, as I go down a different one to Cara's house.

Chapter 16 - Tate

I sit on the couch in front of the fire, phone resting in my hands.

"Don't look at me like that, Axelle. I'm trying to come up with something witty but nonchalant to say."

Axelle continues to stare at me, her dark eyes judging me.

"It is not that easy. I need to sound casual, yet interesting, but like I'm also not trying too hard."

Axelle walks away, clearly lost her faith in me.

"Knock, knock!" Marielle calls from the other side of my door.

"Come on in, Mari," I look up to her walking in, dragging Dax with her.

"Who were you talking to, Tate? I don't want to interrupt anything," she asks, looking around the room, like she's just caught me with a girl in my room past curfew.

"Just Axelle, who has been no help at all. What can I do for you two?"

"Your mom has a list of errands for us to run for the festivities tomorrow, but there's no way we can get it all done. Any chance you can run to the bakery to check on the extra desserts and then confirm that the children's entertainers for the family events will arrive by noon?" Dax asks me, as he passes me a note with my mother's familiar, tidy script written on it.

"Yeah, sure, I can do that. Only those two? You guys can handle the rest?" I ask as I take the paper from his hand.

"Yep, just those. Everything else is ready for tomorrow, just these last minute things. It looks like it's going to rain soon, so most of the prep work is being done inside and they'll move it all outside tomorrow morning," Marielle adds.

••

I slip into my car, errands completed. The bakery is on track to finish all the requested desserts tonight, ready for delivery tomorrow, and the children's entertainers are packed and ready to go. They were running through a practice when I stopped by. They're quite good. Upbeat and catchy. The children will love them.

The rain is starting to come down, dark clouds rolling in, hiding the sun.

I grab my phone and text Harper.

Me: Hey Harper, it's Tate. How's your day going?

Harper: Hi!!! I'm just about finished up at the gardens. All the work had to be done in the greenhouses, making it sweaty and cramped, but we got it all done!

Me: That's great. Do you have a ride home? It's starting to rain pretty heavily now.

Harper: Gah, seriously? Shit, no, I'm walking. But it's ok, it's not too far

Me: I'm really close to you, I'll come meet you at the garden gates.

Harper: You don't have to do that, I don't want to be an inconvenience

Me: You could never be an inconvenience, Harper. I'll be there in 5 minutes. Take your time coming out.

I toss the phone on the passenger seat, and pull out onto the main road that leads to the castle. Most people have retreated inside because of the rain, something that will work in my favour picking Harper up from a place where so many people could recognize me.

I make it to the gardens quickly, finding a parking spot right near the gates. I grab an umbrella from the pocket in my door and head out to wait for Harper. Delphine at the gate sees me, curtsies quickly, but continues closing down, anticipating no more visitors in lieu of the rain.

Luckily there's no one else around, so I just wait under my umbrella near the front for Harper. It doesn't take too long before I see Yves driving her up in his golf cart. I have known Yves most of my life. He came to work here before puberty hit me, and he has been a calming presence in my life ever since. A good friend to the entire family, he's become more like family himself than someone we employ.

"Hi there, Yves. Hope you were able to get your work done today, despite the rain," I call out when they're close enough to hear me.

"Hello, Tate. We managed just fine, and everything will be gorgeous tomorrow."

"Hello, Harper. Are you ready to go?" I step closer to her side of the golf cart, so she can duck right under my umbrella.

"Yes! Thank you again for coming to get me! It's not a far walk, but honestly, I hate getting wet."

Shit.

Don't think about Harper being wet.

Don't think about Harper being wet.

Yves nods and smiles at me. "Goodnight you two."

"Goodnight Yves!" we call out together.

I lead Harper over to my car, thanking the maker there's no one else around.

Harper directs me to her sister's house and she's right, it wouldn't have taken her long, but I still wouldn't want her walking home in this weather.

I get out to walk her to the door. Fully intending on leaving her there.

That is, until she looks up at me, with those gorgeous Arctic eyes framed by thick, dark lashes, and asks "Would you like to come in for a bit?"

"Yes, I would."

Chapter 17 - Harper

I'm not sure what possessed me to ask Tate to come inside. I should have thanked him for the ride and said goodbye. That would have been smart. But, noooooo, Ms. Vaj took one look up at him, standing there with water running down the side of his face, collecting on his eyelashes, since he insisted I take the umbrella with me out of the car, and invited him inside.

This is ok. Friends have each other over all the time. We are friends.

Cara and Theo aren't home yet, so we make our way inside and I wish we had a chaperone like we lived in the 1800's.

"Would you like a cup of tea?" I offer, leading us into the kitchen.

"Yes, please. I could go for a cup after being out in that rain."

I put some water in the kettle, set it on the stove and turn the gas on. I grab two mugs, putting a tea bag into each one.

"Do you take milk and sugar in your tea?" I ask, trying to keep my voice from wavering.

"Just a bit of each, please." Tate tells me, as he leans across from me against the island. He rolls the sleeves of his light blue button down shirt up, and I try to ignore how the muscles in his forearm bunch and tense and he settles back against the island. God, why was that so fucking sexy? They're arms. Just arms. Ok fine, they're not *just* arms. They're super sexy Greek god arms. I need to stop staring at his arms before he notices and thinks I'm a weirdo with an arm fetish.

I might be.

The kettle whistles as it boils, and I turn around to pour the water into our cups.

I clear my throat. "Can you pass me the sugar bowl from behind you, please?" Maybe if I act super casual, like making tea is way more exciting than his stupid, sexy arms, I'll forget how much I want to touch his arms. With my fingers. With my tongue. With my teeth.

Gah, get it together, Harper!

Tate places the sugar in my hand, letting his fingers graze mine as he does. I swear electricity passes through the two of us. He stands up straight, angling his body so he's directly in front of mine. I involuntarily turn back around to face him and take a step closer after placing the sugar on the counter behind me, completely eliminating the space between us.

We're both breathing heavily.

His nose flares slightly.

His fists clench and unclench as he stares at me, eyes flicking down to my mouth and then back to my eyes.

I can feel my heart in my throat.

My feet are tingly.

My nipples are so hard they could cut glass.

"Fuck it!" he says, and then he moves. He crashes his lips onto mine and cups my cheek with the palm of his hand, angling my face a bit.

Then he growls.

He. Fucking. Growls.

And that sound is my undoing. It unleashes a primitive part of me, wanting him to consume me. Needing him to consume all of me.

We are a mass of tongues and teeth and hands. My right leg is hooked around his left hip, while my hands roam his back, his shoulders, his neck.

He holds me tight to him, one arm wrapped around my back while the other has moved from my cheek to the back of my head.

I can feel the hard muscles in his back strain as he devours me, his thick, hard cock pressed into the softness of my belly.

I can't feel anything besides him.

I can't think about anything besides him.

I only want him.

I'm on fire for him.

We lose ourselves in each other, only living in that moment for the other.

When he pulls away, we're both breathing hard, gasping for the breath the other stole. He rests his forehead against mine, eyes closed, holding me just as tight.

When we've both calmed down, he trails his nose from my temple down my cheek until his lips meet mine again.

This time, the kiss is gentle, pure.

Slow and seductive.

He sweeps his tongue against my bottom lip and I let him in.

This kiss.

This. Kiss.

This is the kiss.

If before we were a raging inferno, setting everything ablaze in our path, burning so hot we left nothing but ashes behind, this kiss feels more like sitting in front of a wood stove on a cold, snowy day, cuddled up with someone under a thick blanket.

This kiss feels warm.

This kiss feels like home.

This kiss feels like a word that I refuse to let myself think, because that would be insane.

When Tate pulls away this time, his lips don't leave mine completely. I can feel him smiling against my lips, making me smile too.

He moves his head so that we're cheek to cheek and he sighs contentedly.

"I have wanted to do that since the very first time I saw you," he whispers in my ear.

"Really?" I whisper back, barely audible.

He pulls away, just enough to look into my eyes. "Yes, really. I couldn't breathe when I first saw you sitting on the bench." He tucks a piece of hair behind my ear. "You are the most breathtakingly beautiful woman that I have ever seen, and for some unfathomable reason you wanted to talk to me."

"Have you seen you?! Tate, you're gorgeous. I'm shocked I was able to speak to you!" I laugh as I recall how nervous I was when I saw him standing near me the first time.

He studies me for a minute. "But, you'll be leaving soon." He says it as a statement, not a question.

"Yes. I need to get back home. Probably should leave soon."

Kissing him was wonderful, magical, but I can't just ignore reality.

His phone rings, and his whole body sags. He leans his forehead against mine again, but he doesn't pull out his phone to answer it.

"That'll be my mother or sister. I need to get going. I wish I could stay but know that I can't. Will you be going to the party at the castle tomorrow?" he asks, not moving away from my body, like he can't bear the thought of leaving.

"No, we're going out of town to Theo's parents instead for their annual Sova Day party. They don't live far, but it's an all day event, so I'm told," I reply.

He nods his head against mine, and finally pulls his body away from me, putting some space between our bodies.

"Ok." Just that simple word, and he manages to sound both disappointed and relieved.

He takes another step away from me. "I should go. We have some work to do for our own party tomorrow, and if I don't leave now, someone is bound to call repeatedly until I get home."

I walk him to the front door, where he gives me another tender kiss.

"Goodnight, Harper. We'll talk soon. Enjoy your day tomorrow."

"Goodnight, Tate. Happy Sova Day."

Chapter 18 - Harper

"You're being quiet tonight, Harp," Theo comments.
"Usually, you're full of stories from your day."

"Oh, what? Sorry. Just thinking," I tell him, hoping to
appear like my body isn't vibrating, full of the energy left
behind from Tate's kiss.

"Hmmm, something's up," Cara comments, tapping her
finger on her lips. "I know you. You're hiding something,
and judging by how you're jiggling your foot, it's juicy!
Did you see Tate again?!" She gasps and points at me.

"Nooooooo," I draw out the word.

One look at Cara and Theo and I know I haven't fooled
them.

"Ok, fine, yes. I saw Tate today. He drove me home from
the gardens because it was raining. And holy shit, Cara, I
thought your car was sexy, but damn, his car gave me a
lady boner. But then he walked me to the door and his
wet skin gave me a real life for real lady boner and I
invited him in, and then instead of drinking tea we ended
up kissing, and holy mother of God it was the hottest kiss
of my life!" I slap my hand over my mouth to stop
anymore words from pouring out.

"What kind of car does he drive?" Theo asks.

"A black one," I reply drily.

"Oh. My. Gosh. Harper!" Cara yells in my ears, slapping my arm with each word. "Finally! I have been waiting for you to get some! And then what happened?" Cara is still squealing at octaves much higher than my ears would appreciate.

"We only kissed. I'm leaving soon, Cara. We've been over this. I can't start something with him. I think I should start planning to return home soon. I need to figure out where I'm going to live, find a job, get back to real life," I reply, feeling dejected.

"How about we'll sit down next week and start looking for apartments. But, this weekend let's just enjoy ourselves and celebrate. Have fun. Just *be*."

"Ok, you're right Cara. Let's *be* this weekend, and then it's back to real life."

■■■

Tate: Good morning, beautiful. I just wanted to say hi and hope you have fun with Theo's family today.

Me: Good morning, handsome! I'm glad it's sunny out today! Is your party outside, too?

Tate: Both inside and outside. The sun is almost as brilliant as your smile.

Me: Laying it on a bit thick there, Romeo

Tate: Sorry, but now that I've let it out, I don't think I'll be able to stop.

Tate: I need to go though. I just wanted to say good morning. I wish I was able to see you today. Maybe we can get together next week?

Me: That would be nice. I'll miss you today. Have fun! Byeeee

∎∎

Theo's parents live about forty-five minutes east of Croix in a small town called Angelique. It's a picturesque town, settled around Angelique Lake, a lake so blue it doesn't look real.

The town is decorated in light blue and amethyst, the country's colours.

Theo's parents have already set up tables of food, and people are milling about eating and drinking. Pop music is playing through an outdoor Bluetooth speaker and kids are running around, playing some sort of elaborate game only they know the rules to.

"How are you enjoying your time in Sova, Harper?" Theo's mother, Estelle, asks me.

"It's been so great! Everyone here is so nice and friendly! I've actually been volunteering at the Royal Gardens with the head gardener there. He's been so kind to me, letting me tag along and ask a billion questions about every plant. He has reawakened a love of plants that I shut down years ago," I tell her. I wish a little that I was at the castle to see everyone's reactions to the flowers I put hours into this past week.

"How long will you be here for? Theo tells us you've already been here for a few weeks now. Maybe there's someone keeping you here?" Estelle wiggles her eyebrows.

"I've made a few friends here, that's for sure, and I will be sad to leave them, but I'll be leaving sooner rather than later. Cara and I are going to spend this week looking for an apartment so I can get back to my life," I sigh.

The lines of what my "real" life is are starting to get blurry the longer I spend here. It takes a lot of effort to not think about Tate and how hard leaving him will be.

"Why not stay? You could apply for a working visa," Theo's dad, Dane, chimes in.

"I have never considered that. Hmmm, maybe I'll look into it. Thank you for the suggestion."

I spend the day eating way too much food, getting to know Theo's family and enjoying the sunshine. After the crazy that was this week, it's nice to sit back and relax. A group of children have started a spontaneous talent show. Some of them do a dance they saw on TikTok that I am absolutely not cool enough to know, and then a cousin sings her rendition of *The Sign* by Ace of Base and totally nails it. Unfortunately, Theo's uncle Edward is currently attempting to sing Justin Timberlake's *SexyBack* and I will never unhear it or scrub his choreography from my brain. Shudder.

"This is so fucking terrible. On behalf of my entire family, I am very sorry you're being subjected to this," a man says to me, beaming a megawatt smile in my direction. This is a dangerous man. He's sexy, and he knows it. Bright green eyes, dark hair shaved close to his head on the sides and longer on top. Roman nose, sharp cheekbones and deep voice. He's a little shorter than Tate, but not short by any means. He's charming, knows how to charm, and probably is very successful in charming plenty of women into his bed. And now that charm is aimed right at me, and I would be lying if Ms. Vaj wasn't taking notice.

"You're Geoffrey, right?" I ask, even though I know for certain who this is. Theo's cousin, known womanizer, and a man Cara highly recommended I stay away from.

"I am, and you are the lovely Harper. Besides being subjected to *this*, are you having a good time here today?" he asks, still smiling, still showing off his pearly whites.

"I am. You guys sure know how to throw a party!" I laugh. It really has been a fun and lively day.

"Perhaps I can offer you a drink and we can find a spot for a private party?"

I have to applaud his direct approach. But, regardless of Ms. Vaj's initial interest, because come on, this man is sex on a stick, I have no desire to get sweaty with him. My mind has been wholly occupied by Tate, despite trying to not be.

"I thank you for the invitation, but I have to pass. I'm quite enjoying my time mingling and stuffing my face with Estelle's baking." I rub my belly, hoping to give off un-sexy vibes and make him hurry away.

"If you change your mind, I'll be around." He looks me up and down slowly, winks and then strides away.

Maybe a food baby is a turn on for him?

"I don't think I have ever seen anyone successfully turn Geoffrey down so quickly. Does Tate have anything to do with this turn of events?" Cara asks, approaching me from behind.

"Yes and no. I'm sure Geoffrey would be an absolute beast in the sack, and a night I would never forget, but that's not really my thing. I need to focus on getting my life back on track and, yes, Tate makes things complicated."

"Theo and I were talking, and we think we should head back to the city for the ball at the castle tonight. We'd both like to go, and seeing how you'll be leaving soon, we thought it would be something fun for you to do. Plus, I really want to see all the hard work you did on the gardens!" Cara is beaming at me. She's proud of me, and that makes me feel incredible.

"Are you sure you wouldn't mind leaving?" I absolutely do not want to pull them away when they're having fun with family, but I would love to see the castle and dress up.

"Totally fine with it. It was Theo's idea, actually, so you don't need to feel guilty. We've been here for hours already. Let's get some dinner, which I believe Dane and Estelle are beginning to set out, eat quickly and go. We'll have plenty of time to get home, get changed and to the castle for seven," Cara tells me as she hooks our arms together and practically skips towards her husband.

After consuming more food than I have ever eaten in one meal before (European mamas are no joke about making sure you are not hungry), I find myself being passed around from person to person hugging and kissing cheeks and saying goodbye. Little kids hug my legs, aunts tell me to visit again soon before subtly reminding me that they have a son. An uncle "accidentally" grabs my boob while coming in for a hug. Geoffrey hugs me a little too closely, lips lingering a little too long on my cheek as he says his goodbye.

By the time we make it out of there and into Theo's car, it's almost 6 p.m.

Traffic is busy leading into the city, no doubt plenty of people heading exactly where we are.

"Cara, can you tell me more about the royal family? I feel like I don't know much about them, and I'm about to go to their house. I've met the Queen, and I know the King is the actual sovereign and that they have three children. Beyond that, I know almost nothing."

"Well, the Sovan Royals are all really nice people. They stay very down to Earth, making themselves visible and available to the public. It's not uncommon to stumble into one while out and about. It's possible you saw one while in the gardens or walking to the market, and you just didn't realize it."

I think about that. I probably have seen the princess or a prince while at the castle setting up for today. Now I feel like a dolt for not even knowing what they look like.

"The princess is the oldest right, so she'll inherit the crown?"

"Yep! And she's so awesome! Princess Marielle. She has dark hair, radiantly gorgeous, and is engaged to Dax Keer, a Viscount from a very old aristocratic family. He's tall, dark and handsome, and also extremely friendly and kind. They've done a lot of work together with various charities, focusing on family and LGBTQ+ issues."

"I wonder if the royals and aristocrats bought all the good genes with their pools of money. They're always good looking," I chuckle.

"Next is Prince Jerome. He's probably the most frequently spotted in town, but also the quietest. He doesn't necessarily shy away from the public, but he doesn't go out of his way to engage with them either. There was some sort of scandal with an ex-girlfriend a few years back. Babe, do you remember?"

"Hmmm," Theo taps his fingers on the steering wheel as he thinks. "Something to do with his girlfriend sneaking stories and photos to the tabloids. Apparently, she was hoping he'd never find out that she was the source and could convince him to marry her *and* make millions selling photos and information. Unfortunately for her, he kicked her to the curb, despite them being together for years and he obviously loved her. At least she had the pile of money the tabloids paid her to keep her company. He hasn't been seen with anyone romantically since."

"That's horrible!" I cry out. "How could anyone treat someone they claimed to love like that? That poor man, I can understand why he'd be wary of dating after going through that."

"Lastly, there's Prince Simon. He is, unsurprisingly, also tall and hot. He's married and his husband Corvin is an absolute hoot. Corvin is big, loud and the life of any party. Prince Simon is quiet, wickedly smart and prefers to observe. He also loves animals and spends as much of his free time as he can at animal shelters and playing with random dogs in dog parks. Seriously, one time I was out for a walk with my friend Danielle and her dog, and Prince Simon was rolling around on the ground with like five dogs!"

I laugh as I imagine a prince covered in grass stains and dog slobber.

These Royals sound completely different than I was expecting.

Chapter 19 - Harper

I pull on the lace dress Cara bought me on one of my first days here, completely shocked it still fits after all the food I forced into my body today. I sigh as I look into the full length mirror in the bathroom. I'm happy Theo suggested we go to the ball tonight. I love dressing up, and I haven't had a chance to since I got here.

I pair the dress with some simple silver hoop earrings and a chunky blue bracelet for a pop of colour. Cara loaned me a pair of brown wedges to wear, which I am thankful for since most of my nice shoes are in the trunk of my car at the airport.

I had my hair up earlier, but now I want to leave it down, using a curling iron to create some soft beach waves. I decide to go a little heavier on the makeup since this is a special event. I freshen up my foundation and mascara, add some blush and eyeliner and even apply some lipstick I stole from Cara.

"Wowza! Harp, you look incredible!" Cara says, as she steps into the bathroom with me.

"So do you! Holy! That dress is magnificent!" Cara is wearing a light blue maxi dress with long sleeves, billowing down to her wrists. It's daringly low, cutting down the middle between her breasts before meeting the belt of the empire waist. It's flowy and makes her look magical.

"Ladies," Theo's voice booms from the main floor. "We need to get going if we want some of the good champagne!"

"That's our cue to go! Are you ready?" Cara asks, looking at me in the mirror.

"Absolutely! Let's go, sister!"

We make our way inside the ballroom at the castle. It looks like half the country turned up tonight. It's called a ball, but it's really just an adult party in a ballroom. I can easily imagine women wearing huge ball gowns here in the 1700's, doing some sort of fancy dance where they barely touch, and seeing a flash of wrist beneath a glove was enough to make a young Earl try to whisk a young Lady out to the gardens for a stroll.

And maybe it's time to stop reading so many historical romances.

Or maybe I should binge *Bridgerton* again.

I'll probably choose the latter.

Queen Janelle is at the far end of the room, standing near a man whom I assume is King Louis IV. He looks familiar, but I can't quite place him. Something about the way he holds himself and his eyes. Maybe Cara was right, and I've seen the royal family around as I've been working in the gardens. Perhaps I've seen him from afar and had no idea I should have acknowledged his presence.

Queen Janelle raises her glass to me and smiles, so I raise mine back and hope my smile conveys how delighted I am to be here tonight.

Cara, Theo and I walk around the room and I point out the flowers in vases that I had a hand in choosing. The roses the Queen approved look phenomenal and I'm glad we settled on them for tonight.

"Would you ladies excuse me for a moment? I see some colleagues that I'd like to speak to," Theo says, kissing my sister on the cheek and walking away toward a boisterous group.

"He says a moment, but what he really means is a good hour. They'll start talking about some new procedure, someone will bring up a football match, and then next thing we'll know, they'll all be drunk, talking about something inane like how loud a bullfrog is."

"I'm not sure how comfortable I am knowing that that's how the nation's top medical experts act when they get together."

"They'll just use this as a *learning opportunity* for their interns and give them more work tomorrow."

Theo's father's suggestion of applying for a work visa and staying for a bit longer wiggles its way to the forefront of my mind. That might not be such a bad idea. Maybe Yves could hire me, and I could get paid to go there everyday.

Cara and I help ourselves to some more champagne and make it our mission to try all of the food. I regret that decision when I bite into something with cilantro in it. Vile, disgusting cilantro.

We see Yves, and I introduce him to my sister and we chat quickly about me staying longer. Cara points out some important people, some families of children in her care at work and introduces me to a few of the friends she's made. Cara has a whole entire life here. She's happy here. She fits in here seamlessly.

I go to take another sip of my champagne but notice it's empty already. That might explain the happy, tingly feeling in my fingers.

"I'm going to use the washroom, I'll be right back," I tell Cara and leave her with a group of her friends from work.

There's a bit of a line to get into the bathroom, so I text Tate as I wait.

149

Me: Hey you! How's your day been going?

Tate: Better now. It's been long. I'm quite honestly ready for bed.

Me: Poor baby. Can you sneak away soon?

Tate: Probably not for another few hours. How has your day been? All partied out?

Me: Almost. I think I have another hour in me before I turn into a pumpkin

Me: Maybe we can see each other tomorrow for lunch?

Tate: Absolutely. Nothing would make me happier than seeing you.

The line has moved and it's my turn for the washroom. I can't stop the smile that feels permanent on my face after reading that last text from Tate. My heart is louder than my brain. I can't stop these feelings. I'm honestly not even sure if I want to stop these feelings anymore. Maybe staying for a bit longer and seeing where things go with Tate wouldn't be such a horrible idea. I love being close to my sister again, and I truly don't have any reason to rush back to Toronto, or go back there at all, really.

I've lost sight of where Cara is when I round a corner, smacking directly into a hard wall of man.

Tate.

There are people all around us, but all I see is him.

He's wearing a suit today, looking so different from the Tate that I've been used to going on walks with. He had dress pants on last night, but this is a full three piece suit. He wears it well. Very well. It's obviously been tailored to fit him exactly. The jacket stretches across his broad shoulders, his pants cling to his muscular thighs. This image of him will be my new favourite late night muse between my sheets. Tate in a suit is perfection.

"Harper! What are you doing here?" He wraps me in a full body hug, which shocks me because he's never hugged me. He held me last night, but this feels different. Friends do not hug their friends like this and smell their hair as they caress their cheeks.

"Theo suggested we come here for the party, so we left his parents' early. What are you doing here? I thought you had your own family party to be at." I'm confused. I don't remember him telling me that he was coming to the castle. His text messages sounded like he was still at his own party.

"Shit." Tate looks around, puts his hands on my shoulders, and takes a big breath in. "Ok, look, there's something I need to tell you, and I have about thirty seconds because Princess Marielle is making her way over here."

I look around the room frantically. There is a striking woman, in a dress that probably cost more than my car, wading through the crowd toward us. Judging by how many people say hi to her and curtsy, I'm guessing she's the Crown Princess.

"Tate, why is Princess Marielle coming here, and what does it have to do with us?" Oh my god! I smack myself on the forehead. "Are you engaged to Princess Marielle? Cara told me that she's engaged to a tall, dark and handsome man, and hello!" I wave up and down his body, fluttering my hands like a crazy person.

"Fuck, no. No," Tate says adamantly, as he rests his forehead against mine, something I'm beginning to think of as his signature move.

"Shit, she's closer. Ok, look, I have to just say this very quickly and I am begging of you to not run off until we have a chance to talk, ok? Please?" Tate has stepped away from me a bit, but still has his hands on my shoulders.

I look at him wearily, unsure of what is about to happen, but know it's going to be huge. "Ok, what is it?"

"Fuck. Shit. Ok, Princess Marielle is my sister," Tate forces out.

"Excuse me? What did you just say? The princess is your *sister*?" My head is spinning, I feel like I'm floating. "So, that means that you are…"

"A prince. My full name is Prince Jerome Louis Gebert Tate of Sova." He's looking right into my eyes, searching them, hopeful.

All I can do is stare back, trying to process those words. But my time is up.

"Hello there. I'm going to go out on a limb here and guess that you are Harper?" Princess Marielle asks in, in a voice so soft and sweet my brain wants to believe this is all a dream.

"Umm, yes, hello. I am Harper. And you are a princess…I mean, you of course are a princess. A sister," I ramble and stumble through the thoughts swirling around in my head. "His sister. Oh my god, I've never curtsied to you, Tate. Prince Jerome! Shit! I probably should have curtsied. How the fuck do you curtsy? Shit! I just swore a lot to royal people. Siblings. Royal siblings because you are his fucking sister, and you're a princess so he's a prince." I'm breathing so heavily that I think I'm hyperventilating. Does breathing into a paper bag really help? Does the castle have a paper bag?

"I like you. I'm guessing Tate forgot to mention that small detail?" Princess Marielle smiles, and it's the same big smile that Tate gives me when I answer his lightning round questions in an unexpected way.

I nod my head, not trusting myself to use words at the moment.

"I just wanted to come over here and say hello and meet you for myself. My mother adores you, and this one," she hikes her thumb in Tate's direction, "can't stop smiling, and we all know it's because he can't stop thinking about you. And goodness, now that I've met you, I can certainly understand why he's smitten with you. You are absolutely stunning," Princess Marielle says easily, like my whole world isn't being rocked.

I force a small laugh out, hoping I don't look quite as freaked out as I'm feeling.

"I have to go mingle, but Harper, I am so glad that we met. I hope we can get together soon, maybe in a not so busy setting? Let's have tea soon, okay?" Princess Marielle looks at me, open, genuinely hopeful that I'll say yes.

"Umm, that would be nice. I think I'll be in Sova for a little bit longer."

And just like that, I agreed to a tea party with a real live princess. What even is my life now?

Princess Marielle swoops in for a hug, and it's warm and nice, and surprisingly not as awkward as I thought it would be.

"Ok, bye! I assume I'll see you tomorrow for breakfast, Tate? Dad is making his famous bacon and Corvin is already promising to bring mimosas, which since it's Corvin making them, he's basically just bringing champagne to drink at nine in the morning. Bye!" Princess Marielle flutters away with a dainty wave.

We stand there in silence for a few minutes. Me in shock, Tate obviously unsure of what to say.

"Can we go somewhere and talk, please?" Tate asks, looking at me through his eyelashes.

"Ok. Lead the way. I'm assuming this is your house, so you'll know where to go?"

"We can go up to my apartments, it'll be quiet, so you won't have to be worried about being ambushed by any more family members."

I wave my hand to tell him I'll follow him. He looks at my hand, and I know he wants to hold it, hold onto me, but he keeps his distance. He lets out a sigh and starts walking.

Tate leads us past some guards and through the servants' hallways so no one will see us. The hallways are narrow and made out of dark stone. This is exactly how I pictured a medieval castle looking.

We walk up a few winding staircases, down a few halls, past another set of guards, and emerge into a wide hallway with plush amethyst carpeting and light blue wallpaper. Golden chandeliers hang from the tall ceilings every ten feet.

"This is my family's private wing. No one is allowed up here but us and our guests," Tate tells me as we walk to the third door on the right. He opens the door to let us inside.

"These are my rooms. This is the living area, with my office through that door. Bedroom is there," he tells me as he points at doors. "And the kitchen and eating area are down that hall. A small powder room is there, and I have a full bathroom through my bedroom. Welcome to my home." He tells me, sounding nervous as I look around.

The space is huge, fit for a prince. Ornate, however, it's not ostentatious. He's decorated it simply, filling the space in with pictures of him and his family and some souvenirs from travelling. If I didn't know now that he was indeed a prince, I would just think I was in an ordinary man's home. Wealthy for sure, since his couch looks like it would scoff at my beloved couch, but normal. It's homey and comfortable.

There's a fire going in the fireplace and there's a faint smell of cedar.

It feels like Tate in here.

The man in question is taking off his jacket and laying it over one of the chairs to the side of the couch.

"Sorry, I just needed to take that off. Suits are a part of my everyday life, but they're restrictive. I feel much better when I can take it off at the end of the day. Feel free to take things off and make yourself comfortable too."

I gape at him, my eyes bulging out of my head.

"Oh shit, no! I didn't mean that I want you to get naked, I mean, yeah, I would want that, I just meant like take off your shoes or something." Tate gulps, and I watch his Adam's apple bob up and down.

Well, looks like I'm now adding Adam's apples moving to my *surprising things I find sexy* list.

"Tate, it's ok. I totally get it. If I was at home, I'd be putting on sweatpants and tearing off my bra. But, maybe since I'm not at home, I could just take off my shoes?"

"Yep. Yes. You should probably leave your bra on," Tate mumbles, probably not intending to say that last part out loud.

I sit on the couch (yeah, way more expensive than my couch. I still love it though. Or, I did love it. Stupid fucking Levi), crossing my left leg over my right so I can undo the shoe and slide it off. I'm glad that Cara let me borrow these, but my feet are killing me now. I guess living in sandals and running shoes for three weeks has ruined me for anything with a heel.

I get the first shoe off and glance at Tate, who is staring at my legs.

The way he's looking at me makes me glad I shaved.

I take the second one off quicker and tuck my feet under my body as I settle into the corner of his couch.

"Please sit down with me, you're making me more nervous by standing there."

"Right, sorry. Ok, I'm sure you have questions," Tate raises an eyebrow, letting me know I'm free to start us off.

"Ok, let's see. Why did you tell me to call you Tate?" I ask first.

"Technically I should have introduced myself as Prince Jerome, but you were talking to me like I was just a regular person, and it felt so nice. To have all your attention on *me* and not on my title. Tate is the name I go by in my personal life, and it just felt right giving it to you. My family and closest friends all call me Tate. The public knows me by Prince Jerome. You never felt removed, like the public does to me. I wanted you to know Tate."

"Why didn't you tell me?"

"I wasn't trying to lie to you or trick you. That honestly was never my intention. I have met so many people that have only been interested in talking to me, have tried to get to know me because of my title and to get close to the Crown. It's hard to know who you can and cannot trust when this is your life. I have few true friends. But you didn't know who I was. We talked and laughed and acted like regular people. And Harper, it felt so fucking good to know that I, Tate, made you laugh. I knew you weren't laughing because you thought you had to, or that you didn't agree to go for a walk with me and my dogs because your Prince asked you. You wanted to spend time with *me*, and I don't know, it was nice."

"Why did you kiss me?"

His head snaps up to mine, eyes staring into mine so intently that I have to look away, afraid of the feelings that I can see swirling around in his irises.

"You make me happy. You make me feel alive. You make me feel, and it was torture being near you and not having you. I kept telling myself that I couldn't touch you. You're only here for a short time, and you didn't want me like that, but I thought about it, about you, incessantly. You took over my life. Every day, all I thought about was you. I had to jerk off in the shower every morning, imagining you writhing beneath me just so I could make it through my meetings without embarrassing myself and coming in my pants halfway through the day when thoughts of you inevitably popped into my head. I kissed you because I was too weak to stay away any longer."

Holy. Mother. Of. God.

I feel like I'm on fire, burning all over for him.

I need to shut this down. Find a way to turn off these feelings.

"Tate," I begin, unsure of what exactly I'm going to say.

He forces a giant puff of air through his closed lips.

"Harper, it's ok. I know this is big, probably too big. I just don't want you to hate me." Tate looks down, sad and lost.

"Tate, no. Listen to me. I'm freaked out, like totally freaked out, and nervous and shocked, but I don't hate you. Not even a little bit."

Tate looks back up at me, glassy eyes shining in the reflection of the fire.

"I'm just not sure where to go from here. I like you. A lot. More than I want to admit, but I'm not sure what to do right now."

We sit still for a few moments, letting the weight of the moment settle.

"Were you ever going to tell me that you're actually Prince Jerome?" I ask quietly, almost afraid of the answer.

Tate studies the fire for a moment before he answers. "I don't know. I wrestled with that for a while. I wanted to, badly, especially when I knew I couldn't just pretend my feelings no longer existed, but I knew that you were leaving soon. I argued with myself that it wouldn't matter if you never knew, that it might work out better if you never knew, because you were leaving."

"I came here to find out who I am, and now I feel like I'm going to be leaving with more questions," I admit.

Tate just looks at me, waiting for me to sort through my thoughts.

"I think I can offer you friendship," I tell him, although I'm not sure how true that is.

"If friendship with you is what you can offer, I will greedily take it. Any portion of you that I can have will make me happy. If that's being your friend, we'll be friends. Best friends, casual friends, friends who send each other memes every once in a while and say happy birthday from across an ocean, I will take it. I can't lose you from my life completely, Harper. You have come to mean so much to me in the last few weeks, and I can't stand the thought of not knowing you anymore."

I look up at him, searching his earnest eyes.

"Friends?" I tentatively ask and hold out my hand.

"Friends," he replies, taking my hand in his, barely shaking it, rubbing his thumb across the back of my hand.

Chapter 20 - Harper

Tate leads me back down through the secret passageways in the walls, bringing me outside to a private patio near the parking lot.

"I'll wait with you here until your sister comes." Tate leans up against the outer wall of the castle.

I take out my phone to text my sister.

Me: Hey, I'm out at the cars, can you come find me. Sorry, it got too busy to find you in the ballroom

Cara: Yes! I was looking for you! Where did you wander off too??

Me: I'll tell you when we get home. It's a story

Cara: Okie dokie artichokie. Let me just get this big lug outside before the docs decide more tequila is the answer

"Cara is dragging a drunk Theo out now. You can go. I'm going to make my way over to their car," I tell Tate, unsure of how to make this goodbye not awkward. Or sad.

"I'll wait here until I see you get in the car. Is Cara ok to drive? I can drive you all home." Tate has his worried face on.

"Cara barely drinks, so she'll be fine. If not, I can drive. Goodnight, Tate. Please tell your mother that I thought the flowers looked beautiful."

"I will. She will be on cloud nine from your praise. Goodnight, Harper."

I walk away, resisting the urge to turn around and look at Tate one more time, even though I can feel his eyes on me the whole time.

■ ■

Cara and I help a very drunk Theo into the house.

Theo is a large man.

Cara and I are not large people.

This is a catastrophe waiting to happen.

Drunk Theo is also very handsy with his wife.

"Babe, you…you are so pretty, with a pretty face," Theo slurs as he runs his hands up and down Cara's face, smooshing her cheeks together.

"Harp, if you could go ahead and get that door open quickly, that would be great."

"I'm trying, but it's hard to unlock a door when you can't stop laughing!"

I finally get the door open, and Cara all but shoves Theo inside. He tumbles in and Cara and I drag him to the couch.

"He's just going to have to sleep here tonight," Cara decides, looking at him with a hilarious mix of love and disgust on her face.

"Sleep! I loooove sleep. Let's get naked!" Theo springs up from the couch, trying to pull his shirt off over his head, but manages to get stuck in it, like a two-year-old.

"Ah! Babe! Save me! A monster has me! I'm going to die without touching your boobs one last time!" Theo yells out, reaching out trying to honk her boobs.

"Stop that! No boob grabbing for you!" Cara slaps Theo's hands away from her.

"Ok, sorry. I just love you so much," Theo wails, starting to cry.

"Christ, what did this man drink?" I ask Cara, staring at him incredulously.

"Who the fuck knows!" Cara cries, throwing her hands up in the air. "Doctors are insane! All I know is that at the end they were throwing back tequila shots like eighteen-year-olds that haven't learned the horrible truth about tequila!"

We eventually get Theo settled on the couch, Cara taking off his shoes and pants, putting his shirt back on and leaving his boxers on, much to his chagrin.

It doesn't take long before Theo is passed out, snoring louder than Grandpa used to.

Cara puts a garbage can on the floor near his head, just in case.

"Fucking tequila," Cara mumbles as we make our way to the kitchen and settle on the stools.

I pour us some water, mostly to buy myself some time before Cara demands answers.

"Ok, so something major happened. But, before I tell you, I want to remind you that if you scream, you might wake up your darling husband who will either start crying again or will try to honk your boobs, two things I know you want to avoid."

"Oh my god, this is going to be good. I'm ready! Go!" Cara yells and I shush her.

"Alright, so…I saw Tate at the party."

"You got some sausage at the party!? That would explain why you vanished!"

"No, and for Pete's sake, stop calling it *sausage*! Call it dick like a fucking lady." I take a big breath before continuing. "We didn't sleep together, didn't even kiss, there was a hug, and that was really nice. Like the nicest hug I probably have ever experienced because he's so big and warm and smells so good."

"Harper, you're rambling, which tells me that this is something you're really nervous about. I'm here to listen, I promise that I won't yell or judge, ok? Just spit it out."

"Tate is actually Prince Jerome."

"*WHAT*?!"

"Cara! No yelling!" I yell back at her.

"I'm sorry, but what the actual hell?! You need to explain that."

"I was walking back from the bathroom when I literally walked into Tate, like my whole body bounced back in hilarious cartoon fashion. Anyway, he was there, and I was so happy to see him, but then he started to panic. Next thing I knew, Princess Marielle was walking toward us, he was explaining that he's her brother and now I have vague tea party plans with the Crown Princess of Sova!"

Cara blinks at me a few times then grabs her phone. After typing for a few seconds, she clicks on something and holds the phone up to me.

"Is this Tate?" she asks, showing me a picture on her phone.

"Yep, that's Tate alright."

The picture is one of him in a suit, looking delectable at a charity event last year.

"And this man kissed you and gives warm, nice smelling hugs?" Cara presses.

"Yep," is all I can get out.

"Are you going to see him again?" Cara asks, setting her phone down.

"I told him that we can only be friends. Kissing him was a mistake. He's a damn prince and I'm a nobody. We live in different worlds, on different continents. It would never work. It's probably best that we just end things now. It'll save us both some feelings in the long run." I start crying, big ugly sobs. Tears and mascara and snot are running down my face.

"It's ok, love, it'll all be ok," Cara says soothingly as she rubs my back.

I hope she's right.

Chapter 21 - Tate

Me: Good morning, Harper.

Harper: Good morning

Me: I hope you slept well. My family is already downstairs being very loud and obnoxious.

Harper: I slept a bit

Me: Are you ok?

Me: I'm here if you need to talk.

Me: I'm sorry, Harper.

■ ■

Half the people sitting around the table are drunk, again or still, I'm not entirely sure. Corvin drank half the mimosas he made already, and it's only a quarter after nine in the morning. Marielle's hair looks like a rat's nest, and Papa is burning more bacon than not, practically falling asleep standing up at the stove. Dax is covering his ears, like life is too loud for him.

Maman and Simon are both somehow fresh-faced and smiling brightly, even though I know for a fact they drank too much last night.

And then there's me. Sitting here, pretending to be present, but really, I just want to curl back up under my covers and stay there.

Harper never texted me back.

I think I broke our friendship.

"Tate, where did you sneak off to last night after we saw Harper?" Marielle asks me, obviously hoping for some juicy gossip.

"You talked to Harper last night? How is she, dear?" Maman asks sweetly.

"Ma, you were right! Harper is absolutely adorable! I can't wait to see her again!" Marielle adds, oblivious to my growing discomfort.

"You met Harper last night? No fair, I want to meet Harper too!" Corvin wails. Someone needs to hide the rest of the mimosas from him.

"Why didn't you introduce her to us? Oh, were you too busy with her?" Simon asks suggestively.

"I invited her to tea, we can all meet her!" Marielle tells the others.

"Enough!" I roar, chest heaving. "Just, enough. Please. We talked, and it didn't go well. Please, just enough."

"Oh, Tate, I'm sorry. Maybe I can talk to her," Marielle suggests.

"No, I think you've done just about enough, Mari! Because you decided to waltz over and introduce yourself, I was forced to tell her I'm a prince very quickly and awkwardly, barely giving her any time to hear my words before you came over and invited her for tea, forcing royalty onto her. It was understandably too much crammed into five minutes and she freaked out. Now, I don't even know if we're on speaking terms. So please, just stop."

"But –" Marielle starts, but our father cuts her off. "Marielle, listen to your brother. He, and Harper, need some space right now." Papa looks at me, "Son, what would you like to do?"

My father is such a gentle soul. He has always known when to push, when to hold back and when we need time to process.

"I don't know. She said we can't be anything more than friends, so for now I need to respect that and give her some time. But it hurts. Really badly."

"Love can son, but it can also heal."

■■

I spend the next few days as a zombie.

I eat food without tasting it.

I shower and assume I clean myself, but really have no fucking clue if I put shampoo in my hair or not.

I don't shave.

I live in sweatpants.

By Monday afternoon, the dogs have had enough and force me outside. They need to get out and run, so I take them to the castle's walled-in section on the west grounds. Originally, this was a medieval hedge maze, but apparently too many drunk party goers got lost in here and a King kept finding half naked people sleeping on the ground, too drunk or stupid to find their way out. So, it was torn out completely in 1725. It's gone through a few different redesigns and purposes, mostly a safe place for royal children to play, but it's currently a giant run for my dogs.

"You were right, Axelle, the fresh air is nice."

Axelle is still mad at me though, so she runs away, chasing after her brother.

"Hello there, Tate," a voice I would recognize anywhere says from behind me.

"Hi, Yves," I reply, not even bothering to turn around.

"What are you doing over here?"

"Just checking on the grass. Looks like I'll have to get someone in here to mow later today." He steps up beside me, studying the grass.

172

"Did you enjoy the festivities on Saturday?" I ask.

"I did. I didn't stay late, the wife wanted to get home before the masses left and clogged up the roads," Yves chuckles.

"Probably a smart idea. It was a great turn out." I shuffle my feet, like I'm a little kid again. "Hey, Yves, have you heard from Harper lately?"

Yves looks at me for a beat, then back to studying his grass. "She texted me yesterday to tell me she wouldn't be able to come back to the gardens. Something about needing to look for apartments. I think she's getting ready to head home to Toronto."

No, no, no. I need more time with her. I need her to forgive me and look at me. She needs to laugh with me and tell me we're ok. She can't leave yet.

I clear my throat, clogged with emotion. "Do you know when she's planning on leaving?"

"I'm not sure, son, but if I were you, I wouldn't wait too much longer before telling her I love her."

"I'm not in love with her, Yves. We're friends."

"Sure. I'll pretend I believe that. I wouldn't wait too long to tell her how much of a good friend she is, then. Wouldn't want to wait too long before telling her how much her friendship means to you, making sure she understands how much of a good friend you want to be, so she has all the information she needs before she decides to move."

"She's already decided to go back home, soon by the sounds of it."

"Has she really, though?" Yves asks, turning his head to look over at me. "She may have mentioned something on Saturday about applying for a work visa and wanting to work with me at the gardens officially. I hope that's still her plan, and the apartment talk meant nothing." Yves claps his hands together, "Well, I better head on back and make sure the lawn team knows to come in here."

"Uh, yeah, see you later, Yves."

She wanted to stay here, in Croix? Did I completely ruin that by not telling her the truth of who I am? God, I can be a fucking idiot sometimes. Not knowing what else to do, I take the dogs back inside and start preparations to get away to my country home in Montfret.

Chapter 22 - Harper

The days pass by in a blur. I haven't left the house, or been at all productive.

Theo forced me to shower this morning, under threat of kicking me out of his house because of my stench.

Today is Tuesday, and I would normally be helping Yves in the gardens, but being there would be too difficult, so I told Yves I wouldn't be able to come anymore.

I feel almost as heartbroken over that as my break up, if you can even call it that, with Tate.

I miss Tate. He's been in my thoughts constantly. I'm still not sure how I feel about everything.

He never actually lied to me, but he did omit the truth. Although, if I'm being honest, I can totally understand why he did that.

I can't imagine living my life under a microscope like he has. Having everything you do criticized and publicly debated. How *could* you know if someone truly liked you, or just wanted to use you. It would be awful.

I think back to our walks in the woods. He was always open and honest with me when I asked him a question. The only question he didn't want to answer was about his ex-girlfriend, and after what Theo told me about her, I understand why he refused.

I grab my phone off the console table in the living room and head upstairs to my room.

Me: Hi

Tate: Hello.

Me: Lightning?

Tate: Ask away.

Me: What's your favourite season?

Tate: Fall. I love the crunch of leaves under my shoes when I walk in the forest.

Me: Why do you go by Tate, and not another of your names?

Tate: Jerome Louis Gebert are all traditional, legacy royal names. They were given to me because it was expected. We've had 3 kings named Jerome and a couple of Princes. The name has been used many times. I'd be just another Jerome in a long line of Jeromes. Same goes for Louis and Gebert. Great names, plenty of great men named both Louis and Gebert in Sovan Royal history, but I'd be, again, just another Louis or Gebert. But, Tate is different. Tate is the name that my mother really wanted for me. She fought really hard to give us unique names, but when Marielle was born, my grandfather wouldn't allow it. He was a big fan of tradition, something my mother and father are not so strict about. So, we were all given long royal names and Maman tacked on a unique middle name to the end. So, I chose Tate because that's what they wanted to name ME.

Me: That makes a lot of sense. I'd probably feel the same way

Me: But Marielle goes by her first name?

Tate: Yes, Marielle Louise Laurel Nicolette Alice, she's lucky and got an extra middle name.

Tate: And Simon Fracois Etienne Taylor.

Me: Will you be expected to give your children a billion names too?

Tate: Yes, probably. Although Maman and Papa won't push for it like my grandparents did.

Me: If you could be any animal, what would you be?

Tate: An eagle. I'd love to be able to fly, to soar above the trees, but not be too worried about being eaten.

Me: Sorry, but the correct answer here is obviously a house cat. Just lay in the sun all day and push shit off tables

Tate: Ok, I'll give you that, that would be pretty fantastic!

Me: I should get going

Me: I'm glad we talked

Tate: Me too, Harper. Any time.

• •

Me: Would you rather, for 1 day and 1 day only, be invisible or be able to fly?

Tate: Hmmm, this is really tough! We've already established my dream of flying, but being invisible would let me walk among people and they would have no idea that the Great Prince Jerome was in their presence.

Me: Tick tock oh great one, you have to choose

Tate: I could be completely naked and no one would know!

Me: Yeah, but what if someone accidentally grabbed your dick because you're waving it around, which you obviously would because you'd be secretly naked (do not even attempt to deny that you wouldn't wave your dick around), and then someone would have a grasp on your invisible dick, hurting you and confusing them. It would be a naked dick catastrophe!!

Tate: Would they be able to grab it though if I'm invisible?

Me: You'd be invisible, not a ghost

Tate: Oh, yeah, in that case I would have to choose flying.

178

Me: What's your biggest fear?

Tate: Not being appreciated for being me.

Me: Heavy, dude. I was thinking spiders or like needles *shiver*

Tate: I'm going to guess that you don't like spiders?

Me: Spiders are actually super cool! Have you ever seen a little peacock spider dance?? OHMYGOD adorable!!

Me: Needles though. No. Nope. Don't like them

Tate: I guess that means you don't have any tattoos?

Me: No tattoos for this gal! I'd probably start stabbing the tattoo artist if they came anywhere near me with their needles

Tate: What's scarier, clowns or ghosts?

Me: Clowns. They're so creepy! With their big painted on faces and stupid shoes that are obviously designed just to trip people

Me: Shit! What about ghost clowns!

Me: Tate! I'm about to go to bed, and now I'm scared!

I dance around the kitchen, humming an old Britney Spears song. The sun is shining, the birds are singing and I feel good.

I woke up when I heard Theo and Cara moving around, starting to get ready for work.

Being the awesome person that I am, I already have two travel mugs of coffee ready for Cara to bring to work and a coffee sitting out for Theo to drink before he heads over to the hospital.

I'm putting some bread into the toaster when I hear Theo's big feet clomping down the stairs. Cara's still in the shower, and in about ten minutes she's going to come tearing down the stairs yelling that she's going to be late, like she doesn't do this at least 60% of the work week.

"Hey Theo," I say as he comes into the kitchen. "Want some toast?"

"Ummm, yeah sure," he replies warily. "Why are you up so early, Harp?"

"I figured I slept more than enough the last few days, time to get up and at 'em!"

I hand Theo his coffee.

"Thanks. I could get used to this. Usually, I'm the one rushing around in the morning making coffee and packing you picnics." He takes a drink of his coffee and sets the mug down on the counter. "Now, are you going to tell me the real reason that you're up and so chipper?"

"I guess I just got tired of being sad. There's no reason to be sad, really. Tate and I are friends. So, we hit a bump in our friendship road, so what. Onwards, right?"

"Sure," Theo replies, raising an eyebrow. "And now's the part where you give the actual real answer."

"Fine. Tate and I were texting all day yesterday, and it made me happy. Makes me feel like maybe we can really move forward and have a real friendship."

Theo studies me for a moment. "*Can* you be just friends with him?"

"Yes. Yes, absolutely. Most likely yes."

"Want me to pretend I buy that?"

"I would appreciate it if you would," I answer and flash him a giant, probably crazed looking smile.

"I'm going to be late!" Cara flies into the kitchen, as predicted.

"Actually, Harper made you coffees and the toast is about to pop, so you'll be fine for time." Theo tells his wife, kissing her on the top of her head.

Someone knocks on the front door.

"I'll get that, you eat quickly." Theo points to his wife and then the toast that just popped.

We can hear rumbly, masculine voices coming from the foyer, Theo sounding surprised, but happy, speaking with the early morning visitor.

"So, why all the nicey-nice this morning?" Cara asks, shoving toast in her mouth, crumbs going literally everywhere.

"I'm feeling happy and positive and wanted to spread that love today." I shrug, hoping she has to leave for work before she can ask any more questions.

"Hey, Harp, you have a visitor!" Theo calls out, his footsteps coming closer to the kitchen, with a second set following behind.

Shit.

I know two people well enough here that they'd want to visit me, and I don't think that Yves knows Cara's address.

"Your Royal Highness! Welcome!" Cara all but yells at Tate.

"Please, call me Tate. You must be Cara?" Tate politely says, reaching out to shake Cara's hand.

It pleases me in a bratty sister way to see Cara fumbling and attempting to curtsy. I feel a lot better knowing that she clearly has no idea how to curtsy either.

182

"No need for that, please. I insist. I'm only here to speak with my friend Harper."

"Oh yes, of course Your Royal Tate." Cara stumbles around the island, grabbing her husband's arm. "Theo and I have to finish getting ready for work out here. Bye!"

"I am very sorry about her!" I say, covering my face with both my hands.

"I can tell you two are sisters. At least she didn't swear forty times, like some other person I know when she first knowingly met a member of the Royal Family," Tate snickers.

"I don't like you right now."

"Not even if I brought you a blackberry pastry?" Tate holds out a white bakery bag.

"I like you a little bit. Now gimme!" I wiggle my fingers at him, and he hands over the bag.

I've wanted to try one of these since he first mentioned them weeks ago. I quickly open the bag, tear off a piece and pop it in my mouth.

"Oh my god, Tate!" I moan. "This is unbelievable!"

Tate's eyes darken as he watches my mouth move. His tongue darts out and he licks his bottom lip.

"I should maybe reconsider giving you treats."

"Nope! You have to give me all the treats!"

Tate takes a long breath in through his nose and slowly breathes it out his mouth. "I just wanted to come by with that and say hi. So, hello."

He's adorable. I can't even pretend like I don't feel looser and happier with him around.

"Hi, Tate. Thank you for bringing me a treat. That was very kind of you."

"I also wanted to let you know that I'll be out of town for a bit. Just in case you wanted to know. As my friend."

"Where are you going?"

"My house in Montfret. It's a small town about an hour and a half east of here, near the mountains. The house has a gorgeous view of the lake that sits at the base of the mountains, and the mountains themselves take up the entire landscape. It's my absolute favourite place in the world, even more than my spot in Croix forest with the swans."

"Sounds absolutely magical! I can totally see why you'd love it there!"

"You should come, you'd love it too."

"Oh, umm, I don't know…" I begin to answer him. What I really want to say is yes, jump up and down and tell him I'd go anywhere with him. But, I'm trying to be smart here.

"Yeah, sorry. You don't have to come. That just came out before I had a chance to think it through," Tate says, rubbing the back of his neck.

"She'd love to go!! She's going to go!" Cara yells, trying to run into the kitchen as Theo pulls her back.

I glare over at my sister, wishing I had laser eyes like I dreamt about once.

"Harper, seriously, you should go. It's so nice out there, and you could explore the mountains and more of the country. And you and Tate are friends, right? Seems like a perfect plan to me!"

Yeah, laser eyes would be fantastic right about now.

"Cara, come on honey, we have to get going or you will be late. Harper, text us and let us know what you decide," Theo jumps in, saving me with his thoughtfulness.

"Ok, bye, but for the record, I think you should go!" Cara can't help but add in. "Tate, it was really nice meeting you, finally. I hope to see more of you when you two come back from the mountains."

And then they're gone. And Tate and I are alone.

But we're friends, so this is fine.

"Harper, seriously, you don't have to come. I would love for you to join me, but I understand if you would rather not. Please do not feel pressured to come, simply because I asked."

I take a moment to study him. He's a good man. He makes me laugh and we enjoy each other's company. We're adults. Adults who have decided to be friends. We can keep our hands off each other. Because we're friends.

I'm going to keep telling myself that until I believe it.

"You know what, that might actually be nice. I've only ever really seen Croix and Theo's parents' house. How long are you thinking of going?"

"Really? You want to come?" Tate asks, beaming. "I was thinking maybe four days, but my plans are flexible. I really just need to get away to clear my head and focus on writing a speech. I've been having some trouble writing it and my father suggested I go up to Montfret. I think it'll help."

"Four days sounds nice. I can just relax and explore on my own so I don't interrupt you."

"You could never be an interruption, Harper." Tate looks me up and down, adding in under his breath, "but maybe a distraction."

"Tate…"

"I know, friends. Sorry. I'll behave. I promise. I really do want to be your friend, Harper."

"I'll need to pack, can you pick me up in maybe an hour? I'd like to get a shower in too," I ask, starting my packing list in my head.

"Absolutely. I plan on bringing the dogs, so I have to go get them and pack their stuff. I'll be back in an hour."

■ ■

Me: I decided to go with Tate

Me: tell me that was a good decision

Cara: YES!!!!!!!!!!!!!!!!!!!!!!!!!!!!!!!!! Sausage time!

Me: No sausage! We're friends, Cara. We have to just be friends

Cara: Ok, then enjoy your time away with your friend

Cara: I think this was a good decision. Even if you remain only friends, you and Tate clearly have something special. You can tell that you get each other. Don't push that away, even if it's just friendship

Chapter 23 - Tate

I have Axelle and Mars' bowls, food, toys and blankets packed. I already packed my bag, so I'm just double checking to make sure I haven't forgotten anything vital. My house in Montfret is fully stocked, with an equally full closet as I have here at Croix castle. I texted my staff to let them know that I'm on my way up, and because I think that Harper would appreciate the privacy, I give them all the week off. They work hard, keeping the house in tip top shape, and they deserve a break. I do make sure to ask Stefan, my chef, if he could leave meals for a few days for us and have the pantry stocked so that Harper has some options.

"Hey, Tate," Marielle pops her head in my open bedroom door. "Are you heading out now?"

"Yeah, just about ready to go. Harper is coming with me, so I'm going to pick her up first."

"Harper is going with you?" Marielle asks, trying so damn hard to hide how interested she is in that bit of information.

"Yes, Harper is coming with me. We're trying to be friends."

"And bringing her to your remote house in the mountains, alone, is the best plan for testing the waters of a friendship with a woman you want to have sex with?"

"Yeah, probably not." I scrub my hands down my face. "But it'll just have to be ok. She wants friendship, so I'll give her friendship."

"I'm sorry I pushed the two of you. I honestly thought it would help," Marielle says contritely.

"It's ok Mari, I know. I should head out though." I whistle for the dogs to follow me out to the hall.

"Wait!" my sister calls after me. "You should pack some of my tea! You said she'd like it."

"That would be nice, I'll tell her it's your version of an olive branch."

Marielle packed me enough tea to last Harper a month.

Maman cut some roses and a variety of other flowers and made Harper an obscenely large bouquet.

Corvin packed us some mimosas, i.e. a champagne bottle and a very small bottle of orange juice.

Simon wants me to ask her if she would like a kitten from the shelter he was at yesterday.

Dax put a whole box of condoms in my bag, even though I told him I wouldn't need them.

Papa just gave me a hug.

189

My father is currently my favourite.

I load the dogs into my SUV, an older Porsche Cayenne. I love my cars, but this one has a special place in my heart. I think of this one as my "family" mountain car, so basically when me and the dogs drive up to Montfret. It was my father's car, but when I passed my driver's test, he gave it to me. It was my first car and I baby it. I keep it washed, polished and vacuumed. I have a chart recording everything that gets done to it, tracking all work, fluids and repairs. I've kept it going for fifteen years and have no plans on letting it go anytime soon.

I debate about where to put the flowers.
If I put them on the front seat for Harper, it will make this look like a romantic getaway, but if I leave them in the back, she might be upset she didn't get to see them right away and they might get crushed.
I put them on the front seat.
Then take them out and put them in the back.
I'll tell her they're back there, letting her decide. It takes some of the romance out of the equation. At least I hope it does.
"Axelle, why didn't you tell me it would be this difficult?"

Axelle doesn't even wake up to help me with my problem. She just lays there with her eyes closed, waiting for me to get this show on the road.

Mars huffs at me, and I'm choosing to take that to mean the flower placement is good.

"At least Mars wants to help. Thanks buddy!" I rub him behind his ears, then close the back door, first making sure that the blanket I spread out for them across the back and folded down seats is laying perfectly flat.

Only the best for my babies.

It's possible that I spoil them.

We make the short drive to Harper's, and the reality of what's about to happen hits me.

I barely stopped myself from reaching out to hug her, feel her smooth skin and kissing her senseless when I was there this morning. Now I have to be around her, alone, in my favourite place in the entire world and just, what, pretend that I don't have feelings for her? I told her that I would be her friend, and I meant it, I will never try to force anything on her, but damn, this is going to be rough.

I pull up to the house and take a moment to force air in and out of my lungs.

"I'm acting like a coward, aren't I, Axelle?"

Once again, she doesn't deign to respond to me.

Mars lets out a supportive bark.

I get out, start walking to the door, but turn back around halfway, grabbing the flowers from the car.

"Hey Tate! I'm almost ready," Harper tells me as she opens the door wide for me to come in.

"My mom sent these over for you. I thought you might like to get them in some water before we go," I tell her as I hold the bouquet out, trying my hardest to sound casual, but giving her flowers is romantic, no matter how I spin it.

"Oh my gosh! I love these! She totally didn't have to do this for me! Are these the yellow roses from inside the rose greenhouse?! I can't believe she remembered how much I loved them!"

"My mother will have locked in every opinion and compliment you gave her about those roses. She can never seem to remember that I don't like mashed potatoes, but will never forget your love of those roses."

"You don't like mashed potatoes? How can it even be possible to not like mashed potatoes?" Harper asks me, voice going up in pitch like I declared that I hate sunsets.

"Potatoes are dry and starchy, and it never matters how much butter or gravy I put in my little mashed potato volcano, they are always dry."

"I'm not entirely sure we can be friends anymore."

"You'll get over it. Just means you can eat my mashed potatoes. Do you need a hand with anything?"

"If you wouldn't mind grabbing that bag for me, I'll put the flowers in water and then meet you in the car."

"Sure thing. I'll see you in a minute."

Chapter 24 - Harper

"I've never seen this car before. It's fancy!" It's a big SUV that likely costs as much as a house. I love it.

"This is my baby. There's a decent chance that if I had to choose between Simon and this car, I'd choose the car. I'd feel bad about it for a bit. But, come on! Look at her!"

Tate seems so relaxed, so casual. He's smiling freely, has dark sunglasses on and is wearing a well-loved grey t-shirt and jeans. Jeans! I have never seen him in jeans, but damn does he ever pull them off. I couldn't help but stare at his ass as he was walking back to the car.

"And how exactly do you think Simon would feel about getting pushed out of the family for a car?" I ask, attempting not to laugh.

"I would just hand him a kitten and he'd get over it. Get in and let's go."

And this is about the time that I recognize how much of a mistake I made in agreeing to go with my friend Tate. I watch as he starts the car and shifts into drive.

Me: I have a problem

Cara: And what's that sugar pie?

Me: TATE IS DRIVING A STICK!

Cara: Oh shit

Me: He has a t-shirt on so I can see his forearms as he shifts!

Cara: Yeah, that's going to make things a lot HARDER

Me: Fuck, he just shifted again! Do guys know how sexy it is to watch them drive standard?? Like, did he choose this car on purpose so I could watch him control this machine like an absolute boss and turn me on?

Cara: I don't know. Men seem to be oblivious. Obviously, you'll need to jump out of the car or make him pull over for dirty side of the road sex

Cara: Whatever you do, don't imagine how well he'd handle your body like he handles that car. Smooth, in control, commanding

Me: I hate you!

Cara: What?? I was helping! I told you not to imagine those things. It's not my fault you can't follow directions

Me: I'll let you know when we get there

We talk on and off for the drive.

Tate points out historic buildings, interesting details and teaches me about the different regions we drive through. I also learn that it is an international phenomenon to yell out "cow!" whenever you drive by a cow.

195

I wonder if cows ever look up and moo out "human!" to their fellow cows.

"How about a lightning round?" Tate asks, when we have about a half hour left of the drive.

"Yes, absolutely!" I clap my hands together and reply cheerily. I have come to love these lightning rounds. I only felt self-conscious during that first one when he asked about where I lived and I didn't want to talk about Levi. Since then, they have become something that I look forward to doing with him. We have learned a lot about each other this way, and they're just honestly really fun and silly.

"What about I will ask five questions, and then you ask five questions?" Tate asks, glancing back and forth between me and the road.

"That sounds like a good idea. You go first since it was your idea."

"What is your favourite day of the week?" Tate asks.

"Hmmm, see, my first reaction is to say something like Saturday because it's the weekend, and that seems like it should be my answer. No work, just a day to myself to do whatever I wanted, but that doesn't feel right. If I push that first reaction aside, I think my real answer is Tuesday."

"Why Tuesday? That's very random. I was absolutely expecting Friday or Saturday!"

"And that's why! There are a lot of expectations and there's just so much pressure on Fridays and Saturdays. What are you doing Friday night? Better be something exciting to shake off the week, and you better have a full Saturday planned where you do all the things! Now, don't get me wrong, Fridays and Saturdays are awesome, but Tuesday is low-key. Tuesday isn't demanding. Tuesday just comes in quietly and does its Tuesday thing. And, let's not forget that taco Tuesday exists! That right there should be enough to warrant Tuesday as the winner of the days!" I exclaim.

Tate takes his eyes off the road and studies me for a second.

"That sounds like more than just a love letter to Tuesday, sounds like maybe a metaphor for life."

"Huh, maybe. I just think that Tuesday is undervalued and underappreciated. We need to appreciate Tuesday a little more."

"Yes, I agree. Tuesdays are great."

Our eyes lock, only for a second, but it feels like so much more. I can feel so much more in that look.

"Question number two, what is your favourite ice cream flavour?" Tate asks me.

"Oh, that one is easy! Moose tracks!" I yell out, waking up the dogs who perk up immediately. They must think they're getting ice cream. I cover my mouth with my hand. My volume even surprised me.

"What exactly is moose tracks?"

"Oh my goodness, Tate! It is the best! Vanilla ice cream, chocolate fudge ribbons and little tiny peanut butter cups! It is so good!"

"Clearly I will have to try some. Question three, do you snore?"

"If you ask me, I absolutely do not. If you ask Cara, she will tell you that I do and that I sound like a dying trombone. However, I'm pretty sure she's lying."

"If you wake me up with your trombone death snoring, I'll let you know. Question four! If you could haunt any place in the world as a ghost, where would it be?"

"Well now you're making me think of ghost clowns again!" I shriek.

"That's your own damn fault," Tate laughs at me.

"Ugh, ok. If I was a ghost, and we're going to assume here that I died super old and it was ok, or that I died in a hilarious way and I'm ok with my unexpected death because it was so funny, I think I would haunt a museum, like a big one like the ROM in Toronto. I'd hide in suits of armour and make them dance around, or pick up super old Greek pots and make it look like they were going to fall and break in front of huge crowds of people, totally freaking them out, but then I would just place it back on its little pedestal. It would be hilarious! Maybe I'd become a travelling museum ghost and I would visit museums all over the world, moving their ancient Greek pots. The media would go into a frenzy, speculating about how all these pots are flying up into the air, almost crashing on the ground and then just floating back to their spots. Oh! I'd bring a permanent marker to the Louvre and just wave it around in front of the Mona Lisa's face, making people freak out because they think a possessed marker is going to draw a moustache on her!"

"Wow, that was a lot more than I bargained for. I'm not going to lie though, I really want you to become a travelling museum ghost. Please promise me that you'll do that?!"

"Oh yeah, I am totally going to do that as a ghost! I'm going to be the funnest ghost the world has ever seen! But if you see Dan Aykroyd or Bill Murray suiting up, send me a message to get out of there before they suck me up in their ghost vacuum thing!"

"You have my word. Alright, here's my last question for you. What's your favourite snack food?"

"Chips. Absolutely, totally, positively chips. Almost any kind will do, I just really love chips. I'll open a bag, shove a handful in my mouth, fill a bowl so it's overflowing and then shove another giant handful in my mouth before putting the bag away. Chips are the way to get on my good side." I just really love chips and make no apologies for that.

"Note to self, keep some chips on hand to make Harper happy, got it. We have about ten minutes left in our drive. Do you want to ask your five questions now, or would you rather save them for later?" Tate asks me.

I appreciate how respectful he is of me and genuinely wants my thoughts and opinions on stuff, even if it's something as small as when to do my lightning round question. He makes me feel valued and important. As a friend. Only friendly feelings happening over here. Yup.

"I think I'm going to save them. That way I have time to come up with some and I don't just blurt out the first five things that come to mind. I want these lightning questions to be the Rolls-Royce of lightning questions."

"That's a lot of pressure to put on your questions. I am going to judge your questions for their Rolls-Royceness now, you know that, right?"

"Oh, well shoot. I did not think that through," I grumble.

We pass through a medium-sized town before the scenery changes to farmland again. Tate and I shout "cows!" at the same time, falling into laughter together.

"We are just about at my house. If you look there," Tate tells me, as he points to the right, "you can see the lake. My house is there. I have six acres, with the two acres immediately surrounding the house walled in. Most of those acres are forest, with a smaller portion of it lawn and a garden some distant relative put in and my mother likes to maintain when she visits. The dogs love coming here, because they can explore the forest without being leashed and I don't have to worry about them since the walls are so high."

We turn down a country road, the mountains looming ahead of us. The lake is brilliant blue and sparkling. There is farmland on one side and forest on the other. I assume Tate's house is on the left with the forest. As we get closer, I can see an absolutely massive brick wall.

"What's that wall? Is there some kind of fortress or something before your house?" I ask, picturing a medieval wall and gate house, protecting the city from attack.

"That's the wall around the house," Tate tells me, sounding slightly bewildered at my question.

"That wall is like a thousand feet tall!" I cry out.

"It's actually just twelve feet tall. This manor was once the home of the Earl of Monfret, who married into the royal family sometime in the fifteen hundreds, then he became the Duke of Monfret and it's been a royal household ever since. But, in times of war, siege or disease, the entire town of Monfret would come here for safety and refuge, hence the giant wall. Now though, I use it to keep Axelle and Mars happy and safe since it's a little too tall for them to jump over."

Tate pulls into a driveway, stopping at a wrought iron fence, also a thousand feet tall, and presses a button on a remote he has clipped to his sun visor.

"Holy shit! Tate, we need to discuss your flippant use of the word house. This is not a *house*! This isn't even a mansion! I don't even know what to call this place! What's the right word for a massive house that isn't a castle because it isn't castle shaped, but is totally a castle!?" I start to freak out, my voice getting louder and louder as I talk.

"Uh oh, are you about to swear sixty times in a two minute long run on sentence?"

"Yes! I can't even process the size of this *house*!" I exclaim.

"Technically, it's called a manor. But, I think that sounds pretentious, so I just call it a house. Honestly though, it really is just a house. My house. This is where I spend the majority of my time when I'm not needed in the city or out on a diplomatic tour. It's big, and yes, maybe a little absurd, but it's a house," Tate says bashfully.

"Ok, fine, it's a house…that ghost me could easily mistake for a giant museum and start haunting. So, get ready to be included on my museum haunt tour!"

"I think I could live with that. Let's go. I'll give you a tour so you don't get lost while you're haunting."

Tate gets out and opens the door for the dogs, who come barreling out and are gone in a flash.

"Wow, you weren't kidding about them being fast!" I hold my hand up to my forehead, blocking out the sun, looking for them. They are nowhere to be found, not even little doggy shaped specks in the distance.

"Told you so! They'll run around for a while and come to the back door when they're ready. Let's grab our bags and head in."

I take my bag out of the car and follow Tate up to the colossal wooden door. The house is made of rough, light grey stone. There are three main sections, what appears to be the main part of the house and wings extending off to the left and right. Each section has a peaked roof, with the middle section being the largest, but the wings appear to have more windows.

We enter through a wide porch room thing, which was maybe where a guard used to be posted at some point, or maybe the former Lord really liked his privacy while he drank his morning tea outside.

The foyer is even more impressive than the outside. Marble floors, giant wooden columns that extend from the floor to the ceiling, where oak beams matching the columns run the length of the room. The largest pedestal table I have ever seen is sitting in the middle of the room with a bigger bouquet of flowers than the Queen sent me this morning. Pink and blue hydrangeas with white roses fill the vase and add a touch of femininity to the masculine space.

A massive marble staircase leads up to the second floor, splitting at the midway point, the center section continuing straight up and then branching off towards each wing of the house. An amethyst carpet runs up the middle of the stairs, making them look plush and warm.

"Tate, this place is absolutely beautiful! There's a decent chance that I'll never leave this room!"

"Perhaps wait for the rest of the tour before you choose your squatting location. Come on in, Harper."

Tate shows me the kitchen, small dining room, great dining room, great hall, living space, library and the main office. He leads me down to the basement to see the old servants' quarters which includes itty bitty bedrooms, offices for the butler, housekeeper and head chef, a dining room for staff and kitchens where food was prepared for staff before being brought upstairs. The kitchen is massive, so big that it feels wrong to call it a kitchen, like it needs its own word.

"We don't use the basement anymore in the way it was intended, but we keep it cleaned and preserved for historical accuracy and for tours. I do have staff, but nowhere near the number that once worked here, and no employees live here anymore."

"Thank goodness, because those rooms are tiny! Could you imagine sleeping down here, knowing that the Lord and Lady of the household were upstairs sleeping in a bed that was bigger than your entire bedroom?" I ask, imagining how terrible that would feel.

"No, I really could not. We have some staff that stay at the castle, but they have their own apartments in a separate wing with proper accommodations. It's interesting to see how my ancestors lived though, even if I don't agree with it."

Tate, and the entire Sovan Royal family it seems, is a surprise. Cara told me they were quite normal, but I wasn't expecting this sense of humility.

"You mentioned tours. Do you give tours here often? Is a tour group going to come tromping through here soon?" I ask, looking around like I might find a chipper guide holding one of those thin, bendy flag poles so people (i.e. me) don't get lost.

"No, there are no tours scheduled right now. Typically, we run tours throughout the summer and around the holidays, and a few other events sprinkled during the year like a Mother's Day tea, Father's day hike, and a spring and fall equinox ball. They are quite fun events. I bet you would love to attend them, maybe you'll be here visiting your sister and could come for one of the balls. You probably won't still be here for the next autumn ball," Tate rambles, sounding nervous.

"Maybe one year I could make it." I smile as I reply, touching his arm lightly. "For now, let's continue *our* tour."

Tate smiles back at me, thankful that I moved us past a sensitive topic. I'm not oblivious to the fact that Tate would like me to stick around for a bit longer. And I would be lying if I said I wasn't feeling a connection and desire to be around him more. I still haven't decided what to do, either go home to Toronto soon and start job hunting for, well, basically any job that will hire me, or apply for a visa and stay here a bit longer. Yves said he would love for me to stay at the castle gardens. It would be amazing and perfect, but something is holding me back from taking the steps to make that a reality.

If I was being honest with myself, and I totally do not want to be, I would admit that I'm scared. Scared to start over. Scared to find a job. Scared to fail. Scared to love. Scared of not knowing who I am. I'm starting to get a sense of the person I'm becoming, or maybe the person I was always meant to be, but I just haven't quite been able to sit down and make a plan, which is wholly unlike me. And that's the scariest part of all.

Tate leads me back upstairs to the foyer where we go up the stairs.

"These stairs are ginormous! I bet I could lie down, and you could still walk around me!"

"How badly do you want to stop and lie down on the stairs?" Tate asks, grinning ear to ear.

"Honestly? Really badly! But, I also want you to continue to think I'm super cool, so I'm not going to do it in front of you. I'll wait until you're gone."

"For the record, you could probably also do somersaults on the landing before the stairs split off, if you wanted to try that too." He winks at me, and Ms. Vaj waves at him, happy to see his playful side.

We stop at the somersault landing, and Tate informs me that the center staircase leads to his personal office and a formal sitting room, where the Lady of the house would have received guests for tea.

"If you go to the left, it'll bring you to guest suites. You can choose to have a room there, or if you go to the right, you'll find my room and two other bedrooms. You can choose one of those if you prefer. You'll have more privacy in the guest wing, but the rooms are nicer in the family wing. Let's go take a look, and then you can decide."

I follow Tate to the guest wing first. There are six rooms here, all tastefully decorated in neutral colours and patterns. They're lovely, large and well appointed with a king size bed, ensuite and small sitting area. If I had to sleep in one of these, I would be very happy, since those beds look absolutely heavenly. But, I'm curious about the other rooms, trying to convince myself it's simply because Tate said they were nicer and definitely not because it would be closer to him.

On our way to the family wing, we stop off to see the sitting room.

"You are welcome to use this room as you see fit during your stay. Make this your space. You can camp out here with tea or books, or tea *and* books, or use it however you

208

please. Of course, you're welcome to any room in the house, but I thought you might like to have a space just for you close to your bedroom."

"That is incredibly thoughtful, Tate. Thank you for thinking of me like that. This room is super cozy, and I can totally see myself hunkering down in here!" I am just so blown away by the consideration of this man. The walls are painted the same light blue as the Sovan flag, and three deep, velvety soft looking amethyst couches surround a large stone fireplace. The floors up here are the same oak as the columns and beams from downstairs. A light grey rug fills the space under the couches. Bookcases line the walls on either side of the door and windows make up the entire opposite wall, giving way to a spectacular view of the gardens and forest below. I can see Axelle and Mars rolling around in the grass wrestling, looking like they are in absolute doggy heaven. There is a pond with a small waterfall near a wildflower garden and a large rose garden right under the room against the side of the house. I make a mental note to go sit on the bench by the pond with a book later today.

We check out Tate's office, the room right beside the sitting room, which matches the style of his room at the castle. Masculine, minimalist, but still personal. There are framed pictures of him and his family all over the room.

Hiking, climbing mountains, and exploring a cave, as well as simpler ones like them enjoying a picnic together and one of them sitting around a campfire. Seeing the Queen with a dirty face and wearing track pants while roasting a marshmallow is making me sentimental. I used to love camping with my mother.

"And this room over here is mine. Nothing really special, just a spot to sleep and keep my clothes." Tate shrugs as he walks in. The smell of Tate overwhelms me in here. His bed is probably the biggest bed I have ever seen. Neatly made, with a navy comforter and light blue sheets and pillows. It looks normal. He has a fireplace in here, the stone matching the exterior of the house, just like the other fireplaces I have seen, as well as a small sitting area with a navy loveseat and two oversized matching chairs. He has a small writing desk with a lamp, a notebook and a pen meticulously lined up.

I clear my throat. "Can I see the other bedrooms?" I ask, needing to distance myself from his personal space. It's making me feel too much, and is making Ms. Vaj far too excited picturing him and his nocturnal activities in that bed.

"Sure, there are two other rooms, so take a moment to look at both. I'll meet you back out here in a moment." Tate excuses himself and walks back into his room, so I walk across the hall to look at the other rooms. They are just as big as his room, making them noticeably larger than the guest rooms. Just like his room, these rooms have their own fireplace, ensuite, sitting area and writing area. The beds both have white pillowcases and sheets. The bed in the first room has a yellow comforter, while the other bed has a moss green comforter.

I'm not sure what to do.

I'll only be here for a few days, so taking a smaller guest room won't be a big deal, and seriously, it's still a gazillion times bigger and nicer than any room I've ever had. I should take a guest room and put some distance between Tate and I. But, that feels wrong. Thinking about being that far away from him makes me feel nauseous and itchy. Which is absolutely bananas since I've never slept in the same building as him before.

But, that moss green blanket is calling my name. The room is beautiful. Would it be too difficult, too tempting, to be sleeping right across the hall from Tate?

Chapter 25 - Tate

Watching Harper wander around my home has been an interesting adventure in feelings. It feels so good, so natural having her in my home. I'm usually much more cautious about inviting people into my personal haven. Even though I have only known Harper for a matter of weeks, I didn't think twice about inviting her. It took me over six months to invite Celeste here. But, Harper seemed to fit right into my life, and she looks damn good in my house.

In fact, she looked so good in my bedroom that I needed to give myself, and my dick, a moment to calm down. I couldn't help but imagine Harper spread out on my bed. Her creamy skin against my blankets, hair fanned out behind her on my pillows. Our bodies intertwined, her legs wrapped up in my darker ones.

My cock throbs as I picture her naked on my bed.

I pace around the room, shaking out my arms. I need to get it together. Harper only wants to be friends, so I need to get better control over my body. We are going to be together, alone, for four days and I need to be able to be in the same room as her without a hard-on.

I think about football and trees and skipping rocks across the pond.

Eventually, I find myself calm enough to go back out and see her again. I can hear her footsteps across the hall. I can't stop the smile that breaks out across my face as I picture her checking the rooms out, touching everything she can, thinking I don't notice her assessing and cataloguing my home.

I am a little worried about which room she will take. I should have put her in a guest room in the other wing. Kept her far away from me, too far away to be tempting come nighttime. Just that thought makes my heart ache though. I both fear and hope that she'll choose a room across the hall.

"So, what do you think? Have you chosen a winner yet?" I ask, leaning against my doorframe.

Her eyes slowly trail up my body, starting at my crossed ankles and raising up all the way to meet my eyes. There is fire in her eyes. I know for a fact that she is picturing us together, tangled up in the sheets just like I have been. Her pupils are huge, her lips part slightly and she bites down on her lower lip just the tiniest bit.

Fuck, she is not helping my dick stay calm.

"Umm, yeah, I umm, well you know all the rooms are really nice, and did you know that you can see the forest and the gardens and all the nice outside things from the rooms? I mean, obviously you did, this is your house. But all the views are a little different because all the rooms are in slightly different locations, and obviously you know that too. And geez, I'm just a rambling fool, aren't I?" She asks as her cheeks turn scarlet.

"Harper," I begin, making sure she looks directly at me before I continue. "Which room do *you* like the most? Which one made you feel happiest being in?"

"The one with the green blanket!" she blurts out, almost like her brain knew she needed to say it as quickly as she could before she started to overthink it.

"Ok, then that will be your room for the duration of the stay. It's a good choice. You may be able to see a pair of green woodpeckers that have recently made the tree outside that window their home."

Holy fucking shit! She is going to be sleeping and bathing and getting naked in the room right across the hall from me!

Do I rejoice or cry? Happy or worried?

All in equal measure.

"Why don't you get yourself settled in there, and then come meet me downstairs in the kitchen when you're ready for some lunch?"

"Sounds good! I won't be long. I'd just like to get a few things unpacked and freshen up a bit. I'll be right down!" She tells me happily, bouncing on the balls of her feet. God, I love making her smile. Harper being happy is my favourite thing.

■■■

I set out some food for lunch that Stefan left for us. He's a brilliant chef and can work magic with the simplest ingredients. I set out the fruit plate, bread and assorted cheeses on the island that Stefan put in the fridge. I grab a bottle of wine and bring everything to the small dining room.

Harper prances in, singing a tune as she enters the room. "This all looks so delicious! How did you do all this in the few minutes you were down here?" Harper asks me, looking around in wonder.

"While I wish that I could take the credit for all of this, my chef is actually the brilliant mastermind behind our meals."

"Oooh la la, a private chef, eh? I feel so fancy! Where is this chef of ours?"

I like it way too much how she says *our chef.* Like we're here together. Like we share a life together. Like she's mine.

"I assumed that you would appreciate some privacy, so I gave the staff the week off."

"How many people work here?"

"When I'm here Stefan comes in as well. He does have a very popular restaurant in Montfret, and I appreciate that he makes time for me. However, on a regular, everyday basis I have Annie and Max who keep this place clean, and the landscapers Elle and Zachary. During the holidays and summer, and when we have special events, we employ a larger team of cleaners, gardeners and catering staff. I believe Annie made sure the library and your sitting room upstairs are fully stocked with a variety of books."

"You told them about me?" She asks, grinning at me.

"Well, yeah. A little. I let them know that my friend was coming up with me for some peace and relaxation. I asked Annie to fill some shelves with her favourite books so you would have more variety than what I have and the boring books my ancestors collected." I'm starting to feel nervous. Maybe I overstepped. Maybe she'll read into that, likely because there is something to read into, even if I won't admit it. I start putting food on my plate to distract myself.

"Thank you, Tate. Once again, you have proven to be extremely considerate. Ok!" she claps her hands together and sits up straighter. "Lightning round time!" Harper pops a grape into her mouth.

"Alright, I'm ready," I tell her. I place a piece of Havarti on a slice of bread and take a small bite as I wait for her question.

"Ok, first question, if you could control one element, like fire, water, earth or air, which one would it be and why?"

"Hmmm," I rub my chin. "Can I create water myself, or would I only be able to draw water from a source?" I ask thoughtfully.

"Ooooh, I'm not sure if follow up questions are technically allowed in a lightning round," she teases me, "but I'll allow it. I think you'd have to draw it from somewhere."

"Ok, then next follow up question, can I create fire myself, or do I need a spark?"

"I think if we're following the same rules, you'd need a spark, but a spark is pretty simple to create. Like, maybe have a metal ring and have a rock, smash them together to get a spark and then you can turn it into fire without kindling and all that other fire stuff."

217

"Fire stuff?" I laugh. "Clearly I need to take you camping to teach you about fire stuff."

Our eyes meet, and suddenly what I said in jest doesn't seem so funny. Seems like a promise involving a different kind of heat.

"Anyway, in that case, I think I would choose fire. Think of all the ways that I could help people. You'd be a travelling museum ghost and I would be a travelling fire starter. I'd go to cold climates and make sure they're warm, help people cook their food and also control forest fires, preventing devastation to crucial forest systems and habitat loss."

"That seems like the perfect Tate answer. Ok, here comes question number two." Harper says as she mimes winding up to throw a baseball.

"Is a hotdog a sandwich?"

"For the record, you think this is a Rolls-Royce question?"

"Oh yeah, absolutely! It's going to tell me so much about you!"

"Ok, feeling some pressure here. It is…not a sandwich…" I ask, slightly worried that I got it wrong.

Harper just stares at me, face in a neutral poker face.

I can feel sweat starting to bead on my forehead. I have to resist the urge to fidget as I wait for her verdict.

218

"You sir," Harper begins, still not giving anything away. "Are absolutely…correct! A hotdog is totally not a sandwich! It's a hotdog, in its own little hotdog category!"

We both laugh, huge, full belly laughs.

"Ok, ok, moving on to question three," Harper gasps out between laughs.

"Alright, yes. Moving on." I take a few breaths to sober up.

I pour a little bit of wine into each of our glasses, as Harper places some more fruit, bread and cheese on our plates.

"If you had to eat a crayon, which colour would you choose?"

I blink at her a few times. "That was absolutely not an expected question."

"I'm giving you a silly one before I throw a couple hard, personal ones at you," Harper replies sweetly, batting her eyelashes at me.

"Magenta."

"Why magenta? You said that rather quickly."

"I don't know, it just looks delicious." I shrug.

"You mentioned that you came here to focus on writing a speech. What's your speech about and why have you been having a hard time writing it?" Harper asks me next.

"For the past five years, I have given a speech at my old high school's graduation. It means a lot to me, and I absolutely love being there, but this year, I just can't seem to put into words what I want to say. I pride myself on not recycling speeches or giving speeches that are filled with pretty words without emotion and sincerity behind them. Every time I sit down to write, either nothing comes out or I find myself using my old words." The more I talk about the speech, the heavier the weight feels in my chest. I don't want to disappoint the families or be without any real inspiring words for the kids, some of which I know could really use them.

"Ok, then let's work it through."

"You want to help me?" I ask, surprised that she would want to use her relaxation time this way.

"Of course, silly! This is what friends do!" Harper beams at me. "So, let's both imagine ourselves as eighteen-year-olds, about to go out into the world, probably being super nervous but also excited. So nervouscited!"

"Nervouscited is not a word."

"It is now! Ok, so nervouscited eighteen-year-old me would have loved if someone told me that it's ok to not have a perfect, exact plan, and that a lot of adults don't know what they're doing. It's a hard time in your life because you're expected to know what you want to be when you grow up, because suddenly you're grown up and tossed out into the world! You just have to go out and learn in a high-pressure environment, if you choose to pursue post secondary education, and be a grown up, but still not knowing how to make real food!"

"Harper, it's ok if you don't have an exact plan."

"I'm starting to understand that. You know, it's like this thing that Cara has been trying to teach me, to just be. Enjoy yourself, enjoy life and *just be*. She doesn't mean don't work, don't do all the boring adult stuff that we have to do, but to stop sometimes and appreciate what you have and where you are. Instead of rushing around non-stop, take an hour and go for a walk, allow yourself to examine the plants on the way. Or just sit in the sunshine or give yourself time to do your hobby just for the fun of it."

"That's actually really good advice. I could talk about the importance of balance between school, career and mental health. That taking time for yourself is just as necessary as studying and writing a report. What do you think about that?" I ask, genuinely interested in her opinions.

"I think that's a great idea! We need to normalize talking about mental health and brain breaks. Too many people push themselves too far, and then they fall apart.

It's ok to say you're not ok and that you need some time to relax, calm your body and step away for a bit."

Harper's eyes are wet, and I feel like this is something personal for her now.

"Thank you for being here to bounce some ideas off of, truly. I feel like I have a good place to start now," I tell her earnestly.

"Alright, here's my fifth and final question for this round! If you weren't a super special prince," she waves her hand around in front of me. "What would you do for a living?"

"I think I would be a teacher. I love engaging with the students when I visit schools. Seeing them learn a new concept, their eyes lighting up when they have that aha! moment and figure a problem out, is such an amazing experience. We had a STEAM event last month, and the enthusiasm they had when explaining their projects to me was infectious and delightful. I was so proud of them, and I can't wait to see what they come up with next." My voice wavers a bit at the end, my emotions surprising me a little.

"If you're finished here," I motion to her empty plate and wineglass, and she nods, "let's take this stuff into the kitchen. I'd like to start on my speech, and you are welcome to do as you please."

"I think I might go explore outside a bit," Harper says as she picks up her plate and the empty fruit bowl. "The sun is shining, and I'd love to get some good ol' vitamin d!"

"The dogs came in and ate and ran back outside, so they may like to join you."

"Axelle and Mars are always welcome to join me as I get lost in forests!"

I ignore how her words make my heart stutter, how I imagine her spending time with us more and more. How badly I want her to spend time with us.

Chapter 26 - Harper

Tate and I part ways after tidying up after lunch. He goes into his office to write his speech, and I grab my (Cara's) shoes and head out back for a walk. I can hear birds singing unfamiliar songs and I get the sudden urge to become a birdwatcher. Maybe I'll ask Tate if he has some binoculars I could borrow and see if there are any books about birds in the library. There are probably lots of European birds that I have never seen or even heard of before.

I'm either getting really cool and discovering new hobbies, or I'm getting really lame and trying to fill in my time before I find a new, cool hobby.

Nope, birds are cool as shit.

I'm a birdwatcher now!

Axelle and Mars run a couple circles around me as I slowly make my way to the pond and then race off into the trees.

I want to be like them. Free and happy, excited over the simple things in life.

I make a stop off at the wildflower garden, breathing in the sweet smells of spring.

A bee flies from flower to flower, making her little pollen pants bigger and bigger with each stop.

I've missed working in the gardens with Yves. I don't know if I've ever felt so happy or at peace while working than when I've been at the gardens.

"Hey little bee friend, is it stupid that I want to completely switch gears, leave an industry that I have actual experience in for something that I might not find a good paying job in and have no education in?"

Mrs. Bee just buzzes around me, oblivious to my identity crisis.

I leave the flowers, making sure to pet as many of the petals as I can to go sit on the bench. The sun is shining down on my face, warming me in its afternoon glow.

I pull out my phone and take a few pictures of the grounds, sending one of the pond to Cara.

Me: This is my idea of paradise!

Cara: Gorgeous! I'm assuming that's at Tate's house?

Me: Yep! Gosh, Cara, you should see this place! It's ginormous! I'm going to get a million steps in today! I'm fairly certain I got like 40,000 steps just getting a tour

Cara: I expect more pictures! Any cool chandeliers?

Me: The size of the chandelier in the foyer is both awe inspiring and terrifying! I'll send you pictures of it later

Me: What if I stayed in Croix for a bit longer? Theo's dad mentioned something about a work visa, and I think that could be really cool especially since Yves said I could keep working with him

Cara: YESSSSSSSSSS!! Stay with me forever!! Ohmygosh!!

Cara: Theo thinks I've lost my mind cause I'm dancing around like a drunk toddler

Me: Maybe you shouldn't be in charge of other people's children

Me: I don't know how the visa process works, or how quickly I would get one, or even how long it lasts. Maybe I'll talk to Tate about it

Cara: I bet Tate will have a lot to say about you staying here. I guarantee he'll want to help

Me: We're friends

Cara: Uh huh. And there's definitely no chance he's part of the reason you want to stay

Me: ….no

I put my phone away, ignoring the next few messages from a gloating Cara.

If I did stay longer, maybe Tate and I could be more than just friends.

Or it would get messier when I did eventually leave.

226

I huff out a breath, annoyed by my confusion, and get up from the bench. I've been sitting there for a good hour, and now my butt is killing me.

I whistle for the dogs and they follow me inside through the patio doors off the kitchen, immediately both going for their water bowls, drinking greedily.

After a quick stop in the bathroom (aka after I looked behind four wrong doors, wandered around for ten minutes and then finally happened to stumble upon the bathroom), I make my way to the library.

I find a few books about local birds and decide to bring them upstairs to the sitting room. The library is great, but that sitting room is calling me. Might have something to do with the fact that Tate called it *mine*.

• •

I am now an expert on Sovan birds.

Ok, not really, but I looked at a lot of pictures of birds that live here, and could probably recite a few facts.

My back cracks as I stand up. "Well, that's a new sound. Let's just pretend we didn't hear that and my thirties aren't breaking me," I tell the room as I leave and knock

227

on Tate's office door. It's open halfway, but I still think it's rude to just walk in.

"Come on in, Harper," Tate says to me, without looking up.

"I don't want to bother you, but I was going to make a cup of tea and I wondered if you wanted one. And also see if you could show me where the tea lives."

Tate types out a few more words and then closes the lid of his laptop, smiling at me.

"I absolutely would love to join you for tea. I made some great progress with the speech today, but I need a break."

Tate and I walk side by side down the stairs and into the kitchen.

He's happy and jaunty, whereas I'm pretending I'm not out of breath from the marathon that walking around this house is forcing me into.

"Do you remember when I said my sister has a special tea blend?" Tate asks, as he opens a cupboard and takes out two mugs.

"Oh my gosh! That has a totally new meaning now that I know she's a princess! I thought she just mixed two loose teas together herself or something!"

"Well, you're actually not too far off. She partnered with the Sova Tea Company to create her ideal breakfast blend. With the help of their head tea specialist to make, and I'm quoting my sister here, 'a tea that wakes me up and gets me ready to savour the morning'. It's cheesy, but a perfect tagline."

"That's so cool! I'm completely jealous of your sister! Maybe I can try it sometime," I say wistfully.

"Actually, Marielle sent me with some for you to try."

"Oh my goodness! Shut up! Yes! I want to drink princess tea!" Now I'm yelling. There is no stopping my voice from getting higher, nor is there any way to stop my feet from bouncing.

Tate scoops some of his sister's tea blend into a tea infuser for me, setting it in a mug and then gets out a tea bag for himself. When the kettle boils, he pours the water, passing the cup over to me and hands me the sugar and milk.

"You mentioned that your speech is coming along well?" I ask as I wait for my tea, taking a seat on a barstool at the island, Tate following my lead.

"Yes, very well thanks to you. I have most of it written, and then will need to go over it and revise it, but I'm happy with what I have. I hope it'll inspire at least a few of the students."

God, he's adorable when he's being humble.

"I bet it's amazing! I'd be inspired by you," I say. "I mean, by a speech you gave. Because you're inspiring and great and I like it when you talk to me and say things to me…" I trail off, hoping he'll ignore my lobster of a face and move on before I blurt out how hot he is or that Ms. Vaj is very inspired by him. But instead he smiles like the Cheshire cat, knowing exactly what Ms. Vaj is thinking and ok, yes, what I'm thinking as well.

"How about you drink your tea, friend?" he says, pushing the cup in my direction. I pull out the infuser, adding some milk and sugar to it.

"Holy shit, Tate! This is the best thing I've ever swallowed!"

"Maybe so far," Tate says, winking at me.

Oh lawdy! Ms. Vaj is on fire right now!

I shift in my seat, but that just puts pressure on Ms. Vaj, and that is totally not what I need right now.

Or, maybe that's exactly what I need right now.

No! We're friends. Calm your titties, Ms. Vaj!

Tate is biting his bottom lip, eyes raking over my body. I imagine how his hands would feel on my skin. How he'd take his time to feel my body below his, from my legs all the way up to my neck, probably making a couple of stops to rub between my legs, just for a moment as a tease, and again once he reaches my breasts, just giving them a gentle squeeze and rubbing my nipples between his thumb and finger a few times. I imagine how the rough stubble on his face would feel against my face, my neck, my breasts, between my legs. I remember how good he smelled, how strong he felt the one time we kissed. How soft his lips were.

I have played that memory over and over again, mostly at night when I'm alone in my bed.

I wonder if he does too.

I stifle a moan, but find myself turning a bit towards him, leaning into his space a little bit. He copies me, both of us gravitating towards each other, unable to stop the pull between us.

The dogs run into the room, Axelle chasing Mars as she tries to pull a toy out of his mouth. We jump apart like we were just caught doing something we shouldn't be.

I clear my throat and he rubs the back of his neck.

There's silence for a few seconds, until Tate says, "Stefan left a few dinner options for us in the freezer. Would you like to take a look at what he made, and we can pop one in the oven?"

"Oh, umm, yes. Dinner. Let's go see about the dinner food stuff." Smooth Harper, real smooth.

Tate opens the freezer, and after looking through the options we both decide on giant stuffed shells. Pasta is always the right choice.

As we wait for dinner, we make ourselves comfortable on the coffee coloured sofas in the living room. I set my tea on a dark cherry wood side table and sit down in the corner of the couch, tucking my feet underneath my body. Partly because it's super comfortable and partly because I need to put some physical space between Tate and I. I'm not sure exactly what would have happened if the dogs hadn't come barreling into the kitchen when they did, but I know it wouldn't have been something friends do.

And I will totally admit that I'm confused right now. I want Tate. Badly. So badly it hurts. My whole body is sensitive and reactive when he's in the room. But, I'm still not sure if pursuing anything would be a good idea. I want to stay here for a bit longer, but realistically, a bit longer doesn't mean long-term. And I'm a long-term kind of gal.

I really do need to make some sort of life plan.

"Hey Tate," I begin, a little nervous to actually have this conversation and start mapping out a plan. "How would it work to get a work visa here? Theo's dad mentioned it, and Yves said he would love it if I would work with him at the gardens some more."

Tate sits ramrod straight. I watch as his Adam's apple bobs up and down as he swallows. He wipes his palms on his thighs.

"You want to stay in Sova?" he asks, voice cracking just the slightest bit at the end.

"I've been thinking about it. I really like it here. Cara's here. Working in the gardens has been so amazing!" I look down, avoiding Tate's gaze. "And I've made some friends here. I don't know how long I would stay for, but I don't think I'm ready to leave just yet."

"But you do still want to return to Toronto at some point?"

"Probably. I don't know if I *want* to return or if I feel like I *should.* It's my home, I was born and raised there. My whole life has been there. But now that I've been here, I'm not really sure where I feel at home. I don't know if any of that makes sense. I feel lost, but starting to feel like I'm not drifting quite so aimlessly these days."

"I think that home is a fluid term. There are many different kinds of home. Toronto is your home because that's where you were born and lived your entire life. Canada is home because that's the country you were born into and your nationality. Nothing can change that, nor should it. But, that doesn't mean that you can't make somewhere else home too. It would never take away the feelings of home that Canada holds for you. Home is where you're happy. How does Cara feel now that she's been living here for a year? Does she feel like Canada was never home or like she replaced home?" Tate asks.

"Cara loves it here. And I know that she loved growing up in Toronto. I just feel like a failure. I failed at my career. I failed at my relationship with Levi. I failed at being an adult." I start to cry. I've tried holding it all in, but my feelings are bursting out of me now.

"Shh, Harper, it's ok," Tate says soothingly as he moves to sit beside me, gathering me in his arms. "You are not a failure. Not in any way. Sometimes things just don't work out, and it's stupid luck that two major things imploded at the same time, but that's not because of you failing. You were greatly affected by it, yes, but you didn't fail. Business was business and Levi is just an asshole, two things that you did not cause to happen. This opportunity right here, right now is something people rarely take advantage of, or even understand the greatness of what they are dealing with. You get to actively and intelligently decide the next path you take. You're in a position where you are free to choose. The world is open to you. I will help you in any way that I can, as I'm sure your sister will."

"I don't want to be a burden though, relying on other people when I'm supposed to be an adult and already have all this stuff figured out," I reply glumly.

"You're not a burden by asking for support. There's a difference between freeloading and getting support. You staying at Cara's or me helping you with visa paperwork or Yves hiring you is working within your support system, your village. We want to help you. That's what you do for people you love," Tate says, quickly adding "and for your friends. Friends help each other out."

"I don't really have a reason to go back to Toronto. All of my stuff is there, and I probably should go back to deal with it, and I will, but I think I want to stay here longer. Will you help me sort through what I have to do?" I look up at Tate, realizing just how close we're sitting. Our thighs are touching and his arms are still around me.

"It would be my pleasure to help you, Harper."

The way he says *pleasure* makes tingles erupt all over my body. He purred the word.

"Thank you, Tate. You're a good friend." I need to pour a bucket of ice water on this fire.

"Hmm, yes," Tate mumbles as he pulls away from me, moving back closer to his corner of the couch. "I'll look into what you need to do, and maybe speak with the

Minister of Immigration and Citizenship on how to expedite your application with the Canadian embassy."

"You can do that?" I ask-yell.

"I'm a prince, Harper, I can do that."

"Thank you!" I throw myself into his arms. "I'm so lucky to have you in my life!"

We hug for a few seconds before it turns into more of an embrace. We hold each other, my hands slowly moving across his upper back and shoulders, my right hand snaking into his hair. God, his hair is soft.

Tate slides his left hand across my lower back until it settles on my left hip, his arm is wrapped around my body, holding me close to him. He runs his right hand up my arm and onto my neck, holding it as his fingers gently whisper across my sensitive skin there, making me break out in goosebumps. I can feel Tate lower his head into the crook of my neck, his lips millimeters above my skin. We stay like that, both just feeling. Both breathing as hard as we can. Both hearts beating in time with each other.

"I want to stay here forever," Tate finally breaks the silence, "but I know I need to let you go."

I run my fingers through his hair again, making him groan.

"You're right. We should go check on dinner," I reluctantly agree, forcing myself to take my hands off him and backing away.

"Let's go eat," Tate says, trying to smile, but it doesn't reach his eyes.

Chapter 27 - Tate

That last hug with Harper almost broke my resolve. I was so close to putting my lips on her neck. So close to tasting her again.

I'm amazed I had enough blood left in my brain to remember that we're just friends and that I couldn't kiss her.

My dick might be mad at me right now, but I'm glad we didn't cross that line.

We make awkward small talk as we eat. I know the food is delicious, anything Stefan makes is, but I don't taste any of it.

I keep reliving the feeling of Harper in my arms. She was so warm and soft. She smelled like absolute fucking heaven.

Being here with her is torture, but it's the best kind of torture. Having her near me feels amazing, and even if I can never have her, I'll never want to give her up. She's already a part of me. I wasn't lying when I said that I would greedily take any piece of her she was willing to give me. I'll be like a stray dog following her around, hoping for scraps. And I'll do it with a big, goofy smile on my face.

"You'll have to tell Stefan thank you from me! That was delicious!" Harper says as she diligently scrapes all the sauce off her plate.

Don't watch her lick the fork. Don't watch her lick the fork.

I watch her tongue as it glides around the tines and back into her mouth.

Fuck, I watched her lick the fork.

"I will be sure to pass the message along. It will make him very happy to hear how much you enjoy his cooking. Would you like to play a game of cards with me after we clean up?"

"Ok! I know three card games, Go Fish, War and Crazy Eights. I can almost guarantee that you'll win," Harper laughs as she sashays into the kitchen with her dirty dishes.

"Let's play War to start us out, and then we can play Go Fish and I'll mop the floor with you!" I tease her.

■■

"You cheated!" Harper yells at me.

"How exactly does one cheat at Go Fish?" I ask, laughing under my breath.

"You said you didn't have any fours when I asked! I think you deliberately kept it for yourself!"

"I didn't have a four when you asked! Besides, why would I deliberately keep it? I had no idea I was going to need a four to win."

"Oh, I think you did! You sir, are a dirty cheat!"

"Careful, some might construe that as treason," I tell her. I actually have no idea if that would even count as treason or if I could convict someone for treason like that these days.

"Pfffft," Harper blows out a puff of air. "You're just trying to throw me in the dungeons to cover up your crimes of cheating at a children's card game. But I'm on to you now, buster!" Harper wags her finger at me.

"Oh no, you caught me." I reply deadpan. "See, I wasn't really sure if this whole being a prince thing was going to work out, so I thought I would test out a life of crime. Guess I'm not a good fit for a crime lord and I should stick to being a prince."

"Definitely stick to princing."

"Princing isn't a word."

"It's a word now because I said it," Harper replies. A yawn cuts off whatever she was going to say next.

"Ok, let's get to bed before you pass out down here," I tell her as I stand up and offer her my hand to help her up off the floor where we have been sitting around the coffee table.

Harper takes my hands, but quickly lets go once she's standing.

I can't blame her for putting some distance between us, but it stings a bit.

We walk upstairs quietly, casting glances at each other and then looking away quickly.

All too soon, we're standing in front of her bedroom door.

I put my hands in my pockets so I can't touch her.

"Well, goodnight, Harper. Sleep well. If you need anything, you know where to find me." I hitch a thumb over my shoulder.

"Goodnight, Tate. I'll see you in the morning."

Harper opens her door and walks inside, gently closing the door behind her.

I let out a big breath I didn't realize I was holding.

Now just to make it through another few days.

■■■

Marielle: How's your little sleepover going?

Me: She's warm and soft and in her own room sleeping.

Marielle: And how exactly do you know that she's warm and soft?

Me: I hugged her. I made myself let go and didn't let it go any further than a hug, even if I desperately wanted it to. Then we ate dinner, played cards and I walked her to her bedroom and said goodnight from the hall.

Marielle: Just out of curiosity, which bedroom is she staying in?

Me: I don't think I want to answer that.

Marielle: She's sleeping across the hall, isn't she?

Me: ...maybe

Marielle: Yeah, you're not going to remain just friends for long.

Me: Be quiet.

Chapter 28 - Harper

I wait until I hear Tate go downstairs before I get out of
bed to avoid any awkward *just woke up and now we're
standing in the hall looking at each other* moments.
I couldn't fall asleep, thoughts of Tate kept playing
behind my closed eyelids. I eventually had to resort to
pleasuring myself while imagining it was his fingers
between my legs, pumping into me aggressively,
whispering dirty words in my ears. I could almost feel his
large hands on my skin. My fingers became his fingers as
I played with my nipples. I came so hard and so fast that
it was a miracle I didn't scream the house down. I had to
press my face into a pillow to muffle out the sounds
coming out of me.
So yeah, I'm going to try to avoid him for a little bit this
morning until I am fully awake and can appear
composed.
I jump into the shower before I go down for breakfast.
That way I can blame any blushing that's bound to
happen on the temperature of the shower.
The bathroom is gorgeous, with slate tiles and a
freestanding clawfoot bathtub. An aqua coloured glass
vessel sink sits atop a slate countertop with dark

cherrywood cabinets. Pewter fixtures match a pewter pendant light hanging in the middle of the room. White fluffy towels subdue the dark, masculine feel of the room and the large window beside the tub gives a gorgeous, almost ethereal view of the forest.

While a bubble bath in here would be absolute perfection, I think this morning calls for a shower.

After a quick shower and shave (which we will not dwell on or comment on how diligently I did so), I hop out and towel off. I'm prepared to put my hair in a wet braid, but luckily for me there's a hair dryer in the cabinet under the sink.

I take more time than normal drying my hair, making sure it lays nice and smooth against my back, and carefully apply my makeup (we're not dwelling on these either, by the way).

Smells of bacon and eggs waft up from the kitchen when I open my bedroom door.

Great, now he's cooking for me.

As if Tate wasn't already the sexiest man I've ever met, now he's making me breakfast and it smells bloody amazing!

Tate has his back to me when I walk into the kitchen, facing the stove as he places more bacon in the pan.

A teapot sits on the island and there is a plate of scrambled eggs sitting out. The toaster pops and he expertly plucks the pieces out, buttering them before he flips the bacon over.

How is this man single? Holy heavens above, he's every person who's attracted to men's dreams come true, and honestly probably even those who aren't into men.

"This all smells so great! I can't believe you made us breakfast. I was prepared to eat cereal," I tell him as I take the plate of toast to the island to join the other food.

"I like cooking. I rarely get to do it myself and when I do, it's usually just for me," Tate replies, looking bashful. "Please help yourself. This bacon is just about done. I made a pot of my sister's tea. I hope that's ok with you."

"Mmm, thank you!"

I begin loading my plate with the fluffiest eggs I have ever seen outside of a restaurant and Tate takes the bacon out of the pan, dealing with the grease before he joins me. I place a giant mound of bacon on my plate alongside my eggs. I've never been one of those women who are afraid to eat in front of men. Fuck that noise. Food is delicious and I want to eat it. If a man can't handle the fact that I eat more than a garden salad without dressing for dinner, then he doesn't deserve to know me. Salads are delicious, but I want the dressing and I want a big salad. And carbs. And fat. And dessert.

We sit contentedly side-by-side and enjoy our meal. The silence isn't suffocating. I feel at ease to sit here with him. I don't feel the urge to fill the space with chatter like I usually do with people other than family. Our connection has always felt natural. Becoming close friends felt as easy as breathing.

"If you don't mind, I'm going to go straight to my office to finish up on my speech."

"Oh, yeah, that's fine! I was thinking that today I would explore the forest. Yesterday, I mostly just stayed near the pond, so now I would like to go a bit further."

"That sounds like a great idea. The dogs would love to go out with you, although I make no promises that they'll stay with you."

We clean up the kitchen and go our separate ways. I call for the dogs and we head out the back door together. They, of course, take off as soon as their little feet hit the grass.

It doesn't take long before I'm under the canopy of the trees. The tall pines guarding this area like sentinels from above, the sun filtering through their boughs before it softly illuminates the ground below. I can hear animals scurrying around on the forest floor (let's assume here that they're squirrels and nothing to worry about) and birds up in the trees. I should have asked for binoculars! Tomorrow. Tomorrow I will be a serious birder (a new word I learned from one of the books I read yesterday. Look at me using lingo for my new super cool bird watching hobby!) and bring binoculars and maybe a little book to record what I have found.

I wander around for a couple of hours, taking in the fresh air and beauty nature has to offer.

This feels like home.

That thought is both jarring and comforting.

I can see the house off in the distance, so I make my way towards it before I get lost and need to embarrassingly call Tate for a search and rescue.

Axelle and Mars meet me at the door just as I'm letting myself in.

"Hey! I'm glad you're back. I have two pieces of news to share," Tate tells me excitedly.

"Ok, let's hear it!" I match his enthusiasm as I take off my shoes and place them near the back door.

"First, I finished my speech! It's all done and ready to go. I'll probably look it over a couple of times before the big day, but I'm happy with the way it's come together."

"Tate! That's so awesome! I'm so proud of you!"

"Thank you, that means a lot to me," Tate says, grinning at me. "The second piece of news is for you. I have a contact at the Canadian embassy who is waiting to meet with you about a visa and will personally see that the paperwork is put through quickly."

"Oh my gosh! For real!? Tate, that's amazing of you!" I squeal as I launch myself at him. Tate catches me easily as I wrap my legs around his waist. He holds me tight to him and I cling to him.

"Harper," Tate murmurs my name, pressing me closer into his body.

He's so hard. His biceps bulge as they hold my body up. I can feel his abs and pecs flex against me. His hard cock pulses against my softness.

"Tate," I whimper into his neck.

"We need to either let go of each other right now and go to separate areas of the house for a while, or I'm going to fuck you."

I moan into his skin. This is it. I know that no matter what happens right now, things will never be the same. This moment has been inevitable since we met. No matter how many times I have said that we were just friends, I know that I have been lying to myself. We've never been just friends.

"Don't put me down, Tate."

"I need you to tell me you want me. I need you to tell me yes," Tate whispers in my ear.

"Yes, Tate. I want you so badly," I admit.

"Thank fuck!"

And then Tate's lips are on mine. He pushes his tongue into my mouth and I moan at the feeling.

I grip onto him tighter, needing to be closer. Needing to feel all of him.

Tate must get the hint, because he slides me down the front of his body, kissing me as soon as my feet touch the ground and then he's pulling me along as he races towards the stairs and to his room. I marvel at his agility, and later I will be impressed that he didn't smash us into any walls running through the house like I know I would have.

"Still yes?" Tate asks, looking into my eyes when he stops us in the hall outside his bedroom door. "You can still say no. Always remember that you can say no."

"Yes, Tate. I want you. I want all of you. I think that I will always want you," I confess before I take his face between my hands and kiss him, pouring out all of the feelings that I have kept pent up inside of me.

Tate picks me up again and walks us over to the bed, laying me down gently, kissing me softly before he steps away.

"God, you're fucking beautiful, Harper." Tate's eyes travel down my body, searing me with the heat in his gaze. He pulls his shirt off in one fluid motion, and holy hell, Tate shirtless is even better than I imagined. If I was a cartoon character, my tongue would be rolling down to the floor and my eyes would be popping out of my head. "You have a tattoo." I look up at him, raising my body up to a sitting position so I can see him better. "It's beautiful. You're beautiful, Tate."

Tate's tattoo covers almost the entirety of his left side. A mountain range wraps around his ribs, from his back to his mid-chest. Pine trees line the front of the mountains, with a lake off to the right side. The way the tattoo artist has done the shading makes the water look like it's gleaming in the sunlight.

"Thank you. It's Montfret. It's the view from my balcony," Tate points over to a set of French doors on the opposite wall. "It's my favourite place to get lost and think. I can just be me here. No pretending. No pageantry. No dressing up and smiling even if I don't agree with what is being said. I got this tattoo to remind me of that feeling. That no matter where I am, I'm always Tate."

I lean forward and run my fingers along his ribs, tracing the lines of the jagged peaks of the mountains, down to the subtle waves in the lake.

I can feel Tate shiver beneath my touch, making me bolder in my exploration. My other hand joins in as I feel all the taught muscles I have been dreaming about for weeks.

Tate unbuttons his jeans, sliding them down his legs, looking at me before he removes his black boxer briefs.

"Holy gods!" I exclaim when I see him in all his naked magnificence.

Tate is huge. Like, Adonis would be jealous huge. And fit. Not so muscley that I'm worried about him crushing me, but every muscle is defined and strong. He's going to make me orgasm just by standing there.

"Now it's your turn," Tate says, climbing on to the bed, running his hands up my legs until he reaches the waistband of my jeans.

He stops and looks up at me. I nod, letting him know he can take them off. He unbuttons them slowly, torturing me. I am more turned on than I have ever been before. Tate kisses down my legs as he slowly peels my pants off my body. Once they're off, he throws them to the floor, joining his clothes in a heap. He kisses his way up my other leg until he reaches my hip, kissing across my stomach before he starts to roll my shirt up. I help him by taking it all the way off, too impatient to have his hands on my skin.

I unclasp my bra, but Tate takes over by sliding the straps down my arms and oh so slowly pulls the bra away from my body.

"Fuck," Tate says reverently.

"I'm glad you like," I reply, feeling bolder than I ever have before.

"I can't even put together the words to express how much I like."

I look down at his thick cock bobbing between us.

"I think I have an idea," I say, raising an eyebrow.

"I need you to know that I absolutely did not bring you here to get you into bed. I did not expect sex from you," Tate tells me seriously.

"I know. I didn't come here assuming this would happen."

"Good. Because I happen to have a box of condoms. And while I grumbled at Dax's presumptions when he put them in my bag, I'm really glad that he did."

"Ha! I'd say something about assuming, but it looks like he was absolutely right!" I laugh. I should be embarrassed that his family assumed we'd end up having sex, but well, here we are, so…

Tate gets off the bed, opens his bag and grabs the box of condoms.

"Looks like your family thought we'd be having a lot of sex!" I laugh as I point at the jumbo box of condoms.

"Yeah, sorry, Dax likes to be prepared."

I watch as Tate rips open a wrapper and rolls the condom down his thick length.

I take my underwear off faster than I ever have in my entire life. My whole body is vibrating with anticipation. Tate prowls over to me and I am trapped in his gaze. I couldn't move even if I wanted to. But I most definitely do not want to go anywhere. Ms. Vaj would murder me if I left right now.

I lay back down on the bed as Tate holds up his body above mine. He runs his hands up my legs until he reaches my already soaking wet pussy. He slowly slides a finger inside as his other hand continues its path up to my breast. He rolls my nipple between his thumb and finger, pumping his finger in and out of me.

"You're so fucking wet for me," Tate groans. "You're so perfect." Tate kisses me slowly, winding his tongue with mine. He kisses the side of my mouth, my cheek, across my jaw, all while pumping his fingers in and out of me. I've never been this wet before. Never been this ready. Never wanted anyone as bad as I want Tate.

"God, Tate, that feels so good," I moan.

"You ready?" he asks, his voice huskier than I've ever heard it before.

"Yes, Tate, fuck me," I plead.

Tate takes his fingers out, grasping his cock instead, while his other hand cups my cheek as he slides himself into me, and it's the most glorious mix of pleasure and pain.

It's too much. It's not enough. It's everything.

"Oh my god, Harper, you feel so good. I might need a moment," Tate murmurs as he rests his forehead against mine.

We lay there for a moment, both of us breathing in and adjusting to the new sensations.

"We haven't even moved, and this is already the best sex I've ever had," I tell him. "I'm not sure if that's really sad for me or if it's something really good for us."

"I know what you mean," Tate says as he kisses his way down the side of my face. "And I think I know why we feel like this." Tate kisses me on my lips.

"Oh yeah? And why's that?" I ask breathily as he moves back to kissing my neck.

"It's because," Tate punctuates his thought with a deep thrust.

"You," *thrust.*

"Are," *thrust.*

"Mine." *thrust.*

I moan in response as he picks up speed, thrusting deep into me each time.

"And," I say, holding his face in my hands. "You are mine." I kiss him deeply.

"Say that again," Tate growls into my mouth. "Tell me I'm yours again."

"You, Tate, are mine. And I am yours."

Tate licks up the column of my neck, making me moan. He slides his hand down my body to my clit and begins to gently rub it.

"Fuck, Tate, I'm not going to last long."

In response, he licks his way down to my nipple, gently nipping it at, then sucking it into his mouth, at the same time putting more pressure on my clit.

I arch my back and cry out. Tingles spread across my body as my orgasm builds. All it takes is a few more swipes of his tongue and thumb, and I erupt and scream.

"I can't hold back anymore, I need to come."

"Yes, Tate, yes. Fuck me until you come!"

Tate turns into an absolute animal, pounding into me so hard the headboard smashes into the wall. He roars into my neck as he finds his release and crumples on top of me.

"Well, I hope you didn't have any other plans for the day, because I don't think I can move," Tate tells me. I laugh as he peppers kisses all over my face.

"I would be very happy to stay here with you."

And I would. I have no desire to get up and leave this bed. I feel absolutely content. And it's not just because I can't feel my extremities at the moment.

We lay together for a while, drawing patterns on each other's skin.

My stomach growls, reminding me we missed lunch.

"Let's get cleaned up and then go eat," I suggest, trying to bring my limbs back to life.

"I suppose we should. I think rehydrating is probably a good idea too."

Chapter 29 - Tate

Today has been unbelievable. I can't stop touching Harper. Part of me can't believe I actually get to touch her. This feels like a dream, and at any moment I will wake up and have to go back to being just friends.

"Would you like a sandwich? Stefan put some sliced ham in here, and we still have some of the Havarti we could use," I ask Harper as I start pulling stuff out of the fridge.

"That sounds great! Can I help in some way?"

"You can get a couple of plates down, if you wouldn't mind," I tell her, pointing to the cabinet with the plates. We work together, side by side making sandwiches.

Such a simple task, but it feels otherworldly doing this with Harper. What should be a mundane task is fun with her. She brings a light to my life that I didn't even realize was missing. I didn't know I was living in a shadow, but now I feel like the whole world is lit up and I can see in technicolour.

I pour us tall glasses of water. I was being serious when I said we needed to rehydrate. I was a sweaty mess in bed with Harper.

That was the best sex I have ever had. I need to do it again, and maybe last longer than a few minutes. I'd feel embarrassed about that, except it felt so fucking fantastic.

We sit at the island to eat our late lunch, and I inhale my food and guzzle down my water. Harper slides over half her sandwich.

"You clearly need more food," she says with a wink.

"I want to tell you about Celeste, my ex," I tell her after I finish eating the sandwich she gave me.

"You don't have to, Tate. I don't expect you to talk about her. Theo mentioned it was a very public, very bad breakup. I wouldn't blame you if you didn't want to talk about her."

"That's the thing," I reply. "Normally, I don't want to talk about her. Ever. She hurt me so badly that I still immediately shut down any mention of her. But, I want to tell you. You make me feel like I can open up and share. I want you to know all of me."

This is difficult. I don't like people looking at me with pity. But, Harper is different. She makes me feel whole.

"Celeste and I met when we were kids. Her family comes from old money. No titles, but wealthy and ran in the aristocratic circles that attended events and balls with my family. Celeste was always beautiful. Even as a child she turned heads. Sleek dark hair, big mocha-coloured eyes, olive skin and long legs. Everyone wanted her, and she

258

wanted me. When we were twenty-four, we found ourselves bored together at a party for some charity. I can't remember what it was for, but I do remember it being dreadful. We snuck a bottle of wine and hid in a sitting room so our parents wouldn't find us. One thing led to another, most definitely aided by the wine, and we slept together. For a year, we snuck around together. We weren't together, but we weren't not together." I pause for a moment and Harper lays her hand on my arm, silently lending me her support.

"After a year, Celeste wanted more. We were having fun, and I didn't have a good reason to say no, so we started to attend events as a couple. The press ate it up. Until Celeste at age twenty-five, I had never publicly been in a romantic relationship. Things were great for about a year and a half. We started to get serious, and she started to drop some hints about marriage. But I wasn't ready. Something kept telling me to hold back. Marriage is a big deal, and an even bigger deal when you're a member of a Royal Family."

"I can imagine. So many more things you'd have to consider, compared to us normal, boring commoners," Harper says, being supportive but also preventing me from going too far down the sinkhole thinking about Celeste opens up in me. I squeeze Harper's hand.

"After that, Celeste started to act a little off. She was jumpy when we were out in public and pushed for marriage more. Her dad invited me golfing, which I hate by the way but went to be polite, and he started telling me how beneficial our marriage would be. He was pushing it hard. It made me feel like I was nothing more than an antique lamp at an auction house. I told Celeste that I wasn't ready for marriage and to stop pushing me for it." I take a drink of my water, needing a moment to compose myself.

"That's when the tabloids really seemed to get interested in me. At first, I thought nothing of it, since every once in a while, tabloids and magazines will run a story about us, create some sort of scandal or an old photo will resurface that they try to make a big deal out of. But these stories were different. They were targeted, personal and had some photos that the paparazzi would never have been able to take. After weeks of this, The Sova Sun published a story detailing my sex life. Considering that I had been with the same woman for two and a half years at this point, and they included some photos of me from inside my house, I started to question their source. Celeste swore she didn't know anything, but one of the photos was of me in my bathroom here, with just a towel wrapped around my waist after a shower. It was only

Celeste and I in the house, and I think you'll agree that there's no way paparazzi could get a photo like that from outside this house."

"Oh my god! Celeste took that photo and sold it to the tabloids?!" Harper cries out, her hand over her heart, "I can't even imagine doing that to anyone, especially someone I loved!"

"Mmhmm. Eventually, Celeste admitted everything. Her father had made some bad stock market investments and lost most of their fortune. He tried to make it back through gambling, but he ended up losing it all. She tried to force me into marriage so they'd have access to my family's money to save her own family. When I told her I didn't want to get married, her dad became angry and told her to do whatever it took to save their family. She came up with the idea of selling information and photos to the tabloids." I huff out a laugh. "She actually thought she could sell stories about me and my family, not tell me and that we would still get married."

"What a bitch! Where is she?! I bet I could take her!" Harper stands up abruptly like she's going to march into battle, hands fisted at her sides.

I grab hold of Harper's hand, pulling open her fist and threading our fingers together. "Harper, it's ok. It all ended four years ago. I kicked her out of the house.

Literally. I escorted her to the gate and shut it on her face. She called her dad to pick her up. I haven't seen her since. She is not allowed at the castle, nor is her family. They tried to launch some campaigns against my family, tried to sue us for slander and bad mouthed us to whoever would listen. Fortunately, they had no basis for legal recourse, and people saw through them very quickly and realized what she did to me. The truth that Celeste and her family are truly terrible people was evident to everyone. But, she did make me nervous to invite people into my life, and I haven't dated since. Until you."

"Pffft, no pressure at all," Harper says, looking around the room.

"Hey, no. Look at me." I pull Harper back down to sit on her stool. "I'm not trying to put any pressure on you. Whatever this is that we have feels real and special to me, but I know that we have some obstacles. I want to be happy with you, for however long and in whatever way that looks like."

Harper looks at our linked hands for a few seconds before whispering, "It feels real to me too. You make me happy." She looks up at me with the biggest smile now, and it takes my breath away.

"It seems really early to be having a *where is this going* talk, but I think we probably should, considering who I am and your short-term residency here." I clear my throat, absolutely terrified of what this conversation will bring, but know that it's important.

"Yeah, we should probably be adults about this. That's the adulty thing to do, right?" she asks with a grimace, closing one eye tightly like it will offer her some kind of emotional protection.

"Alright, so," I begin. "I really like you. A lot. You make me feel alive, but also calm and grounded all at the same time. I can talk to you about anything. Beyond my family, I can't think of another person that I have ever felt this safe with. I want to spend time with you. I want to learn all about you. I want you. Do you remember the swans we saw the first time we met?"

"Yep! They were swimming, and you got all sappy telling me about how they're mates and they swim around in each other's orbits," she tells me, grinning wide.

"Yes, well, I'm about to get sappy again, because you feel like my swan. Wherever you go, I am drawn to follow. I am hyper aware of you. I know where you are in the room. I find you when I'm not even looking for you. I always want to be with you, in your orbit." Oh man, I have it bad for this woman.

"You think," Harper's eyes fill with tears and chokes back a sob. "You think that I'm your swan?"

"Yes, I mean, I know that probably doesn't make much sense…"

"You're my swan too! I'm a little afraid, but I want to be with you." Harper hugs me from across our stools. Her unexpected launch hugs are becoming one of my favourite things.

Harper is so warm. So soft. She smells so good. Her skin is so soft.

No, come on man, stay focused.

"I sense a but coming here," Harper says warily as she pulls away from me.

"Not a but, more like something that we need to be aware of."

"Ok…is this where you reveal that you wish I was an actual swan?" Harper asks, biting the inside of her cheek, looking like she's trying really hard to not laugh.

"No, no, nothing like that," I laugh. "Being with me, and this applies even if this," I move my hand back and forth between us, "wasn't happening and we remained as just friends, will mean that the media will become very interested in you. I haven't been in a relationship for four years, Harper, the media is going to go crazy over us." Fuck, it didn't really hit me until I said it out loud. "The media, the paparazzi, are going to be watching us like hawks. Everything we do, even separately, will become

264

interesting to them, and the tabloids are masters at spinning the smallest thing into a scandal. Living in the public eye is not easy, and I understand if you'd prefer to step away from us now to protect yourself."

Please don't step away. Please don't leave me. I love you. *I love you*?! What the fuck?

Ok, yes, maybe I do have some loving feelings toward her, but nope, not going to say that right now. Need to keep those thoughts locked away.

"So, you're telling me that we either have to, what, break up or my life will never be the same and someone is going to follow me around taking pictures of me picking my nose as I walk down the street?" Harper cries out.

"Probably shouldn't pick your nose regardless of the paparazzi, but, yeah, I guess that pretty much sums it up."

"Ok, this is fine. I like you, you like me, but I don't like paparazzi, that just sounds horrible, but maybe it won't be all that bad. I mean, I'm boring and normal but you're not boring or normal and they know that. Oh god, they'll probably hate me for being normal and find pictures of me from when I was like fifteen and made the horrible decision to have bangs, and let me tell you, Cara did not know how to cut bangs!" Harper is breathing rapidly now, her face is splotchy red.

265

I stand up and pull Harper off her stool, leading us over to the couch. I sit us down close so our bodies are close, but facing each other so we can talk.

"I've had to deal with the media and public scrutiny for my entire life, and sometimes I forget that people aren't used to cameras in their faces and can't just shrug it off. Whatever we decide between us, is for us, you understand?" Harper nods her head. "We are the ones who decide what our relationship looks like and feels like. The media will be interested in us, I will not be able to prevent that, but I will protect you as much as I am able to. If you decide that it's too much, I will never hold that against you. You tell me what you want to do, how you want to proceed from here, and I will follow you."

"I don't want to walk away from us, Tate. We've just found each other, and I can't fathom the idea of not being with you," Harper says, and I breathe a huge sigh of relief. "But, I'm also scared of being torn apart by people who don't know me. I don't think I could handle being publicly attacked by a tabloid." Harper looks up at me, her eyes huge.

"What about if, for now, we don't hide, but we also don't flaunt anything. Like, we'll be seen together in public, but keep displays of affection to a minimum. We act

266

polite and respectful. Wave to people, smile for cameras, but keep our private moments private?"

"So, you're thinking that if we act like boring adults, they'll get bored of us and leave us alone?"

"Yes, essentially. There will be initial interest, but if we don't give them any fodder, it'll die down."

"Ok. But, there's still the issue of me leaving. At some point. Probably. I may or may not be here for a while. I clearly have no idea what is going on with my life or where I will live. Are you sure you want to entangle yourself with the hot mess that is me?" Harper shakes her head. "I might be bad publicity for you, Tate."

"First of all, I absolutely want to entangle myself with you," I wink at her. "Secondly, you are not a mess. You are human, and sometimes our lives have messy moments. I want to be with you, mess and all. Ok? I need you to know how much I want *you*."

"Well, if you're absolutely sure, then ok. I really like you, Tate," Harper says as she leans in and gives me a sweet kiss.

"I really like you too. But remember, if my life gets to be too much, just tell me ok, don't hide your feelings. I want to know."

"I promise, Tate. As for where I'll be living, can we just put a pin in that? This is very odd of me to say, but let's just see what happens. I have no current plans to leave Sova, so let's just be together and see what happens." Then I kiss her with everything I have, hoping that this happiness won't be ripped away from me.

Chapter 30 - Harper

"We need to move." I force my eyes open and try to move my arms, but they are jelly.

"Mhmm."

"At the very least, we need some water."

"Mhmm."

"Has anyone ever told you that you are an amazing conversationalist post-orgasm?" I ask, attempting to sound haughty, but fail miserably since my vocal cords are also jelly.

"Mhmm," is Tate's witty retort.

We're sprawled out on the couch, clothes literally everywhere. I'm amazed we didn't break the couch after the gymnastics we just performed on it.

My need for the bathroom wins out over wanting to stay cuddled up with a naked Tate, and trust me when I say that was a battle Ms. Vaj fought hard to win. I drag myself up and start putting my clothes back on. I grab my phone from the floor where it fell when I threw my pants and slide it into my back pocket.

"I'm just going to go freshen up, I'll be right back," I say as I lean down and press a kiss to Tate's lips.

"Mhmm. And tell Cara I say hi," Tate says, smirking up at me.

"Who says I'm going to talk to Cara?" I ask, even though I absolutely planned on it.

"You're either going to play a game on your phone while you're in the bathroom, or you're sneaking off to tell your sister about the best sex of your life."

"Who says it's been the best sex of my life?" I ask, placing my hands on my hips.

"You did. Repeatedly. Loudly."

"Yeah, ok, fine. You're the best sex I have ever had and I'm going to tell my sister all about it and you. Happy now?"

"Yes, Harper. I am very happy right now. Go talk to your sister and I'll make us a snack." Tate gets up, and the sight of him standing before me, gloriously naked is almost enough to bring me to my knees. Again. Wink wink, nudge nudge.

No. Bathroom, then text Cara, then eat a snack. A regular snack, not a Tate snack. Stand down, Ms. Vaj!

I text Cara as soon as I make it into the bathroom.

Me: You were right, Sovan sausage is fantastic

I put the phone on the counter as I take care of business. It doesn't take her long to text back.

Cara: YES!!!!! YESSSSSSS!!! TELL ME ALL THE THINGS!

Cara: I bet his cock is huge! It's massive, isn't it?

Cara: ARE YOU GOING TO BE A FUCKING PRINCESS?????!!!?!?!?!?!?!

Cara: Does this mean that you're staying in Sova????!!?!

Cara: Or is this a casual thing? Are you ok with it being a casual thing?

Cara: HARPER LEE JONES, YOU BETTER ANSWER ME RIGHT NOW BECAUSE IN CASE YOU HAVEN'T NOTICED, I'M FREAKING THE FUCK OUT OVER HERE!!!

Me: Cara Lynn Morteau!! Calm your little horses! I'm going to apply for a visa so that I can stay here longer and continue to work with Yves. I don't know exactly how long it will be for, but I will make sure to tell you, so you don't need to get worked up about that

Me: We were behaving really well, staying in friend territory. But, then a hug turned into more, and the next thing I knew, we were humping like rabid teenagers and sex obviously had to happen at that point. And yes, we're talking MASSIVE cock, like monster massive!

271

Me: But, it was more than the sexiest penis I have ever seen. It just felt so good, and not just in a the sex was mind blowing (it was btw), but in a it was right, like we felt right.

Cara: It sounds like you two have something really special. So, tell me, where are you going from here? Casual sex? One time thing, got it out of your system and now you'll go back to the just friends thing? Going to be more than friends?

Me: We're going to be together, like together-together. Can I call a thirty-one year old prince my boyfriend? That word doesn't seem right. I'll figure that one out. I don't want to hide what we have, what we are, but I also don't want to be mauled by paparazzi. So, we decided to continue just being us. In public, we'll keep our hands to ourselves, but in private we'll be sickeningly cute and cuddly.

Me: I'll go back to working in the gardens with Yves, stay with you a bit longer, if you don't mind, and then we'll just see where this goes

Cara: YOU don't have a plan? And you're ok with no plan?

Me: Yep! And actually, I like not having a plan. This feels right.

Cara: It sounds like you do have a plan, but maybe you're not quite ready to admit it?

Me: Yeah, maybe. I don't know. I should go though. I'll check in with you before we leave

Me: Also, Tate says hi!

▪▪

We spend the rest of the day lounging around the house. Tate found some sea salt kettle chips in the pantry and had a giant bowl waiting for me when I came back from the bathroom, which were delicious. Chef's kiss!

We're up in my sitting room, sitting on opposite ends of the couch. Tate has his long legs stretched out in front of him, propped up on the table, whereas I'm laying across the couch, my feet in his lap. He's absentmindedly rubbing my feet as we each read a book. Annie has excellent taste in books, and I'm going to have to take this one with me when we leave.

Tate's phone beeps as a text message comes in. He picks it up, groans and quickly puts it back down on the arm of the couch, face down.

"Who was that?" I ask curiously.

"My family text thread. Marielle wants to know how things are going here. And probably very soon someone

273

else is going to chime in asking about you, and then someone will make a lewd comment, Marielle will join in, Maman will say something subtle but prying. So now I'm trying to decide how much information is needed to satiate their interest without giving them too much, which would in turn make them more chatty and ask more questions." Tate runs his hands through his hair.

"They love you very much. I happen to think it's sweet," I tell him. I wish I had a big family, prying into my life like that. I have Cara, but parents invested in my life would be nice too.

"Pass me your phone," I tell him, sticking my hand out toward him.

He unlocks his phone and hands it over to me without asking any questions. He trusts me. It hits me like a punch to the gut. This man that has been so hurt before, that has to be closed off just because of the nature of his life, trusts me completely. That seems like it should be too much. Like it should scare me, but really, it just makes me happy and like I need to protect him.

"Can I jump into your family messages and say hi?" I ask, wanting to make sure he knows and is ok with what I'm about to do.

"Harper, if you haven't already noticed, you own my heart and have my life in your hands. If you want to talk

274

to my family, I want you to talk to them. But, I'm warning you, they are going to go insane and you are going to be bombarded with questions, many of them likely personal and embarrassing if Corvin and Marielle team up."

I just smile at him. Old me would have made a pros and cons list, planned out how we would tell his family about us dating, and probably would have waited a while before doing so. But this me wants to jump right in, feet first. I know I'm falling in love with Tate, I probably already am in love with him, and there doesn't seem any way to stop that train.

All aboard the love train! Choo choo!

Man, I am such a nerd.

Me: Hello everyone, this is Harper

Marielle: Harper! Hi! I am so excited right now!

Simon: Hello, Harper. It's nice to finally "meet" you. Marielle won't stop gloating that she's actually met you and I haven't.

Corvin: I don't know babe, I don't think this counts. Marielle still gets bragging rights

Maman: What about me? I met her first!

Corvin: Ok, first place goes to Janelle, second place goes to Marielle, and Simon, you get third place

Papa: Now, wait just a minute. I saw Harper at the Sova day party before Marielle met her, so what about me?

Corvin: Ok, ok. Janelle first, Marielle second, Louis third (sorry, but I think actually speaking to her gives Mari an extra point), Simon is in fourth, then me in fifth. Dax is last since he hasn't made an appearance yet

"Wow, you weren't kidding!" I show Tate the messages. "Think they'd even notice if I never responded?"

"Nope, they'll just keep going like that if you let them. It's one of my tricks, give them a talking point and then back away slowly."

Me: I know everyone has questions. Yes, Tate and I are now dating. Yes, we failed horribly at just being friends. No, I will not be giving any details. I'm going to be incredibly awkward when I officially meet all of you. Probably for a while. It's just part of my charm. We're going to go for a walk now. You probably won't hear from us for the rest of the night.

Marielle: I knew it!! I knew you wouldn't stay just friends! Honey! You owe me twenty euros!

Simon: You bet on them sleeping together?

Marielle: Obviously. Dax thought they'd make it another night.

Corvin: Well, I was banking on the first night, or first thing the next morning. Why else would I send you with such a giant bottle of champagne?? I'm a little disappointed in you two

Me: Sorry, we actually haven't opened the champagne. But, Princess Marielle, your tea was superb! Thank you for sending me some!

Corvin: Kiss ass

Marielle: Hush, Corvin! I am so glad that you liked it, Harper! I will make sure you get as much as you need!

Dax: Whoa, what'd I miss?

Simon: Tate and Harper are fucking.

Maman: Simon! Manners please!

Simon: Sorry, Maman. Tate and Harper have made sweet love, and now the entire family is competing over who knows Harper better. Soon there will be bets on who Harper will like the most.

Me: Ok, well, you guys have fun clamoring for my love. I look forward to meeting everyone soon. Goodnight

Marielle: Goodnight, new bestie!

■■■

We put in another of Stefan's amazing looking meals into the oven, this time it's a mouth-watering moussaka, and

Tate preps a Greek salad, adding in way more feta than a sane person would want, as per my request.

I started some bread earlier, so now I'm prepping it to go in the oven.

We spent a couple of hours outside before coming back in to get ready for dinner. We left the walled-in area of the property, much to the chagrin of the dogs, and Tate brought me over to the lake. It's even more beautiful up close. You can see the mountains reflecting on the surface of the water, as if the lake was made of glass. It just might be the most beautiful place I have ever seen.

"Tate?" I ask after I slide the bread into the second oven (yes, this kitchen has a double oven! Have I mentioned how amazing this house is!?).

"Yes, love?"

Love? Well, that's new.

I like it.

A lot.

"I'm really happy you invited me here."

"I'm really happy you came."

"Is it weird that I think you're my best friend? That I even thought that before today happened," I tell him, feeling all kinds of self conscious.

Tate slides the salad to the middle of the island and walks over to me, so we're standing toe-to-toe. He lifts my chin up with his fingers so we're looking right at each other. "You're my best friend too, Harper." Tate kisses me slowly, deliberately. He knows what I need, like he's already proficient in my body. He doesn't demand control, but I happily give it to him anyway.

Chapter 31 - Tate

I wake up before Harper, so I lie here like a total creep and watch her sleep. I could do this forever. Just watch her breathe in and out slowly, completely at peace. The sun finds its way into the room through gaps in the curtain, illuminating her hair. She looks like an angel, sent just for me.

I know, without a shadow of a doubt that Harper is the one for me. My body knew it before I allowed my brain to catch up. A magnetic pull has always existed between us, from that very first moment I saw her sitting on the bench. I should have just walked away, but I *couldn't*. Everything about her was pulling me in. She's my swan.

"Mmmm, good morning," Harper mumbles as she stretches out. I watch as she arches her back, her arms raising above her head, pulling her shirt up to give me a peek of her creamy skin.

"Morning, love. Did you sleep well?" I ask, attempting to be a gentleman this morning and ignore my dick who is screaming at me for morning sex. For someone who has gone years without sex, he's a demanding bastard now.

"I sure did! For having such a hard body, you're surprisingly easy to cuddle into. And you're warm, like really warm. Not too hot like a furnace that had me uncomfortable all night, but like cozy warm that made me want to burrow into your body." Harper continues to mumble, sounding more asleep than awake.

"I like you first thing in the morning. And for the record, you're warm and cuddly too and you do not snore like a dying trombone," I tell her, kissing the top of her head.

"Yes! Suck it, Cara!"

The words *suck it* are my undoing. I slide my hand up her shirt, cupping her breast.

"Hmm, is there anything I can help you with, your Royal Highness?" Harper asks playfully.

"You know, usually when someone calls me that when I'm out and about, I brush it off as being nothing more than a title. When I'm addressed as His Royal Highness Prince Jerome during an event, it makes me feel proud and strong, like I'm a leader. However, when you call me that, here in this bed, with your sweet little nipple between my fingers, it makes me want to please you, to follow your orders and serve you." I roll her nipple between my fingers for emphasis, kissing her neck slowly.

"Is that so?" She says, licking her lips slowly, drawing the tip of her tongue over her bottom lip, so very agonizingly slowly. "Well, in that case, Your Royal Highness, best you kneel before me and prove your loyalty."

"That's the hottest fucking thing I have ever heard," I growl as I crash my lips into her, kissing her with all the heat that has built up in my body since I woke up next to her.

I slide my body off the bed, kneeling as I pull her body to me.

"You, my Lady, are wearing far too many clothes for me to worship you properly," I say, as I slide my hands up her bare legs, disappearing under the cotton of her little lilac coloured sleep shorts.

"That seems like a problem you need to address immediately, Your Highness."

Fuck, I am never going to recover from this woman, probably never recover from this moment.

I move my body away from the bed a bit, knowing that any amount of friction is going to set me off.

I pull Harper's shorts down, noting with a groan that she didn't put her underwear back on after our before bed sex marathon last night. This fucking woman.

Harper looks me right in the eyes, giving me the most regal look that I have ever seen.

"Now, lick," she tells me, spreading her legs open wide.

I don't waste any time. What Harper wants, Harper gets. I slide my tongue against her swollen folds, making her moan and clutch the sheets in her hands.

I plunge my tongue in, and fuck is she ever sweet.

"You're so wet, so fucking wet for me," I say against her body, flicking my tongue out against her clit to make her squirm.

"Mhmm. Don't stop. Don't ever stop."

I couldn't stop if my life depended on it right now.

I flick her clit with my tongue again and then suck it into my mouth, making her moan louder. Oh, she likes that. I do it again. I can feel her body tensing up. She's getting close already, but I'm not prepared to stop just yet.

I move my mouth a little lower, sucking one of her swollen lips into my mouth.

"Oh my god, Tate! Whatever you're doing, please just do that forever!"

I pull the other lip into my mouth, giving it the same treatment before moving back to her clit. As I suck it into my mouth, I slide a finger into her, pumping into her. I can feel her inner walls squeeze me tight.

"Come for me, Harper. Come like the Queen you are!"

And she does. Her whole body quivers as her orgasm takes over her body.

"Holy fuck, Tate. That was unbelievable. There's a good chance that I died and this is heaven."

Once Harper's breathing returns to normal, I climb back on the bed to lay beside her.

"That was the best way to wake up," Harper murmurs as she nuzzles up to me. "Now for you."

"You don't have to do anything Harper, that was fantastic for me too."

"Tate, I command that you fuck me," Harper boldly says.

"Well, who am I to deny you, my Lady?" I ask as I reach over to the nightstand and grab a condom from the open drawer.

"How do you want me to fuck you, Harper?" I ask as I line our bodies up, "Do you want me slow and gentle, or do you want me to fuck you fast and hard?"

"Fast and hard. God, please fuck me dirty!"

I slam into her, so hard I swear I can hear the bed crack, but I don't care. She feels so fucking amazing. I need to be closer to her, need more of her. I pump into her warmth as hard and fast as I can. I don't know if I could ever tire of the feel of her warmth surrounding me.

I pull out of her, my dick protesting but he'll be happy again in a second, and flip Harper over, pressing her head down on the pillows, pull her ass up to me, and I slam back into her, making both of us groan.

Fuck, I'm not going to last long like this. I should slow down, but I can't. I fuck her harder, faster. Both of us screaming.

"Tate, come on my back," Harper moans into the pillow.

"Jesus fucking Christ, yes," I mumble as I pull out of her, tear off the condom and grip my cock in my hand. It only takes a few pumps before I'm shooting my come all over her back and ass. Fuck, that's an amazing sight.

"Time to clean me up and make me breakfast."

"Yes, my Queen," I reply, kissing her on the shoulder before I get up to get us a cloth.

Chapter 32 - Harper

"Do you have any binoculars?" I ask Tate as he flips pancakes.

"Hmm, yes, I believe there are some in the outdoor storage room in the basement," Tate tells me, putting a stack of pancakes on each of our plates.

"I'd like to take them out for a walk and see if I can find any birds," I explain. "I've decided to be a birder now."

"A birder, huh? Well, it looks like a beautiful day out there for that. I have some work to do this morning, but if you wouldn't mind waiting for me until after lunch, we could pack a picnic and go on a birding adventure."

"Ok!" I exclaim. "That sounds like a great plan! That would give me some time to read. The book I borrowed from Annie is absolute fire!"

"I'm going to guess here that it's a good thing for a book to be *fire*?" Tate asks, raising an eyebrow.

"Oh, gosh yes! Lots of awesome sexy times in that book!"

"Good heavens, what is Annie reading in my house?" Tate cries out, making me laugh.

"Don't you dare tell her not to bring these books into the house! I'm going to need more of these! They're so good! The main male character is so hot!"

"Should I be jealous of a book? It feels like I should be jealous of this book," Tate asks uncertainly.

"Nope, not at all. I get to actually touch you," I say, rubbing my hand up his arm and squeezing his shoulder.

"Mmmm, maybe I'm a fan of these books," Tate says lazily, closing his eyes.

"Unfortunately for you and Ms. Vaj, I need a break. And I would be shocked if you were able to get him up again right now." I laugh, but actually wondering if he physically could.

No, I said we need a break, Ms. Vaj!

"You call your vulva *Ms. Vaj*?" Tate asks gleefully.

"One, kudos to you for knowing that it's called a vulva. Two, obviously I named her. She deserves a proper name. Haven't you named your cock?"

"Umm, I just call it my dick," Tate shrugs.

"Oh, no, no, good sir. That just will not do!" I say, far too excited about the situation.

"And what exactly would I name him? Mr. Dick?"

"He's a Prince's dick, be more respectful! You should address him as His Royal Hardness!"

Tate just stares at me, mouth hanging open.

287

"How have I never thought of that?" Tate whispers.

I pour a generous amount of maple syrup on my pancakes.

"I can't help but notice that this maple syrup comes from Québec. That's an interesting coincidence," I comment as I cut off a healthy piece to shove into my mouth.

"Hmm, yes, that is indeed an interesting coincidence," Tate remarks, looking at his pancakes and avoiding my gaze.

∎∎

I finished the book, and my goodness was it ever fantastic. I'll have to look for the second book when we get back to Croix. I *need* to know what happens next.

Tate was still working on his laptop, a look of intense concentration on his face, so I opted to leave him be and quietly go downstairs to start picnic preparations.

We're leaving tomorrow, so I gather up the remaining perishables and put together a hodge-podge lunch for us.

I make a small fruit salad, cut up some cheese to go with some crackers I found in the pantry and make some sandwiches using the ham Stefan left for us and the bread I made last night.

Tate comes down as I'm cutting the sandwiches.

"Wow, this looks fantastic, Harper," Tate says, kissing me softly on my cheek.

"Thank you. I made sure to use up the food we had left over. Do you have a bag or something we could pack this in?" I ask him.

"I can do you one better than a bag. I'll be right back!" Tate bounds away, looking like an excited little puppy. He's just so precious. And sweet. And kind. And hot, just so fucking hot. How is this my life right now? If this is the universe cashing in on all the good karma points I racked up over the years, I am a fan of the rewards system it has in place!

"Here we go!" Tate proudly proclaims as he walks back into the kitchen.

"Is that an actual picnic basket?"

"Yes, it sure is! We even have a real picnic blanket to match this real wicker picnic basket."

Tate puts the basket on the island. Opening the lid, I find a folded up red and black plaid blanket.

"This blanket is making me a little homesick," I say wistfully, looking at the Buffalo plaid print.

"Oh, I'm sorry. I can go get us a different blanket to use," Tate says, leaning in to pick up the basket.

"No, that's not what I meant at all. Homesick, but not in a horrible, I'm going to start crying and turn into a

289

blubbering mess, yelling out 'take me hooooome'. More of a this reminds me of home, and I'm a little sad so this is nice, kind of homesick."

"Are you sure?"

"Absolutely! It'll be like I'm sitting on a lumberjack! Let's go!" I start putting the food into the basket.

"Great, now I'm jealous of a blanket," Tate remarks, but helps me load up the basket and carries it for us as we leave the house.

● ●

We're laying on our backs on the picnic blankets, hands laced together between us.

"I think I ate too much," I grumble.

"I told you not to eat that last bit of fruit." Tate turns his head to look at me, laughing.

"Like I could just not eat the last bit of food. I didn't want to make the food sad! Geez, and I thought princes were supposed to be smart!"

"Sorry, looks like Simon got all the brains. Luckily, I got all the beauty."

"I don't know man, Marielle may make me consider switching teams," I tease.

"Ah, but she's happily engaged, so it looks like you're stuck with me!"

Tate rolls over so he's hovering over top of me, making me squirm and giggle.

"Let's pack this up and then go find you some birds!"

Tate rolls off of me and leaps up, helping me to my feet.

"You don't think my new bird watching hobby is stupid?" I ask self-consciously.

"No, not at all," Tate replies without missing a beat. "If it brings you joy, why would I think it's stupid?"

"It's not productive. It's not going to help me in the future or get my life back on track or be helpful in any way," I shrug. Levi would have hated this. He would have told me to stop traipsing around forests and find a job already. He probably would be embarrassed of me.

"I repeat, if it brings you joy, why would I think it's stupid? There are many different ways something can be helpful. Remember our chat about mental health and the importance of taking breaks?"

"Y-yes," I reply hesitantly.

"Well, I think you need this new hobby of yours. You've been through a lot, and honestly, it doesn't sound like you were truly happy for a long time. You deserve some time to relax and enjoy life. I know, for an absolute fact, that you will do great things. You are amazing, brilliant, and kind. You make people happy just by being in the same room as you. Your joy is infectious. Yves and my mother cannot stop talking about how exceptional you are with the gardens. Yves wanting to hire you at the gardens has nothing to do with me, and everything to do with you. Give yourself some time here to enjoy living, then worry about your career and goals."

"So, I should give myself a grace period?"

"Yes, a grace period filled with birds and tea and princes who fuck you so hard that you can't walk straight. Now, let's get going because I think I heard a magpie."

Tate and I spend the rest of the afternoon walking around the forest, pointing out birds and chatting. We play another round of lightning questions.

Spending time like this with Tate feels so nice. Easy. Our conversations flow and there's no weirdness we have to dance around.

It feels like bad luck to acknowledge how amazing he is, how amazing we are.

"What time do you want to leave tomorrow?" I ask, as I carefully step over some loose rocks.

"Maybe between ten and eleven? I'd like to have some time to meet with my father about the report he sent over this morning before dinner tomorrow."

"That sounds good. Early enough that we have plenty of time to get back without having to rush around in the morning."

"Mhmm, and there's no way I'm going to be rushing out of bed with you." Tate looks at me from the corner of his eyes, a flirty smile on his lips.

"Down Your Royal Hardness," I say sternly, pointing at Tate's crotch.

"So, tomorrow is Sunday…" Tate begins, but trails off.

"Yes, it is. Maybe you did get some of those intelligence genes after all!"

"Hush, you. So, tomorrow is Sunday, and Sunday means family dinner. I'm pretty sure that there will be a full house tomorrow, which will be crazy, so I understand if that would be too much."

"Tate, you sound like me. Take a breath and tell me about family dinner."

Tate takes a big breath in and blows it out slowly.

"Would you like to join us for family dinner tomorrow night?" Tate asks cautiously.

"You want me to join your family for dinner? That seems like a big deal. And I know it probably doesn't mean anything to you, but it's a big deal that I'm being asked to dine with the Royal Family. Oh my god! The entire *Royal Family*! What do you even wear for dinner at the castle with the King and Queen! Oh man, I can't just wear jeans and I'll have to know which fork out of like seventeen forks to use and I have no idea what an oyster fork looks like!"

"You can wear jeans. I'll make sure to wear jeans to make you feel better, ok? I promise you that there will only be one fork option, well maybe two depending on dessert. It's not a formal state dinner, but a casual dinner with my family. But, if you'd prefer not to come, I understand. I do not want you to feel like you have to come."

"It's up to me?" I ask slowly.

"Always, love."

"Ok, I'll come. Dinner with your family sounds nice."

"I do not guarantee that they'll behave. Actually, I can guarantee that they won't. But, they'll love having you there."

∎∎

"Would you rather have a bad haircut or a bad hair dye job?"

"And I'm guessing that I couldn't just get it cut again or dye over it to make it look nice?" I ask.

"Come on, obviously not. Have to pick one that you'll be stuck with for a while," Tate reprimands me.

"Ok, ok, I guess a bad dye job. Here's one for you, which is less creepy, babies dressed as animals or animals dressed as babies?" I ask, creeping myself out as I picture both.

"Ugh, gross. That's hard. I think animals dressed as humans is a little better."

"Excellent! Looks like I'll be buying us, Axelle, and Mars matching Christmas sweaters!" I whoop, punching the air.

Tate beams at me. "I like that plan."

It's only as I'm settling in for the night that I realize that I made plans with Tate for Christmas, which is over six months away.

Chapter 33 - Harper

"What are you doing, love?" Tate asks, leaning over me as I sit at the kitchen island.

"I'm writing thank you notes to your staff. I wanted to thank Stefan for the delicious food, Annie for the books, and comment on how amazing the house and gardens look."

"That's very thoughtful of you."

I lay the notes for each five of the staff out on the island for them to easily find.

"The car is loaded. I'm just letting the dogs run around for a bit before I get them in. Are you ready to go?"

"Yes, I think so. I'm going to miss this giant non-castle castle manor house. I'm glad I got to see it," I say, looking around one last time.

"Who says this is the last time you'll be here?" Tate asks, looking genuinely confused.

"I didn't want to assume. Maybe you'd prefer your privacy and peace when you're able to make it up here."

"I am only going to say this once, so I need you to listen to me, ok?" Tate studies me, making sure I'm paying attention. "I know this is early, and insane to be saying things like this, but I know that I will always want you here. This is your home, and you will always be welcome here. There will never be a time that I won't want you to join me here, or anywhere I go. If I come up here to get away from the city or visit the town, or if I have to travel to another country, I will want you to join me. Got it?"

"You called this my home," I say, blinking.

"Yes."

"And this is your home."

"Yes."

"You think of this as our home now? Already?"

"Yes."

"Why?" I ask. My mind is racing, filled with way too many thoughts and I need to know if those thoughts are way off track or if I'm following what he's saying.

"Harper," Tate purrs. "I think we both know what I'm suggesting, but I don't know if I should say the words out loud. I don't want to scare you off or make me seem needy and clingy." Tate moves to stand right in front of me. "Do you want me to say it now or wait a bit longer until a more socially acceptable length of time?" Tate whispers, leaning his forehead against mine.

"Well, if you wait, then I guess it'll mean that I have to wait to tell you that I love you," I whisper back. "But I don't think I can wait. Knowing me, I'll probably blurt it out at an inappropriate time."

I can feel Tate smiling against my head. "So does that mean that you love me and want to tell me now?"

"I love you, Tate. So much, I can't even believe how much."

Tate hugs me close, cupping my cheek in his hand as he presses his lips to my other cheek.

"And I love you, Harper. I love you more than I ever thought possible. You are it for me. Sometimes I feel like I can't breathe when you're around, other times it feels like you are my only reason for breathing,"

I push up on my tippy toes and press our lips together. I have never met anyone that makes me feel like Tate does. I thought I was in love before, but now knowing how Tate makes me feel, I wonder if I ever actually was.

■■■

"Tell me a fun fact about cats," Tate requests as he drives us through a small town.

"Cats, eh? Hmmm, ok, did you know that cheetahs are not considered big cats?"

"Umm, Harp, I hate to burst your bubble, but cheetahs are huge."

"I'm not talking about their physical size, silly, I'm talking about how felines are categorized as either big or small cats. Cheetahs are considered small cats because they can't roar."

"There's no way that roaring is the definition of a big cat. A cheetah is a large animal."

"Sure, they're physically large cats, but they can't roar, which means they aren't considered to be big cats. They can chirp and purr though! Big cats can't purr. Lions, tigers, jaguars and leopards are big cats, all other large cats are small cats. True facts, yo!"

"You're telling me that a cougar is a small cat? Those things are not small little kitties." Tate shakes his head, but chuckles.

"They are the sweetest littlest little kitty-witties ever…except don't ever try to pet one or it'll probably kill you with its giant paw."

"Got it, do not be fooled by the little kitty-witty purring because it will kill me. We're about twenty-five minutes from Croix, I assume I'll drop you off at Cara's so you can unpack and rest before coming over for dinner?" Tate asks as he downshifts, and that will never not be sexy. I have to squeeze my thighs together a bit and look out my window to compose myself.

"That sounds good. What time should I be at the castle?"

"How about I come pick you up for four-thirty? Dinner won't be until six, but I imagine everyone will want some time to, how did you put it, clamour for your love before we eat."

"Dinner is going to be absolutely bonkers tonight, isn't it?" I ask, biting my lip. What on earth am I getting myself into?

"Oh yeah, it's going to be insane. I'll make sure you have wine," Tate says, and his maniacal grin does nothing to reassure me.

Chapter 34 - Harper

"Bye puppies, I'll see you tonight ok?" I tell Axelle and Mars, giving them extra head scratches for being the bestest dogs ever. Something I make sure to tell them in what I'm sure is a super annoying voice. But come on, I dare anyone to try to talk to these sweethearts in anything but a cutesy baby voice. It's impossible.

Tate walks me inside and presses me against the door as soon as it's closed.

"I know I'm going to see you again in a few hours, but I'm going to miss you like crazy," Tate mumbles against my lips.

"Gah, me too! What have you done to me?" I throw my arms around his neck, kissing him back. Apparently our sexnastics on the kitchen island before we left Montfret wasn't enough. I have my legs wrapped around Tate's waist as he holds on to my ass, grinding against me.

"Welcome back, lovebirds!"

"Hello, Cara. I'm going to need a minute before I look at you," Tate calls out as he hides his face in my neck.

"Sure, you and Your Royal Hardness take your time." Cara walks away, cackling.

"You told her about that?"

"Of course I did! That name is way too good to not share!"

Tate sets me down, giving me a little peck on my nose. "I should get going. The dogs are in the car and Papa is waiting for me. I'll go say hello to your sister now that I'm a bit more fit to see people."

Tate steps away, smoothes down his shirt, and in the blink of an eye, I can see his royal training kick in. He stands up straight, pushes his shoulders back, calms his breathing. It's impressive, and unsurprisingly, incredibly hot. In charge, regal Tate is fucking sexy.

We walk into the kitchen to find Cara and Theo acting way too casual to be believable. Clearly they were eavesdropping. Jerks. Although, I totally would, and totally did, listen in on moments exactly like that with Cara, so I probably can't comment.

"Cara, Theo, it's nice to see you again." Tate shakes each of their hands. Cara has apparently gotten over her nerves around royalty, because she throws her arms around Tate and yells, "Nope! We hug now! Welcome to the family!"

"Geez, Cara. Calm the eff down. We just started dating, no family talk just yet, ok?"

"Pffft, nope, totally family," Cara says as she releases Tate from her death grip, "There's no way we're not in family territory after the way I saw you two going at it. Sorry, those are just straight up facts."

"If it wasn't obvious that you two were sisters," Tate says looking between Cara and me, "I would be able to tell from that sentence alone."

"Seriously, man," Theo adds in, "wait until they really get going. It's like they are the same person!"

"Ok, well as fun as this is, Tate needs to get going. Say goodbye to the pretty prince!"

"Bye pretty prince!" Cara and Theo call out together.

I walk Tate to the door, keeping some distance between us. He has to leave at some point and me touching him tends to result in him not leaving.

"You think I'm pretty!" Tate taunts me with a grin.

"Ugh, yes, you are a very pretty prince, and you have to go before your dogs bust out of the car."

"I will pick you up at four-thirty. I love you, Harper."

"I love you too." I lean in for a quick kiss.

A medium length kiss.

Ok, a kiss that turned into a mini make-out session, but who can blame me? He's a very pretty prince!

■ ■

A sport is on tv (football? Rugby? Who knows, something with a ball and men running around on a field), which Theo is way too animated over, so Cara and I slip out and go to what is becoming my favourite little coffee shop.

We order our tea and pastries, and the cashier offers to have a waitress bring it to us so we don't have to stand there waiting for it.

"So, tell me, how are you feeling? A lot has happened over the last few days," Cara asks, settling into her chair. We chose a table in the back corner so we would have some privacy.

"Honestly, I feel good. Great even! Normally I would be panicking at how quickly things changed between us, and I would never have jumped into bed with him without knowing what the future holds, but it just feels so right with him. And I know that's crazy, but I just have a feeling that everything will work out the way it should."

"And the sex?" Cara waggles her eyebrows up and down.

I look around the restaurant, making sure no one is paying attention to us. There is a father with his two young daughters on the other side out of earshot, a man working on his laptop near the front window, and a woman just sat down about twenty feet away from us, but she's preoccupied with her phone.

"Oh my god, Cara! The sex has been phenomenal! It's never been like this for me with anyone else. He's insatiable. And he's huge. I don't think I could ever get tired of his cock, seriously. Usually they're kind of weird, right? Well, not his! I want him all the time!"

I'm blushing now. Just thinking about him turns me on. He's ruined me, but in the best way possible.

"Damn, sis, I'd be jealous of you if I didn't have Theo. Hmm, nope, sorry Theo, I am a little jealous of you!"

"Want to hear more about the house?" I ask, knowing that she'll want to see the pictures I took.

As I'm showing Cara photos, our waitress brings us our food and tea.

"I am so sorry this took so long! We're short staffed at the moment. If you need anything, my name is Amanda and please do not hesitate to ask me for anything!"

Amanda beams at us, gives a little wave and walks away.

"Cara, perms are a bad idea, right?"

"Umm, yes, always a bad idea! Why?" Cara asks me, narrowing her eyes. "Perms and crazy hair things are what you do when you go through a breakup, not at the beginning of a great relationship with a sex god!"

"I know, but just look at Amanda's hair! It's so alive and perky and fun! Mine is so boring. I bet Amanda isn't boring. And she has an amazing ass! I kind of want to be more like Amanda."

Cara tilts her head and studies Amanda.

"Yeah, you're right. I feel like I'd have to go to the gym every day to maybe get close to an ass like that. And her hair is fantastic. It bounces and moves when she walks. Our hair just lays there." Cara runs her fingers through her hair. "Well shit, Harp, now I'm not so sure if perms are a bad idea!"

I go back to showing Cara pictures of the house, the shop getting a little busier and noisier as we enjoy our treats. I look around us as I sit back with my mug in my hands and notice that a few people are looking over at us. More than a few. A lot of people are looking at us. Some are holding their phones and whispering with their friends, glancing at me.

"Hey, Cara, things are getting weird in here," I say quietly.

Cara looks up from her pastry, "Gee, yeah. What's going on?"

"I think I might be able to answer that for you," Amanda says as she reaches our table. "Here, look at this. I have a feeling you haven't seen it yet."

Amanda slides her phone across the table toward me.

I pick it up, Cara leans in to look at it with me, and my eyes go wide.

"Shit, this was not expected," I mumble as I look at the photo.

It's a picture of Tate and I at the Sova Day party at the castle. He's resting his forehead against mine, both of our eyes are closed and his hand on the opposite side of the camera is cupping my face.

I remember this moment exactly. I was so happy to see him, but then was ambushed by the truth of who he is.

"Is this from Sova Day?" Cara asks.

"Yep."

"And this is before…"

"Yep. I didn't realize anyone was taking our picture."

I scan the article, titled *Has Prince Jerome Finally Met The One?*

The article states that we were seen together and caught in a sweet embrace before he whisked me away, presumably to enjoy some "private time" together.

Well, they aren't exactly wrong, but also not really right either.

The journalist has no idea who I am, but speculates that we've been secretly dating for a while and that I am a foreign heiress.

I suppose it could have been a lot worse. Hopefully there isn't an article out there somewhere ripping me to shreds as Prince Jerome's secret lover.

I skipped over the part where they compared me to Celeste. Considering they know nothing about me, they don't really have anything to compare.

I pass the phone back to Amanda and thank her for showing me.

"Prince Jerome comes in here sometimes and has always been super polite. I always like serving him. I respect his and his family's need for privacy. I hope to see the two of you in here together sometime. Have a wonderful day!" Amanda bounces away. Not only does she have amazing hair and an ass that won't quit, but she is so nice!

Amanda is my new favourite. Unlike all these other people staring at me like I'm some sort of sideshow freak.

"Alright, I think it's time to go."

As I'm about to stand up, the woman that was sitting near us when we sat down saunters over to our table.

"I'm sorry to bother you, but I feel like I know you. Did you go to King Hubert High School?" the woman asks, batting her obviously fake eyelashes at me.

"Umm, no, sorry that wasn't me. We were just about to go though, so…"

I took the easy route with my education.

I took the first job I found, and then just stuck with it.

I stayed in a relationship with Levi for three years because it was simple.

What if I want to stay here just because it's easy?

"Harper, I can see your thoughts spiraling out of control. Take a deep breath for me, love."

I follow Tate's lead and breathe in and out slowly.

"I want you here. I like having you here with me. But, above my selfishness, I want you to be happy first. So, if you'd be happier at Cara's, or in your own home here or Toronto or in, I don't know, Wales, then that's what I want for you, ok?"

Tate looks at me, one eyebrow raised.

"Ok. It's just fast. And a lot right now. I think I got worried that it's too much and I'm choosing the easy route," I admit.

"Well, for one thing, choosing to be with me won't exactly be the easy route. It'll be hard. Leaving would be easier."

"I'm not going anywhere, remember?" I reach out and cup his cheek.

"Yes, love, I remember. I do think that from a security point of view, it would be wiser for you to stay here for at least a bit longer."

"Yeah, you're right. I miss Cara and Theo though."

"Let's have them over for dinner," Tate suggests.

"Can we? Really?" I try to keep my voice down, but excitement is controlling my vocal chords now, so I'm yelling.

"Of course we can. Why don't you see if tonight works for them and let me know?"

"Ok! Thank you!" I pepper Tate's face with kisses.

"Eww, gross you two. I don't want to see that while I eat," Marielle says as she takes a seat across from us, Dax following right behind her.

"Need I remind you that I once walked in on you guys fucking in the pool? Ruined a whole summer of swimming for me!" Tate says, covering his eyes, but belting out laughter.

"Yeah, I'm not sorry about that, man. That was some fantastic sex!" Dax says, grinning as he shovels some scrambled eggs into his mouth.

I text Cara asking about dinner.

Me: Would you and Theo want to come over here for dinner tonight?

Cara: Yeah we would!

Cara: Wait! Do we have to dress fancy??

Chapter 39 - Harper

The King, Queen, Simon, and Corvin left early this morning for a tour of the northern part of the country, so the castle seems extra quiet this morning for breakfast. It's funny how quickly I've already gotten used to being here. I miss Cara and Theo, but being here feels right.

"I got a text from Cara this morning. She saw a few people lingering about, and every once in a while a paparazzo tries to sneak their way onto their property, but they're always caught. Seems like interest in the house is dying down," I tell Tate as we sit down to eat.

"Do you want to go back there, then?" Tate asks me timidly.

He's so damn adorable.

I reach out and smooth the wrinkles between his eyes.

"I'd like to get some of my stuff, some more underwear would be excellent. I'd like to stay here a bit longer though, if that would be ok with you."

I'm suddenly nervous. Maybe staying here is a bad idea. I mean, really, we haven't been together, or really even known each other that long.

Panic is setting in. What if I'm making another bad life choice right now?

bring back here with me. Maybe donate the stuff that I don't need."

"You're not leaving me?" I ask, still feeling scared and vulnerable.

"No, Tate, I'm not leaving you."

"You're coming back?"

"Yes. I will always come back to you."

"Ok," I say, pressing my forehead to hers.

"I love you, Tate. Please don't ever doubt that. I love *you*." Harper kisses me, and with the feel of her warm lips moving against mine, I can feel the truth of her words.

"Oh! I know!" the woman exclaims! "I saw you at the Sova Day party! You had a gorgeous lace dress on!" Great, a pushy fan already.

"Thank you very much," I say, trying to figure out how to get her to leave us alone without being rude.

"My name is Claire, and it is very nice to meet you," she says, obviously hoping I'll give her my name, but she is giving me weirdo vibes, so there is no way that's happening.

"It's nice to meet you too, but my sister and I really must be going now. Bye." Cara and I stand up and walk past her and right out the door.

"Something about her was really off," Cara says as soon as we step out of the coffee shop. "Her hair bothered me. The cut and blonde colour seemed fake or cheap or something, but her clothes were clearly designer. Someone who wears Louboutin shoes to get coffee should have a better haircut," Cara laments.

"Yeah, she bothered me too. Guess I should get used to that though. Tate warned me that the media was going to get interested in me. I'll probably have more people approaching me and taking my picture." I shiver. That just feels strange to think about.

Chapter 35 - Tate

"Welcome back, sir," Gabriel says as soon as I step into my apartments. "I hope your time away was helpful with your speech."

"It definitely was. I finished it, and am quite happy with the result. How were things around here? I hope you took some time off and whisked your wife away for a couple of nights like I suggested."

"We did get away, yes. Thank you for recommending that little Italian place, Marta loved it!"

"Excellent! I'm glad to hear it. Anything going on that I should be aware of?" I ask. Gabriel keeps me on track with all my meetings, events, and general goings-on. Basically, he runs my life.

"Actually, there is one thing. A few magazines and papers, both online and print, have picked up a story about you and Harper."

"Already? Wow, that was faster than I thought it would be. Which publications?"

"I've already put the print stories on your desk and the online stories are open on your computer. Nothing substantial, just speculation about the new mystery woman in your life."

I thank Gabriel for his work and tell him to go home. It's Sunday and he should be spending it with his family, not searching tabloids for me.

I sit down at the desk and look over the articles. Gabriel was right, there isn't much out there yet, just fluff and theories, and a beautiful photo of us. If it wasn't from a tabloid, I'd want to frame this picture.

Sighing, I push the papers to the side of my desk and turn off the computer. I hope the media is as kind as they can be to Harper. I know what it's like to be the focus of a media shitstorm, and I absolutely do not want Harper to be in the middle of one.

I walk over to Papa's office for our quick meeting before dinner, trying to put my worries about the media out of my mind for now.

I knock on the door and wait until I hear my father tell me to come in before I enter. I learned that lesson the hard way.

"Son! It's good to have you back!" Papa says as he gives me a bear hug.

"It's good to be back, although I'll miss Monfret. I need to get up there more often."

"I bet you'll miss being up there," Papa says suggestively.

"Shit, not you too! I expected this from everyone else, but not you," I complain as I throw myself onto his couch.

"I take that to mean that you and Harper had a lovely time?"

"You know damn well that we did."

"We all just want you to be happy, and it seems like you've found that with Harper."

"Yes, I think I have," I reply, rubbing my thumb along my upper lip. "She's coming over for dinner tonight."

"Is she? Does your mother know?"

"No, not yet. I told Michel though so he'll know to prepare her a plate. If I told Maman, or anyone really, I'd have to listen to them talk incessantly about Harper and our week together and answer a million questions. It's best to surprise them."

"Your mother is going to be mad that I knew before her," Papa chuckles.

"Yes, well, I'm sorry about that. I am bringing Harper over here early though, so I figure the family will have lots of time to interrogate us and talk about us like we're not there."

"Good plan, son. We should discuss these reports before you have to go get Harper then." Papa opens his case full of reports and assessments from the ministers, and we get to work.

Chapter 36 - Harper

I've been watching the cars drive by and people walking on the sidewalk since we got home. I swear the red BMW that's now sitting across the street drove by the house a few times first.

Maybe the SUV of Levi's lady friend made me suspicious of all unknown cars parked outside my house. Stupid fucking Levi.

Tate will be here soon, so I pull myself away from the window to go get changed.

I pull on a dark wash pair of skinny jeans (whatever gen Z, you can pry my skinny jeans from my cold dead hands), and pair it with an emerald green short sleeved blouse I stole from Cara. I put on a simple gold chain with a small heart locket and some big hoop earrings. I figure it's a nice mix of casual and respectful. I check my makeup, brush my hair and put on extra deodorant.

I hear a car pull up and let out a sigh of relief when I see that it's Tate. Although, there are a few other cars parked along the street now and that red BMW is still there. I'm getting too paranoid. "People are allowed to park cars places, Harper," I chastise myself.

I reach the door just as Tate's about to knock. Throwing the door open, I pull him inside and quickly close it behind us.

"Miss me?" Tate asks, hugging me close.

"I really did. But also, there are a lot of cars out there and weird people keep looking at me and I'm getting freaked out that people are going to start taking our pictures."

"Ah, I take that to mean that you saw the papers?"

"Papers? As in plural? As in more than just one?!" I cry.

"I saw one article online, actually a lovely waitress at the coffee shop showed me since everyone was staring at me and whispering."

"Gabriel found a few. Basically all the same photo and non-story. I'm sorry Harper, I didn't think we would become so interesting so quickly." Tate pauses, biting his bottom lip. "Is it too much?"

"No! No, that's not what I'm trying to tell you. It's just something I have to get used to now, right?" I ask nervously. It'll be fine. Yep. Totally something that I'll get used to. Remember, do not pick nose in public.

I take a big breath, pull up my big girl undies and tell my brain to chill out.

"We should get going. I'm already super nervous, and waiting around is just going to make me worry more," I say, reaching for a pair of flats I borrowed from Cara (as in I am totally stealing because they are cute!).

I call out a goodbye to Cara and Theo and we leave.

I swear I can feel people looking at us as Tate opens the car door for me.

I swear I can hear pictures being taken.

I swear I'm losing my mind.

"Are you ok?" Tate asks, searching my eyes.

"Yeah, I guess I'm just paranoid about people watching us. Some weirdo approached Cara and I when we were out today, and she freaked me out. Everyone was whispering and pointing and, I don't know, I guess I just have the heebie jeebies," I tell him, craning my neck to look out the back window and at the cars parked along the road.

"Did she threaten you?" Tate asks seriously.

"No, nothing like that. She was just overly friendly. She wasn't mean or rude, but it was very uncomfortable. But, it's ok."

"You still want to come over for dinner?"

"Yes, let's go, Your Royal Highness!"

"Harper," Tate murmurs, "we don't have time for that right now."

"I was just being respectful. Geez, get your mind out of the gutter!"

The castle is blissfully quiet and empty when we get there. I was kind of expecting footmen to meet us at the car, a butler to open the door for us and maids to be scurrying around carrying long feather dusters.

It's entirely possible that my love for old movies and fairy tales helped create an entirely different picture in my head for tonight.

I'm glad there's no one around. Makes my nerves die away and this does indeed feel like a normal family dinner. Tate even wore jeans and a faded black t-shirt, just like he promised he would.

Tate leads me through some giant rooms, whose purpose I could not tell you, and down a very long hallway.

Corridor? I need to learn proper castle terminology.

Voices start to filter out to us and Tate laces our fingers together, sensing that I need some extra support.

I can do this.

They're just people. Totally normal people.

As soon as we walk into the room, their normalcy smacks me in the face.

They're all dressed casually, no suits or gowns in sight.

Ok, sure, the sweater that Queen Janelle is wearing probably cost a few hundred dollars, but it's still just a sweater.

"Harper! Look, everyone! Harper is here!" Marielle yells out, having spotted us first.

And, the nerves are back.

Marielle jumps up from the couch where she was sitting beside her fiancé, Dax, runs over to me and wraps her arms around me in a bone crushing hug.

Her excitement is infectious and I find myself hugging her back, my nerves forgotten.

"Hello Princess Marielle, it's very nice to see you again," I croak out.

"Oh, no, no, no. None of that. I'm just Marielle to you. I mean, we are practically family now, right?"

I look over to Tate, my eyes wide. "What is with our families? We legit just started dating!"

Tate looks towards the ceiling, sighing heavily. "We are never to let Cara and Marielle in the same room. Agreed?"

"Oh yeah, they're never meeting!"

"Harper, it is a pleasure to meet you." A man walks forward, gently pushing Marielle out of the way. "I'm Simon," he says, reaching his hand out for a handshake.

"Hello, Simon. I'm currently trying to convince Theo to surprise Cara with a kitten for her birthday, so we may need to team up later!" I tell him excitedly. Cara loves cats, and I was shocked that they didn't have any pets at all. My sister needs a cat.

"Yep, I like you," Simon says simply, then motions behind himself, "This is my husband, Corvin. He's probably the one you should be worried about teaming up with your sister."

"Hey! That's not fair!" A shorter, but equally attractive man calls out from where he is still sitting on the couch.

"Actually, that's probably accurate."

"Hello, Corvin!" I call back to him. He seems like a bundle of energy and laughs.

"And I'm Dax. I'll do my best to keep Mari away from your sister," a man says, making his way over to us. He has dark brown hair, coffee coloured eyes, is clean shaven and 6 feet tall. Sovan genes are ridiculous. How can so many good looking people be from one little country?

"Hey! You're supposed to be on my side!" Marielle shouts at Dax.

Dax chuckles as he stops at Marielle's side, kissing her cheek. "I'm always on your side, hun."

"You already met my mother, Janelle," Tate says as he takes my hand and walks us across the room to where the Queen and King are standing.

"Harper, I am so pleased that you are joining us tonight. I can't tell you how happy I am to see you again." Queen Janelle takes both my hands in hers.

How have I forgotten how soft her hands are? Thank the maker I used hand lotion today!

"Hello Harper, I'm Louis, Tate's father. No titles or pageantry here, ok? Just Louis and good food." Louis smiles at me, and his whole demeanor is warm and inviting. I can see so much of Tate in Louis. He has the same dark hair, same striking features and the same calm aura. Being in his presence is soothing, something I will need during this dinner.

"That sounds good to me," I reply, smiling. I can feel my body loosen up. I was so tense and worried about being accepted by *the Royal Family*, but I really didn't have anything to be concerned about. They're genuinely happy and nice.

Tate links our hands together again and leads me over to the couch.

"Ok everyone," Tate says looking at his family. "We have an hour before dinner. Get all of your questions and comments out now so we can enjoy our meal."

319

And boy, they do not disappoint.

This is a lively bunch. They are so comfortable as a group, clearly very involved with each other's lives, but in a way that tells you they love each other fiercely and will support you in whatever way you need.

With a father that walked out on us when Cara and I were barely out of diapers, and a mother who left the world too soon, I feel a little jealous of their dynamic. My heart craves a family like this. The fact that they're willing to invite me in means more than I can possibly ever express.

"Will you continue to work with Yves, dear?" Queen Janelle asks me. Her use of the sweet endearment makes me choke back a sob. She's so lovely. So kind. No one could ever replace my own mother, but the Queen makes me feel like maybe I could feel that kind of love again.

"Yes, I'm planning to. Tate has arranged a meeting for me with the Canadian embassy about a visa, so hopefully I can get that processed and officially start working with Yves."

"I think given the recent interest in you, it might be wise to go with someone when you're out and about," King Louis tells me.

"You think I need to enact the buddy system now? Already?" Ugh, that's going to suck. I can feel my freedom slipping away from me.

"Safety in numbers dear." Louis winks at me. "Sova may be fairly casual and used to seeing us around town, but you're the new shiny toy, and people will want to approach you and take your picture."

"Great, so I need bodyguards to run errands. Fuck my life. Oh, shit! Sorry for swearing!"

Tate erupts in laughter, "Oh love, considering the way you reacted to Marielle, that was tame for you! Besides, if you haven't noticed, Corvin swears way more."

"No I fucking don't! Asshole," Corvin adds in helpfully.

"Don't worry, we're not at a team of six dudes in suits and sunglasses flanking you level yet, but you probably should go with one of us or an assistant when you go out," Tate says. "I have a full week of meetings scheduled, would you mind waiting until next week to go to the embassy?"

"I can go with her tomorrow," Simon says casually. "That is if you'd rather go sooner, Harper."

"You'd volunteer to go with me?" I asked, shocked at how easily he offered. He doesn't even know me.

"Sure. I don't have anything planned for tomorrow." Simon shrugs.

"Ok, then sure, that would be great! Thank you, Simon."

Louis (man, that feels weird, like I'm committing some sort of crime by not calling him King) leads us all into the dining room. I'm happy to see that it's not a giant table like you see in pictures. There are only 12 chairs and not the 1200 I was picturing.

A delicious smelling roast with mashed potatoes, green beans, a garden salad and bread are sitting on the table for us.

It's all just so normal. Maybe one day I'll stop being surprised by the normalcy of Tate's private life.

People start passing bowls around the table, and when Janelle offers the bowl of mashed potatoes to Tate, I take it from her instead.

"Thank you, love." Tate leans over to kiss my head.

"Well, if there were any lingering concerns about Harper's feelings toward Tate, I give you Exhibit A. Harper knew that Tate hates potatoes." Simon snaps his fingers as he points at us from his seat across the table.

"You hate potatoes? Since when?" Janelle asks.

"Since I was old enough to tell you that they're gross, Maman. Geez, and you claim you know me." Tate rolls his eyes, but smiles.

We eat our meal, chatting with each other, often over top of each other.

My phone rings, and I embarrassingly fumble for it.

"Oh my gosh, I am so sorry! No one ever calls me!" I finally pull it out of my pocket and see my sister's name on the screen.

"It's Cara. She knows I'm here, so something must be wrong. I need to take this."

"Absolutely, go ahead, love."

"Hello? Cara?" I ask, answering the phone.

"Harper, we have a bit of a problem," Cara tells me, her voice sounding worried.

"What's wrong? Are you ok? Is Theo ok?"

"We're fine. But, there are a lot of people outside the house. They started showing up a little after you left. Just a few at first, but now there are at least fifty people out there, and some with really big cameras!"

"What the heck?!" I relay what Cara told me to the royals.

"Shit. Tell her to close all the curtains and get away from the windows," Tate says. "We'll send the police over to disperse the crowds. Tell them not to go anywhere tonight."

I tell Cara what Tate said, and we hang up, promising to check in with each other soon.

"Seems like someone found out where you live, Harper," Simon says, looking down at his phone. "Someone was there taking pictures when Tate picked you up. I'll send a link to the group chat so we can all see it."

I lean in close to Tate so I can see his phone as he opens the website Simon sent us.

There are photos of Tate getting out of his car, me pulling him inside and us walking back out to his car with his hand on my back. There are even a couple zoomed in shots of us inside the car.

Someone was in fact out there watching us. I knew I could feel someone's eyes on me.

An image of the red BMW flashes behind my eyes, but I push it away. There's no way to know who it was. Cara said some people had really big cameras. It could have been a paparazzo from really far away.

My phone dings with a text message from Cara. She sent photos of the crowds on their front lawn.

"Crap, Tate! Look at all these people! That's insane!"

"I called the chief of police. He's sending some officers over to Cara's house now. That should get rid of most of the crowd. He'll send officers by regularly to check on their house, and we'll have a couple of guards posted on the street too," Louis tells me, in serious King mode now.

324

Shit, I don't like this. Cara won't like this. This fucking sucks. Why can't people just leave people alone?

But, we have no choice at the moment. Keeping Cara and Theo safe and uninteresting to the paparazzi is what's important now.

"Ok, thank you," I reply lamely. I text Cara back letting her know the plan.

"You should probably stay here too," Louis adds. "At least for the night."

"I can't go home?"

"I think it would be best not to, at least temporarily. People will move on and away from your sister's house if they don't see you there for a while," Janelle says with a sad, knowing smile on her face.

"You can borrow some of my clothes," Marielle tells me. I can tell that she's worried about me, but also very excited. I can almost see her thoughts of slumber parties and girl talk floating around in her head.

"I would appreciate that, thank you very much."

I worry my lip. "Should I postpone going to the embassy?"

"Hmm, no I think you should still go. Hiding will make you seem even more exciting and elusive. Being out, doing normal things will help you seem like a boring adult," Tate replies.

"I'm going to be the most boring adult that ever adulted!"

"I'm suddenly not as excited about our field trip tomorrow," Simon says drily.

"Too late to back out now! You're stuck with me!"

"Good. Tate would probably turn all mopey again if you changed your mind." Simon laughs as he talks about his brother.

"When were you mopey?" I ask Tate, turning to face him.

"When all he wanted was to kiss you and hold you because you're warm and soft, but you just wanted to be friends!" Marielle cackles.

"Aww, that's actually really cute," I tell him, squeezing his hand.

"Yeah yeah, I was sad. Now I'm happy. Let's all talk about the stupid shirt that Dax is wearing instead."

"You don't like my shirt?" Dax asks, looking down at his chest. "Paisley is a classic."

Tate winks at me, the conversation flowing around us.

Yeah, I could get used to this.

∎∎∎

"Do you want one of my t-shirts to sleep in?" Tate asks from his ginormous walk-in closet. Seriously, that thing is the size of my first apartment. I'm afraid of going in and getting lost. I'd make a left at the shoes and end up in ties and have no idea how to get out.

"That would be excellent, thank you!"

I peel off my clothes, waiting for Tate to emerge with something for me to wear.

"I could get used to seeing this," Tate whistles as he walks into the bedroom.

His eyes freely roam my body as I stand there in my bra and underwear.

Feeling bold, I hold his gaze as I unclasp my bra, letting it fall to the floor.

"Fuck," Tate drags out the word. "Underwear too."

The authority in his voice has me obeying immediately. Who knew I liked being told what to do. When he uses that deep, gravelly voice on me, I'm completely at his mercy. He controls me and I want to please him.

I keep my eyes trained on his as I slowly slide my underwear down my legs, kicking them to the side.

"Now turn around," Tate says, staying where he is. He hasn't moved, hasn't approached me, and for some reason that makes me dripping wet.

"Mmm, look at that ass. It looked so fucking pretty with my come all over it. I can't wait to get my hands on it again."

327

Oh holy fuckballs.

I can hear Tate take a few steps so he's standing closer to me. My hearing is trained on him. I can hear every breath he takes. I can hear him lift his hands and rub the stubble on his jaw.

Picturing him looking at me, staring at me, is making me quiver.

I have never felt anticipation like this before. My skin is buzzing.

Tate reaches out and gently runs a single finger down my spine, goosebumps erupting in its wake.

"The question now though is where do I start with you, hmm?"

Tate slowly walks around me so we're standing face-to-face.

"I could touch you here," Tate whispers as he leans in close and runs his finger along my jaw. "Or here." His finger makes its way down my neck across my collarbone and right down the middle between my breasts.

"Or," Tate looks at me, and I swallow. "I could start here." He trails his finger down lower, over my belly, dipping in my belly button, down, down, until he's pressing it on my clit.

"Oh my god, Tate," I moan.

But he doesn't stop there. He pushes his fingers inside, finding it soaking.

"Looks like you might want me to start here."

Tate moves his finger inside me slowly, in and out, in and out.

I'm amazed I'm still standing up. My legs feel wobbly. I'm not entirely sure I'm breathing.

Just when I can feel the energy inside me building, he takes his finger out. While holding my gaze, he lifts his hand up between us, lightly rubbing my bottom lip.

"Lick it," Tate demands, eyes burning into mine.

I flick my tongue out, gliding it around his finger. Tate pushes his finger into my mouth and I suck on it.

"Do you like tasting yourself? Tasting what I can do to you?"

"Yes," I murmur.

Tate pulls his finger out of my mouth and continues to walk slowly around me until he's standing directly behind me. I can feel his breath on my neck.

"Do you have any idea what you do to me?" Tate asks against my neck. "I think about you all the time. I can barely get my work done because I'm thinking of you. Your laugh. Your smile. The noises you make when you come. All I want is you. I'm desperate for you, Harper."

"Then show me."

Tate kisses my neck and across my shoulders. He wraps one arm around me, palming my breast and rubbing my nipple. The other hand snakes down my body, finding my clit once more.

"I'm going to make you come like this, and then you're going to come on my cock."

I lean against Tate's body as he touches me. I'm an absolute mess for him. I can feel everything. I feel alive.

"You're so fucking beautiful, Harper. You're the sexiest woman I have ever seen. God, you're so fucking wet for me."

Tate rubs harder, faster now. I can feel his cock pressing into my back, grinding against me.

"Oh my god, I'm going to come."

And then my body explodes. Energy bursts inside of me. Flashes of light detonate behind my eyelids.

I sag against Tate, not able to hold myself up any longer.

"Nope, I'm not done with you just yet. Hands on the wall."

I take a few steps to the wall, and I do as he asks.

I can hear the rustling of Tate's clothing as he starts taking pieces off.

I peek over my shoulder to see Tate rolling a condom on.

"Goddamn, you're hot. Fuck. This is going to be fast and hard. Just seeing you standing there, waiting for me is enough to get me off."

Tate rubs his hands down my back, grabbing my ass on the way down.

"Ready?"

I can't speak, so I nod.

Tate lines us up and eases himself in slowly. It's torture. It's heaven.

"Fuck, fuck," Tate mumbles as he picks up speed. "Hang on tight, love."

The sweet nickname and the rough pounding of his hard cock is too much for me. He's going to make me come again already. God, he's fucking magic.

I let myself go, feeling all of him as he fucks me. I can feel his hard chest pressed against my back, sweaty and warm. I can feel every inch of his dick sliding in and out of me.

"Tate, you're going to make me come again, just like this. Ah, fuck!"

I've never orgasmed just from sex alone. I've always needed my clit rubbed, but this fucking man with his huge fucking cock is hitting me just right. I explode around him, squeezing him tight.

"Shit, holy shit, Harper, yes!" Tate growls into the back of my neck as his orgasm takes over his body.

"Think anyone heard us?" I ask, laughing.

"We'll find out over breakfast if they did."

"I really love your family, Tate."

"Good, because they really love you. Let's get ready for bed for real this time." Tate kisses me sweetly, and I fall even more in love with him.

Chapter 37 - Harper

The early morning sun streams in through the curtains as Tate and I leisurely move our bodies together. We take our time exploring one another. Slowly feeling our two bodies move as one.

A text message comes through on Tate's phone, but he ignores it as he kisses me, his tongue running along my bottom lip.

"How can it just keep getting better? How is it this good?" I ask as I rub my hands up his strong back.

"I don't know, love. I've never felt like this before. I don't think I was whole before I met you."

"I love you, Tate. I love you so much."

"I love you, too. I'm so happy you're mine."

We don't rush ourselves. We take our time, and when we finish, it's the most complete I have ever felt.

After we've cleaned ourselves up and are ready for the day, Tate picks up his cellphone to finally read the message that came through a half hour earlier.

"Fucking Simon," Tate grumbles and passes me the phone to read the message.

Simon: When you're done pounding into your girlfriend, tell her I'm ready to go.

"Ha, oh my god! We weren't even being loud that time!" I say, covering my face as I continue to laugh.

"No, but Simon is a dickhead and he probably just assumed."

"Yeah, well he was right, so…" I shrug.

"Let's go get breakfast and then you and Simon can head out. I have a meeting in about thirty minutes."

Tate texts his brother, letting him know we'll be downstairs and to find us there.

∎∎∎∎∎∎∎∎∎∎∎∎∎∎∎∎∎∎∎∎∎∎∎∎∎∎∎∎∎∎∎∎∎∎∎∎∎∎∎ ∎∎

"Can I drive?" I ask Simon as he leads us to a shiny silver Audi TT.

"No."

"Why not?" I whine. "I'm a good driver, I promise!"

"No."

"Ugh, Simon, you're the worst!"

"And yet, you already love me." Simon grins at me as he climbs in the driver's side of his car. "Get in loser, we're going shopping."

"Oh my god, Simon! Did you just quote *Mean Girls* to me?"

He's right, I already do love him.

I'm not going to admit it, but it's a good thing that Simon drove. I have absolutely no idea where we're going.

We pull up to the Canadian Embassy and Simon escorts me inside. Everyone knows who he is, so they don't even bother stopping us.

The Canadian Ambassador herself greets us and leads us into her office. My paperwork is already on her desk. I'm not sure exactly what Tate said to them, but the process is insanely fast. Sign here, initial here. Sign this. Simon and I are in and out in twenty minutes, and most of that was just us chatting.

She told me the paperwork would be rushed through, and when I said not to worry and that I can wait, she just nervously laughed and said it would be quick.

It makes me feel awkward, but also extremely special.

"Are you hungry? We could stop for something to eat," Simon asks as we get back in the car.

"Simon, it's probably safe to assume that I'm always hungry."

"Ok, then, let's go." Simon chuckles as he shifts into drive and pulls onto the street.

We pull up to a cute looking restaurant with a red and white striped awning and a few little bistro sets outside on a front patio. A few people sit together, enjoying coffee. They stop when they see us approaching.

"Oh my god! That's Prince Simon and Prince Jerome's new girlfriend!" One of the people exclaim as we walk by and into the restaurant.

Simon holds up his hand to the waitress and he motions over to a table at the back. As soon as we're seated, she walks over to greet us.

"Prince Simon, how lovely to see you again. How are you doing today?" she asks.

"I'm well, thank you Keely. Same as always, whoever is currently here right now, ok?"

"Absolutely! Can I get you something to drink?" she asks, in a sing-song voice.

"I will have a coffee, and Harper, do you want a tea?" Simon looks at me.

"Yes, please! Tea would be fantastic!"

"Coming right up!" Keely walks away and talks to a man behind the bar, who does that man up-nod thing to Simon.

"What *same as always* thing?" I ask, curiosity getting the better of me.

"Corvin and I come in here quite often. When we were dating, let's just say that there were a few places that didn't really like having two men on a date in their establishment," Simon tells me and I gasp. Some people. "So, I made sure to remember the places that were genuinely kind to us. Paul over there, the owner, is a big supporter of LGBTQ+ rights and always marches in the parades. He was the first restaurateur in Croix to hang up a pride flag in his front window."

I look toward the front, and sure enough, there is a large pride flag in the window.

"Now, whenever I come here, I cover the bill for anyone that is already here when I arrive. I won't pay for anyone who comes in after me, because I don't want people to come here just to have their tabs paid for by me. But, those that are already here, they get a free meal."

"Simon," I say, blinking away tears. "That is incredibly sweet of you. You're such a good person."

"Remember you said that when I'm making fun of you and Tate for how fucking loud you guys were last night. Jesus Christ, woman!"

"Ugh, I take it back. You're the worst." I cover my face. Awesome, they did hear us.

"Pfft, whatever. As gross as it is to hear my brother having sex, I'm really happy for you guys. We're going

337

to give you a hard time, but it's because we already love you like family. Understand?" Simon is looking at me intently.

"Yes, I get it. You love me soooooo much!"

"Drink your tea and shut up."

Chapter 38 - Tate

"Hey, Mari, do you have a minute?" I ask Marielle as I step into the library.

"Mhmm, absolutely," Marielle mumbles as she reads a financial report.

She's not even looking at me, some sister she is.

"It's about Harper."

That gets her attention. Her head snaps up and she shuffles her papers away.

"What's up?"

"Harper said that someone approached her and Cara at the coffee shop near their house yesterday, and then suddenly paparazzi are there and her address is leaked. It doesn't exactly feel like a coincidence to me. "

"Hmm," Marielle hums as she bites the inside of her cheek. "The timing is too close for my liking. Do you think that woman followed them home?"

"Maybe," I tell her, not wanting to give away exactly how worried I am about it. "Have you heard anything about Celeste lately?"

"Celeste?" Marielle asks, disgust in her voice. "No, nothing lately. Last I heard, she was vacationing in

Portugal, throwing some stupid party and trying desperately to win back the love of her former friends."

"Ok, can you ask security to be on the lookout for her and family?"

"Absolutely. Do you think that woman was Celeste?"

"I'm not sure. I'm probably just being paranoid over what Celeste did to me and comparing it to our current situation, but there's something about it that's bothering me."

■ ■

"Come on love, you can do it. Keep it up!"

"No, shut your face, you devil-man," Harper grumbles at me from where she's hunched over on the treadmill beside mine.

I convinced Harper to join me in my workout today, something I think she's regretting now.

"How come you're just over there all sexy and glistening, while I'm over here having a heart attack?!"

I chuckle at her. She's too fucking cute.

"Because I work out every day. If you joined me regularly, you wouldn't be dying already," I tell her as I increase the speed on my machine, which earns me a death glare.

"Nope, I'm out. I think I prefer to just watch you work out. Much better for my health." Harper turns off her machine and slumps down to the floor.

I turn my treadmill off as well and lay down beside her. "I bet I could come up with some exercises we could do together," I say, waggling my eyebrows up and down at her.

"Stop being weird, you two," Marielle calls out as she strides into the gym. "As interesting of a workout as this looks to be, Harper I was wondering if you'd like to join me for some tea and trashy tv instead?"

"Yep! Yes, that definitely sounds like something I'd rather be doing!"

I help Harper up and watch her walk away. Damn, those workout pants make her ass look fucking fantastic. Working out without her is probably a better idea. She was very distracting.

■■

"How was the rest of your workout?" Harper asks later that evening. We're spread out on the couch in the apartment. The fire is lit. We each have a book, and it feels absolutely perfect.

"Once you left, and I could actually focus on something other than your ass or your bouncing tits, it was great," I tell her, grinning.

"Perv. Remember that you're the one who invited me."

"And I would do it again."

"Hey, I think I should go back to Toronto soon."

What the actual fuck? Harper wants to leave? I thought she was staying in Sova? Staying with me? I can hear my heart pounding. My stomach is in knots. I sit up straight and look right at her.

"You want to leave? God, I'm so sorry, Harper. I'm so sorry that I ruined things for you here." I'm going to cry. I can feel the air getting stuck in my lungs and my eyes are burning.

"Oh! No! Tate, no! I'm not *leaving*!" Harper scoots closer to me on the couch and grabs my hands. "Oh my god, I'm so sorry I made you think that I was leaving you!"

"If you're not happy, or if it's too much, it's ok. I want you to be happy." Even if it kills me.

"Gosh, no," Harper says adamantly. "I meant that I think I should go back for a few days to get the rest of my stuff. I left most of my stuff at the house or in my car parked at the airport. I'd like to get the stuff that I really want and

Cara: Let me rephrase that, do we get to dress up all fancy??!!?

Me: You can but we'll probably all be in jeans. It'll be us, you guys and Marielle and Dax

Me: You're going to show up in a ballgown, aren't you?

Cara: I'm checking the beading on the bodice as we speak!

Me: Does 6 work?

Cara: It sure does!

Me: Can you bring me some more clothes? It looks like I'll be staying here for a little longer and I have no more clean underwear

Cara: Is that because a certain pretty prince has destroyed all of them?

Me: Quite possibly

Cara: There's only been one straggler outside. Looks like people think I'm too boring to hang around. They're not interested in the non-princess sister

Me: Snort, I'm not a princess, nor will I ever be

Cara: Umm, Harp, if you and Tate got married, you'd be a princess

Well, shit. That's something I need to shove to the back of my mind.

Nope, not going to think about that at all.

I'm not royalty, so I won't actually be a princess.

Right??

"Did you ask Cara about dinner, love?" Tate asks, pulling me from my thoughts.

"Oh, yeah, she's in. They'll be here for six."

"Your sister is coming over?!" Marielle asks excitedly.

"Yes! This is going to be so fun!"

"You don't even know her sister, how do you know it'll be fun?" Dax asks, giving her a bewildered look.

"There's no way Harper's sister is anything but awesome, especially since Tate doesn't want us to hang out."

"Fuck, I changed my mind. No dinner tonight," Tate grumbles.

"Nope! Too late! Dinner tonight is going to be great! Buckle up, buttercup!" Marielle says animatedly.

Tate just sighs in response. "So, what are your plans today, love?"

"I'd like to go see Yves and chat about me working in the gardens. I miss my flowers."

"That sounds like a lovely idea. I have meetings all day, but I'll meet you here for dinner. I have to get going. I'll miss you," Tate says as he leans in close for a kiss, lingering just a bit longer than is appropriate given his sister is sitting at the same table as us.

"Oh, I almost forgot. The Crembois graduation is on Thursday. Would you like to come with me?"

"Of course I would!"

"It'll be our first time out in public together."

"Oh shit, it will be! That seems like a big deal!"

"It is a big deal, love."

"You're not helping with my nerves!" I cry out.

"It'll be fine. It's a safe place for our first outing. Actually, I think it's a smart first outing for us. It'll make us seem normal, boring even. It'll help frame you as a responsible adult supporting me. They'll have a hard time spinning this as anything but a committed relationship if we're seen at a high school graduation together."

"Yeah, you're right. Sorry, this is all just really weird for me," I confess. Sometimes this feels so easy, other times it feels like a lot of pressure that I'm not ready for.

"I know," Marielle jumps in. "What if Dax and I went too? That way there would be less focus on just Harper, and the media would see that we're already a unit. Plus, safety in numbers, right?"

"I think that would make me feel a lot more comfortable. Thank you, Marielle," I tell her sincerely.

"Great, thanks Mari. I need to get going. I'll see you tonight." Tate gives me another kiss, this time sliding his tongue against mine, taking his time exploring my mouth.

"Gah, come on guys!" Marielle yells at us.

"I repeat. Fucking. In. The. Pool! You have no right to complain about us! Bye, love."

■■

I take a big breath in and let the aromas of the garden take over my body.

God, how could I have ever forgotten how much I love being outside and in the gardens? I crouch down to smell the sweet fragrances and let them take over my soul.

"Well, isn't this a lovely sight?" Yves calls out as he stops his golf cart in front of me.

"Hello, Yves! I was just about to look for you. Would you like any help today?" I ask, standing up and dusting my hands off.

"I surely would, Harper. You can check on the roses with me. With Queen Janelle away for a few days, I'm taking over in the rose greenhouse."

We get in his golf cart and he drives us the short distance to the roses. I get out this time to open and close the secret gate.

"You know," Yves says as we walk into the greenhouse. "I have known Tate for most of his life. He seems free and truly content these days. I could tell you that he's different with you around, but I don't think that's quite right." Yves studies me for a moment. "I think it might be more correct to say that you help bring out his true self. With you around, he feels like he can be the real him, and he's now allowing everyone else to see what he felt he could show you from the beginning."

A tear runs down my cheek.

"What if he discovers that I'm not special enough for him. I'm a nobody." I drop my head.

"You're not a nobody. You're Harper." Yves wraps me in a fatherly hug, and I breathe in the love.

"Thank you, Yves." I wipe my eyes with the back of my hand.

"He loves you, and I'm going to wager that you love him just as much. Be equals. Be partners in life. If you stick together, you can manage the chaos that is surely going to be surrounding you two soon. I have seen the way the media can take someone down. Don't let it get in between you two, ok?"

"Ok, Yves. I might need another one of those hugs along the way though."

"Any time, Harper. Any time."

Yves and I spend the rest of the day watering, pruning and checking on the Queen's beloved roses.

Yves sends me back with a bouquet of roses for the dinner table tonight.

"For a reminder of the happiness you're here for," Yves tells me as he passes me the flowers.

▪▪▪

"Cara is going to be here soon!" I yell as I jump up and down on the circular driveway in front of the castle.

"I know, love. Remember that time you told me the exact same thing only thirty seconds ago?" Tate replies, attempting to sound irritated, but I can hear the laughter in his voice.

"But, like she's going to be here really soon!"

It's funny how I went almost a year without seeing her, and now I can't even handle a couple of days.

I spot movement at the gates. I can see a guard stepping out of the little booth (portico? Gatehouse? Man! I really need to get a castle dictionary!) and talking to Theo on the driver's side.

I grab Tate's arm and squeeze way too tight as I bounce up and down again. "They're here! Tate! They're here!"

We watch as they drive up the driveway, and as soon as Cara steps out of the car, I attack her.

"Oh my gosh! I'm so happy you're here!!"

"Me too! I can't believe we haven't seen each other in days! I have so much to tell you!" Cara replies, speaking way too quickly for regular people to understand.

Tate and Theo stand side-by-side staring at us.

"You just saw each other," Theo tells us unhelpfully.

"Um, no we did not. How rude," Cara replies to her husband.

"Cara, Theo, we are glad you could join us for dinner tonight," Tate says, slipping into Prince mode.

I hook my arm through Cara's, and we bound up the steps.

As soon as we step inside, I hear Marielle running from across the castle.

"Is Harper's sister here?" Marielle squeals.

"Yes! Marielle, come meet Cara!" I squeal back.

I know that they are going to get along well. It'll feel like I have two sisters.

"Cara! I'm so excited to finally meet you!" Marielle yells as she grabs my sister in a tight embrace. The two women don't even hesitate. Yep, instant best friends. Called it!

"You know, I'm here too," Theo grumbles from behind us.

I turn around and wrap my arms around his waist, laying my head on his chest.

"Hi Theo. Don't worry, I missed my pretend brother too."

Theo returns my hug and rests his cheek on the top of my head.

"You look happy here, Harp."

"I am. I really am, Theo."

"Shall we head into the dining room? I believe Michel was already having the food brought up when you pulled in." Tate gestures toward the small dining room.

We settle around the table, digging into an amazing lasagna. God, I have missed lasagna. I'm glad to report that Levi didn't ruin lasagna for me forever.

We trade ridiculous stories around the table, Marielle and Tate trying to embarrass each other.

It's an amazing night. I feel like my family meter has been refilled completely.

■■

Cara, Marielle, and I sit around the fire in the sitting room, chatting excitedly.

"Ok, Harp, tell me everything," Cara says from her spot beside me. "Well, maybe spare Marielle *all* the details, but I want to hear how things have been going between you two."

"Pfft," Marielle waves Cara off. "Please, we have all heard Harper and Tate at night. I think I have a pretty good idea of *the details*."

Marielle and Cara erupt in laughter, falling over to the side, clutching their stomachs.

"Jerks. Whatever. We're really happy, the sex is super hot, and honestly, guys, I know it's fast and absolutely bananas, but I think Tate is the one. God, nope, nevermind, that *is* crazy to say! We haven't known each other that long. Let's pretend I stopped talking after I said the sex was great, mmkay?" I blabber on, my face flaming red.

"Oh please, Harper. Do you remember how Theo and I met?" Cara asks.

"Yeah, he was in Toronto for a conference, and you met him while he was out eating dinner with some of the other doctors."

"Yep. We met at the bar while he was putting in a drink order and I was waiting for a friend. And then we spent the night together, for what was supposed to be just a steamy one-night stand. But our hearts had different plans, and after a few months of long-distance, I moved here and we've been happily married now for almost a year. When you know, you know."

"Harper," Marielle gently takes my hands in hers. "Follow your path, not someone else's. If what you and Tate have is real, then it's real. It doesn't matter that it's fast. Dax and I have known each other literally our whole lives. Our parents are friends. We dated for a few years as teenagers, broke up and dated other people. No one that came after him made me as happy. No one lit a spark in me like he did. We got back together about five years ago, and immediately I knew it was right. We broke up initially because the entire world told us we were too young to know what love was. Maybe we wasted the time being apart or maybe we needed that time to grow separately so that we'd be even stronger now. Who knows, but we're happy. Despite what the world thinks, only we know what's in our hearts."

I wipe tears away from my eyes. I feel much lighter. I didn't realize how afraid I was of being judged for how quickly things have moved between Tate and me.

"Cara?" I ask, looking at the fire. "Do you think Mom would have liked him?"

"She would have loved him! Besides the fact that he's a very pretty prince," Cara teases me, "I think she would have really liked talking to him. She would have seen just how happy he makes you and that would have made her love him way more than anything. And, I think she would have loved dinner. She likely would have been telling the most hilarious, and probably very embarrassing stories."

"It sounds like she would have fit right in with us," Marielle says with a little smile.

"I think she would have. Mom would have loved it here in Sova," I say. I can picture her going on hikes with us and helping me in the gardens alongside Yves.

"Speaking of liking Sova, how are you feeling about staying here? Do you think you'll still want to go home to Toronto eventually?" Cara asks, voice getting quieter as she speaks.

Going back to Toronto used to feel inevitable. It didn't take me long before I felt like I *had* to go back, not that I actually wanted to. Sova very quickly replaced the feelings of home for me. I lived in Toronto my whole life, but this feels like where I truly belong.

"I applied for my visa, so I'll be allowed to stay here for up to a year, but the Ambassador gave me a wink and told me that it can be extended," I tell them, remembering the gleam in her eyes as she talked to me.

"Sooooooo, are you going to move here, like officially yet, or what?" Cara whines.

"I'm going to Toronto to get the rest of my stuff, so, umm, yeah it looks like I am moving here."

"Yes!! Yes!!" Cara yells out, wrapping me in a bone crushing hug.

Marielle jumps on top of us. "I didn't want to be left out of a cuddle pile!"

"When are you going?" Cara asks me.

"Gabriel booked plane tickets for Friday morning and then we'll return Tuesday morning. It'll be a few days of packing, sorting and donating. Tate is making me go with two guards and an assistant," I say, rolling my eyes, even if I agreed with his reasoning.

"I think going with people is smart," Marielle tells me.

"Yeah, I know. It's just so weird for me. I'm used to doing everything on my own, and you know, just going and doing things. It'll get easier though, right?"

"It will. Interest always comes and goes. Sometimes I need to take someone with me when I'm out, but usually people just leave me alone. That will happen for you too."

Chapter 40 - Tate

Our guests have left, and Harper looks so happy. So beautiful. She hasn't stopped smiling since she invited Cara to dinner this morning.

I settle in on the chair in the living room to pull off my shoes.

"Thank you for letting me invite them tonight!" Harper tells me, as she begins taking off her jewelry. Seeing her things in my space opens up a primal part in me. I like having her in my space. I like having her stuff all over the place, her scent hitting me as soon as I walk in here.

"You are always welcome to invite them over, whenever you want, Harper. You do not need permission, ok?"

"Mhmm, sure."

"You're still going to ask, aren't you?"

"It feels rude not to, considering I'm a guest here."

"You're not a guest here, love," I tell her. I mean it. I want her here permanently, but outright saying it seems too early, so I'll save that for later.

Harper smiles at me, and it feels like an unspoken agreement has been reached. She wants to be here too.

As she looks at me, I can see a shift in her. She stands up a little straighter, smooths the hair away from her face and bites her lip.

Fuck. I'm already half hard just from that fucking lip.

"Tell me," she says as she straddles my lap. "Did you ever think of me before you kissed me?"

"Of course I did, all the time."

She kisses across my jaw and down my neck.

"And were any of those thoughts rated R?"

"Maybe a few," I mumble as she continues kissing and licking me. The ability to speak has completely vanished.

"Do you remember the first time you thought of me like that?"

"Mhmm. Yep. Yes. I do." Yeah, words are gone.

"Tell me about it." She stops kissing me, which helps me get my thoughts in order.

I clear my throat and shift in my seat, but all that does is rub my rock hard cock against her, making me groan and need another moment to compose myself.

"It was the day that I first met you. I didn't even know your name, but I had already memorized your face. And your body. God, I remember that first day I could barely function just from looking at you and wondering what it would feel like to just touch you. Just feel your skin against mine. I think looking at you almost killed me on the spot."

She grinds into me a little, just enough to tease me and I suck in a breath.

"Then that night when I was in my bed, all I could think about was you. I imagined you naked and touching you."

"Be specific, Tate. Be specific and I'll reward you." She licks the corner of my lips, just a quick flick of her tongue.

"Oh my god, ok. Ok. I imagined your tits and playing with your nipples. I thought a lot about what they would feel like between my fingers. And sucking them in my mouth."

"Very good, keep going," she encourages me, grinding her body on my hard length.

"I thought about fucking you. I imagined how wet you would be for me. I knew you'd be soaking wet when I slid my cock deep inside of you."

"Mhmm, you do make me so wet, Tate." She slowly starts to unbutton my shirt and begins to trace one of my nipples with the tip of her index finger.

"Oh Jesus, yes. Fuck, yes, Harper," I mumble. I try to reach for her, but she backs away and stands up in front of me, just out of reach.

"Nah ah ah, Tate, no touching me until I say so."

"Ok, sorry. Fuck. I won't touch, just please come back. Please, please come back here," I plead with her as she stands before me, unmoving.

"I don't know. Can I trust you to be a good boy?" She asks.

"Yes. Yes, I'll be very good. Please, please come back. Please touch me." I need to touch her. I feel like I'm falling apart with her standing over there. My body is vibrating. I need her like I need air. I've never wanted anyone to call me a good boy before, probably would have told someone to fuck off it they tried this whole *be a good boy and no touching* thing with me before, but I crave Harper's praise. I want her to call me a good boy and control me.

She slowly lowers her body back over mine and straddles me again, making me hum in contentment.

"Now, you may continue. Tell me how you imagined fucking me."

"I imagined going really slowly at first, taking my time to explore you. I imagined sucking your nipples and making you moan my name."

"Did you do anything while you imagined fucking me?" She whispers in my ear, tugging my earlobe with her teeth.

"Mhmm, yes. Yes, I did." Words are gone again.

Harper grabs the hem of her shirt and pulls it off her body.

I'm itching to touch her, but won't because I want to be her good boy.

"I'm going to stand up again," Harper tells me and I whimper. "When I do, I want you to unbuckle your pants and slide them off, but you need to stay in your chair. Understand?"

I nod my head and she stands up, watching me. It's so fucking hot. I'm not sure I'm going to make it out alive after tonight.

I do as she asks, undoing my pants and lifting myself up just enough to slide my pants off. I leave my underwear on since she just said pants.

"Tate, you are such a good boy." I preen at her praise.

"Do you know what good boys get?"

"What? What do we get?" I ask, although it comes out in a croak.

"Good boys get rewards. Do you want a reward, Tate?"

I nod again.

"Take off your underwear."

And I do, making sure to stay in my chair.

Harper slowly undoes her pants, and I watch greedily as she does it.

She slides them down her long legs, and my cock bobs up and down in excitement.

She pauses for a moment, assessing me as she stands in only her underwear and bra.

I want her naked so badly, but I don't tell her and don't make a move to remove the remaining pieces of clothing because I'm the best good boy for her.

Looking me right in the eyes, she slides her underwear down to join her pants in a puddle on the floor at her feet.

I groan and lean my head against the back of the chair. I'm going to die like this. Looking at her perfect pussy is going to kill me.

And then she takes off her bra. Her tits are perfect. Magical. Not too big, not too small, just perfect. I can fit one in my hand. And her nipples, her fucking nipples. Pink and perky, already erect. They feel so good in my mouth.

"Would you like to hear a story?"

"Yes," I moan.

She steps closer to my chair, leaning over me and putting her hands on the arms of the chair right behind mine, where I have the chair in a death grip.

"The first day we were in Montfret," she whispers. "I wanted you so badly. I kept thinking about touching you. Kissing you. Fucking you."

I swallow.

"And that night," she continues, "I couldn't fall asleep. I couldn't stop thinking about you. And do you know what I had to do, Tate?"

I raise my eyes to hers. I know exactly what she had to do.

"I had to fuck my fingers and pretend it was you. I wanted your cock but had to settle for my hands."

I groan. I need to touch her.

"Did you think about me that night?"

"Yes, Harper, I did."

"Do you think we were doing it at the same time?" She asks, and I see stars behind my closed eyes. "Imagine if we were in our separate rooms, touching ourselves, moaning each other's names at the same moment."

"Fuck, Harper, I think we were."

Harper straddles my lap again, keeping only a few inches between my dick and her pussy. She's so close. I have to breathe in and out slowly.

Harper runs her hands on my chest and up to my neck, holding me in place.

"Open your mouth," Harper commands me.

As soon as I do, she moves one hand away from my face and lifts up a breast.

"Good boys get rewards," she tells me again as she rubs her nipple on my lip. I slowly reach out with my tongue to lick it, making sure I'm allowed to do that. When she doesn't tell me no, I move my mouth so I can suck her nipple into my mouth, giving it a few hard pulls.

She arches her back and moans.

"Do you want to see what I did while I was thinking of you?" Harper asks in a breathy moan.

"Yes, please show me," I say against her breast, going back to licking and sucking as soon as the words are out of my mouth.

Harper slides one hand down her body to her clit and grabs her other breast with her other hand.

She begins rubbing her clit as she rubs her pussy against my thigh. She's so wet, making me sticky. I fucking love it.

"Show me what you did, Tate."

I remove my right hand from the chair and grasp my cock. Fuck, that feels so good. I watch Harper as I move my hand up and down, slowly at first, but I have to go faster, go harder. It feels so good it hurts.

"Tate, I'm going to make myself come and then you're going to make yourself come. It's going to get all over us. I want your come on both of us, understand?"

I nod, unable to speak again as I watch her pleasure herself.

I slow down a little bit, wanting to enjoy her first.

I lean in slowly and lick her nipple again, pulling it into my mouth. She moans and picks up speed.

Her body tenses and I suck harder. She falls apart on my lap, moaning as she slows down. I grip my hard cock and give it a few hard pulls. I'm so fucking turned on that that's all it takes. I shoot my come all over us, covering both of our stomachs.

Harper presses our bodies together, smearing it between us even more, kissing me fiercely.

It takes a few minutes, but we finally calm down.

"I think we should shower before bed," Harper giggles into my neck.

I scoop her up and walk us both to the bathroom, refusing to let her go even as I get towels and turn on the water in the shower.

I don't ever want to let her go.

Chapter 41 - Harper

"If you have some time before meeting Yves, I'd like to introduce you to your security team and your assistant," Tate says between sips of his morning tea.

"You mean the people that are coming with me, right?" I ask, focusing on the way he said *your team*.

"Yeah, that's what I said," Tate replies nonchalantly. He knows exactly what he's doing here. Sneaky bastard.

"No, you said they are *my* team, like it's a personal for me team and not just a few people that will be going with me this one time. I don't need an assistant and I don't need a *security team*."

"I beg to differ, love. You'll need security, probably from now on. They don't have to stick to you like glue, but it's a good idea to have a few people that you can absolutely rely on at any given moment, and who make you their top priority."

"Why do you have to always make so much sense?" I grumble. "Ok, let's meet with them after breakfast, since Yves is expecting me after lunch. Stupid princes getting their stupid way while looking stupid hot," I mumble as I take a gulp of tea.

"Hello, everyone," I say to the three people standing before me. I give them a little finger wave, feeling incredibly awkward.

"This is Julie, and she will be your personal assistant," Tate tells me and I step forward to shake Julie's hand. Julie is about my age, with long blonde hair that stretches just below her breasts. She has brown eyes and is a couple inches shorter than me.

"It is an honour to meet you Ms. Jones. If there is anything you need, anything at all, do not hesitate to ask."

"Please, call me Harper."

Julie smiles at me. She seems warm and friendly and makes me feel like having an assistant won't be so bad.

"While Gabriel has been my right hand for almost ten years, Julie has been his for the last five. I know that you two will get along well, and Julie knows the ins and outs of our lives, which means you really can ask her anything," Tate tells me.

"Next, we have your security. They are both retired from the army and joined the royal guard thereafter. Their job is to keep you safe. This is Dane," Tate motions to a very tall, very broad man. He has olive skin and brown hair buzzed in typical army fashion. Dressed in all black, he looks the part of a serious security guard. "And this is Sylvia." A short Black woman steps forward. What she lacks in height, she makes up for in brawn. The woman has some serious muscles on her. I think her arm is as big as my thigh. She is a motherfucking powerhouse.

"Hello Dane, hello Sylvia. Thank you so much for joining me. I hope I'm not too boring for you," I laugh nervously.

What exactly do you say when you meet the people being paid to follow you around? Hi, nice to meet you. I don't really want you around, but you have to be, so, thank you I guess, and I'm sorry if I pick a wedgie in front of you?

"There is no such thing as boring, ma'am. We're honoured to be here with you," Dane replies.

"Nope, no ma'aming, ok? Please call me Harper. It would make me feel a lot less awkward about this whole thing."

"Harper, of course." Dane cracks a little smile, and it feels like a huge victory.

"Harper, if you have some time, we should go over your itinerary and plans for the weekend," Julie tells me. She is holding an amethyst coloured binder against her body. I lead everyone into the library, while Tate goes to his office to join a virtual meeting.

Julie opens her binder, which is filled with all things Harper.

370

She has our travel plans printed out and asks for details about where we're going and what exactly we'll be doing.

I don't want to bring too much back with me, so Julie and I make a plan to donate most of my stuff to various women's charities around Toronto.

Julie busies herself checking to see which ones take clothing, which take furniture and which will take bedding.

"What about your car? You mentioned it's at the airport," Julie asks, looking down at her notes.

"Hmm, yes. I suppose that won't fit on the plane," I joke. That car was my first real adult purchase. Before my Corolla, all I had were cheap cars that had passed through a few owners before I bought them. It was a symbol that I made it and was a real adult. But, it's just a thing, right? I have my memories, and what the car represented and how it made me feel will never be taken away from me.

"I suppose we should sell it. Think that would be doable while we're there?" I ask nervously, biting the skin around my nails.

"Absolutely, just leave it to me," Julie says. She's so sure of herself that I literally cannot doubt her. Julie is the best!

"There is one thing," I say looking at Dane and Sylvia. "I haven't spoken to Levi since I left. He tried to call a few times, left some voicemails, but I never returned his calls. He's texted too. At first they were sad and pleading with me to come home, but then they started sounding a little angry. I didn't text back after the first few times. He eventually stopped, so I assume he's moved on. I've let him know that I'll be there this weekend and asked him to not be, but he didn't confirm that he'd stay away."

"Don't worry, Harper. We will be with you the entire time. If he refuses to leave, Dane and I will be there, and we can be very persuasive," Sylvia says, smiling like the thought of violence excites her. Yep, motherfucking powerhouse.

"Ok, one last bit of business for us," Julie says as she claps her hands. "Tomorrow is your first official outing as Prince Jerome's girlfriend. We need to choose an outfit carefully. Although it's a high school graduation, and it's not likely that there will be paparazzi, everyone has a cellphone, and everyone can post on social media. I have asked Marielle's stylist to come by and meet with you with some options for tomorrow. She should be here in a few minutes."

"Ok. I guess I shouldn't wear cut-off jean shorts. A stylist is probably a wise choice for me."

Julie chuckles, shaking her head slightly.

Marielle's stylist, Maxine, is a little pixie. She's barely five feet tall and very thin. She has long, silvery hair and is an absolute spitfire. She talks a million miles a minute, and I think at some point she stops to breathe, but I really can't be sure. Now in her late 40's, Maxine tells me that she has been Marielle's personal stylist since Mari turned 18, when suddenly the world's interest in the Sovan Princess changed. People can be gross, so Maxine made sure that Marielle was dressed well at all times.

Maxine shows me a few different options, but I fall in love with a light blue maxi dress with an oversized purple damask print. It has a scoop neck and thick straps. Casual and respectable, exactly what I was hoping for.

Maxine takes my measurements and pins a few places where she is going to take the dress in.

"I hope you don't mind, but I also made a list of other items to bring you tomorrow morning when I return with this dress. Just a few dresses, blouses, trousers and jackets. After meeting with you, I think I have a good idea of your style. If there is anything in particular you would like, let me know."

"You really don't have to do that," I protest.

"I don't have to, but I want to, dear. Take care of Prince Jerome. He's a good one."

"I will. Thank you for coming here. I really appreciate it," I tell her as we make our way back downstairs.

"I have a feeling that we will be seeing each other again soon, and repeatedly. Goodbye for now, dear."

"Goodbye, Maxine."

Chapter 42 - Harper

"This is a *high school*?" I screech. My high school was a red brick box. Unimaginative, but functional. "This is a mini castle!"

"This school dates back to the 1850's," Tate tells me. "The architecture was a little different from 1960's Toronto."

"True, but still! Oh, wait. Hold up a minute. This isn't just some normal high school though, right? It probably costs like a million dollars a year to attend?"

"Well, you're not wrong, but that's not precisely accurate," Tate informs me. "It is a private school, and there are plenty of wealthy families that attend here, but there is also a very generous scholarship program giving many other families the opportunity to send their children here."

"Hmmm, it's still a mini castle."

Tate just laughs at me. "Are you ready, love?" He asks as he leans over to kiss my cheek.

"Yep, as ready as I'll ever be!"

Tate's head of security, Henry, drove us, with Dane in the passenger seat.

Tate and I are in the back of the SUV. Marielle and Dax are in their own giant, black SUV with their security behind us.

As expected, as soon as we step out of the vehicles, there are murmurs and fingers being pointed in our direction.

Tate links our fingers together and kisses the top of my head, and instantly I can hear the clicks of phone cameras going off.

Ok, first impression went well. I didn't fall out of the car or trip, and our first photos together are of a sweet moment.

I let out a sigh of relief.

As we walk inside, the royals wave and smile at the crowd. Tate greets the staff, and even plenty of the graduates. He's so happy here, in his element within these walls. He's animated and personable. His interest stays on whoever is speaking with him, giving them his full focus.

His hand doesn't leave mine the entire time.

We have seats off to the left side of the stage, sitting with the director and some teachers. Other teachers sit on the opposite side, facing us.

The graduating class fills up the first 3 rows of seating, and their families find spots behind them.

I can see some more people trying to be sneaky about taking our picture. Tate was right, this was a smart choice for our first outing together.

The director gets up and gives a speech to the graduating class, telling them how proud he is of them all. After that, he waves in Tate's direction.

"I am very honoured to introduce Prince Jerome. He plays an important role in the success of Crembois. Please put your hands together and give a mighty Crembois welcome to Prince Jerome of Sova!"

Tate picks up our hands, and places a sweet kiss on the back of mine, earning us a chorus of "aww"s and some more camera clicks from the crowd. He stands up to button his jacket (have I mentioned how incredibly delicious he is when he's all dressed up?!) and gives me a little wink.

"Thank you very much," Tate says when he reaches the microphone in the middle of the stage. "I have had the absolute honour of getting to know these young people for the last four years, and let me tell you, they are an incredible group of people. Whenever I come to visit, they always have something new to show me and teach me. I know for a fact, that each and every one of you will do amazing things. But, I want you to remember something very important. You do not have to do grand things to do great things. Sometimes, the biggest things in life are the simplest. While you are out there studying, writing papers, and changing the world, make sure that you are also giving yourself time for you and the life going on around you. Take breaks. Go outside. Just *be* for a while. Your mental and emotional wellbeing is just as important, if not more important, than a grade on an exam. And if any of your professors have a problem with that, you can send them my way." The audience laughs, and I beam. I'm so proud of him.

Tate finishes his speech by sharing a few stories from his visits with this group of students over the years, finishing with a loud round of applause.

The director moves on to handing out the diplomas, Tate staying up on stage to shake the hand of each graduate, posing for a picture with them as well.

We stay for a bit after the ceremony, mingling with the crowds. Tate introduces me to a few people, including one student's mother who works with the city on their community gardens projects. Tate has to literally pull me away from her.

"Well, love, how did that feel?" Tate asks me once we're back in the car.

"It was weird and scary at first, but by the end I felt safe and almost normal. Something came to me while I was listening to your speech and watching you interact with the students," I tell him.

"And what's that?"

"Well," I start, suddenly feeling nervous. "You once said that you think you'd have liked to be a teacher, remember?"

"Yes, I remember. And I still think it. Being there with them gives me a rush I have never felt anywhere else."

"But, the chances of you leaving Princing,"

"Still not a word," Tate interrupts me, but I ignore him.

"Are pretty low, right?"

Tate nods.

"Ok, well, what about starting your own summer camp or something? I know you're passionate about giving children equal opportunities and providing them with experiences they wouldn't otherwise have, right? Well, you could do that. You could focus on STEAM, maybe having smaller groups for each interest, a new topic every week or so." When I wasn't staring at his ass in those suit pants while he gave his speech, I was thinking about this.

"Hmm, that's an intriguing idea," Tate says while he rubs his jaw. "I like it. Would you help me flush out some plans?"

"You want my help?"

"Of course I do. It was your idea and I value, no need, your opinion."

"Ok, let's sit down when I get back from Toronto and talk shop!"

My phone dings with a text message when we're almost back to the castle.

Julie: Photos and stories already coming out online are looking good!

I show Tate my phone.

"That was fast! We literally just left."

"Yes, but remember, people were most likely posting pictures of us on their social media as soon as we got there," Tate reminds me.

Julie sent a link to an online magazine and we scroll through the pictures. It's mostly screenshots of people's social media, along with their captions and comments. The article (which is really just the author reiterating comments from people's posts) reads:

Prince Jerome and his new girlfriend, Miss Harper Jones, have finally stepped out together for their first public appearance. The couple were spotted at the Crembois graduation service, something Prince Jerome has made sure to attend every year since his own graduation, even giving personal speeches and handing out diplomas in recent years. Miss Jones looked absolutely stunning in a simple blue and purple damask dress (well done choosing Sova colours!), and it appears that Prince Jerome wasn't the only one who couldn't keep their eyes off of her. The crowd was positively smitten with the couple, if comments on social media are to be believed. While no one is quite sure who *exactly Miss Jones is (rumours have swirled around that she is a German heiress, a secret European Princess and an American socialite), those at the graduation ceremony have confirmed that she is either American or Canadian, judging by her accent, and is as sweet as the pie Prince Jerome is known to devour. Considering the looks he was giving her, it seems likely that he does indeed enjoy devouring her as well! No matter who she is, it seems clear that Prince Jerome has fallen head over heels in love, and we can't help but be happy for him.*

"I honestly didn't even realize that I was wearing Sova colours." I look down at my dress. Yep, light blue and amethyst. I bet Maxine did that on purpose, that sneaky little pixie.

"They were right though, you do look absolutely stunning. It seems like our first outing was a success. We should celebrate," Tate says as we make our way back to the castle.

"And how should we celebrate?"

"I think I should devour you like pie."

Tate starts tickling me, and I fall into a fit of laughter.

When we pull up to the castle's front gates, there is a crowd gathered. Some even have signs with my name on it. A lot of people are waving and taking pictures.

This is interesting to say the least. It seems like I've gone from a nobody to a somebody in the span of a few hours. The crowd is overwhelming. They're so loud. There are even people crying.

This is a lot. This is the beginning of what Tate meant when he said his life might be too much for me.

"You ok there, love?" Tate takes my hand in his and gives it a gentle squeeze.

"Umm, yeah," I choke on some saliva like an adult. "It's just that there are people here, like people people. A lot of people. And oh my god, that's a giant me on a poster board! People made a Harper-face sign! I'm fine, this is fine. Totally super fine over here." I take some big deep breaths, which is really just me hyperventilating, but I'm trying to pretend that I'm fine so I'm lying to myself. "We'll be inside soon, and then we can chat. I'm going to roll down the window and wave, but you absolutely do not need to, ok?" Tate says but I only kind of hear him. This will be my life. If I choose to stay with Tate. I will be bombarded with Harper-face signs and people waving to me. People taking my pictures and me being expected to wave back.

Tate rolls down his window and the screams are deafening. But Tate is in Prince mode. He's all big smiles and easy waves, while I'm over here definitely being fine.

People are yelling my name, and I find myself leaning toward the window and waving along with Tate. It feels rude to ignore them. I'm a no one, yet they still came here to see me. The least I can do is smile and wave at them. Guards have cleared a path for us to safely drive through the gates, Marielle and Dax right behind us.

■ ■

"It looks like Harper has made a good first impression!" Marielle says easily as we all sit around in the family's preferred sitting room.

"Yeah, umm, are they going to stay out there for a while?" I ask, biting the nail on my thumb.

"Probably for a little bit. People are interested in Prince Jerome's first love in years. They want to see what's so special about you, and so far, they like what they see," Marielle tells me matter of factly, like this is a normal topic of conversation.

But this is not a normal situation for me to be in.

"Well, glad I got the Sova seal of approval. I think I'm going to go pack. We leave early and I haven't done anything to prepare." I walk away, not even caring that I didn't say bye to anyone.

I can hear the three of them murmuring to each other and make it halfway up the stairs before I hear Tate's big feet following me.

I appreciate that he doesn't speak. He seems to know that I really need silence right now to sort through the feelings swirling around inside of me.

I find my teal carry-on suitcase in Tate's closet, and just as I'm about to bring it out, I see a whole row of new clothes for me. Maxine.

I can't keep it in anymore, tears are streaming down my face and I am ugly crying. Tears, snot, spit, mascara. It's not a pretty sight.

As I crumple to the ground, Tate runs over to me, crouching down with me to gather me in his arms. He doesn't say anything, just rocks me back and forth and rubs my back soothingly.

"I'm sorry," I mumble into his shirt, smearing snot and tears all over his chest. "It just hit me all of a sudden. This is my life, but sometimes it's not. Like seeing that crowd and all these beautiful new clothes, seriously beautiful, like look at that lilac dress, it's just so nice, probably too nice for me. I'm just me and I like how my life is looking but those people and the clothes and princes and a princess best friend and living in a freaking castle is somehow me yet not me? I don't know how I, Harper, fit into this world, but I'm suddenly very expected to be happy and waving to people with signs of my face. My face!"

Tate scooches us against the wall and sits me across his lap. He smoothes the hair away from my face and uses his very expensive shirt to wipe my nose.

"I love you, Harper, so much," Tate begins, taking a breath for courage. "I know that this is a lot. I'm used to

385

it, and yet some days it still shocks me." Tate sighs before continuing. "Is it too much?"

I pause for a moment to think about it. I mean, I just had an epic meltdown over a crowd at the gate and some clothes hanging in the closet. I'd be lying if I said that I didn't think about just leaving. Tate was correct when he said that choosing to stay with him and this life wasn't going to be taking the easy route.

But I love him, so, so much.

He's in my blood. Just the thought of leaving him makes my body ready to push the big red panic button.

Not being with him isn't an option.

"It is a lot," I say, and I nuzzle into his neck, "but it's not too much."

Tate tightens his arms around me.

"Are you sure? I would absolutely understand if it was."

"I am very sure. I had a moment, but I'm good now. It was just shocking and I needed some time to process. I am yours and you are mine and I am here forever."

"I love you, Harper. Thank you for choosing me."

When Tate kisses me, it isn't hurried. It's electric, but not frantic. We take our time with each other, lazily making love. He fills me with love and hope and trust and I hope he can feel all the love I have for him in my kisses.

Chapter 43 - Harper

Given the current media attention on me, Tate wanted me to take a private jet for my trip to Toronto. But that made me feel too pretentious, and I want to project an image of being a normal person who happens to be dating a prince. I won the argument about flying commercial, something that the Sovan Royals mostly do anyway, but he drew the line at flying economy and had Gabriel book us in first class. I wanted to argue against it, but Tate raised good points about security and privacy, things I need to make my priority now.

So, here I am in first class. Flying first class is a whole different ball game. I'm not cramped, no one is stealing my window and it doesn't smell oddly of feet. I'm in my own little private bubble. The air is fresh, everyone is so nice, and the few other first class passengers value their own privacy too much to care that I'm up here with them.

I'm wined and dined, literally since they gave me a glass of wine as soon as I sat down and I ate a delicious, cooked to perfection steak. Steak on a plane!

My flights back to Toronto are vastly more comfortable and happy than my flights to Sova.

When we land in Toronto I feel relaxed, which is an odd thing to feel walking off a plane. I actually slept comfortably and didn't even need that overpriced neck pillow!

I lead the way to where I parked my car, and to my absolute shock, it's still there, not broken into with all my stuff still jammed in the trunk.

"We have a car coming to pick us up. I will drive your Toyota and the rest of you will be in the town car," Dane tells us.

I'm glad Dane, Sylvia and Julie are with me. I have a plan, but I also feel lost. I'm essentially giving up my life here, literally packing up my stuff and getting rid of it. Starting over in a whole new country as a whole new person. I'm overwhelmed and even making a plan isn't enough to ground me.

"I texted Levi to let him know that we will be there tomorrow at nine a.m. He only responded with an 'ok' so I'm not exactly clear on whether he'll be there or not."

"That's fine, we'll deal with him when we need to," Sylvia responds, that wicked smile on her face. Yep, I'm going to let Sylvia loose on Levi for sure.

I hand my car keys over to Dane when the hired car pulls into the garage. My Corolla doesn't exactly sound happy about starting again after sitting for too long, but he gets it going and he follows us to our hotel.

It's around 4pm when we settle into the hotel, if you can call it simply a hotel. The Fairmont Royal York is no Super 8. Our executive suite is massive and so nice that I'm afraid to touch things. Our suite has two bedrooms, and Dane absolutely insists that I get a bedroom all to myself and that he will sleep on the couch for security purposes. I try to convince him that he is too large for a couch, but he silences me with a look. Sylvia and Julie share the other bedroom.

"It's a gorgeous June evening, can we walk around, maybe go get a bite to eat?"

Dane and Sylvia share a look, and I prepare myself to be told no, so it is a complete surprise when Dane tells me yes.

We all wash up and get changed. I, obviously, have been rocking my sweatpants. First class or not, I needed the ultimate in comfy clothes for the plane rides.

We walk around and I act as tour guide for my little group of Sovans. Obviously I take them to see the CN Tower and point out the Rogers Centre where the Blue Jays play (go Jays!). I point out some cute little cafes, shops and places Cara and I used to go when we were teenagers. Being back here is nice, nostalgic. Oddly enough though, I don't feel relieved, like I'm finally home. More like a *yeah, it's nice to be back here for a visit*. I'm happy that I'm here, but I don't want to stay.

We choose a little Italian place, and the welcoming scent of garlic and cheese makes my stomach growl.

"Harper? Is that you?"

I spin around at the sound of my name, and I can't believe my eyes.

Sweaty Neck! What are the odds of running into him?

I close the distance between us and don't even hesitate as I throw my arms around him.

He wraps his arms around my body and squeezes me in a tight bear hug.

"Robert! I can't believe you're here!"

Dane catches my eye, looking intently at Sweaty Neck, clearly trying to gauge the security risk. I just wave him off.

"Robert, I would like to introduce you to some friends. This is Dane, Sylvia and Julie," I say pointing them out. "Everyone, this is Robert. He was my plane buddy when I flew from here to Germany on my way to Sova."

I see it when it clicks for them. I told them all about Sweaty Neck on the way over.

Sweaty Neck is here for a night out with his wife, a delightful woman named Susan.

"Would you guys like to join us?" Susan asks.

"I wouldn't want to interrupt your date night," I reply.

Susan is the sweetest. She looks like she would bake you cookies and give you a warm glass of milk after a long day. You'd spill all your secrets, because who wouldn't after warm milk, and she would say just the right thing to make you feel better and top it all off with a warm hug. The world needs more Susans.

"You wouldn't be, dear. I'd love to get to know you. Robert has been worried about you."

Sweaty Neck looks down at the ground sheepishly. Aww, what a guy!

"If you really wouldn't mind, we would love to! Right everyone?"

Everyone nods, and Julie is the only one to give me a verbal response. They're probably just agreeing because I'm the boss. Eesh, that makes me feel weird. I'll need to make sure to get them a donut or something to show my appreciation.

We sit around the table, sharing stories and laughing like we're all old friends. A few people look at me, but no one yells my name or takes my picture. This is nice.

"I was wondering how you were doing in Sova, which got me googling Sova the other day, and do you know what I found?" Sweaty Necky says as we dig into our food.

I groan, knowing exactly what he would have seen.

"It sounds like maybe I didn't need to be worried about you at all, eh? Seems like you were able to find your way."

"Yep. Being in Sova and with my sister has been really good for me," I hedge.

"I'm sure it has been. I bet that Sovan Prince is also helping. I've never met him or Levi, but Prince Jerome gets my vote," Sweaty Neck laughs at himself.

"Yeah, well, you don't have to worry about casting any ballots. Levi and I are completely over. Prince Jerome and I are happy, but that's all I will say about it, ok?"

"My lips are sealed." Sweaty Neck mimes locking his lips and throwing away the key.

"Are you back here for good, then?" Susan asks confusedly.

"No, just back here for a few days to tie up some loose ends. I've decided to relocate to Sova."

"Good for you! You seem much happier than the first time we met," Sweaty Neck comments. "I'm happy that you're happy, Harper."

"Thank you. And I am so happy that we're here together!"

"I'll cheers to that." Sweaty Neck holds out his glass, and we all clink our drinks together.

Chapter 44 - Tate

"Sir, do you have a moment?" Gabriel asks as he walks into my office. He's already closing the door, making his question moot, but I appreciate that he at least tries to act like he cares about my response.

"Of course, come on in." I wave him in, even though he's already taking a seat across from me.

"Security has reported seeing Celeste around town. Most of the sightings have been in the east end of the city, where she bought a house a couple of years ago. Mostly doing normal things like shopping, meeting with friends and going for a walk. However," Gabriel pauses, which has me sitting up straighter, "she has also been spotted closer to the castle. She was seen in a cafe down the street from Cara's house, but with a blonde wig on. We don't know if she was just trying to hide from us because she didn't want to cause trouble, or if she's trying to hide for nefarious reasons."

"Gabriel, I don't like that. Harper was approached in that cafe by a woman with blonde hair. She said the woman was pushy and made her feel uncomfortable." I rub the back of my neck. My stomach is twisting itself into knots.

There is no good reason that Celeste would try to talk to Harper.

"I don't like it either, sir. I spoke with Dane as well as security here. Dane and Sylvia won't let Harper out of their sight, although being in Toronto right now is working in our favour. We put some of our people on Celeste and have alerted the police department to be on watch. They'll watch her every move and report anything suspicious immediately to Henry."

"Thank you, Gabriel. Keep me posted. If you have any recent photos of Celeste, especially of her with blonde hair, please forward it to me."

"Of course, sir. And don't worry. We all know what Harper means to you. We'll protect and support her just like we do you."

"And this is why you're the best, Gabriel. Remind me to give you a raise."

"Nah, I don't need a raise, but I will take some of that whisky you hide in your drawer."

"Done, grab me some glasses."

Chapter 45 - Harper

Levi's car is in the driveway. Fuck! I was really hoping he would be gone like I had asked. But, I'm not surprised he ignored me. He was always ignoring my wishes.

Julie reaches over and squeezes my arm. "He's here?" She asks.

I nod. "Yeah, I think so. I guess I should knock, right? Probably rude to just waltz in." I blow out a big puff of air, force myself to stand up straight and get myself into battle mode.

I am strong. I am tough. I am happy. Levi is the worst, Tate is the best. I am fucking sunshine and Levi is a stupid cloud I blew away.

OK, here we go.

I knock on the door and immediately hear Levi's footsteps, like he was waiting for me and jumped up from the couch.

My couch. Stupid fucking Levi.

"Harper, hi," Levi says as he opens the door, with a huge smile on his face.

Is he fucking kidding me right now? How does he look this happy to see me?

"Levi," I nod at him. "May we come in please so I can get my stuff?"

"Who are these people?" Levi demands accusingly. Like he has any right to be mad that I brought people to help me.

"These are my friends. They are here to help me. Just let me in, Levi," I sigh.

He steps aside letting us in.

"Look, Harper, I was hoping we could talk. We didn't really get to talk about what happened or work on our problems."

"Our problems?" I snarl. "We didn't have any problems! You had a problem! You decided instead of talking to me, the best plan would be to stick your dick into someone else ON MY COUCH! You single-handedly ruined any chances of us talking through any problems when you cheated on me. Now, let me get my stuff in peace and I'll be out of here as soon as I can."

I'm breathing so hard I can hear it whooshing in and out of my lungs. My face feels hot and my hands are clenching at my sides.

"Harper, come on. You don't belong in Sova with some *prince*," Levi spits out the word prince like it's poison on his tongue. "Yes, I know all about your little fling. You belong here, with me. We've been together for years. I

397

had a plan and I made you a very important part of that plan, and now you're just throwing it all away! I had a plan!"

"Levi, you're a fucking idiot. I'm not throwing anything away. We weren't happy and you, now listen up because this is extremely important, you cheated on me! Even if I thought we were super duper happy, cheating would immediately end everything, including your precious plan. And it did! My current relationship status is of no concern to you. Understand?!"

"I am going to give you one more chance, Harper. You either come back now or I won't give you any more chances!" Levi is yelling at me now.

"In what world would yelling at and threatening me make me want to forgive you and come back?" Geez, this man is delusional.

Levi goes to grab my arm, but Sylvia steps between us.

"Sir, I am going to ask you one time to step away from Miss Jones. If you do not, I will not warn you, but I will subdue you. I am far more lethal than I appear."

Levi looks Sylvia up and down with a smirk. "Yeah, I doubt that."

Faster than the human eye could possibly track, Sylvia reaches out, grabs Levi's hand and wrenches his thumb backwards, making him fall to his knees and screech louder than a soldier getting his leg cut off on the battlefield.

"I highly recommend that you leave before Syl gets mad," Dane chuckles.

"Fuck you, Harper!" Levi sputters as he gets up, tripping over his own feet, "You'll regret this!"

"I already do, Levi. I sincerely wish I had left you years ago. Now, if you don't mind, I have work to do. Leave."

Levi looks like he wants to argue, but one look from Sylvia has him scuttling out the front door. I breathe a sigh of relief when I hear his car start and drive away from the house.

Over the next few hours, the four of us comb the house for my things.

We pack up any items I want to bring back with me in suitcases that Julie magically procured, and put anything to donate in boxes.

Julie clearly marks the contents of each box, and writes where each box is being donated to.

We have far more things to donate than I want to keep, giving Julie lots of work. She seems to thrive on this though.

"What about the couch?" Julie asks after we tape up the last box.

"I don't want to bring it with me. I don't even think I could bring it with me." I loved that couch, but I don't want anything to do with it now.

"I've been in contact with a local company that will professionally clean furniture and then donate it to a low income family. It's a nice couch, someone should get to enjoy it."

"I love that idea!" I exclaim. Have I mentioned how wonderful Julie is? I know I scoffed at the idea of having a personal assistant, but Julie is awesome. I'm never giving Julie up.

"Perfect. I already made plans with them, so I will confirm when we are done here. I also have a moving company set to arrive in," Julie checks her watch, "twenty minutes to load everything up and bring it all to the various charities. Some places are not open right now given it's the weekend, so I have a storage unit to store those items until Monday." Julie claps her hands twice. Julie likes clapping to punctuate her sentences.

"Wow, that's amazing! You're amazing!" I gush over her. I might have a woman crush.

∎∎∎

Sunday is our day off. No Levi, no moving, no dealing with all the logistics like we have to do tomorrow, just a day off.

I take my little group down to the harbourfront. I introduce them to poutine and beavertails. They are all equally weirded out but also quickly obsessed with both. I mean, can you really blame them? Poutine is french fries, cheese curds and gravy. It's wonderful and anyone who says they don't like it is lying. Beavertails are giant pastries with sugar, cinnamon and your choice of toppings. They are ginormous, gooey and the best things ever. They are always worth getting. Always.

We catch a Jays game and find another random restaurant to eat dinner at.

It feels like this has been a perfect goodbye to the city I grew up in.

■ ■

Monday is insane. It is the antithesis of Sunday.

Julie is already on the phone when I stumble out of bed at 9am.

I take a peek at the checklist she has written and left out on the coffee table.

Looks like a full day. Shower. Tea. Do all the things. Got it.

After my shower, and Julie has confirmed drop offs for the remaining items, including my couch, we enjoy a quick breakfast in our room.

"We have a meeting at your bank to transfer funds to the bank of Sova, where an account is already set up for you. You can choose to keep some money here if you'd like, total personal preference at this point."

"Umm, ok," I say helpfully. Shouldn't I have been needed to open up a bank account?

But Julie continues, unaware of my internal panic.

"You'll likely want to cancel any Canadian credit cards you have, and we'll ensure that any debt is paid off. As well as student loans."

"Umm, Julie, if I had the money to do that, don't you think I would have done so already?"

"It's being taken care of by Prince Jerome. You just need to sign some paperwork."

Me: You're paying off my student loans and debt????!!!?!?!

Tate: And good morning to you as well. I am so happy to hear from you. I love you so much. I saw a beautiful butterfly yesterday, but it's beauty came nowhere close to matching yours.

Me: Stop being weird and answer me

Tate: Yes Harper, all debts are being taken care of. I didn't mention it because, A) it's a drop in the bucket of my wealth, B) it will be nice for you to not carry that debt over with you, not to mention the interest rates, and C) I love you and I can, so I did.

Me: You didn't think to ask first?

Tate: I did, but I knew you'd say no. You can thank me when you get home

Me: Who says I'm going to thank you??

Tate: I'll accept a thank you blowjob.

Ugh, even though I'm irritated with him, I'm now super turned on.

I put my phone away, and turn to Julie. "Ok, what's after the bank?"

"We'll go to the Toyota dealership and see about selling your car. Are you still ok with that plan?"

Ok, maybe Julie isn't all that oblivious to my internal freak outs.

"Yeah, that sounds good. I want to donate any money from the sale of the car to local women's shelters."

"That sounds like a great idea!" Julie claps her hands.

Julie fills me in on the rest of our day. Things like letting my doctor and dentist know that I'm moving and no longer need their services and setting any mail to forward to me in Sova. Boring things that I'm glad Julie thought of because I never would have.

Harper's plane landed twenty-two minutes ago. Not that I'm checking my watch constantly.

OK, yes, my eyes have been looking between my watch and the door in arrivals at the airport since I got here, but come on, can you blame me?

I can't believe how much I have missed her.

I've missed sex with her, obviously, but it was also missing the way she wiggles her nose when she thinks or the way her eyes light up when she talks about the gardens.

My security team insisted on coming with me today, and while I fought against a whole team of six people, I'm glad that Henry insisted. As soon as I arrived at the airport, people started to swarm. Henry is right behind me, with three others flanking him to keep people at bay. The two other members of the team are hiding discreetly in the crowds.

I wave politely, smile easily, but I can't help but glance around and worry that Celeste is out there.

I've been feeling uneasy since Gabriel told me that she's been seen around town.

Finally, the doors open up and a few people make their way out.

I see Sylvia first, she stops to scan the crowd, eyes finding mine quickly. She doesn't smile, but I see a little quiver of her lips and eyes get just a bit softer. Behind her is Julie, and then finally Harper, followed by Dane. I'm thankful that her team is being so careful and watchful, but mostly right now I'm just thankful that she's home.

At the risk of sounding like a pop song, my life was lonely without her beside me the last few days. I've gone thirty-one years without knowing her, but now I don't think I could survive without her.

Harper doesn't notice me at first, which is good because it gives me a chance to unroll the sign. I lift it up, and the second she sees it, her eyes narrow at me. She's trying so hard to hold back a smile, her face is twitching like a mouse.

"Seriously? You brought Cara's sign?" She calls out to me. She's frozen in her place, about twenty feet from me.

"This sign is way too nice to not be used again!" I hold the poster board covered in glitter with *Harper* written on it higher. I'm going to be covered with glitter, probably forever because glitter is basically permanent, but it's so worth it.

"Ugh, it's a good thing you're cute." Harper finally unglues her feet and runs to me. I drop the sign and catch her as she launches herself into my arms.

"Welcome back, love," I murmur into her hair as I hold her close.

"I missed you so much! I'm so glad that's all done and over with."

My lips meet hers, and what was meant to be a quick kiss has morphed into a passionate make-out session. I groan as she slides her tongue against mine. Fuck, she tastes so good. I need her. I need more.

I press my hard cock against her, making her moan again. She sucks my lower lip into her mouth, making me feel weak.

"We should probably stop since we have an audience," Harper says into my lips.

"I don't care. I want you. Now."

"You'll care when your naked butt is all over the tabloids," Harper laughs.

"Fine. But as soon as we get home, I'm fucking you so hard you won't be able to walk straight for days. Deal?"

"Sounds good to me!"

Harper gives me a chaste little peck, which seems comical considering the way she was just sucking on my tongue and extremely close to making me come in my pants like a fifteen year old.

I pick up the sign and take her hand, leading the way to the cars.

I can hear people giggling and whispering. I can see people angling their phones at us. They probably got that whole thing on video, meaning it'll be all over the internet very soon. But, I can't find it in me to care. Harper is home, that's all that matters. She's home with me and all feels right in the world.

■■■

My family wants to talk to Harper for fucking forever about her visit to Toronto.

Marielle is particularly interested in the charities she donated to.

Maman asks about what flowers were in bloom. That is a long discussion.

Corvin wants details about the food. He's making Harper promise to take him for beavertails.

I just sit here, watching Harper. I gently play with her hair as she chats. I study the slope of her nose, the way her long neck moves as she talks and nods. The few freckles on her cheeks and nose that have come out with the sun. How the neckline of her shirt hits just above the swell of her breasts, but when she leans forward just a bit, I can see a hint of cleavage. I study that neckline a lot as she speaks.

Finally, there's a break in conversation.

"Well, it's getting late, and I bet Harper is tired from all her travelling, so I should probably get her upstairs," I say, stretching and standing up from the couch.

"Mhmm, no one here believes for a second that you're going upstairs to sleep," Simon says, crossing one leg over the other.

"Whatever, you guys, we're going upstairs. Goodnight." Harper has turned slightly pink. Fuck she's cute. I wonder how far down that blush extends.

"Goodnight, everyone. I'll see you all in the morning," Harper says, giving my family a little wave.

I have to fight myself to stop from throwing her over my shoulder and running up the stairs to our room. I somehow manage to walk with her, matching her speed, but really my dick and head have joined forces and are yelling at me to hurry the fuck up! Need Harper. Bed now. They've gone full caveman.

As soon as we reach our door, I push Harper inside, making her squeal. My dick jumps at that sound.

I walk Harper into the bedroom, prowling after her. Her eyes are big, pupils dilated so large that they look more black than blue. Her lips part slightly and she slides her tongue out to lick her lips. She wants me just as much as I want her.

"I have been thinking about this since you got on the plane," I tell her, as the backs of her knees hit the bed.

"Oh yeah? I take it that you've missed me?" Harper asks coyly.

"Mhmm." I reach out and trace the line of her jaw, making her mouth open a little bit more.

"Now that I'm here, what would you like to do to me?"

I groan. Oh, the things I would like to do to her.

"First of all, we're both going to have to lose some clothing."

I start by pulling her shirt off, I am a gentleman after all and believe wholeheartedly in ladies going first. Her bra is next, and I can't stop myself from touching her breasts. They fit perfectly in my hands. Harper throws her head back and moans, giving me access to her neck. I lick up the smooth column of her throat until I reach her lips. I capture them in mine and kiss her hard.

Harper undoes my pants as I kiss her, fumbling a bit. I help her slide them down and then I turn my attention to her pants. My shirt is next, and finally we're both naked. Her body feels so good pressed against mine. She's smooth and warm.

"I believe that I owe you a thank you," Harper says, sliding her hands around my hips to my ass, grabbing it.

"Mmm, yes, you do. It's the polite thing to do," I say, my voice huskier than I intend, but she's looking at me like I'm her next meal and I'm a mess of need now.

Harper moves a hand around to my cock, squeezing it twice, and holy fuck that feels amazing.

"Harper," I warn, "there's a chance that this is going to end very quickly."

"Then I guess I better get started on my thank you."

Harper drops to her knees, gazing up at me as she licks around the head of my cock.

"Fuck, that is the best fucking sight in the world. Shit, yes, love, take it all in. Show me how much you love my dick."

And she does. Holy shit, does she ever. Harper moves her mouth down my length until I hit the back of her throat. Fuck. Fuck. Fuck.

She bobs her head up and down, swirling her tongue around and sucking as she goes.

I grab onto the back of her head, needing to feel her as she moves.

Her other hand gently cups my balls, kneading them gently.

I'm a goner. This feels so fucking amazing.

"Harper, love, I need you to stop," I manage to get out. "If you keep going, I'm going to come right now, and I still want to fuck you."

Harper looks up at me again, and it's a goddamn miracle I don't explode at that sight. She takes me out of her mouth, but licks up the entire length one last time before standing up.

"Was my thank you acceptable?" Harper asks, batting her eyelashes.

I can't answer her, I just crash my lips to hers, forcing us to fall onto the bed. I kiss down her body, making sure to stop at each breast, licking and kissing her breasts and nipples before making my way down her belly and to her wet pussy.

"Your thank you was so good that I need to thank you for your thank you." I wink at her, and then lower my mouth to her. She's so wet, my face is soaking immediately.

"Fuck, Harper, you taste so good."

"Make me come, Tate. I need to come!"

I suck her clit into my mouth, nipping it just a little bit, making her moan. Her breaths are coming quickly.

I slide two fingers inside her, and pump them into her as I continue to lick and suck at her clit.

So good, so fucking good.

"Tate, now," Harper pants. "I'm going to come now!"

I can feel her inner walls tense around my fingers. Her clit is swollen and pulsating in my mouth.

"That was amazing. Like, holy shit. You're the best at orgasms. Ten out of ten for you. I'll give you a gold star when I get back the ability to move," Harper babbles with her eyes closed and an arm thrown over her forehead.

"I'm not done with you just yet," I say as I crawl back over top of her body.

I'm so fucking turned on, I can't think straight. Nothing exists in this moment except us. I grab onto my hard cock and rub it in her wetness.

"Fuck, that feels good," I groan.

"Mmm, do it again. I like feeling you play."

I trace her pussy with the head of my cock, nudging it in just inside her opening and then back out, rubbing it along her clit and then back inside a bit.

"Harper, I need to fuck you. So bad. I need to stop, but you feel so fucking good that I can't."

"Then fuck me. God, that feels so good!"

I can feel her walls squeezing my head, and I swear to god I see stars.

"I need a condom," I mutter

"I've been on the shot for years, and I always used a condom as well. I'm safe. I'm clean. If you're ok, I'm ok."

"I've never had sex without a condom. Ever. I get regular check ups. I'm clean. Besides, you're the only woman I've been with in four years."

"Then Tate, fuck me!"

I answer with a roar and push my cock into her as hard as I can.

"Holy shit! Holy fuck. Harper! This feels so fucking amazing!"

This is better than amazing. This is everything.

I need a moment to calm down, or this is going to last like ten seconds.

I focus my attention on Harper and move as little as I can, but even that is a lot because I can feel everything now.

I kiss her. Her lips, her cheeks, her neck.

I focus a lot of attention on her breasts. I just really love her breasts.

"Harper, I can't, I need to move."

"Yes, Tate, yes! Fuck me hard and come inside me. I need to feel you inside of me."

A few thrusts is all it takes for me to explode. I can feel my come hitting her inner walls. I can feel her squeezing my cock, pulling out every drop.

We're both breathing hard, sweat covering our bodies, glistening in the waning sunlight.

"That was the best ever," Harper mumbles.

"Mhmm. That was incredible." I think I say that coherently, but I really have no clue.

"I love you, Tate."

"I love you too, Harper." I kiss her deeply, slowly. Our bodies still intertwined together.

"Next time you have to go to Canada, can I come with you?" I ask, feeling shy.

"Of course you can! I'd love to show you around!" Harper kisses my cheek sloppily.

"Where would you take me?"

"I'd show you all the sights in Toronto. We'd obviously get beavertails and take pictures to send to Corvin to make him jealous," she giggles.

"Obviously. Where else?" I'm hoping she gives me some ideas for a plan that's starting to form in my head.

"Hmm, well, if we have time, I'd like to take you to meet my family, particularly my Aunt Mary and my cousins Sadie, Emily and Cameron. We all basically grew up together. We got into so much trouble! Aunt Mary really helped Cara and me out when my mom, her sister, got sick. And after mom passed away, even though we were technically adults, Aunt Mary took us under her wing and made sure we had everything we needed." Harper sniffs, but smiles. "Happy and sad memories mixed together. Every summer, we used to go to a little cottage resort in Muskoka for a week. Each family would get their own cottage, and we would spend the week on the beach, kayaking, catching frogs and going into Algonquin park to hike. It's been years since we went though, each cousin's life getting busy as we got older. I miss it."

There it is. Just what I was hoping for.

"Maybe we can arrange to go there again. Get all the cousins together again for a week."

"Yeah, maybe. That would be fabulous. Slightly harder now though since Cara and I are here and not just a couple of hours' drive away."

"Ah, but you're forgetting the whole you have a prince wrapped around your finger thing," I tell her, winking. "I'm sure we could work something out."

Chapter 47 - Harper

I'm aimlessly wandering through a native wildflower garden. There is a winding stone pathway, looping around different sections of the garden. The lavender is in full bloom, and it smells absolutely heavenly. I feel so relaxed, I might just fall asleep right here.

"Hey, Harper, we need to talk." Tate's voice is cold, hard. Distant.

He's standing a few feet away from me, looking tense, like a snake coiled up, ready to strike if you get too close. He's not at all loose and happy like he was when we parted ways after breakfast.

"Umm, ok. What's up?" I ask nervously.

"Just, let's just go to my office and talk."

He turns around abruptly and walks away from me.

This is bad. What happened? What did I do? We were so happy at breakfast, we literally made Simon gag on his toast because we were being so cute and obnoxious.

I follow Tate's retreating back, like a puppy that knows she's about to be kicked, but wants its owner's attention anyway.

"Tate, can you stop and just tell me what I did?" I call out when I can't take it anymore. I feel like piranhas are swimming around in my body, feasting on my internal organs.

Tate stops, but doesn't turn around. He rubs the back of his neck, his nervous habit.

"Just, if you're mad at me, I'd rather you just tell me now. Please don't drag this out." Tears start running down my face, and a few sobs slip out.

At the sound of my sobs, Tate turns around quickly, reaching for me.

"Shit, no, Harper, I'm sorry." He wraps me in a big hug, his warm body pressed against mine.

He strokes my cheek, and wipes the tears away.

"I'm not mad at you. You didn't do anything wrong," he soothes.

"Then why are you so angry?" I ask, my voice quivering.

"Something happened. I am not mad at you, not even close to it. I know this is not your fault. At all. But, I know that you're going to be mad, and I am mad for you."

"Tate, what are you talking about?"

Tate shifts his body weight from left to right. And then from right to left. Stalling. I have never seen him stall before.

"Some pictures have been leaked," he finally says.

"Of us?" I think back to his welcome at the airport. Yeah, I bet there were more than a few pictures being posted after that.

"No, not us. You."

"Pictures of me? I don't understand."

"I think it's best if we go up to my office and talk about this. You can see what I'm referring to, and we'll make a plan with Julie, Gabriel and our head of PR. We're in this together, ok?"

I think I mumble a response, I'm fairly certain I nod my head, but honestly I have no idea. I'm a jumble of thoughts and feelings.

I wrack my brain the entire walk to Tate's office. What have I done since I've been here that could be so scandalous to warrant this kind of response from Tate. I guess my yoga pants are super tight on my butt?? Maybe they don't look as nice as I thought they did?

Tate pulls me along into his office and sits me in his chair. His computer is on already, the pictures branding themselves onto the screen.

They're not from when I've been in Sova.

These were taken about 3 years ago.

I slowly glance at Tate, his eyes already on me. His eyes have softened, he's lost that hard edge of anger. Now he looks like he wants to soothe me, hold me. Like my pain is his pain.

There are two pictures.

I can still feel the lace. It was itchy, but I put up with it because he said I looked hot.

In the first picture, I'm on all fours. The camera is angled from above, so you can see almost my entire breasts, my nipples barely covered by the lace of the black bra. My hair was longer then, it's hanging over my shoulder and laying across my back. You can see my ass, the thin strips of the matching black lace of the thong do nothing to cover my bottom half. I'm essentially naked, with only the barest scraps of see-through material covering my most private places.

The second photo might be worse. It used to be my favourite of the two, but now I hate it.

I'm kneeling on the bed, hair wild around me, obscuring part of my face as it hangs in loose waves around my shoulders and between my breasts. My lips are parted. I have one hand cupping a breast pushing it up, testing the limits of the bra, and my other is flat on my stomach, the tips of my index and middle finger just inside the thong that barely covers anything.

My stomach clenches and I taste metal in my mouth.

I bolt out of the seat, running toward the bathroom, barely making it to the toilet before I vomit.

I keep heaving when I feel Tate crouch down behind me and gently gather my hair to keep it out of the way. I'm crying as another wave of vomiting takes over my body. When I'm finally done, Tate wipes my mouth with a tissue before I stand up at the sink to rinse my mouth out. Tate searches my eyes, worry etched into his face.

"Do you think you can sit down and talk? Julie and Gabriel are in the office now."

I hide my face in his chest, shaking my head. I fist his shirt in my hands as I cry. Tate doesn't say anything, he just rubs my back and kisses my head.

"I'm sorry. I'm ok. I'm just shocked. Let's go, I don't want to keep them waiting." I step away from Tate, but he grabs my arm and pulls me back to him.

He tips my chin up with one finger, "You have absolutely nothing to be sorry about. Nothing. Those are private pictures and they were shared without your consent. You have every reason to be angry, but no reason to be sorry, understand?"

I nod, unable to speak.

This time Tate allows me to lead us back into the office. He sits me in his chair, and when I protest he just raises an eyebrow and stands beside me.

I'm happy to see that someone turned the computer off. I don't think I could look at the photos again.

I'm introduced to George and Arianna, the family's lead PR agents.

"I'm sorry that we're meeting under these circumstances," Arianna says kindly, "but we are happy to finally meet you." She gives me a warm, yet shy smile.

"Well, looks like we're about to get to know each other very well, very quickly," I joke, but it falls flat.

Arianna smiles at me again. "Why don't you start by telling us who you think could have leaked the photos."

I glance over at Tate and sigh. I can't seem to look at him as I say, "It was Levi. He was the one who took those photos at the beginning of our relationship. I honestly had forgotten all about them."

I tell the team what Levi said when I was there to get my stuff.

Tate doesn't say anything, but I can feel the anger radiating off of him.

"He actually said the words 'you'll regret this'?" George asks.

"Yes. He was really angry. I assumed they were empty words said in anger, but it looks like he meant them."

Julie agrees with me, explaining how Sylvia had to take him down.

Tate already knows all this, since we discussed it over the phone after Levi left, and at length with our security team when we returned, but it doesn't look like it's any easier for him to hear this time around.

"I can't believe he would do this. How did he even do this, and so quickly!" I ask, feeling exasperated.

"Some people are just terrible, and unfortunately, it's rather easy to find a bidder for a private photo like that," Tate answers. His eyes are hard. He must be thinking about Celeste.

We talk some more about what to do, discussing a few options. Ultimately, we put together a statement condemning the sharing of private pictures and those who did so without my permission.

George and Arianna weave some magical PR terms together to ensure that the statement makes us sound like a unit, like the entire Royal Family is standing behind me and is appalled by the sharing of the photos. Arianna insists we emphasize that the Royal Family is not condemning the taking of the photos, but instead it is the sharing of them without permission that is the problem.

I can't even begin to express how much better that makes me feel. I'm still a little worried that Tate's family, especially his parents, are going to look at me differently now though. That they'll judge me.

We say goodbye to everyone and make our way through the inner door to our private space.

"What do you want to do, love?" Tate asks quietly.

"I want to take a nap. I just want to be alone for a bit. I think I need some time to process everything and I don't think I'm ready to face anyone just yet."

"You want me to leave?" Tate asks dejectedly.

I want to console him, tell him that he's not the problem, that I'm the problem, but I can't. I don't have it in me to be strong for anyone right now.

"I just want to sleep," I finally say, avoiding eye contact.

"Ok, I'll check on you in a little bit." Tate gathers my body to his in a loving hug. One that I can't even reciprocate.

"I love you, Harper. Don't ever forget that."

"I love you too." But my voice sounds void of any emotion.

Tate releases me and walks toward the door, glancing back at me, worry and panic clearly written on his face. As soon as he closes the door behind him, I change into sweatpants and a grey cotton t-shirt. This is a time that comfort over fashion is needed.

I hear my phone ding with a text message. Glancing down, I see that it's Cara, but I can't even muster up the energy to talk to her.

I know she's seen the pictures. I know that she's worried, but I close my heart up tight and place a thick brick wall around it. If I let myself feel anything at all, I'll crumple. Not feeling anything is better right now.

My phone dings dozens of more times. Probably more from my sister and the royals, but I wonder how many are family or old friends who want to get in on the gossip first hand.

I ignore them all. I get in bed and stay there all night.

Chapter 48 - Harper

It's been a week since the photos were released. The Royals have all banded around me, refusing to speak with journalists and saying the same things when asked. "We support and love Harper. We condemn whoever released those photos without her permission. Please respect our family at this time as we work with authorities to penalize those responsible."

The photos that Celeste sold to the tabloids four years ago resurfaced as well. People delighted in discussing our bodies, like our lives are a game to them.

I was hoping that interest would go away, but it seems people are just getting started. It feels like my body has been printed in every tabloid and in almost every newspaper all over the world, not to mention all the online magazines, tabloids and gossip sites.

I've been glorified, praised, slut shamed and vilified. Everyone seems to have an opinion on my body, and whether I'm good enough for Tate.

I'm sitting in the solarium, a giant dome of glass with rich hardwood floors and plants filling the space, making it feel more like a jungle than part of a castle. Usually this space relaxes me, calms me, but it's not working its charm today.

I scroll through my phone, seeing my body and name everywhere.

I stop when I see an article titled *Is Harper Good Enough for Prince Jerome? Cast Your Vote Now!*

Cast your VOTE?! Like anyone other than us gets to decide our compatibility and happiness. What the actual fuck?!

Against my better judgement, I open the article.

Stupid fucking choice, Harper.

We're seeking to find out if the people of Sova think Harper is good enough for our beloved Prince Jerome, or if she should pack her bags and move back to Canada with her dirty tail tucked between her legs.

My dirty tail? Like I'm a canine skank for having taken personal photos? I bet most of the people answering this thing, probably even those who wrote it, have done something similar.

I make the stupid decision to look at the results so far.

Harper and Tate are happy. I'm happy for them. Let's leave them alone - 14%

Harper cleary needs to take some etiquette classes, but let them be - 23%

Prince Jerome should have some fun with her, but she's not fit for royalty - 41%

Harper is a slut, Prince Jerome should dump her immediately - 22%

Well, that's depressing. And, since I seem to be on an idiocy spree, I read some comments. Because why the fuck not?! I'm apparently out to hurt myself, might as well take a peek at what the trolls are saying.

Mrs.Olive.Reynolds: *I knew that Harper was bad news as soon as we saw her. She's not even Sovan! She cannot date our Prince! She needs to leave and never come back!*

FlowerPower1974: *I don't see what the big deal is?!? She's a beautiful woman, and she's showing off her beautiful body. Leave her alone!*

CheeseyPeasy69: *GODDAMN! HARPER IS SO HOT! GOOD JOB PRINCE JEROME!*

Lila18532: *I wonder if maybe Harper released these herself?? I mean, they look personal. I bet she wanted to get some attention.*

ReturnOfThePat: *if she ever gets tired of Prince Jerome, she can keep me company ;)*

Shell-ey: *I think everyone is being too hard on them! To whoever released these pictures without her permission, shame on you! You are a horrible person*

FrankiePJ: *oh baby, come over here and suck my cock. I bet you like it dirrty girl. I'll spank you and make you forget about the pansy prince*

I turn off my phone and slam it down on the cushion beside me.

I pull my knees up to my chest and wrap my arms around them.

I take in huge gulps of air. Everything hurts. My eyes, my head, my heart. I feel like I'm shattering, but I have no idea how to glue the pieces back together.

I let the sobs take over my body. I have cried so much over the past week, and somehow I still have more tears to come out.

"There you are," Corvin says as he walks into the solarium, Dax right behind him.

"We've been looking for you," Dax adds. "Looks like we're here just in time."

"Just in time for what? To see me fall apart and be a complete mess?" I snap. I don't mean to be rude, but I'm just done.

The guys don't take any offense to my mood. They sit on either side of me, cuddling in close.

"Simon and I met when we were doing our undergrad at University," Corvin says. "We met our second year. I was drawn to him immediately, but I kept my distance because he's a prince. And brilliant. And so hot I thought he was out of my league." Corvin runs a hand through his hair. "One day, I was eating lunch between classes, and Simon just sat down at my table. He didn't ask, he just sat. I swear I fell in love with him at that moment. We struck up a friendship, but it didn't take long before it grew into something more. By the end of University, we were living together and were inseparable. We knew that we were made for each other."

"You two are absolutely adorable together," I say, and even manage a small sincere smile.

"I'm glad you think so," Corvin says. "But a lot of people didn't agree. I come from a poor family, like barely able to feed ourselves sometimes kind of poor. The only reason I was even able to attend University was because of a rugby scholarship. I never would have been able to afford to live, let alone attend classes and buy textbooks,

430

if it wasn't for rugby. It didn't take long before the media came after me. They attacked me. Attacked my parents. Attacked my neighbourhood where I grew up. Every single bad thing we ever thought about ourselves, the media said as a joke. They said I wasn't good enough for Simon. Called me a gold digger. Called me so many names, actually. But Simon stuck by me. The whole family did. And that's not even mentioning all the hate we received for being gay. A whole group of people protested once, early on in our relationship. Like literally had homophobic signs and marched in front of the castle yelling. They couldn't accept that a prince was gay." Corvin rolls his eyes, but I can see the lingering pain in his eyes.

I remember Simon telling me how some restaurants didn't want them eating there when they were dating. "I'm sorry Corvin. That's truly awful."

"It was. But now, it's better. No one protests, people don't yell obscenities at me as I walk down the street. People are mostly happy to see us together. Some people were even inspired by our story. I like to think that we helped out a lot of people who were wrestling with their own sexuality. It helps seeing yourself in others who come out on the other side."

"Do you think people will eventually leave me alone?" I ask tentatively.

"Yes, I do. You're amazing, and soon people will realize that you are the best thing to ever happen to Tate. And besides, most of the hate is probably just from jealousy. You looked fucking hot in those pictures, Harp!"

I cover my face with my hands.

"Corvin! You can't say that!" Dax yells, and I hear what sounds like Dax hitting Corvin on the head.

"Pfft, of course I can. It's true, and besides I'm gay, so it's fine for me to say." He shrugs.

"Thanks Corvin. Telling me your story actually did make me feel better. I bet the media loved you though, right?" I ask Dax. "Marielle told me that they thought you were too young to be so serious when you were teenagers, but it was probably better the second time around as adults, right?"

"You'd think so, but no." Dax rubs his chin. "The first time, they said we were too young. And we were stupid enough to believe them. The second time, they were outraged that I'm *only* a Viscount. I bet even if I was a prince from another country, they still would have found something to gripe about. They're never happy. But that's the thing Harper, they're never happy. They will always find something to complain about and blow way out of proportion."

"I doubt they were this mean to Janelle when she started to date Louis," I say. She's just so poised and proper. She's what the media wishes I was.

Corvin and Dax look at each other over top of my head, each of them grinning.

Dax pulls out his phone and texts someone.

"We need the skinny dipping story," Corvin says as Dax types.

"The skinny dipping story?" I ask them.

"The skinny dipping story!" They reply in unison.

■■ ■■

Queen Janelle sits across from the three of us. She has a beautiful red dress on. Her hair is perfectly slicked back. Her nails are painted red to match her dress and her shoes are spotless, even though I know she just came from the gardens.

She's the epitome of grace and elegance.

Except for the story that she's sharing.

"Oh my gosh, it was absolutely hilarious! Louis had convinced me that no one was home. That it was late enough and no one would see us. I wasn't too sure, because even at two in the morning people are always around, and the fence only came up to our waists. But, I trusted him. So, we were standing in the middle of the yard, stripping down when we thought we heard a noise. We paused for a moment, but nothing happened, so we resumed. We tried to stay quiet, but as soon as we jumped in the pool, the giggles took over and I couldn't stop them. Louis grabbed me, crushing our bodies together in an attempt to silence me. I'm sure you can guess how well that went." Janelle pauses her story, breaking out in a case of the giggles as she remembers. "I heard rustling from inside the house, snapping the giggles out of me, but again, nothing happened. So, we were in the pool. Naked. Only the light of the moon to keep us company. I'm sure you can guess what two twenty-three year olds were getting up to?" She arches a brow and I nod. "Well, just as things are heating up between us, and about to get, ahem, very interesting, a light turned on and blinded us. We jumped apart, which only served to expose our naked bodies to the group. The family was lined up against the sliding glass doors, noses pressed to the glass."

"Wait. Wait a minute here," I say, holding up my hands. "You were at someone else's house? I assumed you were at the pool here!" The castle has an indoor pool that can be opened up to the outside with a retractable wall.

"Oh no, dear. It was someone else's house. Someone we didn't even know." Janelle throws her head back as she laughs. The couch shakes as Corvin and Dax laugh along with her.

"Wait, wait," Corvin says between laughs. "It gets so much better!"

Janelle takes a few breaths to calm herself. "So, this whole family is staring at us, and we're just standing in the shallow end of the pool facing them. The water is only up to our waists. Our clothes are on the patio, right by the doors where they're standing. Then I noticed that one of the sons, because yes, of course they had two teenage sons, was taking pictures of us. The flash was going off constantly. He must have used up an entire roll of film!"

"How did you get out of there?" I ask, entranced by the story, laughing along with them.

"Louis decided that he was going to try to charm them, get the camera from them and then we'd all move on and forget what happened. Unfortunately, what the father of the family saw was a tall, naked man walking towards him at two in the morning, and the man panicked! He opened the door just as Louis reached the patio, and let out these two huge rottweilers! They chased Louis around the yard, barking at him. One of the dogs even got a bite in on his ass!" Janelle loses it now. Laughing so hard she can't breathe.

"A dog bit him on his naked ass?"

"Yes! Just as the other son very helpfully found another roll of film! They got pictures of the whole thing. I was just cowering in the pool, covering my body as well as I could, trying to figure out how to get out. Eventually they called the dogs back in, and we scrambled to get our clothes on and left."

"Oh my gosh! That's the best story I have ever heard!"

"And the media hated me for it. The family sold those pictures to the highest bidder. The media ran with this story about how I'm a bad influence, and that I made him go skinny dipping and I got him viciously attacked. Meanwhile, Louis was the one who talked me into it! He was always talking me into taking risks, and when we got caught, the media blamed me. I was the scapegoat for their perfect prince. And still, even now, those pictures will resurface from time to time. Someone will discover them again and try to turn it into a scandal, usually when there's political strife or someone gets the idea to abolish the monarchy."

"Our point here, Harper, is that we've all dealt with this. I mean, Janelle was literally naked in the tabloids, at least you had *something* on," Corvin teases me.

436

Maybe they're right. They've all been attacked and vilified, yet they stuck it out and their relationships stayed strong. If they can do it, so can I.

"Hey guys, you have to see this!" Marielle yells out as she runs into the room.

"What is it, dear?" Janelle asks, worry immediately evident on her face.

"Tate yelled at some reporters! Look!"

Marielle shoves her phone in front of our faces.

"Oh my god!" I gasp, my hand covering my mouth.

Chapter 49 - Tate

I'm on edge. Harper hasn't really looked at me or touched me or laughed in a week. I've been giving her space, because that's what she said she needs, but it's killing me seeing her this way. Especially since I know it's all my fault. If she wasn't dating me, her mostly naked body wouldn't be splashed on tabloids all over the world.

Well, my fault and Levi's. Stupid fucking Levi. I hate that guy so much.

I need to clear my head. Sitting here brooding isn't going to help anything.

"Axelle! Mars! Walk!" I yell out for my dogs. I hear their nails clicking on the wood floor immediately.

I hook their harnesses on and we walk over to Croix forest.

I had hoped that the fresh air would help, but everywhere I look in here reminds me of Harper.

The trees, the trails, even just the sounds of the birds bring forth memories of being here with her.

The dogs and I veer off to a path that Harper and I never took. It doesn't help, but I pretend that it does.

"Do you think she's going to leave, Axelle?"

Axelle tips her head from side to side. Probably trying to come up with the best way to break the news to me.

The dogs put up with my slow, mopey walking for a bit longer. We meet back up with the main path, and we head back towards the castle.

"What's that?" I ask my dogs, like they'll actually answer me one of these days.

I can hear shuffling and murmurs. It sounds like a group of hikers around the bend.

I move the dogs over to the side so that the hikers will have a place to pass us.

But it's not hikers.

It's worse. So much worse.

Journalists. And I'm guessing that they're probably not from any reputable papers.

"Prince Jerome! How do you feel about Harper's photos?"

"Are you and Harper still together?"

"Is Harper good in bed?"

"Did you know about the pictures? Does she have any more?"

"Will Harper be posing nude next?"

Fucking tabloid reporters.

Normally I politely wave at them, answer a few questions vaguely, smile broadly. I have never been rude to a journalist, tabloid reporter or not.

But today, something in me just explodes.

I can feel my temperature rise, my breaths become ragged and my vision blurs.

Who do these people think they are? They have no right to ask these questions or speak about Harper, any human being for that matter, this way.

They're crowding into me now, shoving their cameras and recording devices into my face.

Mars growls behind me, and I pull on his leash to keep him close to me.

"Those pictures of Harper were shared without her consent. How dare you judge her for something she did in private years ago. Can everyone here seriously say that they have never done anything in private that could easily be turned into a scandal? Pictures, words shared in bed, positions, toys, the person you brought into your bed?! The man who shared those photos, and yes, we know who he is, shared them with the world because he was angry he was caught cheating and Harper left him. They were shared out of hate, even though they were taken out of love. No one has the right to judge Harper for taking those photos or her body, or me for loving her. She has given *me* the consent to see her and love her, not any of you. Shame on all of you. Now leave me alone!"

I push past the stunned group. Some of the reporters follow me with their phones, still recording me. I can hear them talking loudly behind me, a few words making their way to me, but I ignore them.

I just need to get back home. I need Harper.

But what if she doesn't want me anymore? What if my little tantrum just made it a hundred times worse for her?

Fuck!

I drag the dogs to do another lap of the forest in an attempt to calm myself down.

Chapter 50 - Harper

I've made myself shower, dry my hair and eat real food.
After living off of tea and toast for a week, I devoured my
lunch when Michel brought it up to me.

I don't know where Tate is, so I start a fire and try to read
a book while I wait for him.

I read the first paragraph four times before I give up.

Holding it feels nice though.

The door opening and slamming shut scares me.

"Tate! Geez, what did the door do to you?"

"Oh, Harper. Sorry, I didn't know you were in here."

Tate runs his hands over his face.

I walk over to him, which apparently shocks him because
he stands ramrod straight. When I wrap my arms around
his back, he barely loosens up enough to hug me back.

"I'm so sorry for shutting you out this week," I say into
his chest. "I shouldn't have done that. It was just so
much, and I just froze. I'm sorry."

I can feel the muscles in his back relax, and he finally
gives me a real hug.

"I fucked up, Harper."

I lean away from him a bit, just enough to look in his
eyes, "What do you mean?"

I pull him toward the couch and have to push him and make him sit down. I sit down right beside him, our thighs touching.

"I was in the forest, and I was cornered by some reporters. I yelled at them, Harper. Like, yelled. I've never raised my voice to them before. I just made this so much worse for you. I'm the one who should be sorry. And now you're going to leave." Tate starts to cry, his shoulders shaking as tears fall on his lap.

I wrap my arms around him, and pull his big body into mine. "I saw."

His head snaps up, his eyes finding mine immediately. "You saw?"

"Yes. Marielle found a video online and showed it to us. Since you just came home now, and this was about thirty minutes ago, I'd wager that it was posted as soon as it happened."

Tate tries to pull away from me, but I don't let him.

"I just couldn't seem to help it. They were asking all kinds of horrible questions, attacking me with their words, and I just snapped at them. I'm so sorry. The media is going to eat this up."

"Tate, look at me," I tell him. Once he raises his head again and meets my eyes, I continue. "I am proud of you for standing up to them. It sounds like they were being bullies. You didn't say anything mean or unnecessarily rude. You were defending me, and I could never be mad at you for that."

"You're not mad?" His voice is so quiet, I almost don't hear his question.

"No, not at all." I lean my forehead against his, like he has done to me countless times. "We're in this together, right? I am yours and you are mine. We are a team and we are stronger together."

"Are you back?"

"Yes, I'm back. And I am so sorry I checked out for a week. I promise I won't do that again."

"It's ok. I understand. But please know that you can always talk to me."

"I know. And I will for now on. I did have a nice chat with Corvin, Dax and your mom about the media," I tell him.

Tate grins. "Did Maman tell you the skinny dipping story?"

"Yes she sure did!"

We laugh together, both gasping for air.

"Man, I never get tired of that story!"

A knock on the door sobers us up.

"Come in," Tate calls out.

Gabriel walks in with a look of concern on his face.

"Gabriel, I'm sorry about me yelling at the reporters. We'll issue a statement about it soon."

"Oh no, that was fantastic, sir. I think we just leave that one alone. They deserved it. I'm actually here for another reason."

Oh come on, what now?

"Celeste has been arrested for attempted breaking and entering," Gabriel tells us.

"What?!" I shout.

"Where was she trying to break in to?" Tate asks, much more calm than me.

Gabriel flicks his eyes over to me before answering, "Cara's house."

"What?!" I shout out again.

Gabriel turns his tablet to face me. "Is this the woman you saw at the cafe?"

I look at her for a second. "Yes, it is. She approached me and Cara right after we got back from Montfret. She was really pushy and made me feel icky."

"This is Celeste," Tate says, voice void of emotion. He's trying to stay calm, but I can feel his foot bouncing on the floor.

"Celeste? But I thought she had black hair and wasn't allowed around here."

"We believe she's been wearing a wig when close to the castle as a way to avoid detection," Gabriel tells me.

That explains why Cara thought her hair looked weird. It wasn't just the colour or the cut, it was just straight up fake.

"Why was she trying to break into Cara's house? She has to know that I'm staying here," I ask, trying to piece the puzzle together.

"That's what the police are working on right now. She cannot get out of the charge. She was caught right in the middle of working a lock pick into the door by an officer." Gabriel looks down at his phone for a moment, then back up at us, smiling. "Who wants to go pretend to be police officers? The detective leading the case has offered to let us watch the interrogation."

- -

I feel just like a cool, badass cop. We're behind a one-way mirror in a little room. The walls are brick, painted off-white. I have a little styrofoam cup of bad tea and a man with a serious moustache is in the other room talking to Celeste, AKA Claire, over a rickety looking metal table.

"Look, we caught you in the act of breaking in. You're going to be charged. We also found some interesting items in your car. Care to discuss them?"

Celeste just stares at him.

"You drive a red BMW M8, correct?"

The red BMW! I knew it was following me!

Gone is the bubbly Claire I met at the cafe. In her place an ice queen.

The officer sighs. "Are you really going to make me ask you about every single item?"

Celeste continues to stare at him.

"Ok, so first up we have all these photos of Harper Jones, Cara Morteau and Dr. Theodore Morteau. Why do you have so many photos of them?"

More staring.

"And this is what appears to be a contract between you, a Levi Metz and the Sova Sun to purchase photos, exclusive rights to more photos in both of your possession and an interview with both of you concerning Prince Jerome of Sova and Harper Jones."

"What the fuck?!" I yell. Thank goodness the room is soundproof. "She was working with Levi?"

Tate looks at me, his mouth hanging open. "Our exes teamed up?"

"And then," the officer continues, "there's the matter of the rope we found. Looking like we're adding attempted kidnapping to your charges."

"I wasn't going to do anything to her!" Celeste finally says. "I just wanted to talk to her. Maybe tell her to back away from my man. She stole him, and I was looking for proof that she's not good enough for him, ok? Levi was kind enough to find that proof."

Tate and I just look at each other.

"Man, our exes suck!" I say.

■■■

Celeste ended up getting charged with stalking and attempted breaking and entering.

I watch with glee as she is handcuffed and hauled down the hall. Tate looks relieved, like he can finally stop worrying about her.

"What's going to happen to Levi?" I ask the officer.

"Well, he didn't commit a crime and his contract with the Sova Sun was legal. However, you could charge him with slander. I hear he's a lawyer?" The officer asks, and I nod my head. "Depending on his influence, you may or may not get anywhere with it. My personal opinion, and this is off the record," the officer looks from side to side, making sure we're alone. "He's a bastard, and you should throw everything you can at him. That is no way to treat a lady, especially not our future Princess."

The officer squeezes my arm and shakes Tate's hand.

"Tate?" I ask.

"Yes, love?"

"I'm not actually going to be a princess, right? He's not the first person to say that to me."

Tate tilts his head slightly, studying me for a second.

"Well, yeah, you would be. If we got married, you would become Princess Harper of Sova."

I blink at him a few times before finally finding the ability to form words again. "But I'm not actually royal. I'm just a regular person. Wouldn't I be like a Duchess or a consort or something?"

"No, you would become a princess. The spouse of the sovereign and the spouses of the five people next in line for the throne get a royal title. Dax will be a prince when they get married and will become King when Marielle ascends the throne. Corvin is already Prince Corvin. We just remember who the actual sovereign and blood members of the royal family are. You would become a princess. Did you really not know this?"

"Umm, no! That is something I was not prepared to process."

"Don't worry love," Tate says, pulling me into his arms. "We have some time before that happens. Lots of time to process."

Chapter 52 - Harper

"You have to be quiet, love!" Tate tells me as he covers my mouth with his hand.

"It's hard to be quiet when you feel so good!" I say into his palm.

Tate pulls out a little bit and slams back into me making me moan again.

"See! Shhh!"

"It's your fault! Stop being so good at sex and I'll be quiet. Besides, you're the chatty one, maybe I should tell you to be quiet."

Tate wiggles his eyebrows up and down and picks up speed. Oh my god, it feels so good. Tate sucks my nipple into his mouth and I find my clit. Together we work my body into a frenzy as he continues to fuck me as hard as he can.

"Yes, Harper. That's it, love. Come for me. Come all over my cock!"

I slap Tate's arm. "See! Chatty!" I point at him. Tate sucks harder, making me lose all sense of worry about the people gathered downstairs. I moan as my orgasm builds.

"Yes, yes, Tate!" I explode on him, my walls squeezing him as he pounds into me, his own release following mine.

I smooth out my dress, finger comb through my hair and walk downstairs.

"Seriously, Harper? At my birthday party?" Cara asks as soon as I take a step into the living room where her friends and family are gathered.

"Umm, yeah….sorry?" I shrug. I'm not sorry. "I'll show you some spots in the castle you can sneak away with Theo during my birthday in a few weeks."

"Deal!" Cara shouts.

"It might be time to cut back on the wine, sis," I tell her. Something is different about her. She's extra happy. Yes, it's her birthday, but there's something else.

Cara pulls me into the kitchen, away from everyone else. "Actually, I haven't had anything to drink. Won't for a while." Cara bites her lip.

"Oh my gosh! Cara! Are you pregnant?" I whisper-shout, grabbing onto her shoulders.

Cara nods her head vigorously, tears streaming down her face. "Yes!! I have only told you and Theo. It's still early, so I won't be telling anyone else for a while, but I had to tell you."

I hug Cara as we jump up and down. "I am so happy for you! I'm going to be an Aunt! I'm so excited! You're going to be the best mom! And of course I won't tell anyone."

"I assume you'll tell Tate, like as soon as he comes downstairs after he deems it long enough after you to not be suspicious."

"Umm, well…."

"It's ok, you two are a package deal. I'd be a little upset if you didn't tell him." Cara shrugs. She's already accepted him as family.

I spot Tate talking to Theo, and give them a little wave. "Well, just to make your soon to be hectic family life a little bit more hectic, we got you a birthday present. Simon helped."

Cara's eyes grow large and a smile takes over her face.

"Happy birthday, Cara!" Theo says as he sets a cat carrier on the island and opens the door. Two tiny kittens nervously walk out. They are long haired calicos, one with a bit more orange and white, the other with bigger splotches of black with bits of orange and white mixed in.

"These two were brought into a shelter that Simon was helping in," Theo explains. "Their mother, a street cat, was hit by a car a few weeks ago and unfortunately didn't make it. The shelter took these ladies in and deemed them healthy enough now for their forever home. Simon immediately thought of you. These two sisters, who lost their mother too young have been strong and fought to survive. They are now the sweetest, happiest kitties."

There isn't a dry eye in the house.

"I love them so much!" Cara is crying, clutching both kittens to her chest. "Thank you. I'm going to name these kitties Lynn and Lee."

"Those are our middle names," I say, my heart bursting.

"Yep! And just like us, they'll stick together and help each other on this crazy path of life."

■ ■

I crawl into bed beside Tate.

"Thank you for coming with me tonight," I say.

"You don't have to thank me. I'd go anywhere with you."

He kisses the top of my head as I snuggle into him.

"Oh yeah? What if I wanted to go to Iceland in winter and see the northern lights?"

"Then I would buy the biggest, puffiest coat I could find and go with you."

"What if I wanted to go to that hotel where giraffes can stick their heads in the windows while you eat in Nairobi?"

"I'd go with you. Actually, that sounds awesome! Let's do that!"

"What if –"

"Love, I will follow you anywhere. You want to go to Costa Rica or Norway or to Antarctica to see some penguins, fine. I will follow you. You own all of me. I live for you. I need you. You are mine and I am yours." Tate cups my cheek in his hand. "Forever, you are mine."

The End

Epilogue

"When you said you were going to rent a car for our visit, I pictured us picking up a Hyundai or something from the rental counter at the airport. I didn't even know things like this existed!" I exclaim as we speed away in the car.

"Ah, but remember that I'm a super special prince and you're a super special princess, so we get super special things."

I roll my eyes at him. "Again, I'm not a princess."

"Semantics. Either way, why would I get a Hyundai when I could get this amazing Porsche 997. Listen to this baby purr!"

Tate guns it on the highway, leaving the city in our wake.

"Did you get a standard on purpose?" I ask, watching as he shifts gears.

"Maybe," Tate smirks, and I know that he did in fact get a manual transmission just to get to me. Sexy jerk.

We drive down the highway, enjoying our freedom. It's been a crazy 14 months since Levi sold my photos to the tabloids.

We charged Levi with slander, and won our case.

Levi's father, much to my surprise, was not at all pleased with Levi's actions. In fact, he fired Levi from the firm and made a public statement that he denounced his actions and treatment of me and the Sovan Royal Family.

Take that, Levi's plans!

Tate and I launched the Sova STEAM Camp we were working on. We kept it small this year but will add new programs each year. It was well received, and the children have really been enjoying themselves.

I have stopped reading articles about me and Tate, and definitely haven't read any comments sections. I'm so much happier now. Freer. The tabloids rarely publish anything of note about us these days anyway. Some super sleazy online magazine wrote an article about the one-year anniversary of my photos, but it was mostly ignored by the public. Those photos will be out there forever, but I'm not letting it get to me.

I have continued working with Yves in the gardens, that is when Tate and I aren't travelling around the country on royal tours. Between Tate and the gardens, I feel like I have finally found my place in life.

The scenery begins to change as we enter cottage country. The air smells clean and fresh. Nothing can come close to the feel of being in Muskoka.

"I can't believe you arranged for all of us to come here! I haven't been back here in years!"

Tate contacted the owners of Wildflower Cottage Resort on Petal Lake to book us in for a private week. My mom and her sister would bring the kids up here for a week of fun and sun every summer starting when we could barely walk. We grew up on the shores of this lake. We learned to kayak and fish here. We would hike in nearby Algonquin Park during the day and roast marshmallows by the fire at night. It was a week that we looked forward to all year, we counted down the days to return as soon as we left. We stopped coming after my mom got sick, grief and adulthood getting in the way of summer fun.

"It's my pleasure, love. I'm glad that everyone was able to make it. Cara, Theo and baby Thomas should already be there, as should your cousins. We're the lollygaggers here."

The resort looks exactly as I remember it, if not a bit run down. The same owners are here, taking me by surprise. They must be into their 70's now.

"Harper! You made it!" Cara squeals, passing Thomas over to Theo so she can charge at me with a giant hug.

"Is everyone else here?" I ask looking around.

458

"Yep! Sadie and Emily are unpacking in their cottages and Cam is grumping around in the forest looking for wood. He didn't want to pay the $10 for a bundle of firewood. I suggest we stay away from his fire. All the wood is soaking wet from the rain yesterday and his fire is going to be all smoke!"

Cameron has always assumed that he's known best. Suggesting to Cameron that he does something a different way usually ends in grunts.

Sadie and Emily are twins, born in March of the same year as Cara, two years after Cameron.

"Harper! And the Prince!" Mae's sweet voice reaches me as she runs out of her cottage.

"Mae! Sweetheart! I am so happy to see you!!" I throw my arms around her and hug her tight.

Mae is my cousin Sadie's daughter. She's ten years old now and has grown into a beautiful young lady.

"Mae, this is Tate. Tate, this is Mae." Tate joins us, shaking her hand.

"It is an absolute pleasure to meet you, Mae. I am thrilled you were able to join us this week. Please let me know if there is anything you need or desire while here."

Tate is laying the Prince act on thick, but Mae is eating it up.

I look behind Mae and see Sadie and Emily coming. I rush over to meet them halfway. We throw our arms around each other in a three-way hug.

"Oh my god, Harp! He's so much more handsome in person!" Emily gushes.

"And look how good he is with Mae!" Sadie adds in.

Tate is paying close attention and looks completely engaged in whatever story Mae is telling him.

"Yeah, he's pretty fantastic!"

Tate sees us watching him and gives us a little wink and a wave.

"Fuck, Harp, how can you even function? I think I almost orgasmed from that!" Emily says as she fans herself with her hand.

We fall into a fit of laughter.

It feels so good to be back here with them.

Cameron comes back with his bundle of wet sticks, and not wanting to make him feel bad, we all gather around his smoky fire pit.

Whenever possible, we sneak some firewood we bought into his fire.

The owners, Jack and Linda, come over to greet us and meet Tate.

"I am so happy to see you all back here, with a few new members in the group!" Linda says, waving to Tate and the kids.

"Thank you very much for accommodating us this week. I truly appreciate it," Tate says to our hosts.

"Of course, Prince Jerome! We are thrilled you wanted to come here to Wildflower and bring this lot back to the lake! Especially since we won't be here after this summer."

"Oh no! Are you closing Wildflower Cottages?" Cara asks.

"We're hoping to sell so we can retire," Jack tells her. He has a grandfatherly vibe to him. Always has, even thirty years ago. "Linda and I aren't getting any younger, and we'd like to enjoy the time we have left on this planet relaxing and having someone else take care of us for a change!" He laughs his full belly laugh. Santa would be proud of his laugh.

"You're selling?" Cameron perks up. "That's interesting."

"Yes we are, boy. We haven't officially listed, but we've started to spread the word some. We would like to pass the torch on to someone for next season. So, if you know anyone willing to take this place on, please tell them about us."

Cameron tells them he will, but has turned his attention to the fire, stroking his chin.

Tate spends the evening getting to know my family and I catch up on gossip from my cousins.
We barbecue some burgers, make s'mores and enjoy the sun setting over the lake.

■■■

Yesterday the entire family ventured into Algonquin park to do the Beaver Pond Trail, a fairly easy trail with some spectacular beaver dams. We didn't see any beavers though, which disappointed me greatly. It was easy for Mae to keep up, and Cara had little Thomas in a carrier. However, today Tate the outdoorsman wanted a challenge. We packed a full lunch, plenty of water and headed out to do Centennial Ridges, a much longer, much harder trail. The 10km loop is worth it though. It has some spectacular views and lookouts.
"I saw you and Cam talking a lot yesterday. You seem to be getting along well," I say as we near the crest of a hill.
"Yes, he's a great guy. A little rough on the outside, but once we got talking, we found we have a lot in common. He wants to buy the resort."

"He does?!" I shriek. Some birds flutter away, out of the trees. Oops, sorry for scaring you, birds!

"He does. And I've offered to join him as a silent partner."

"You have?!"

"Yes, I have." Tate's eyes crinkle at the corners, clearly enjoying my shock.

"What else have you been up to?" I demand, stopping at the top of the hill, ignoring the breathtaking view for a moment.

"Well, let's see," Tate lets out a puff of air. "I paid off Cara's house, and all of her and Theo's debt."

"You paid off Cara's house?" I stare at him, jaw on the ground.

"Well, yeah." Tate rubs the back of his neck. "I wanted to a year ago, but Cara made me wait."

"Wait for what?"

Tate ignores me, continuing to detail his generosity. "I have also set up a trust fund for Thomas and will set one up for Mae when we get home."

I blink rapidly in response. "There's more isn't there?"

"I also bought one of Emily's paintings."

"I didn't know that you had seen her paintings."

"I haven't, so perhaps it's more accurate to say that I have commissioned a painting."

"A painting for what?"

"As a wedding gift."

"For whom?" I ask, confused by this conversation. This man is incredible. Confusing, but incredible.

"For you. Roses, like the ones you and Maman picked out for last year's Sova Day party."

Before I can say anything else, Tate drops down to one knee. The view of the sparkling water below and the canopy of trees that we're standing above pales in comparison to seeing Tate kneeling in front of me, holding open a little black box. The ring inside is a gorgeous princess cut diamond surrounded by smaller diamonds and amethysts on the band.

"Harper," Tate says, reaching out to hold my hands in his. "We met in a forest, so it only seems appropriate that the next stage of our lives begin in one too. I fell in love with you before I even knew your name. You make me complete. You make me happier than I ever thought possible. You make me feel like *me*. I love you with my whole heart. Will you please make me the luckiest man in the world and be my wife?"

Tears fill my eyes. I'm nodding before I can get words out.

"Yes, Tate. Yes I will marry you! You make me so happy! I couldn't imagine spending my life with anyone else. I love you so much!"

Tate slides the ring on my finger and stands up and kisses me.

"I love you, Tate."

Tate rests his forehead against mine. "I love you, Harper. You are mine and I am yours. Forever."

Acknowledgements

I still can't believe I wrote a whole book! I might be in shock over that fact for the rest of my life.

This book started because I couldn't get a scene of a woman and man pretending they didn't want to kiss each other while making a meal out of my head. I could vividly feel the tension between them. I could see how his arms would flex while chopping. I imagined her needing to wipe the drool away, because for some reason, forearms are in fact extremely sexy. So, I wrote the idea down. And then I wondered how they got there, who they were and what was going to happen next. Before I knew it, I had 20,000 words and a real book was starting to form!

I wouldn't have been able to do this if I didn't have such an amazing support team.

To my amazing husband Steve, thank you for being my favourite person! You cheered me on as soon as I said "I want to write a book" and kept me going as I stared off into space and tried to make fictional people seem real.

To my children, although you absolutely cannot read this book for a very long time, you were always very excited to hear about how my book was coming along.

To Jamanda, thank you for being so incredibly supportive of me and being around to bounce ideas off of (even if you're awake when I'm asleep).

To my friends Amanda, Shari, Lauren, Marina, Amy and Shelby. Thank you for being excited when I told you about my book. I am so fortunate to have such fabulous friends!

And finally, to my sister Sarah, for being my real life Cara. Thank you for listening to me rant, sending me books in the mail and supporting me when my car accidentally swerves into a bookstore or garden centre and I HAVE to go in.

About the Author

Becky Tzag writes swoony, sexy contemporary romance, filled with easy to love characters and ridiculously close families.

She lives in Ontario, Canada with her fabulous husband and three children.

Becky survives off tea and chips and usually has a book in her oversized purse (along with delicious purse snacks).

You can find Becky on:

Facebook – Becky Tzag's Reading Buddies
www.facebook.com/groups/beckytzagauthor

Instagram – @beckytzagauthor

Manufactured by Amazon.ca
Bolton, ON